A FLAME
IN HALI

BOOK THREE OF
The *Clingfire* Trilogy

A FLAME IN HALI

BOOK THREE OF
The *Clingfire* Trilogy

MARION ZIMMER BRADLEY
AND
DEBORAH J. ROSS

DAW BOOKS, INC.

DONALD A. WOLLHEIM, FOUNDER
375 Hudson Street, New York, NY 10014
ELIZABETH R. WOLLHEIM
SHEILA E. GILBERT
PUBLISHERS

To Ben and Trude Burke,
visionaries for peace

ACKNOWLEDGMENTS

Special thanks, once again, to my editor, Betsy Wollheim, to Ann Sharp of The Marion Zimmer Bradley Literary Trust, to Sherwood Smith, and to a multitude of others who have shown me how life can be lived with dignity, respect, and serenity.

DISCLAIMER

The observant reader may note discrepancies in some details from more contemporary tales. This is undoubtedly due to the fragmentary histories which survive to the present day. Many records were lost during the years following the Ages of Chaos and Hundred Kingdoms and others distorted by oral tradition.

AUTHOR'S NOTE

Immensely generous with "her special world" of Darkover, Marion loved encouraging new writers. We were already friends when she began editing the DARKOVER and SWORD & SORCERESS anthologies. The match between my natural literary "voice" and what she was looking for was extraordinary. She loved to read what I loved to write, and she often cited "The Death of Brendan Ensolare" (FOUR MOONS OF DARKOVER, DAW, 1988) as one of her favorites.

As Marion's health declined, I was invited to work with her on one or more Darkover novels. We decided that rather than extend the story of "modern" Darkover, we would return to the Ages of Chaos. Marion envisioned a trilogy beginning with the Hastur Rebellion and A FLAME IN HALI, the enduring friendship between Varzil the Good and Carolin Hastur, culminating in the signing of the Compact. While I scribbled notes as fast as I could, she would sit back, eyes alight, and begin a story with, "Now, the Hasturs tried to control the worst excesses of *laran* weapons, but there were always others under development . . ." or "Of course, Varzil and Carolin had been brought up on tales of star-crossed lovers who perished in the destruction of Neskaya . . ."

Here is that tale.

Deborah J. Ross

PROLOGUE

Rumail Deslucido had cheated death before, but now it had come for him at last. He lay on a cot, as sagging and creaking as his failing body, in the dingy room that had been his refuge and his prison, and waited. Each breath had become a battle to suck air into his scarred lungs. With each passing moment, his heart stuttered as if it, too, trembled with the exhaustion of having lived too long.

The door opened and the girl from the village stepped in, carrying a basket of bread and an earthenware jar. He sipped the broth as she spooned it for him, then lay back. She spoke to him, things of little consequence, not worth the effort of listening. Her voice faded, mingling with the memories of other voices. Sometimes he spoke with men long dead—his royal brother . . .

Ah! There was the unbowed golden head, the eyes brimming with fire and victory. Once again, they stood together on a balcony while below them, the white-and-black-diamond-patterned banners of Deslucido rippled in the breeze. The morning sun burnished the King's hair to a natural crown. He spoke, and his words painted visions in Rumail's mind, hope for a time when these Hundred Kingdoms might be united into a single harmonious realm. No more incessant warfare, no more petty bickering while men bled out their lives upon the ruined fields. Rumail's *laran* talents would be celebrated, his place as Keeper of his own Tower, so long denied by those head-blind purists, secure. . . .

The bright sky darkened, the vision blew away like winter-dried leaves, and now Rumail stood on the battlefield at Drycreek, where his brother's army had clashed with that of King Rafael Hastur. His brother's soldiers paused to gaze skyward. Hovering above the enemy, Rumail's mechanical birds released showers of glowing green particles, as eerily beautiful as they were deadly: bonewater dust, forged by the concentrated power of Gifted minds, bought at great cost from a renegade circle.

Even as Rumail watched the luminous poison drift toward the unsuspecting enemy, he wished there had been some other way to stop the Hastur King and his witch-born niece, Taniquel Hastur-Acosta. By treachery and psi-wielding servants of their own, they had turned the tide of battle.

I had no choice. None of us had a choice.

Rumail had relived the scene a thousand times, from the first moment victory slipped away to the sudden shift of the wind that blew the bonewater dust back upon their own forces. As if it were yesterday, he remembered that mad scramble of retreat, men and beasts perishing within a heartbeat, with thousands more doomed to a lingering death. He himself had narrowly escaped. Wounded, barely able to maintain a psychic shield against the toxic dust, he had clung to the merest shred of hope.

He should have perished there, immobilized and helpless. But he did not. He had escaped death then, as he had before, as he would again. The gods had another destiny for him, not as one more nameless body on a field no one dared cross for a generation or more.

Now, in his memory, he stood high upon a Tower balcony, wrapped in the crimson robes of a Keeper. At last, he commanded a circle of his own, and no matter how its workers might despise him, they would obey. Their Tower was sworn to his brother the King, and it was by his orders they now mounted their attack upon a Hastur Tower.

Screams echoed through the caverns of Rumail's mind. Around him, walls shuddered under blasts of psychic lightning as each Tower unleashed its terrible weapons upon the other. Stones burst into unnatural flame. He sensed the dying minds of his own workers and, echoed from afar, those of their enemies. Blue flames shot skyward, rocking the foundations.

Rumail remembered stumbling from the ruined Tower, wandering in a daze, now a disembodied spirit in the Overworld, now ragged and half-starved, through the wild lands where none knew him.

Now the memories flickered through his mind like candles guttering in a winter wind. He looked upon the homely village woman he had taken to wife, gazed down upon the rounded face of a newborn son, then another and another. The years blurred together. He looked upon the bright eyes of his sons and his own vengeance mirrored in them. Felt a distant wrench as his oldest son's mind flared and fell into silence. Saw the weathered face of a traveling tinker, bringing news that King Rafael Hastur had died under mysterious circumstances.

Heard the voice of his second son: *"Father, Felix Hastur of Carcosa has claimed the throne and he has a healthy heir, his nephew Carolin."*

"Then Carolin, too, must die," Rumail had said, *"so that their line be obliterated. I will send my youngest son, my Eduin, to Arilinn Tower, there to train as a* laranzu, *the perfect weapon against this Hastur Prince."*

Eduin . . .

"La! There!" said the village girl, smoothing the hair back from Rumail's forehead. "Feeling better, are we?" He had no energy to favor her with a response, for the past pressed even closer now.

The face of his youngest son drifted behind Rumail's closed eyelids and it seemed that once more he wandered in delirium, his body racked to the core with lung fever, his lungs weakened by his battlefield ordeal. When word reached Arilinn of his illness, Eduin had rushed to his side. Rumail felt the touch of his son's trained *laran.*

Father, please! You must live, if only to see yourself avenged upon the Hasturs!

Live . . . he heard his own mental voice, dim and far off. *Yes, I must live. And make sure that next time,* you *do not fail me.*

Eduin had cringed under the mental onslaught. His weakness, his guilt shone through. Rumail stormed through each memory, each moment of betrayal. When Carolin spent a season training at Arilinn Tower, Eduin had a dozen chances to strike—a slip of the knife, a fall from a balcony, a heart suddenly stopped as his fingers closed around Carolin's starstone. . . . At each crucial moment, however, something had stayed his hand.

It wasn't my fault! Eduin had cried. *Always, Varzil Ridenow interfered, suspected me, protected Carolin. . . .*

No excuses! With all the force of his Tower-trained mind, Rumail struck. Eduin, caught between desperation and hope, was without defense. Rumail penetrated his son's mind, deep into the core of his *laran* talent, grasped and *twisted. . . .*

You will know no rest or joy until Carolin Hastur and everyone who aided him is dead.

When the deed was done, Rumail had opened his eyes to see his two remaining sons, Eduin the *laranzu* and Gwynn the assassin. Eduin had become his instrument, wedded utterly to his purpose.

Rumail sent his sons back into the world. *"Find the child of Taniquel! Kill Carolin Hastur and anyone who stands in your way!"*

Fragments of *laran* memories rose in Rumail's memory, things he had sensed from afar, linked to the minds of his sons. Gwynn struggled on a muddy riverbank with Carolin, then locked in a psychic battle with Varzil Ridenow, who had foiled the assassination attempt. Varzil's mind pressed against his: *Who sent you? Who?*

Even now, Rumail heard the echoes of Gwynn's final, anguished thoughts: *WE WILL BE AVENGED!*

From afar, Eduin surged with triumph as he uncovered the identity of Felicia Hastur-Acosta; his hands moved, setting a deadly trap-matrix; he fled the ruins of Hestral Tower, hunted . . . outlawed . . . Rumail could no longer tell whether these memories were Eduin's or his own—the cold, the fear, the constant need to hide, to keep moving. . . .

Father, I am here . . . waiting for you. . . .

Rumail blinked, as one vision overlapped another. Gwynn beckoned to him, and behind that ghostly form stood another, the sons he had lost in his quest for vengeance. In each face, he saw the light of recognition and welcome. There his brother stood, golden and kingly, beside his own son and heir . . . there the general who had led them . . . there the men fallen under the bonewater dust. Waiting, all waiting for him to join them.

I cannot die, not yet, not while Carolin Hastur still sits on his throne! What accursed sorcery guards him?

Eduin's shadowy form shimmered in the old man's sight.

You were right, my son. Without Varzil Ridenow, you would have succeeded.

With the dregs of his strength, Rumail struggled for speech, but could not form the words. His vocal cords, like his body, had gone numb. Grayness lapped at him, hungering.

We are waiting for you. . . .

"Sir, you must rest." A light voice, girlish.

Rest. Soon enough. Rumail closed his eyes, summoning the *laran* that had once been his in full measure. He had trained at Neskaya Tower before its fall, before Varzil the Good had rebuilt it with the help of Carolin Hastur. He could have been a Keeper in his own right. Should have.

No time for that now. His thoughts were becoming disjointed, falling into rust.

The Hasturs. Must be destroyed, he sent. *Kill them . . . kill them all!* Across the leagues, he sensed Eduin's response.

Varzil Ridenow, Rumail insisted, even as his thoughts frayed into tatters. *He is the key to Carolin's power. Without his strength . . . Hastur will fall.* . . .

Yes, Eduin replied, with a hatred that mirrored Rumail's own.

Avenge us . . . the ghostly figures pressed even closer now, their voices growing as strong as if they stood before him. *Join us* . . .

"Swear—" Rumail could not be sure whether he projected the command mentally or spoke it aloud. His breath whispered through his throat, the faintest of sighs. "Swear it will be done!"

The grayness rose about him and the faces grew clearer, their skin and clothing as colorless as the landscape beyond. The Overworld closed its jaws about him, and this time there would be no return.

I . . . swear . . .

BOOK I

1

That year, the long Darkovan winter seemed to last forever. Month after month, ice clouds masked the swollen Bloody Sun. Snow fell, hardened like glass, and then fell again, until the compacted layers encased the land in armor. The passes through the Venza Hills above Thendara closed. Even traders, whose livelihood depended upon travel, lost all desire to venture beyond the city walls. *Comyn* lords and commoners alike barricaded themselves behind their doors, hunkering down for the season.

Midwinter Festival came, and with it, a flurry of merrymaking. King Carolin Hastur threw open the doors of his great hall for a tenday, with music and feasting enough to lift the heart of the meanest street beggar. He had but lately moved his seat from Hali, where his grandfather had ruled, to the larger metropolis of Thendara. Hastur Kings had lived here, too, the last being Rafael II at the time of the Hastur Rebellion. By moving his court to Thendara, Carolin let the people know that he meant to rule all of Hastur. He was no longer Hastur of Carcosa or Hastur of Hali, but High King in Thendara. To celebrate his new seat, he distributed holiday largesse with a generosity that inspired thanksgiving in some quarters and suspicion in others. When he appeared in public, whether addressing *Comyn* lords or commoners, he spoke of the Compact that would bring about a new age of peace and honor for all of Darkover.

The traffic of carts and wagons through the traders' gates dwindled. Grain merchants raised their prices, hoarding their shrinking supplies. One bleak gray tenday followed another, and the festivities blurred into memory, pale against the unrelenting cold. King Carolin established a series of shelters, much like those maintained along mountain trails for travelers, where poor people might find refuge in the bitter nights.

Distributions from the royal granaries to the poor continued for a time. On those days, people gathered in the darkness before dawn, shivering in their layers of woolen cloaks and shawls, jackets and much-patched blankets, clutching their jars and baskets. Their breath rose like plumes of mist. On some mornings, each was given a portion of grain, dried beans, and a measure of cooking oil or sometimes honey. Lately, there had not been enough for everyone.

Thick dark clouds hung low above the city, as if the sky itself were frowning. The King's guards, warmly clad in Hastur blue and silver, cleared the area in front of the doors and funneled the people forward, one by one. They gave preference to the weakest, the women and the elderly. More than one man was turned away, especially those wearing thick, fur-lined wool over their ample bellies.

"Why throw away good food on the likes of them?" shouted a man who had been pushed to the side. He pointed to a woman clutching a pottery jar now filled with grain. Her skirts and shawls were so thread-bare that several layers showed through in patches. She looked like an overdressed doll, except for the pinched thinness of her cheeks; clearly, she wore every tattered garment she owned.

"She'll only waste it—"

"And *you'll* only sell it to some wretch who's even poorer or more desperate," the guard at his elbow replied. "The King means this food to go to those who truly need it. You don't look to me like you've ever gone hungry."

"Zandru's scorpions upon you!" Cursing, the man jerked his arm free from the guard's grasp.

"Not so long ago," one of them grumbled, meaning the reign of King Carolin's cousin, Rakhal, "things were different. There were avenues open to a sufficiently resourceful man, bargains to be made, favors exchanged. More than one of us had a friend in the castle. But those times are gone. There's no doing business with Carolin's bunch." He shrugged philosophically. "As soon as the roads open in the spring, I'm off for Temora. There's nothing here for the likes of us."

"You mean we'll have to turn honest to earn our bread!" a third man joked. Waving to the others, he disappeared down one of the side streets.

"*They* don't go hungry. Or cold, or in want of any comfort." A stranger who had been standing a little apart from the others moved forward. He glanced toward Hastur Castle and then the rich residences of the *Comyn* lords. The sun was not yet full up and shadows lay in frigid pools along the streets. Tower and Castle blazed with light, powered by *laran*-charged batteries.

"They throw us a bit of bread and expect us to be grateful. All the while they sit up there with their satin cushions and their heated rooms and their matrix screens. Poison and plague and spells of torment, they care nothing—nothing—"

"Come, friend," the man bound for Temora said, holding out his arm. "Come. I'll buy you a drink."

"A drink will not cure what ails this city." The hooded man pulled away, lips drawn back in a snarl. The hood of his shabby cloak partly masked his face, revealing only the line of an angular, cold-roughened chin.

The other man paused, eyes narrowing in appraisal. The stranger's clothes, though stained and torn, had once been of good quality, and he did not hold himself like a man accustomed to the gutters.

"Then let me see you home, away from—"

"Home?" The hooded man's voice rasped, dark and bitter. "It is *their* doing that I have none. But the time is coming when it is *they* who will beg for bread and sleep on cold stones—"

"Hold your tongue, man!" the man hissed. "Or if you cannot, then go your way alone, for I'll not be a party to your seditious talk. It's one thing to take the King's largesse or strike a bargain with his men, and quite another to stand here in the open, courting treason with such words. Any one of those guards could hear us, and they're Carolin's to a man." He strode away without a backward glance, as if eager to distance himself from any troublemakers.

The first man, the one who had been so angry, gave the hooded man a coin. "Best get out of the cold." Then he, too, departed without waiting for thanks.

The hooded man stared at the coin in his palm, while the people who'd been given food hurried away and those who had come too late turned back with sagging shoulders. His hood concealed his expression, but something in his carriage kept even the grumblers at a distance.

"You there!" one of the guards called as he locked the granary doors. "We're done for today." He added, in a more kindly tone, "Come back tomorrow, earlier next time, and we'll try to give you something."

"I don't need anything from the likes of *you*," the man snarled. "You and your accursed sorcerer masters—"

The guard's face hardened and he took a step forward. The hooded man whirled with surprising quickness, spat out a curse, and scurried away. The guard turned to his partner, who still wore the sash of a cadet.

"Keep an eye out for that one. I've seen his kind before. They make trouble wherever they go."

"We have enough of that this winter without some madman drumming up more," the boy replied, shaking his head. "Should we tell the captain?"

"What should we say, there's yet another malcontent on the streets? We'd as well inform him the sun came up, or there is an excess of mice in the granary!" The first guard barked out a laugh. "Come on, let's get back to the barracks. A drop of hot spiced wine sounds good to me."

"Friend."

Sound shaped into word, repeated now, along with a gentle shake of the shoulders. Eduin's head felt as if it had swollen to several times its normal size, and with each pounding of his pulse, an answering jolt erupted behind his eyes. Hands slipped beneath his arms, lifting him. He opened his mouth to protest, for the slightest movement only intensified his headache. He realized his eyes were still closed, and a bright light shone directly on his face.

Day.

He mumbled a curse. It had been day when he found oblivion beneath the tavern bench, but now it was day again. Probably not the same one, but he neither knew nor cared.

"Come on, sit up, that's the way," came the voice again.

Go away. Leave me be.

Thought came slowly, as if the cheap ale still flooded his veins. Somehow, he found himself on his feet, eyes slitting against the brightness. He made out the blurred shape of a man—one head, two arms, two legs—enough to convince him this was probably real and not another drunken hallucination.

"Aldones, you stink," the stranger said. "But you're soaking wet and I can't let you stay out here. Night's coming on. It'll be a cold one, enough to freeze Zandru's bones."

To freeze. It was a painless death, he'd heard. To sleep and never wake, not with some interfering stranger yammering at him. It sounded wonderful.

No more forcing down ale so raw a dog wouldn't touch it, guzzling the stuff until the knot in his belly finally eased and the voice in his head fell silent. No more petty, demeaning jobs or stealing small coins, begging for the next round. He'd long since ceased to care about a bed or food or the taunts of the gutter urchins. The only thing that mattered was the next drink, and the next. And stillness, blessed stillness.

His body was moving now, partly by its own reflexes, partly propelled by the gentle, uncompromising hands. About him, an alley came into focus. He didn't recognize it; he could have been anywhere in the poorer areas of Thendara. Or Dalereuth or Arilinn, for that matter.

No, not Arilinn. For in that place, he could not hide. They would know him, no matter how dirty or drunk he was. They would know his mind, the *leronyn* of the Tower. Even with the psychic shields that long ago had become as automatic as breath, they would know him because he had once been one of them.

Here in the anonymous squalor of Darkover's largest city, no one would think to look for him. Here he could drown himself in a river of ale. No one would know if he lived or died. No one would care. Only in the bitter winter would some passerby or alehouse keeper pull a nameless drunkard out of the snow, for no one could survive such nights.

"We're almost there," said the voice.

"Wh— where?" His voice came out in a croak.

He felt rather than saw the stranger's smile. "Someplace safe."

They passed between two buildings, deep in shadow. A wind, ice-tipped, gusted down the narrow space. It would snow again tonight. His body shivered, and he thought how he might crawl into a drift and pull it over himself like a blanket of costly wool, gather it to him until it turned warm and dreamy. He would have to be thoroughly drunk to do it, almost in a stupor, or the pressure in his head would stop him. He had tried several times to seek permanent oblivion, but each time, his second conscience, like an old and evil companion, kept him alive, chained to its own purposes.

A door swung open and warmer air surrounded him. He put out one hand to catch his balance and touched the cracked, weather-splintered planks. Inside, light flared. He staggered free of the stranger's grasp and slumped into a crudely wrought chair.

He was in some sort of servants' quarters, an old scullery perhaps, though he could not make out anything beyond a rickety table along one wall. A pitcher, its rim cracked and jagged, sat beside an equally decrepit bowl. He couldn't make out the rest of the room's contents without turning his head, and that meant risking another wave of nauseating pain.

"Drink," he pleaded, gesturing with one hand.

The stranger bent over him, and it seemed a mantle of blue light rested across his shoulders. The hood of his cloak hid his face. He placed one hand on Eduin's forehead.

Rest. Rest now, and forget. We will speak tomorrow.

— ✦ —

Eduin woke again to a dim, watery light. He had been drifting in and out of strange, restless dreams in which faceless men pursued him, and each time he tried to hide, he was discovered. Now he lay on a crude pallet on the floor of a room that should have been strange, but felt familiar.

Aside from his physical discomforts, the urgency of his bladder and the thick cottony film in his mouth, he could not remember a time when he felt more at ease. More inwardly still. It was as if a voice that had been raging at him, night and day, had suddenly fallen quiet.

He sat up, his spine crackling, muscles stiff. The light came through a window, layers of oiled cloth instead of glass. A candle, thick and irregular, shone from the other side of the room. On the floor beside his pallet, he spied a mug. It contained water rather than wine or even rotgut ale, but he drank it down. There was a faint lemony taste that cleared his head and eased the dryness of his throat. It gave him the strength to haul himself to his feet, to the door and outside. The drifted snow burned his bare feet. The alley was deserted, and he discovered with some surprise that this mattered to him. He relieved himself against the side of the building.

As quickly as he could, he scurried back inside. There was no fireplace, only a small stone brazier filled with ashes. Still, the walls kept out the worst of the wind.

Heartened, he explored his surroundings. The pitcher contained more of the lemony water, and beside it was bread, only slightly moldy on one side, and hard cheese. He could not remember when he had last eaten. Chewing slowly, he finished it all, except for the moldy part. Once he would have eaten that, too, but now the smell disgusted him.

Several circuits of the room revealed no trace of its owner's personal effects. The floor was bare wood, stained and gritty with dried mud. The sleeping pallet was of the poorest sort, layers of straw and blankets too tattered for any other use, laid over a frame of wooden slats to keep it off the floor. The back of the door bore a row of wooden pegs, some broken off like rotten teeth, and here his own jacket hung. The worst of the surface filth had been brushed off and the padding stuck out in threadbare patches. He found his boots shoved into a corner. As he pulled them on, he reflected that for all appearances, the room was his, and yet he had no memory of ever being here before. Certainly, if he had come upon the few *reis* for rent, he would long since have spent them at the ale shops.

Again, he remarked on the clearness of his head and the unwonted silence in his mind. He felt no craving for drink, although there was every reason why he should. His memory presented him with numberless mornings in which his first and only thought was how he was going to get drunk again. In his time in Thendara and before that on the road, he had known many men who lived as he had, stumbling from one stupor to the next. They swore the only cure for the nausea, the headaches, and the nightmarish visions was more of the same.

Eduin had never drunk to escape the aftermath of drinking. This was what he had sought, this blessed stillness. Was it some property of this room, although it seemed ordinary and shabby? He saw no trace of a telepathic damper. From experience, he knew how useless a damper was against his inner tormentor. Properly attuned, it would keep psychic energy from entering or emanating from the room. It could not protect him from what already lay within his own mind. He had used one when he lived in a Tower, first at Arilinn, where he was trained, and later at Hali for a brief time, and then Hestral until its destruction.

Hali. Only a short half-day's ride from Thendara, it might have been on another world. At the far end of the city, at the foot of the mysterious cloud-filled lake, a Tower lifted toward the heavens, a finger of graceful alabaster. In it, as in every other Tower, psychically-Gifted men and women joined their minds to work unimaginable feats, everything from the creation of weapons to the healing of hurts. Relays sent messages across the reaches of plain and mountain; *laran*-charged batteries powered aircars, lighted palaces, and guarded the secrets of kings.

Hali. *She* had once been there. Might still be, for all he knew.

Pain washed through him, but not from any physical cause.

Eduin sank down on the pallet and buried his face in his hands. His breath came ragged as he struggled for the control he had learned in his years as a *laranzu,* a master of the psychic force called *laran.* Images flashed behind his closed eyes, bits of memory he had washed away with the bottle. The pale translucent stone walls that created the sense of light and endless space . . . the ever-restless mists of Lake Hali . . . Dyannis warm and supple in his arms.

Sweet and bitter, feelings he had thought long dead stirred in him— longing and loss and things he could not put a name to. He lay back upon the pallet. Soundless weeping racked him. Some long time later, it seemed that someone held him, rocked him, stroked his matted hair.

For this pain, too, there will be a healing.

Again, he slept.

He wandered through a dreamy landscape of gently rolling hills and a knoll overlooking a river. Although he could not remember ever having been here before, something about the place tugged at his heart. The air was almost luminous, the warmth hypnotic. Time itself seemed to be holding its breath. Tree branches stirred and dappled brilliance danced across his face. Around him drifted transparent shapes, like figures of the Overworld. They drifted in and out of his sight. He felt no sense of threat.

He thought he heard singing in sweet bell-like tones, so faint it might have been only the breeze through the leaves. Shapes took on substance. Out of the corners of his eyes, he glimpsed slender bodies and cascades of silvery hair. Eyes and skin glowed with colorless radiance, as if sculpted from moonlight.

No humans moved with such grace, for these people were *chieri*, of the race that was already ancient in the times lost to memory, when humans first came to Darkover. It was said that in the madness of the Ghost Wind, they left their forests to take human women as lovers, appearing as fair, proud elfin lords, and from that time, the blood of the *chieri*—and their *laran*—flowed through *Comyn* veins.

Their voices came clearer now as they sang through the slow, stately movements of their dance. Four moons swung through the pellucid sky, drenching it in multihued pastel light.

Part lament, part joy, the words resonated through Eduin. His body felt strangely light, as if the *chieri's* song transmuted his mortal flesh into glass. He found himself moving among them, these people whom no man had seen for hundreds of years, known only by legend. Their blood flowed in his veins, sang in his *laran*, his very soul. They turned to him with those knowing, luminous eyes, and held out their hands in welcome.

The Yellow Forest and the White, the slow, slow turning of the stars . . . the pain of exile, the seasons in their cycle like the beating of an immense living heart. . . .

And most of all, the endless dance of sky and tree, of hands and voices intertwined, so calm and sad and joyous as to break his heart, fading now. . . .

Fading. . . .

Eduin's next waking came more quickly. His senses had grown even sharper, as had his hunger. He had slept deeply, wandering in dreams that slipped away with each passing heartbeat. A rank smell arose from his body, a miasma of stale sweat, gutter filth, and the sodden reek of ale. His gorge rose at it.

There was no food, only the full pitcher. With an effort, he gulped down the water, which he now recognized as a dilute tincture of *kirian,* a psychoactive distillate used in the Towers for treating threshold sickness and other psychic maladies.

Eduin frowned as he finished the last of it. Only someone with training would know how to make the stuff, let alone administer it properly. It was clearly beneficial in his case. He could not have fallen into the hands of anyone with Tower training. If he had, he would not be in such a hovel, nor would he still be at liberty.

No, that transgression would not be soon forgotten.

His unknown benefactor had done more than refill the pitcher. Charcoal glowed in the little brazier, giving off a comforting warmth. The pile at the end of the table turned out to be clothing, a heavy tunic and drawstring trousers, worn and crudely-patched, but clean.

Set on top was a disk of fired clay, a token to one of the local bathhouses. Gathering up the clean clothes and token, Eduin pulled on his jacket and slipped into the street. He recognized the establishment by the stylized rabbit-horn on its sign, twin to the one stamped on the reverse of the token.

The woman who guarded the door inspected the token. "This one includes soap, towels, and shave. Haircut's extra." She squinted at him.

He thought of telling her he hadn't stolen the token, as she so clearly suspected. He had spent too much of his life creating trouble where there was none. The last thing he wanted was to be hauled before the *cortes* for trying to steal a bath. "That will be fine," he said meekly.

The tub was barely an arm's length across. Its wooden walls had gone velvety with age and stank of sulfur, but he didn't care. The water was deep enough to cover his shoulders. Looking down, he scarcely recognized the body as his own. When had he become so wasted, his skin so sickly pale and pocked with the small red bites of body lice? Where had the scars over his ribs come from—some altercation with a man who had even less reason to live than he had?

Sighing, he rested his head against the rim of the tub as the heat sank deep into his muscles. His hair trailed into the water.

How long he lay there, drifting in and out of consciousness, he could not tell. The water grew cool. He roused himself, noticing the puckered skin on his hands, and reached for the soap. By the time he had lathered his body twice and his hair three times, the water was scummy with grime. A bucket of rinse water stood in the corner. He hauled himself out and doused himself, though it left him shivering. He dried himself on the coarse towels left for his use and wadded his old clothes into a bundle. Filthy as they were, they might be worth a *reis* or two for rags.

Dressed now in the clean clothes, he folded a small bundle into the waist of his pants. His fingers lingered upon it for a moment. Within its wrapping of grime-stiffened silk lay the one possession he could never sell, no matter how desperate. Although its discovery would surely betray him as an outlaw *laranzu,* he dared not let it leave his person. The pale blue starstone had been given to him upon his arrival at Arilinn Tower. Throughout his training, he had used it to concentrate and amplify his *laran,* so that it had become a crystalline extension of his own mind. Were it to be lost or stolen, or fall into the hands of anyone but a Keeper, the shock might well stop his heart.

Eduin couldn't remember the last time he had been shaved by someone else. The barber, a wiry old man with more hairs jutting from the warts on his chin than from his head, hummed as he worked. When he reached for Eduin's still-damp hair, Eduin protested that he had not paid for a haircut.

"Ah, but it would be a crime to let you go, so clean and fine, with locks like these. You couldn't pick out those tangles, not even with a horse comb. Besides, a man likes to take pride in his work."

Eduin mumbled his gratitude, for it was not merely the haircut that deserved thanks, but the man's kindness. It had been a long time since his life had included such luxuries.

He spent the next few hours wandering the streets. The neighborhood was familiar, yet it seemed he had never seen anything above the gutters. When he returned to the room, he found the door ajar.

A man, tall and thin, looked up from where he was bending over the table. He wore a short cloak with a hood pulled snugly about his face. Eduin had no doubt this was his mysterious rescuer.

"I am glad you came back," he said, "so that I might thank you for all you have done for me."

"No thanks are necessary," came the reply. The voice sounded familiar, as if he had heard it in his sodden dreams. "For like has called to like, and mind answered mind."

"I—I don't know what you're talking about," Eduin stammered, suddenly alarmed.

"But you do. For who else but a fellow *laranzu* would recognize what you truly are?"

The man reached up and pulled back his hood, revealing an angular, weathered face and a head of the bright red hair of the psychically-Gifted *Comyn*.

2

Adrenaline shot along Eduin's nerves, terror born of years of hiding. Only a member of the *Comyn,* Darkover's telepathic caste, would have such flaming red hair or be able to pick up Eduin's own *laran*. Eduin could hardly remember half the things he'd done during the past year, yet he would have staked his life—for what little that was worth—that his psychic shields had not slipped. They were as much a part of him as his own breath or the sound of his heart in the stillness before the dawn. From the earliest stirrings of his powers, he had been drilled in keeping his innermost secrets. And so he had, even from his own Keepers at Arilinn and Hali. If those men, the most powerful and highly-trained telepaths on Darkover, had not been able to penetrate his barriers, then surely this bedraggled stranger could not, regardless of his bold words or the color of his hair.

"I don't know what you're talking about," Eduin repeated.

"Let us not descend to petty games," the stranger said. "We hold each other's fate in our hands. I am called Saravio."

Eduin's glance flickered once more to the man's flame-colored hair and to the hood now lying about his shoulders. *I am called,* he'd said. Not, *I am* or *My name is.* What was he hiding? Could he also be a renegade from a Tower with a price on his head? Did he guess that Eduin was in a similar position?

"You can call me Eduin," he said, keeping his voice mild.

Saravio had not offered his family name, which need not have any devious intent. Many illegitimate offspring of great *Comyn* lords found a home in the *laran* circles. There, at least, a man's ability counted more than his titles.

After a pause, Eduin asked, "By the way, which Tower did you train at?"

"Truth for truth, my friend. I will name my Tower if you name yours."

"What makes you think I trained at a Tower?" Eduin snapped. "You found me in a gutter, hardly a fitting place for a mighty *laranzu*."

Saravio laughed. "And your hair is the color of mud and not of fire, but what of that? Keep your secrets, then, and drink yourself to death or freeze because you have not the wit to come in from the storm. If, on the other hand—" In a quicksilver shift of mood, his eyes narrowed. "—if you have been sent to spy on me, you will wish you had given yourself to the snow."

Without warning, Eduin felt a burst of psychic power from the other man's mind. He recoiled. Telepathic contact meant discovery, and discovery meant death. Instinctively, he parried the probe, reaching for skills he had not used since he left Hestral Tower.

Ah! Then you are an exile, like myself. Saravio's mental touch was gentler this time, compassionate.

This is not safe, Eduin muttered silently. There was no escape. He had already revealed himself. Yet what had the other man said about each of them holding the other's fate? Curiosity stirred.

"Are you a fugitive, too?" He spoke aloud, for the ingrained fear of mental communication was still strong. If Saravio had picked up his unguarded thought, he gave no outward sign.

"In a sense," Saravio replied. "There is no price upon my head, if that's what you mean. I am an outcaste by my own conscience." He glanced at the paper-covered windows and the city beyond.

"My Tower, Cedestri, cast me out," he added in a voice low and poignant. "For they had become agents of evil."

Eduin frowned. Cedestri Tower was, he believed, some two or three days' journey from Thendara in the direction of the Dry Towns. During the brief time he was at Hali, he had heard it mentioned as researching the extraction of trace minerals from sand, hardly dangerous or controversial.

Saravio's eyes went unfocused. "When the rebuilt Towers of Neskaya and Tramontana signed the Hastur's accursed Compact, many who could not abide by it found a welcome at Cedestri Tower. But in the end, Cedestri proved no more enlightened than any other. They dismissed me."

"The reach of the Hasturs is long," Eduin said, choosing his words carefully, probing for a response. "I fear there will come a time when all Darkover bows under the yoke of their rule and the Towers will become their pawns." He lowered himself to the pallet. "I am no friend to the Hasturs or their Compact."

Once he might have been, for he had known Carolin Hastur when they were boys together at Arilinn Tower, where the young Prince spent a season during the time Eduin received his first training. Despite himself, he had liked Carolin, with his easy generous ways. He wondered if that was why he had never succeeded in ending Carolin's life, or if that had been a combination of bad luck and the infernal meddling of Carolin's other friend, Varzil Ridenow.

Saravio sat down. "What is your story, friend? Why do you hate the Hasturs?"

Where could he possibly begin? Better to keep to the latest incident, Eduin decided. His outlawry was more than sufficient reason to harbor a grudge against the Hastur family.

"In the days of King Carolin's exile," Eduin began, "Rakhal the Usurper sent an army to force Hestral Tower, where I had lately come, to make *clingfire* for his wars."

Briefly, Eduin told what happened next. The Keeper of Hestral Tower had refused, saying the old stockpiles of the caustic incendiary had been destroyed and he would make no more. Neither would he use the immense psychic force of his trained circle to actively defend the Tower. He was content to merely nullify each attack and hope that with time, Rakhal's men would go on to easier prey. Remembering, Eduin felt an echo of his outrage.

Days of siege had followed one another, with starvation drawing ever nearer. Finally, made desperate by the Keeper's inaction, Eduin seized the opportunity to defeat Rakhal's army. In secret, he assembled a circle of the strongest workers. Together, they sent spells of terror and madness into the minds of the enemy. He would have succeeded if he had not been discovered and taken prisoner by Varzil Ridenow.

Eduin made no effort to keep the bitterness from his voice as he related this part of the story. In retaliation, Hastur had ordered Hali Tower into the battle. With the very foundations of Hestral Tower crumbling beneath him, Eduin had escaped his imprisonment.

As Eduin concluded his story, Saravio nodded, his lips pressed together. In that moment, Eduin recognized a sort of kinship.

We are like brothers, he thought, *made unfit for the ordinary world by our talents and training, cast out by those very Towers that made us, forced into a life of hiding.*

It had been so very long since another human being had understood what it was like. Even his father—

Eduin broke off the thought. One hand went unconsciously to his temple. "I thank you for your help last night. Now I will be on my way."

He dared not linger. The risk of discovery was too great, for even another fugitive might be tempted by the rewards of betrayal. Zandru knew, there had been enough times when Eduin would have sold himself for the price of another drink.

Keep moving, stay out of sight, had been his watchwords since that desperate flight from Hestral Tower.

He closed the door behind him. With any luck, they would never meet again.

Outside, the brightness of the day stung Eduin's eyes. Otherwise, he felt remarkably well. How long that would last, he could not tell. He would use the time to scrabble together some money, perhaps rent a room such as this, lie low for as long as he could.

For the next two days, he found work hauling water and charcoal for a smith whose apprentice was laid up with lung fever, earning a meal and a room for the night. The urge to drink gnawed at him from time to time, but he forced himself to ignore it. Instead, he curled up on the straw pallet in the shed behind the smithy, hugging himself, holding on.

As long as the pressure in his head did not return, he repeated to himself, he would be all right. He could think, begin to plan.

Hours crept by. At night, he roused to gulp water from the ice-crusted bucket and crawl shivering back to bed. Lying there, waiting for sleep to return, he thought of the dream of light and song. Already, the memory was fading. He could not quite remember where he had been or with whom he had danced, why he had felt such soaring joy. His heart ached with a longing he had no desire to drown in drink. Instead, he clasped it to him like a precious thing, that half-remembered beauty.

Midway through the third day, the smith had no further need for him. Eduin decided to try one of the livery stables, where he had found work mucking out stalls when he was not too drunk. A couple of them might still hire him. As he made his way to that district, something shifted within him, like a cloud passing before the sun. Pressure brushed his temples and his belly tightened.

Kill the Hasturs . . . Kill them all . . .

No, it could not be. Not after so many days.

Failed . . . whispered the familiar, relentless voice. *You have failed.*

His stomach knotted. Bile filled his mouth. He shook like a palsied man. Gods, he wanted a drink. He *needed* a drink.

Before he could reach the nearest tavern, the compulsion struck again in full force. He staggered, falling against the side of the building. The edges of rock and mortar jabbed his side through the layers of his clothing. His thoughts cleared, pain pushing back the craving for an instant. The desire for drink receded a fraction and an even deeper craving came roaring up in his belly, the crushing urgency to find—to destroy—

Kill . . . K–k–kill . . . The syllable fractured like the clacking pincers of a Dry Towns scorpion.

Crying out, he crumpled against the wall. Though he tore at his face with his hands or covered his ears or drank an ocean of ale, he could not shut out the silent, insistent demand.

Escape was impossible. It always had been. What a fool he had been, to think it might be otherwise.

Despair raced through him, wave after wave so deep he could not contain it. How long he lay there, half propped against the crude wall, half sprawled in the muck of the gutter, he could not tell.

Eventually, his thoughts began to stir, along with renewed thirst.

Drink—drink would ease the noose around his soul. Just this once. Not enough to get stinking drunk, just to take the edge off so he could think straight.

A couple of hours mucking out stalls at one of the poorer stables and the sale of his bundle of filthy clothes brought him enough to buy a pitcher of ale, the cheapest he could find.

In the ale house, Eduin found a rickety table jammed against a corner that smelled of mildew. At the bar, men quaffed their drinks and laughed, telling coarse stories. He was content to be left alone.

He drank quickly at first, as he usually did. The first gulps scoured his throat as they went down. He closed his eyes, waiting for the familiar warmth to seep into his belly. Another gulp, and then another. Soon he no longer tasted the stuff; his throat seemed to open up and draw it in. Relief spread through him, a softening of the driving need. Sighing, he poured the last of the pitcher into his tankard and downed it.

He staggered only a little as he went up to the bar for another. One of the men was telling a story about a drunken farmer and his long-suffering *chervine*. Eduin found himself laughing, a chuckle that shook his body, rolling through him. Someone slapped him on the back. "Another round for this fine fellow."

Eduin accepted another full tankard and lifted it in salute. It flowed down his throat like honey. Someone began a song, others stamping or clapping their hands with the beat.

> *"Here's to the man who drinks good ale*
> *And treats his friends as well, oh!*
> *Here's to the man who drinks good ale*
> *For he's a carefree fellow . . ."*

Eduin slapped down the last of his earnings for another pitcher. One song rolled into the next. He retreated to his corner, content to hum along from the shadows. The world went swimmy except for the blessed stillness inside. Slumping against the wall, he cradled the pitcher. It sloshed reassuringly and then it did not slosh at all. He tipped it over. In his doubling sight, it seemed to be empty.

That did not matter, it was enough to simply sit here . . . to lie here, on the floor, wedged in between table leg and wall, his body curled around a knot of blissful silence.

Voices reached him, but he waved them away, *Let me sleep.* They went away for a time, then returned, more annoying and insistent than before.

"On your feet, friend . . ." The voice—voices—had a peculiar echoing quality. "Closing time. Do you have a place to go?"

Then he was upright, hard hands digging into his armpits, the world tilting and whirling about him. His legs moved beneath him as if they belonged to someone else.

"Lea' me alone . . ." *So warm, so still.*

"I'll take care of him." The voice was ale-roughened but familiar—the man who'd bought the round of drinks.

"How 'bout another?" Eduin asked.

"Better take him to the King's shelters," the man said, placing a hand on Eduin's shoulder. "Out of the cold, just the place—"

No! There would be *Comyn* youth serving as cadets, City Guard everywhere. He'd be recognized—

Eduin jerked away. "Don' need no charity. Not from you, not from no stink—no king!"

"Easy there, friend. We're just trying to help—"

"I can get home—jus' fine—on my own." Eduin rushed for the door before they could stop him.

A blast of cold, damp air shocked across his face. He fought to keep on his feet, staggered a handful of steps, then collapsed in a tangle. He hauled himself upright, twisting back toward the ale house. A man stood silhouetted against the brightness inside.

Then the rectangle of yellow light winked into shadow.

Eduin saw only a few lights, the faint flickering of candles from windows high above, a single torch burning low in the next block. No moons shone, nor any stars. A wind, ice-tipped, sprang up, threatening worse to come.

Find someplace dry and out of the wind, he urged himself. *Then sleep, just sleep . . .*

Half-crawling, half-stumbling, he worked his way toward the guttering torch. The few doors he passed were shut tight. He searched for an archway, an alcove, anything that would provide a little shelter. None appeared, but now it did not really matter. The night was not so very cold. The wind was no more than a little breeze. His body came to rest, all of its own, under an overhanging eave. From the edge of his vision, he watched the torchlight sputter and go out.

Darkness took him.

"You there!" Hands dug into his arms, hauling him upright.

He squinted at the unexpected brilliance. A torch—no, several—no, one—lit the night. One man held it while another dragged him to his feet. He gasped, inhaling the acid reek of vomit. The wind blew in cruel gusts, slicing through his clothing, burning on his skin.

"Pah!" the man who held him snorted in disgust. "He stinks to heaven!"

"He's no gutter rat." The second man moved closer. "Look at his clothes."

Eduin noticed the badges on their cloaks, the swords ready to hand, the polished boots, the precisely trimmed hair.

City Guards. By Zandru's seventh hell!

"He's just some poor devil who drank more than he could hold," the second man said, lifting the torch still higher. "We'll take him inside until he sobers up."

"Aye," replied the first. He twisted Eduin around and pushed him in the direction of the Guard headquarters.

In an instant of reflex terror, Eduin's muscles locked.

The Guard wasn't expecting resistance. "Here now, you can't go wandering off on a night like this. You'll freeze to death!"

Eduin turned and ran. Somehow, his legs obeyed him. He burst into a pounding run, heading for the shadowed alleys. His only hope was flight, and he clung to it as a lifeline. Years of finding cover, of skulking and hiding, guided him. The Guards shouted for him to stop, but he kept on, staggering around corners, hardly feeling the bite of the wind or the impact when he slammed into a wall.

Finally, he came to rest at the end of a twisted series of lanes and alleys, some buried to knee-height in refuse and filthy snow. He leaned against a patchstone wall, lungs heaving, ears straining. Moments ticked by, marked by the slowing of his pulse. He heard only normal night sounds, the creak of timbers, the shuffle of a dog nosing in the garbage, the snort and shift of a horse rousing from sleep.

In only a few minutes, the warmth his body generated during that brief flight faded. He began shivering; he had no cloak or any protection. The wind howled down the alley, eerily like the cry of a giant banshee bird of the heights. It seemed to be hunting him.

The Guards were right. He would die out here, on a night like this.

He was still drunk enough to keep off the worst of the compulsion, but not enough to completely befuddle his wits. Leaving the tomblike chill of the alley, he found his bearings. He was not far from the stables where he'd worked. With a little luck, he would be able to sneak inside.

The side door creaked as he eased it open, but no alarm sounded. The air was warm, laden with the smells of fodder and animals. One of the horses startled awake, and two others shifted uneasily in their pens as he passed. Feeling his way through the darkness, he located one of the stalls he'd cleaned out earlier. The horse was an old white mare, sweet and docile. She nickered softly as he piled the cleanest straw in one corner and buried himself in it.

— ✦ —

Gray, filtered light filled the inside of the barn. Horses stamped and buckets rattled. Eduin's head throbbed and his mouth felt thick and sour. His shirt was mostly dry, but smelled of ale and vomit. He cleaned himself as best he could with handfuls of clean straw. The white mare watched him with gentle, dark eyes as he hauled himself to his feet and went outside.

Shivering, he turned to look back toward the heart of the city. Tall buildings and stately towers, the citadel of Hastur Castle, rose above the humbler dwellings. He thought of the life he had lost, of warm, bright rooms, the keen exhilaration of using his *laran*, of the intimacy and comradeship of the circle. Gone, gone forever.

Compulsion roused, gnawed at him like a wild beast. Soon there would be nothing left of him. It would eat him up, heart and dreams and will. As if in response, thirst clawed his throat.

Drink . . . ah, yes . . . murmured the seductive thought, *drink and forget. . . .*

And wake to yet another morning of pounding in his head and bile in his mouth, drinking again as the compulsion pressed in on him, each bout longer and sicker, each time with less hope, to the shambling, sodden creature he had made of himself. This time there would be no gentle stranger to drag him in from the storm, no dream—

No dream.

He did not want to die. Especially, he did not want to die alone. He did not know what to do. He only knew that he could not continue the way he had before.

The dream itself had vanished, swept away by the pulse and throb of pain. But he *had* dreamed it. That much he must believe, or he would surely go mad.

Not for an instant did he believe the vision to be true. It was simply an illusion born out of his own inner longing. Saravio must have induced in him a state of extraordinary euphoria or suggestibility, having learned the technique during his training at Cedestri Tower. Perhaps the *kirian* played a part.

The dream . . . and then the blessed space of freedom. He must find out how it had been done.

3

Eduin paused in front of the weathered door, one hand raised. It was folly to return, like a moth to a candle, but some deep, wordless impulse had defeated all reason, overridden all instinct for survival. Perhaps after so many years of having no hope, only the long dark descent into despair, he could not turn away from that single luminous memory of *chieri* dancing beneath the moons, of himself being one of them.

Before Eduin could knock, however, the door swung open. Saravio stood there, hood slightly askew over his red hair, as if he had just pulled it on. He grabbed the front of Eduin's jacket, still flecked with bits of straw, and pulled him inside.

"Did they follow you?"

"No one follows me."

"You're sure?"

"Yes, I'm sure." Stepping back, Eduin pulled Saravio's hands away. "Do you think I wouldn't know?"

"Yes, of course. You would know." Saravio's posture softened. "Are you hungry?" he asked, as if Eduin had stepped out for a moment instead of the better part of four days.

Saravio divided the heel of a loaf and gestured for Eduin to sit beside him on the pallet. Eduin bit into the bread, finding a dense, chewy interior beneath the stale crust. Ground nuts and some kind of pleasantly bitter seeds had been mixed into the dough. He knew from experience that such a mixture could keep a man going for a long time.

Behind his eyes, the pressure nudged. *Failed . . . you have failed . . .*

The two began talking, Eduin guardedly, searching for an opening. They spoke of inconsequential things, the coarseness of the nutbread, the weather that day, the price of salt. Eduin learned how Saravio had been supporting himself. Although Saravio's voice was quite ordinary, he had been earning a few coins here and there by singing to the sick. The freemate wife of the man who ran the White Feather Inn had a daughter who was dying of a wasting disease. The child could not sleep for the pain. There was nothing to be done, for they could not afford the fees charged by the city physicians, let alone the even more costly charges of the few *leronyn* willing to accept such work.

"Was there nothing *you* could do for her?" Eduin asked. Surely Saravio, like every other *laranzu,* must have trained as a monitor. Perhaps he had even used those skills, albeit in an unusual way, to temporarily lessen Eduin's compulsion spell.

Saravio shook his head. "Naotalba did not wish it. I do not know her will for the child, the reason she surrendered her into the arms of Avarra, the Dark Lady. Yet in her mercy, Naotalba permitted me to ease her pain."

Naotalba? Eduin blinked, momentarily stunned. Of all the possible explanations for Saravio's mysterious behavior, this one was the least expected.

Like any other educated Darkovan, Eduin knew the legends of Naotalba, The Doomed One, the Bride of Zandru. She might have been human once, a sacrifice to the Lord of the Seven Frozen Hells. Her name was invoked as a curse and it was considered unlucky for an unmarried woman to dress as she did in midnight black, the color of a starless sky. In another, more hopeful version, so great was her beauty and her grief at leaving the world that Zandru allowed her to return for half the year, thus bringing spring and summer.

Eduin had never paid any particular attention to any of the stories. They were all superstitious nonsense. What could a mythical demigoddess have to do with healing a sick child?

"She came to me," Saravio said, now closing his eyes and tilting his head back, rocking slightly with the memory. "She spoke to me. I saw the entire world laid out like a tapestry. It was to be mine, she promised, if I would faithfully do her bidding. I awoke the next morning with her kiss upon my brow."

One hand brushed the pale forehead. "I alone of all men was chosen to be her champion. I alone was given the mission of healing the pain of the world. I alone received her gift. I went to my Keeper with the news, for in those days I still believed there was hope for the Towers."

Eduin drew back unconsciously. He could imagine the reaction of Auster of Arilinn, or Hestral's Keeper, Loryn Ardais, or even Varzil Ridenow, who now ruled at Neskaya, to such an announcement. Steadiness of mind was essential to matrix work, and no sane man claimed to commune with the gods.

Why not? he thought. The scorpion-spirit of his dead father whispered its poison nightly into his own ears.

Saravio opened his eyes, hands curling into fists. "Do you know what they said? They *forbade* me to use Naotalba's gift! They cast me out! And why? Because of some idiotic rule about not messing with another man's mind! As if the Bride of Zandru is bound by their petty tyranny!"

Not messing—Eduin knew a moment of panic, for the most fundamental law of *laran* work was never to enter another's thoughts unbidden. He had sworn it on his first day of training at Arilinn.

And broken it, too, at the siege of Hestral Tower, he reminded himself.

But was that so evil? He had lifted the siege and saved the Tower. It was only because of Varzil Ridenow's relentless grudge that he had not been hailed as a hero and been made Keeper permanently. What Eduin had done would be doubly unlawful under Carolin's Compact, which forbade any use of psychic force, or any weapon that killed without exposing its wielder to equal jeopardy, for that matter. Eduin thought the idea ridiculous. Men would always seize whatever power came within their grasp, even if they had to invoke some imaginary figure to justify it.

And yet . . .

He recalled what Auster, the Keeper who trained him, had said; that men devised myth and legend to explain what they could not understand. When he felt the spell his father had laid on him, he sometimes envisioned it as a frozen vice clamped around his temples, other times a slowly turning knife point in his belly. Perhaps Saravio envisioned himself acting upon the will of the demigoddess when he did his healing work. Surely easing the pain of a dying child was a good thing.

Eduin, his interest aroused, asked, "What exactly is Naotalba's gift? How did you use it to help this child?"

In answer, Saravio closed his eyes and began humming. His sense of pitch was not very good, but Eduin recognized a common street song. The melody would have been familiar and reassuring to the child of an innkeeper. Perhaps her own mother had sung it to her as a lullaby.

> *"Oh the lark in the morning,*
> *She rises in the west,*
> *And comes home in the evening*
> *With the dew on her breast."*

As he listened, Eduin felt his own muscles soften and relax. The soreness from the unaccustomed hard labor melted, replaced by a warmth that soon spread along his limbs. His belly felt as full as if he had just risen from a holiday feast. The dull pressure in his head lifted, and within the confines of his skull, he heard only the lilting melody.

His lips curved unbidden into a smile. Surely there could be nothing so wonderful as to sit here, surrounded and filled by this music. He could not remember feeling so safe, so content, so blissful. The knotted ice in his belly lifted like mist from summer fields. The hissing scorpion voice in his head fell utterly still. A wave of inexpressible relief passed through him. Tears rose to his eyes. From his groin, heat thrummed in rising pleasure.

Pleasure . . .

What in the name of all the gods was Saravio *doing*?

Eduin jerked alert, his psychic barriers slamming into place. The physical sensations of arousal receded. He caught his breath in a gasp and realized he had been weeping silently. Saravio was still half-singing, half-humming, his words barely understandable.

"What—" Eduin stammered, "what did you do to me?"

Saravio met his gaze with a blankly innocent stare, devoid of any trace of dissembling. "You? I brought you in from the storm."

"You sang to me, didn't you? Just as you did to the child, just as you did now?"

"You were delirious and might have done yourself injury. I sang to calm you. There was no harm in it, any more than when I sang for the innkeeper's daughter."

"And that's all? You just . . . sang to me?"

Again, that guileless stare, as blank as a child's. "Why, yes, unless . . . You must mean the *kirian*. I had a little remaining to me. Are you angry that I gave it to you without your permission? We are neither of us bound by the rules of the Tower."

"No, I'm not angry," Eduin admitted.

The *kirian* alone could not have eased the spell. Either Saravio was a consummate liar with the best *laran* shielding on Darkover, or else he truly did not know what he had done.

Saravio shrugged. "As you have heard, I am no minstrel. Still, it was honest work and paid for this room, food, a little heat. My needs are few. In the end, Avarra took the child to her bosom and I had not the heart to sing for another. On the day I found you, a man at the King's granary gave me a coin. I wonder if he thought me a beggar. He should have known better, for he understood the evils that beset this city, which only Naotalba can save. But alas, Naotalba had not touched his eyes, as she has mine."

Before Eduin could ask any more questions, Saravio leaned closer. His eyes burned, as if lit with dark fire. He lowered his voice, now trembling with urgency. "I can trust you. You know what it is to run, to hide, to be persecuted for speaking the truth."

Eduin nodded, although he was not entirely sure what Saravio meant. His head might be steadier than it had been in many seasons, but he still had difficulty thinking clearly. The song and its effects lingered, wrapping him in a dreamy lassitude.

"I believe that Naotalba has spoken to you, too," Saravio whispered, his breath rasping between his lips. "Until now, I was the only one who could stand against her enemies, and you see what I have been reduced to. I live in this hovel, the object of charity, with not a single follower to hear her truth. I tell you, my friend, more than once I came close to despair. But Naotalba has kept faith with her servant. She brought *you* to me." Saravio grasped Eduin's shoulders, bringing his face within a few inches. Sweat broke out over Saravio's forehead and his eyes bulged, so that the tracery of tiny red vessels stood out.

"She *has* brought you to me, hasn't she? Or . . . were you sent to destroy her work? Answer quickly!"

Waves of trembling shook Saravio's frame and his cheeks flushed a dark, congested red. His fingers dug into Eduin's flesh like talons.

Along with the shouted words, Eduin felt a renewal of the pressure against his psychic shields. If he failed to give the proper response, Saravio might well throttle him on the spot.

You are right. She has sent me to you, he answered, mind to mind so that there could be no question of deception. Using the force of the Deslucido Gift as his father had taught him, even as he himself had lied under truthspell, he shaped the thought so that it would ring with sincerity.

For a long moment, Saravio did not respond. Eduin wondered if he had said the wrong thing. Perhaps Saravio was so caught up in his own frenzy that he had not received the mental message. The pressure on Eduin's throat tightened.

"You passed her test—when you healed me," Eduin gasped aloud, "and now I am here—to guide you—in your great work."

"I knew it!" Saravio crowed, releasing Eduin. "I knew she would not abandon her chosen one!"

Well, Eduin said to himself as he rubbed his neck, making sure no trace of the thought leaked past his barriers, *Naotalba is as good a god as any, these days.*

For so long, his only goal had been freedom from a quest that he could not possibly fulfill. As a penniless fugitive without any way of making a living, save with those skills that would betray him, he had no hope of putting an end to King Carolin. Now for the first time, he had both respite and hope—hope that with the help of this stranger, however odd he might be, Eduin might rid himself forever of his father's dying curse.

"I knew it—I knew it—" Saravio chanted, bouncing up and down on the rickety pallet like a small child. "I knew–ew–ew–ew it!"

Dark Avarra, the man is not odd, he's raving mad!

Eduin got to his feet, thinking it would be safer to retreat for a time. He had already seen enough of Saravio's shifting moods to suspect how uncertain, how dangerous his temper might be.

Before he could turn toward the door, however, Saravio's body went rigid. His eyes bulged, the whites stark against the dusky flush of his cheeks. He arched backward and fell upon the pallet with a loud thump. For a moment, he lay there, as still as a corpse.

The door lay only a step or two away. Eduin could be gone in a moment, out into the streets and their familiar anonymity. Every instinct shrilled at him to run, to hide. He might have a few hours or days before the compulsion returned. Yet, he hesitated.

Saravio's next breath came as a hoarse gasp. His spine bowed upward, so that he rested on the back of his skull and his hips.

Eduin had trained as a monitor at Arilinn, one of the oldest and most prestigious of all the Towers on Darkover. Although he had not done the delicate work of diagnosis and healing by *laran* in many years, he had not forgotten the techniques.

Do nothing to draw attention to yourself, urged his years of living as an outlaw. *Hide who you are and what you can do.*

Shudders ran the length of Saravio's frame, each wave peaking in a spasm. Eyeballs rolled up in their sockets, parted lids revealing crescents of white. Arms and legs flailed wildly, fell still for a moment, then began twitching again. Teeth snapped together. No breath came from between the lips pulled back in a rictus.

Even through his psychic barriers, Eduin sensed the wild chaos of the other man's nervous system, the agony of his straining muscles, the lungs screaming for air, the frenzied beating of his heart.

Eduin took a deep breath. This man had pulled him from certain death in the snow, had given him a gift beyond imagining. He could not walk away now.

He threw himself down beside the pallet and fumbled at his belt for the starstone in its wrappings. The crystal warmed instantly upon contact with his bare hand.

The world shifted. He had been living without using his *laran* for so long, he had grown blind. Now every detail, every radiant nuance of color and texture, of sound and smell and inner sensing glowed incandescent across his conscious mind. He closed his eyes, ignoring the sting of renewed tears.

Without visual sight, using his starstone to amplify his *laran* senses, Eduin narrowed the focus of his concentration. Saravio's energy body burned like a flame. The channels and nodes that conducted psychic forces appeared as a spectrum of colors—reds and oranges, searing white and dull brown. The brilliance indicated the strength of the man's *laran,* which was considerable.

Rarely had Eduin seen such disorder, such a breakdown of the normal balances. Colors clashed, especially at the centers at the base of the brain. The node at the bottom of the skull pulsed wildly, throwing off sparks that bore a sickening resemblance to *clingfire.* Wherever they touched, they left gaping holes of darkness in Saravio's energy body.

Eduin searched his memory for a similar pattern. Once, in his first year as a fully qualified matrix technician, he had assisted in the treatment of a woman with falling-sickness. At unpredictable intervals, she would become unconscious and her body would jerk uncontrollably, leaving her battered and exhausted, but with no memory of what had happened to her. Otherwise, she appeared normal, except for the odd neural cross-circuits.

Eduin opened his eyes. Saravio's skin had turned blue around his mouth. He could not survive much longer without air, nor could his heart withstand the strain.

Spreading his fingers wide, Eduin reached out his free hand to scan the other man more deeply. Normally, he would avoid actual contact with the patient he was examining. It was too easy to be misled by direct physical touch.

Just then, Saravio's torso heaved upward, contorting so that his arms wrapped around Eduin's neck. Hands dug into the back of Eduin's shoulders with iron strength, pulling him down. Desperately, Eduin pushed away. It was no use. He was held fast. Panic seared him. He struggled for breath. The mingled rankness of sweat and terror filled his nostrils.

Somehow, Eduin managed to slide his free hand in front of his own shoulders. Gasping, he shoved as hard as he could. His hands slipped upward along the slope of Saravio's rib cage. Under his fingers, he felt the hard line of jawbone. He curled his fingers around Saravio's lower face. If only he could make contact with the brain centers that controlled the other man's muscles. Even a moment of relaxation would allow him to pull free—

He shaped his *laran* like a spear point to pierce the tumult.

Almost without effort, Eduin swept through the other man's chaotic barriers. Images flooded him, stark and vivid. He caught a flash of a Tower illuminated by lightning against a night sky, then a blizzard of swirling gray and white, a river in full flood, a figure in a long dark cloak. The eddies died, leaving only the figure turning slowly toward him.

Hands pale as snow drew back the hood and he saw it was a woman. She lifted her face. Framed by hair the color of jet that dipped in a peak between her flawless brows, her skin glimmered like pearl. The faintest tracery of rose on her cheeks and lips was the only color. Gray eyes searched his, yet he knew she could not see him.

Hers was a beauty to break men's hearts, and yet as Eduin looked upon her in that moment, he felt only pity. Pity that such a human woman walked the earth no more, but must descend into the Seven Frozen Hells.

She shaped a word, perhaps *Adelandeyo, walk with the gods,* a formal phrase of parting among the *Comyn.*

Walk with the gods, she must.

Naotalba.

Eduin repeated her name to himself. He thought that if she answered him, if she called his own name, then his heart would shatter.

A gust sprang up at that moment. It whipped Naotalba's gray cloak, churning the snow at her feet into glittering billows. First her body disappeared, then the pale oval of her face. The dark outline of her cloak flared outward, growing in size like a giant maw, opening to engulf the whole world. Around it, the wind raged, streams of sleet and darkness, far worse than any Hellers blizzard. He looked upon a tempest against which no man could stand, a maelstrom straight from Zandru's coldest hell. And it was coming for him . . .

NAOTALBA! NAOTALBA!

Claws like frozen darkness pierced him. In a spasm of terror, he hurled himself backward. The psychic substance of his body stretched and tore. A brassy din reverberated through him.

Eduin found himself back in his physical body, sprawled on the wooden floor. His outstretched legs convulsed for an instant. Then he scrambled to his feet. He ran trembling fingers over his face, feeling the skin damp and hot, as if with fever. He snatched up the filthy scrap of silk and tucked his starstone away. Chest heaving, he looked down upon the man on the pallet.

Saravio lay back on the bed, his breath deep and even. The blue tinge had faded from his lips and as Eduin watched, the iron tension seeped from his muscles. His face relaxed, giving him the aspect of a sleeping child.

Eduin's heart pounded in his ears and sweat ran freely down the sides of his neck and across his chest and back. Gradually, his terror gave way to pity. He knew very well the taste and weight of obsession, the bitterness of enslavement. What must it be like to live, day by day, with such visions, cast out by the very Tower that was his best hope of healing?

If Eduin were to have any chance at ending his father's curse, he must find some way to help this poor, crazed man. Murmuring a prayer he thought long forgotten, Eduin slipped out the door.

— ◆ —

Eduin returned to Saravio's quarters late in the day, as the early dusk engulfed the canyons of the city. The place was very much as he had left it, with Saravio lying on his side, knees bent toward his chest, head resting on his outstretched arm, breathing deep and regular. Eduin sensed rather than saw all this. The battered lantern that he had purchased with part of his day's earnings cast an uncertain light across the room. In his other hand, he clutched a packet of nutbread, the cheapest he could find, and a skin of water. It had taken all of his ragged determination not to fill it with ale instead.

Sighing with weariness, he set the lantern on the crude table and lowered himself to the pallet. He placed one hand on Saravio's shoulder. The physical contact flooded him with *laran* sensations. As Saravio slept, his brain had continued its recovery. Waves of energy rippled through the overlapping systems of nervous tissue and energon channels, slow but steady.

Eduin sent out a mental probe, a simple telepathic thought. It ought to have been as clear as spoken word to the man's awakening mind, but there was no response, not even a flicker of awareness. He had not expected one.

He shook the shoulder gently. Saravio's eyes opened.

"It's you. I dreamed . . . Naotalba . . ."

"Yes, you're all right now. Here, you must eat something." Gently, Eduin helped the other man to sit up.

Like an obedient child, Saravio accepted morsels of bread and sips of water. He took the first few bites tentatively, as if he had forgotten how to chew and swallow. When Eduin sent a gentle telepathic message, Saravio gave no sign, overt or mental, that he'd sensed anything.

The little experiment confirmed Eduin's suspicions. All through the day, as he had labored at mucking out stalls at the livery stables at the city's edge, he had mulled over the morning's events.

Whatever Saravio's talents while he was still at Cedestri Tower, before Naotalba had "visited" him, he was now as head-blind to telepathic contact as any commoner. Coupled with his delusions and unpredictable temper, that would certainly render him unfit for work in a matrix circle.

Eduin thought it likely that whatever caused the seizures had also damaged that part of Saravio's brain responsible for receptive telepathy. Saravio seemed to have no idea of his extraordinary projective empathy, his ability to temporarily override the compulsion spell.

We are two of a kind, Eduin thought with a touch of unfamiliar compassion, *each crippled through no fault of our own. Perhaps together we can make one whole patched-up man and limp through the world.* No, he realized, he would no longer have to settle for a half-existence in the shadows. Life held the promise of much more.

Emotion, hot and bright, came singing up behind Eduin's throat. For the first time in his years of hiding, he had a friend, an ally. He would know moments of freedom, and in them, a chance to think, to plan, to reach beyond the gutters. Perhaps, too, he could help Saravio find peace and a use for his unusual talent. It would be a fair trade.

4

The last of the snow clung to the alleys and back streets of Thendara long after it had melted everywhere else. Here in the poorest sections, shadows clung, chill and secretive, to the broken walls. Grime scummed pools of slushy water. Half-starved children picked through the piles of refuse for scraps of moldy bread.

Eduin, now close friends with Saravio, had moved to roomier quarters. Saravio sang to him whenever he could not bear the internal pressure of his father's dying curse, and he would know a few days of release before the cycle, remorseless and inexorable, began again. Saravio sometimes lapsed into seizures after an episode, although the fits were never as severe as the first. Eduin dared not leave him, for fear that Saravio might stop breathing again. This only increased Eduin's exposure to the euphoria of the song. His craving for drink abated, but at the same time he found himself longing for the moments of physical pleasure that accompanied Saravio's *laran* manipulations, finding ways to draw them out. The allure frightened him, for it was, both in its power and its purity, far more seductive than ale.

With the lifting of the numbing effects of drink, Eduin experienced a renewal of other emotions as well. Whenever Saravio suffered his fits, Eduin felt a mixture of pity, disgust, and guilt. Guilt that he himself had brought this malady upon the friend who sought only to help him. He never inquired about Saravio's willingness to pay this price. Indeed, Saravio always responded cheerfully to his request and afterward, seemed unaware of what had happened. Then Eduin felt shame, as if he were taking advantage of the innocent trust of a child. He thrust the unpleasant feelings from his mind. What choice did he have? Silently, he promised himself that he would use the respite from the compulsion in a good cause. He swore he would find a way to do without the soporific effect. Usually he would feel better for a while, until he was forced to ask Saravio to sing again.

As one tenday blended into the next and the sun swung higher in the sky, heralding the end of winter, Eduin began to wonder if he had exchanged one form of imprisonment for another. As far as he could tell, Saravio's *laran* manipulation did not place his life and health at risk the way drink had, but he was no less chained to it. Sooner or later, the compulsion within his own mind returned, the scorpion roused to spread its poison in his mind and drove him to beg another song. Eduin grew to resent his dependence. Only his quick thinking in representing himself as Naotalba's messenger prevented him from deteriorating into Saravio's abject slave, willing to do anything for yet another ecstatic moment.

At least, there were times, however brief, when his thoughts were clear. There must be a way to free himself of both the enslavement of his father's command and the numbing addiction of either drink or Saravio's euphoric touch. He walked the outskirts of the city, to and from his days of casual labor, and considered his situation.

Gradually, Eduin's awareness shifted. He needed a permanent solution, not a temporary respite that exacted an even higher toll. Perhaps the answer was not to dampen the compulsion but to fulfill it. For so long now, he had regarded it as an impossible task. How could he possibly attack Carolin Hastur while he was reduced to skulking in the shadows, hardly able to earn his bread for fear of revealing himself? He had never succeeded before, when he was the Prince's companion, and Zandru knew, he had had enough opportunities.

Carolin Hastur seemed to lead a charmed life. He had survived every attempt on his life, not only by Eduin and his brother, but by his own cousin, Rakhal, who had seized the throne and sent Carolin into exile. How had the man done it?

In a strange, transcendent clarity, Eduin understood. It was not his fault he had not been able to defeat Carolin Hastur so many years ago. Something had always gotten in the way.

Not something. Someone.

A voice whispered through the hollows of his mind, not the brutal command Eduin knew so well, but nonetheless familiar, subtle and cunning: *Varzil Ridenow is the power behind the Hasturs. Without his counsel . . . Carolin will fall . . .*

Eduin would not be a penniless outcast if it were not for Varzil Ridenow. He would be secure in his position as Keeper, hailed as the savior of the siege of Hestral, and Carolin would long since have been in his grave.

Varzil! At every turning in Eduin's life, Varzil Ridenow had managed to thwart him. It was Varzil who kept Carolin safe from Eduin's careful plans, Varzil who had tried to prevent Eduin's first romance with his younger sister, Dyannis, Varzil who foiled Gwynn's assassination attempt, Varzil who secretly aided Carolin during the Prince's long exile, Varzil who unmasked Eduin's role in the murder of Queen Taniquel's daughter, and betrayed Eduin during the battle to save Hestral Tower.

In order to fulfill his father's command, he must kill Carolin Hastur, whom he once loved, but in order to do that, he must first eliminate Varzil Ridenow, whom he hated still.

As the thoughts roiled in Eduin's mind, the knot of ice in his belly loosened. Triumph shivered through him. For the first time, he need no longer fight the compulsion. Instead, he would use it to fire his own thirst for justice.

Justice . . . and the end of Varzil Ridenow. He would have to go carefully. He had no direct access to any Tower, let alone the most famous Keeper on Darkover. A Keeper of Narzil's ability could not be taken by surprise or killed by ordinary means. Varzil might have the resources of rank and Tower behind him, but even the most mighty *tenerézu* was mortal flesh and blood. Eduin needed a way to bring Varzil down from Neskaya, place him within reach . . . distract him . . .

And in this pursuit, Saravio would be his ally, his helper, his tool.

Traders arrived with the opening of the roads, and a party of rich *Comyn* lords walked the broad avenues in their fur-trimmed cloaks, their heads raised to the spring sunshine. The laughter of the women rose above the music. A bevy of jugglers and street minstrels accompanied them. Two young boys, twins by the look of them, shrieked in delight as they tossed a glittery ball. Their nurse, her ample skirts of fine-woven wool swirling around her, ran after them.

"Look at them," Eduin said to Saravio. They were standing at a corner beside the door of the inn where they'd earned a few coins chopping wood and washing dishes.

Along the street, a crowd in tattered rags, many with weeping sores on their exposed skin, pressed against the City Guards. Despite the clear skies, the air carried a faint prickle like the first intimation of lightning, perceptible only to trained *laran* yet hovering on the edge of the senses.

Saravio still went cloaked. With time and Eduin's coaching, he was rapidly losing the carriage of a Tower worker. No one would mistake him for a peasant, but he passed well among the underclass. He might have been a tradesman or a soldier, down on his luck and on the streets too long, surviving from day to day. Now, he had no difficulty finding work as a common laborer.

Saravio's lip curled in a sneer that Eduin felt rather than saw. "They play while our people suffer."

Our people. Eduin wondered if he could use Saravio's bitterness and the simmering resentments of the people to generate an attack against Varzil Ridenow. "The *Comyn* are nothing but parasites," he pointed out. "But it is the corrupt Towers that sustain their position. Without that power, they would be nothing."

Once Eduin had believed that the Towers ought not to take orders from kings, as if they were some breed of superior servant. Those who created *laran* weapons were the only ones with the right to decide how they were to be used. Such power ought to rule, not to serve. But the Keepers were too bound to law and tradition to see the truth, just as they had turned away Saravio's remarkable gift. Although their reasons differed, Eduin and Saravio found common cause in their hatred of the Towers.

"Stand back!" one of the Guards cried. He had drawn a stout wooden staff instead of his sword, and he pressed it against the foremost ranks of the crowd.

"For pity!" one man cried. His shirt hung loose from shoulders that had once been broad and strong. Now the bones jutted from his body like the beams of a ruined house. "My children are starving!"

"Then you should have stayed where you belong, and not come to Thendara." One of the *Comyn* party, a young man barely twenty, took a step toward them. He'd thrown back his cloak to reveal a tunic of elaborately-patterned cut velvet, ornamented with a golden chain whose price would have fed an entire village for a year. The sun glinted on his pale hair, the color of straw with only a slight tinge of red. Eduin caught only the whiff of *laran* from the boy, not nearly strong enough to be worth training.

"My good fellow," the young lordling drawled, "did you think you'd find the streets lined with food stalls? We have nothing for you here. Go back home."

"Home?" The man spoke with a thick accent. Anguish ripped through his cry, echoed by nods and glances from the people around him. "To what home? To a pile of cinders, all that's left after the *clingfire* fell." With one hand he jerked his shirt open. Gasps surrounded him.

Eduin's stomach lurched at the sight of the man's chest, scarred over where it had been cut half away, leaving his arm a skeletal ruin. He'd seen what *clingfire* could do. Once ignited, it would burn anything combustible, even human flesh and bone, until there was nothing left. The only way to stop it was to physically dig out every single fragment. Someone had saved this man's life, but at the cost of his livelihood.

"What choice does he have?" Eduin muttered to Saravio. "He cannot farm with his arm like that. He came here for help, and this arrogant puppy tells him to go home!"

"I did not come for charity," the man went on, "but to find work."

"Work!" another man, equally ragged, shouted. "Work and justice!"

"I am very sorry for you all," the boy said, clearly shaken, "but it wasn't our fault—"

"Your kind sent the aircars that dropped it!" someone behind the crippled farmer cried.

"Aye, and the root blight what ruined two years' wheat crops till we had nothing left to plant!" came another voice. More joined him as they surged forward, shoving hard against the City Guards. The incipient electrical tension of the day fueled their anger.

The *Comyn* women and children hurried away, their faces white. The City Guards beat back anyone who tried to follow.

Eduin smiled grimly. The legacy of Carolin's predecessor, the brutal Rakhal Hastur, lay all about them: injustice, hunger, disease, the ravages of terrible *laran*-powered weapons.

The time of the Hundred Kingdoms was coming to an end, if not in this generation, then surely in the next. Even a fool could see that. These wars were the dying spasms of an age. Even now, a few powerful families extended their dominion over weaker client kingdoms.

King Carolin of Hastur had become foremost among them. He might have been a good man once, but the world, with all the allure of power, now had him in its grip.

Soon there would be no one to stop him.

His father's words echoed in his memory: *Varzil Ridenow is the key. Without his counsel, Hastur will fall* . . .

The crippled farmer stood, watching where the rich lords had passed. His chest heaved with emotion, his face flushed. Desperation radiated from his twisted body like heat from a furnace. Some of the crowd dispersed, but a number of them, particularly the men, remained. They seemed to be drawn to his intensity, as if he had been telling their stories as well as his own.

An idea formed in Eduin's mind. Gesturing to Saravio to follow, he strode toward the crippled farmer.

"That was courageous of you to speak so to a *Comyn* lord," he said, pitching his voice so that all around could hear him.

The farmer narrowed his eyes. Adrenaline and color drained from his features. His one good shoulder hunched, as if he would slink away.

Eduin restrained him with a gentle touch on the arm. "It is a black day for all of us when a man cannot speak the truth or demand justice."

"Whether he will receive or not it is another matter," Saravio added.

Eduin stepped into the open area in the center of the street. With a simple twist of the ambient psychic energy, he cast a glamour about himself, so that he drew all eyes to him. He could speak in a whisper, and every word would be remembered.

"Whether or not he will *take* what is his due is yet another," Eduin said. The men around him were as clear to his *laran* as if they had shouted their feelings aloud. Anger and curiosity surged above their ingrained fear.

The farmer rubbed his withered shoulder with his good hand, as if measuring his own human power against the sorcery that could create such a weapon as *clingfire*.

"What's the use? What can any of us do against the mighty lords? And what will befall my children if I'm arrested, without even the few poor *reis* I now earn?"

One of the men muttered, "What are we to do? They feast while our children starve." Around him, the other men and women nodded. Their eyes glowed with eagerness.

"And why is that?" Eduin asked. "What gives them the right to take the best of everything for themselves? Are they gods, to decide who shall live and who shall die? Do they burn with the *clingfire* they command?"

"No!" a woman with a pock-marked face cried. "*We* starve! *We* burn!" Her simmering anger flared suddenly.

"I'll hear no more of this treason," a grizzled fellow with one eye patched said, drawing back. Although his cloak was as dirty and ragged as any, he held himself like a soldier. "I fought for King Carolin, who brought an end to Rakhal's reign of terror. Now he and Varzil, him they call the Good, they've got this Compact, they say, that will end these terrible wars forever. Let honest soldiers fight as they can, and leave the wizards to their own."

"Do you really believe that the high lords will give up their best weapons?" the woman rounded on him. "That they care a filthy *reis* about the likes of us?"

"Hold your tongue, woman," the grizzled man rumbled, gesturing toward Saravio and Eduin. "The King's worth a hundred of the likes of them, and if he says he will bring peace to all these lands, that's what I'll hold to."

"Let us speak more of this," Eduin said urgently. "But not here in the open, for their spies are everywhere. Meet us tonight in a safe place—the inn called The White Feather."

"Aye, we know the place," one of the other men, a farmer by his clothing, said. "The folk there are honest enough, or as much as any can be in these times."

Quickly, Eduin set a time. He scanned the dispersing group with his mind. Hope flared in them, an excitement beyond what he'd expected. Someone had gently fanned the embers of resentment into exhilaration. Saravio.

The red-haired man stood with unfocused eyes. Eduin picked up the ripple of *laran* power emanating from his mind, and was monitor enough to sense the almost euphoric response in the crowd.

Eduin spoke to Saravio several times before the other man seemed to hear him. Saravio blinked, as if rousing from a sleep, and showed no sign that anything out of the ordinary had occurred.

"We must make preparations at The White Feather," Eduin said. "The innkeeper's wife will surely remember you with favor."

"How could she not?" Saravio said as they made their way back through the mazework of narrow streets. "Yet, I do not see what purpose a secret meeting will serve. These are poor, ignorant folk. Useless."

"Useless to the great lords in their palaces, certainly. Perhaps even to you or me," Eduin paused for dramatic effect. "But not to Naotalba."

As he'd expected, Saravio jerked alert at the name.

Eduin rushed on. "She brought me to you, didn't she? Just as she has now brought these men—this army."

"Naotalba's army? But, Eduin—these are not soldiers. They dress in rags. They have no weapons, no training. What could they possibly do?"

"That is the wrong question, my friend. It is rather what *Naotalba* can do with them. Do you doubt her power?"

They turned down the street, slightly broader than the rest, which would bring them to The White Feather. Saravio tripped on a cobblestone that had been turned on its end in the muck, jutting upward. Eduin caught his elbow, steadying him.

"I am her servant, always," Saravio declared. "It is not for me to question her ways."

"It is glorious to walk in the path of Naotalba," Eduin intoned. He despised himself for pretending a devotion he did not feel, to feed Saravio's delusions.

Once, Eduin had prayed to Zandru, Lord of the Seven Frozen Hells. Most *Comyn* honored Aldones, Lord of Light, fair Evanda, or the Dark Lady, Avarra. What did it matter which one he invoked if the cause was right? He remembered the woman of Saravio's vision and shivered inwardly. She could be dark or light, hope or despair, depending upon which aspect of the myth he drew upon. She was imaginary, a dream image, nothing more. Surely he need not fear such a thing. . . .

At the mention of Naotalba, Eduin felt an answering ripple of psychic energy from Saravio. For a moment, he allowed himself to enjoy it. It would be a simple enough thing to block the sendings, to keep himself unaffected while those around them felt whatever Saravio sent them. Pleasure . . . pain . . . elation . . . fury . . .

"Naotalba's army," Saravio murmured. He halted at the threshold of the inn and bent his head reverently. "Here it begins."

Naotalba's army, Eduin repeated to himself. A few desperate refugees tonight, perhaps, but tomorrow, their numbers would swell. An army, indeed. One to topple even the Keeper of Neskaya Tower.

5

The flush of pleasure on the face of the innkeeper's wife at seeing Saravio faded when Eduin explained what they wanted.

"The back room? For a private meeting?" She looked from one to the other. Fear lurked behind the bruise-colored hollows around her eyes. The skin of her neck hung in loose folds and her apron, although clean, had been worn almost to tatters and looked several sizes too large for her.

Eduin caught a fragment of her thoughts, the worry about how much ale might be drunk and how much bread eaten, how much she might be able to charge without overstepping the bounds of gratitude.

"We cannot pay you for the room," Eduin said in his most soothing tones, "only for food and drink, but if that is not enough—"

Saravio nudged the woman's mind. "No, no!" she cried, clearly distressed. "What must you think of me? How could I take payment from the man who did so much for my Nance?"

Before Saravio could mention the glories of Naotalba's service, Eduin pulled him away. Saravio was all too eager to stop whatever he was doing to praise his goddess, without any regard to urgency.

"We must make plans for tonight," he told Saravio as they made their way back to their tiny rented room. "These people are frustrated and angry. They lack direction or leadership. Left on their own, they will spend their strength uselessly and then scatter like chaff upon the wind."

Saravio went to the small brazier and poked through the bed of cold embers for any unburned bits of charcoal. "Naotalba's foes are many and we are but few. Yet her might will prevail. This much she has promised me."

Eduin chose his next words carefully. "Listen to me, my friend. There is more at stake than extolling Naotalba's name. She has sent us to transform the world."

"She has?"

"You yourself said it when we first met. It is the Towers who maintain the power of the *Comyn* lords, the Towers who supply them with terrible weapons like the *clingfire* that destroyed that farmer's arm. If we kill one king, even Hastur himself, what then? They will only choose another. But if even a single Tower were to fall—"

"What?" Saravio cried with a surge of his old Tower-born arrogance. "Commoners rise against trained *leronyn?*"

If Eduin were to succeed with his plan to enlist Saravio against Varzil Ridenow, then he must find a better way to convince him.

"Are you defending them?" Eduin snarled, deliberately provoking a confrontation. "Have you been lying to me about how the Keepers treated you, thrust you out, turned their backs on Naotalba's summons?"

Saravio whirled, eyes blazing. The air hummed, taut and dry. Eduin felt the tiny hairs along the back of his spine stiffen. His *laran* senses quivered with the shift in the atmosphere. With that inner sight, he saw the sky lowering, felt the massing of electrical power. This was no natural storm, of that he was sure. He lifted his head, nostrils flaring as if to catch a distant scent. At any moment, the tension would break.

Before Saravio could speak, Eduin raised his arms, spread them wide to the unseen heavens. "Naotalba!" he cried, his voice filling the little room. "Hear our prayers! Come to us—lead us—command us! We are yours!"

Saravio drew back, his eyes wide. Eduin drew breath to repeat his incantation, but just then, the very air split asunder in a deafening thunderous peal. His ears rang with it, even after it had died into rumbles. Through the papered windows, cold white brilliance burst across the room.

"Naotalba! Naotalba!" Saravio fell to his knees, hands outstretched, palms up, head flung back. He shook so violently that Eduin feared he might be on the brink of another seizure. His eyes showed as crescents of white. Again and again, he called out. Each time, the syllables became less understandable, until they merged into a single howl of raw emotion.

Eduin clamped down his *laran* barriers, lest any tinge of Saravio's frenzy seep through. Deliberately, he strode to the door and opened it. Only a portion of the sky showed between the dark outlines of the buildings, yet that strip flickered with lightning. Thunder roared again, light and sound so intermixed that the storm must be directly overhead. The air shimmered with power.

He tasted ozone . . . and raw *laran* power. In his Tower work, he'd manipulated clouds and air currents to either bring rain to a parched region or lessen a torrent. He felt certain that some artifice fueled the storm, but the traces were too deep and subtle to identify. Only a few generations ago, Aldaran sorcerers commanded weather patterns beyond the power of ordinary Towers; some said they were even able to tap into the magnetic fields of the planet. He had never believed it possible, and he did not believe it now, yet some quality of the turbulence overhead, the tension between sky and ground, made him think of armies massing for attack, of weapons being readied.

At Hestral Tower, Eduin had designed and constructed an artificial matrix to focus and direct the natural weather-sensing talent of a young *laranzu*. Whatever happened to the boy, Eduin never learned, for shortly thereafter, Rakhal's army had attacked and all had fallen into chaos. Now he stretched out his mind to the storm, searching, and came away more puzzled than before. It had none of the personal stamp of the young Tower worker, or of any other individual, for that matter.

Eduin drew away from the door, suddenly weary. In the last few tendays, he had used his *laran* more than he had in the last ten years. His muscles quivered, and he knew he should eat, despite his absence of appetite. So should Saravio, who rarely gave thought to such matters. *Laran* work consumed huge amounts of energy, which must be replaced. Eduin's thoughts wandered to his early days at Arilinn, where Lunilla, who acted as foster mother to all the novices, would pester him until he'd eaten enough to satisfy her. She always had a kind word for him, and never guessed the secrets behind his smiles. What would she think if she could see him now?

Useless musings, he told himself. Wherever she was, if indeed she still lived, they would never meet again.

On the floor, Saravio had fallen forward, his face hidden under the fall of his hair. He rocked forward and back, crooning to himself. Fine tremors ran through the muscles of his shoulders and legs. Even through his shirt, Eduin saw the outlines of Saravio's ribs.

You need food and rest, my friend, he thought with an unexpected tinge of compassion. He placed one hand on the other man's back—

Once again, the image of the woman with the face of ice, dressed in a gown of moonless black, rose up behind his eyes, a sending from Saravio's mind.

Naotalba . . . Naotalba . . . Saravio's thoughts battered him like the relentless rhythm of a drum.

This time, however, the vision did not catch Eduin by surprise. His confidence in his own mental abilities had returned along with the rush of memories—of who he had been at Arilinn, at Hali, and especially at Hestral, when he had thrown back Rakhal's army.

Why not use Saravio's own visions to ensure his cooperation? Saravio so clearly needed a cause to which to devote himself. Why not let Naotalba herself supply one?

He would have to proceed with caution, weaving his own intentions into the other man's hallucinations. Closing his eyes, he dropped to the floor and drew out his starstone.

As carefully as he could, Eduin began shaping the visual images. Saravio was so caught up in the frenzy of his belief that he accepted the changes without question. Eduin imagined the woman—Naotalba—lifting her arms in summons. He showed her at the head of an army of men and women, all gazing at her with rapt, worshipful eyes, all ready to die—or to kill—at her command. She pointed to Saravio and from her mouth came the words Eduin placed there.

"You will be my champion. You will lead my army. You will throw down my enemies and bring the dawning of a new age!"

"Naotalba! Naotalba!" Saravio's physical body crouched even lower. In the vision, he prostrated himself before her. *"I am yours to command!"*

Slowly, the pale-skinned woman smiled. Eduin drew the moment out to heighten Saravio's desperate loyalty.

"Tell me, I beg you! How may I serve you?"

Eduin painted a landscape of mental energy. Naotalba and her ragtag army stood upon a ruined plain. Steam rose from rents in the parched earth. The sky lowered, red and congested, above them. A wind, tinged with ice from Zandru's coldest hell, pulled at their hair and clothing. The vision-Saravio moaned and pressed his face against her foot.

"Arise, my general. Arise and see!"

She turned, pointing. Eduin shaped a rocky tor, and upon its peak, a Tower. He imagined it as white and smooth, like Hali. He showed the people crying out in despair. Then lightnings flew from the hand of Naotalba, lacing the air. When they touched the sides of the Tower, the resulting explosions left jagged fissures. Fragments of wall tumbled down and the Tower rocked upon its foundations. The people cheered wildly. They waved their fists and stamped their feet. Frenzy lit their faces.

"Lead us! Saravio, lead us to victory!"

Eduin held the scene as the people rushed forward, but was careful not to direct any action upon the figure of Saravio. This was not from any squeamishness about imposing his own will on the other man. He'd captured Saravio's visions easily enough and shaped them to his own purpose. No, in order for Eduin's plan to succeed, Saravio's commitment must arise from own deepest wishes. It was he who would be the visible spearhead. Eduin could not risk public exposure. Saravio would take the brunt of any reprisals should their plans go awry. In that event, he, Eduin, must be free to try again, and that meant not presenting himself as the leader.

In the shared vision, the figure of Saravio lifted his head. Eduin saw the glisten of imaginary tears upon his cheeks. Saravio looked not like a man demented, but a man transfixed. Awe had given way to acceptance and then to utter joy. A light shone in his eyes, a light not of the flesh but of something beyond. Envy stirred in Eduin, though he scarcely recognized it.

Eduin willed the figure of Naotalba closer. She reached out her ghostly arms and raised Saravio to his feet. Then, bending close, she whispered in his ear.

"Be faithful, O my champion. Be faithful and strong. My enemies lurk everywhere, and those who once betrayed me are ready to rise up again. Will you serve me?"

Saravio's eyes never left her face, but his assent was swift and unequivocal, his obedience complete.

"Then go—go and save my people! Lead them in the ways of righteousness and truth! Throw down the Towers and all the evil-doers who dwell therein!"

When Eduin returned to himself, he was sitting on the floor, his back muscles on the edge of spasm, his hands balled into fists, his jaw clenched. Saravio lay on the cot, gulping air and moaning softly.

Eduin clambered to his feet. His body cried out for food. He went to the shelf where the remains of yesterday's supper lay wrapped—stale bread and cheese, a couple of shriveled apples, along with a half-full skin bottle of sour watered ale. He ate the apples and half the cheese, then forced himself to leave the rest for Saravio. He would have to resume his Tower exercises if he were to do any more *laran* work.

Eduin lowered himself to the cot, curling his body into the empty corner. Saravio had started snoring gently, but Eduin fell into an exhausted slumber. His last waking thought was that the storm had abated.

— ✦ —

They slipped through the shadows along the street leading to The White Feather. The last dusky light had faded from the sky and there were few lamps here. Even the inns and other places that did business after dark waited as long as possible, in order to save fuel. Eduin hugged the sides of the buildings. Saravio went more awkwardly, but he was learning fast.

Even a commoner could have sensed the fear in the streets, lingering after the last of the lightnings had ceased. Fires still burned in several areas of the city, although those in the richer neighborhoods had already been extinguished. Smoke and ozone tinged the air.

They were not the only men abroad at this hour. On their way here, they had passed several others, sometimes singly, other times in groups of two or three.

"They are frightened," Eduin murmured to Saravio, "although they do not know why." He raised his voice and adopted a coarse country accent. "Aye, it's sorcery for sure. My wife's cousin tells of storms like this, and worse, down Arilinn way."

He felt the surge of interest in the group of approaching men. In a moment, they were passed, the seeds planted. As they had rehearsed, Saravio nudged the men's minds. Fear sharpened to the edge of pain. Eduin smiled.

. . . the winter so long . . . unnatural . . . Zandru's curse . . .

Yes, let them think that. Let them whisper. Let the whispers grow and feed upon themselves.

. . . Tower witchery . . . can't trust any of them . . .

Within the inn, they found light and warmth, hard-edged merriment overlying resentment like tinder awaiting a spark. The innkeep's wife brought watered ale and meatless stew, which was all the refugees could afford. She collected their money before she brought the drink, but she hovered just outside the door to listen.

From the moment he threw back the hood of his cloak, Saravio burned with a fervor that drew all eyes. The dozen men already in the room fell silent, as did the handful more who entered after them.

Saravio's first words caught them as easily as netting fish in a stream. Understanding dawned in their faces, along with surging rage. In his speech, they saw the pattern and the reason for it all, not only the obvious horrors of *clingfire* and bonewater dust, of taxes and the ravages of war, but the way the very heavens had turned against them. The killing cold of this last winter, the failure of their crops, the stillborn children, and now the eerie turbulence in the heavens themselves, all had one cause, one origin.

It was, Saravio announced as Eduin had rehearsed him, the work of the accursed *leronyn* in their Towers. Anger burned hot and clear, without hesitation or doubt. All the while, Saravio's deft mental touch roused adrenaline, damped thought, heightened desperation.

"But what can we do?" the crippled farmer was the first to speak. "We have no magical powers, not even swords if we knew how to use them. We are men of the soil—farmers, herdsmen, plain, ordinary folk."

"It's easy for you to say these things," a black-haired man with huge, callused hands confronted Saravio. "At the first hint of trouble, you'll go running. Why should you care what happens to us?"

Stung, Saravio started to reply, but Eduin silenced him with a gesture.

"If my friend did not believe as he speaks, would he be here with you now?" Eduin demanded.

"If we were to go against them," another man muttered, "what chance would we have? No more than a beast in the fields!"

"How do we know you're not one of their spies?" Scowling, the black-haired man got to his feet.

Eduin sensed the quicksilver mood of the group, how quickly their fury could be turned to an easier, more immediate target. He raised one hand to the insulated starstone at his throat, although he feared he could not control so many by himself. Yet he must protect Saravio at any cost.

"Because *I* say so." The innkeeper's wife stepped away from the door frame, hands on her hips. "And you all know me. I'd never sell out one of my own. I tell you, this man is to be trusted. All the time Nance was dying, did any of those fancy lords lift a finger for her? No, it was this man who stands before you, this Saravio, who came every day to ease her passing. Did he have to do that? I say you're throwing away the best thing that's ever happened to the working folk of Thendara if you don't listen to him now."

The black-haired man eased himself back into his seat.

"You want to know what we can do against the Towers," Saravio said. From his mind, Eduin caught the image of Naotalba standing behind him, infusing each word with certainty. "If we are patient, if we are faithful, then we cannot fail. But the time is not yet ripe. You must be my heralds, to carry the message to all who still suffer."

The men looked from one to the other, doubtful. Eduin stepped into the silence. "As has been said, we are too few to go up against the might of a Tower. It would be like storming a fortress with only a kitchen knife. We must bide our time and gather more men to our cause. We will wait and watch. Sooner or later, the accursed sorcerers of Hali must come out from behind their walls. Then we will see that even a man armed by magic can be felled."

And then Varzil will hear of our attack. Carolin will summon him, even if the Keepers do not. That will bring him within my reach . . . and then Naotalba's army will fall upon him. No power on Darkover can save him against men willing to die for their cause.

BOOK II

6

Dyannis Ridenow loosened the scarf that covered her copper-colored hair and gazed out over the Lake of Hali. A spring breeze, chill and laden with moisture, rippled through her cloak. She inhaled, welcoming the reflexive shiver.

Aldones, it was good to be outside again. The winter had seemed interminable, each tenday of confinement more tedious and unbearable than the last. She stretched out her arms. The old women of both sexes who made it their business to mind everyone else's would work themselves halfway to apoplexy if they knew she was here, unchaperoned and dressed in the scullery maid's borrowed cloak and overskirt.

Let them cluck over her; it wouldn't be the first time or the last. She might just spend the rest of the day abroad and give them even more to talk about.

One sacrifice Dyannis had not been willing to make for the sake of disguise was her own boots, fine leather worn to butter softness and fitted exactly to her small feet, which now rested at the very edge of the golden sand. Just beyond, the cloud-water of the lake curled and receded. Instead of the usual gentle waves, the surface looked choppy, torn.

Above, the sky hid behind a blanketing overcast. For an instant, her fancy seized upon the image and she saw not only herself, but all of Darkover, caught and pressed like dried flowers.

Pressed. Yes, the analogy was apt. Her nerves tingled with the electrical tension that had been growing daily. She could almost see the unborn lightning, taste its metallic trail.

The storms had been growing worse since winter's end, both in frequency and intensity. The fire brigades in Hali and nearby Thendara had been run to the point of exhaustion, for the storms never brought rain. Nor did the lightning discharge the electrical tension. Instead, each one seemed to feed upon the one before.

Something had to be done. Even with maximum shielding, the circles at the affected Towers struggled for the concentration that usually came so readily. Sometimes, half the workers were incapacitated due to overload of their energon channels.

So far, the city of Hali was peaceful, but reports arrived daily of increasing unrest in Thendara. What began as a mere spark of temper or drunken quarrel would erupt into a riot filling the streets. Sometimes the City Guards could not restore order and had to let the outburst run its course. Dyannis, who had not worked as a monitor in some time, was called into service along with the other senior *leronyn,* to tend to the wounded.

Many times over the years, since Dyannis had first arrived at Hali Tower as a bewildered adolescent novice, she had sought the lake for the calm that the fresh air and rhythmic motion of the waves always evoked. Now she found the irritation was, if anything, worse here in the open than within the confines of the Tower. It seemed to permeate both air and land, sizzling over her skin. She wanted to lash out at something, to put her pent-up frustration into action. Even as her hands curled into fists, she knew how irrational that was. As a trained *leronis,* she recognized her own increasingly volatile temper as a response to the atmospheric disturbance, but as a human woman, she was still subject to its nerve-grating effects.

Impatiently, she kicked out with one foot, scattering grains of sand into the cloud-waves. The toe of her boot caught on a buried rock and she stumbled. She cursed, brushed damp sand off the leather, then bent to rinse her hands.

The instant her bare skin touched the mist, a jolt of psychic energy surged through her. Gasping, she tripped on the skirts that were two sizes too big for her and sat heavily on the sand. She drew breath, trying to calm herself, staring at the lake that had once been so familiar and soothing.

What in Zandru's Seven Frozen Hells was that?

She felt as if she'd brushed an enormous bank of *laran* batteries, of the sort used to power an aircar or light an entire city, only unstable, so that the merest contact released a burst of discharge.

Impossible! She had touched the cloud-water many times, had even descended a short distance down the lakebed, but never experienced anything like this. Nor had she heard any report of anything untoward or unusual at the lake; but then, it had been a long cold winter, and few had ventured outdoors without need.

The lake was filled with a mist that was neither liquid nor gaseous. It curled and drifted, always in motion, and could be breathed like air, although to do so carried its own dangers. At the same time, the cloud-water conducted sound and light very much like ordinary water.

Dyannis, her heart still racing, forced herself to think, to reason things through. Water also conducted electricity, and so did the lake substance. From what source? Why would the curling mists feel like an overcharged *laran* battery?

She tilted her head to stare at the sweep of sullen, gray overcast sky. Her nerves tingled. Although she could not have put it into words, she sensed a connection between the electrical tension of the sky and what she had felt in that brief moment of contact with the lake waters. She did not believe the unusual storms were the source, but rather the effect.

If the lake were generating psychic energy that bled off into the air and manifested as electrical storms, why had no one noticed before now?

Dyannis frowned, considering the problem. The lake bottom was largely unexplored, true, and for good reason. The cloud-water sustained life, but something in it suppressed the breathing reflex after a time, so that it was not safe to remain submerged for more than the briefest excursion. Perhaps, too, this phenomenon was new, beginning during a particularly harsh winter and growing slowly in strength. She could very well be the first person to walk the lake shore for pleasure since last autumn.

Moments slipped by. The cloud-waves plashed gently. The diffuse overcast light continued unbroken. Somewhere behind Dyannis, a bird called out a three-note song and then fell still.

Dyannis pushed herself to her feet. A step or two carried her halfway to the water's edge. She drew out a locket of filigreed copper on its chain around her neck. Within its silk-insulated interior lay a brilliant blue-white starstone. Without slipping it from its anchoring clasp, she pressed her fingertips to the stone and felt the answering surge of power.

Dyannis placed one palm on sand left damp by a receding wave. Again she sensed the strange psychic energy. Every nerve screamed to jerk away, but she shifted her weight, thrusting her fingers through the coarse grains of sand. Shivering, she forced herself to hold still as the wave returned. Warmer than water, the cloud-stuff swept over her hand.

Her vision went white, as if she had plunged through ice into a winter river. Then the discipline of her years of Tower training took over. Even as part of her conscious mind reeled with the overload, she diverted it, restoring the integrity of her own *laran* systems.

Her first impression, she realized, had been correct. The cloud-water acted as a conducting medium. Just as ordinary water evaporated from the surface of a lake or river, so this energy bled off as electrical potentials, manifesting as worsening storms.

Dyannis found it less difficult to hold still for the next wave. The power came in ripples like the waves themselves, each one building, cresting, and then subsiding. The pulses functioned to collect and direct the energy. With a shudder, she realized that this could not be a natural phenomenon.

Dyannis returned her focus to the rhythmic pattern. By using what her first Keeper had called, "the back door of her mind," she sensed the telltale residue of a matrix lattice. It was faint enough so that, no matter how hard she tried, she could not get more than a general impression.

One inescapable fact emerged. Within the depths of the lake lay a source of immense artificial psychic power that radiated through the cloud-water. How long it had been there, she could not guess. Quiescent, it might have been created at the very beginning of the world, only to awaken in these perilous times.

Despite her training, Dyannis shuddered away from contact with it. The muscles of her belly clenched and bile rose in her throat, pulling her back into her physical body. By now, the drain on her body and mind that accompanied intense *laran* work began to shred her concentration. She had no monitor to safeguard her.

I hadn't planned on doing a little unauthorized laran *work out here!*

With an effort, she raised her *laran* barriers and crawled backward beyond the reach of the water. She'd only touched the surface of what was going on in the lake, but she was not going to solve its mysteries all by herself. She dared not delay. Gathering her strength, she clambered to her feet.

As Dyannis rushed back to Hali Tower, she sent a mental signal ahead to alert her fellow *leronyn*. At this hour, after a night of intense work, many were asleep or resting, their *laran* barriers raised. With the sensitivity necessary to join with other trained telepaths in a circle came an exquisite vulnerability to the intrusion of random thoughts and passions. Experience had shown this could be not only distracting, but destructive when dealing with immensely powerful matrix systems. Many *leronyn* learned to shield themselves with special techniques. For this reason, too, the Tower had been built at the far end of the lake, well away from the city of Hali.

She found one mind awake and receptive to her call, that of a brilliant young *laranzu* from Carcosa. He was younger than she by a few years, in his mid twenties, and of all the matrix workers at Hali, they shared a special kinship of spirit.

Rorie!

Dyannis, he replied in greeting. *What has happened?*

Behind Rorie's thoughts, she heard the fear that her impetuous adventures might have brought her to harm at last.

I am well enough, she quickly reassured him. *I have discovered something—at the lake—and I fear it bodes ill for more than just the Tower. I must tell the Keeper!*

With a wordless acknowledgment, Rorie withdrew to prepare for her arrival.

Raimon Lindir, the Keeper of Hali Tower, was waiting for her beside the outer gates, along with Rorie and Lewis-Mikhail. His appearance, tall and thin, unself-consciously graceful, suggested the *chieri* blood that was said to run in his family. Sometimes his eyes had an almost silvery cast. The deep crimson of his formal Keeper's robe and his fiery red hair contrasted with the paleness of his skin, but there was nothing anemic about his personality or powers. He might be one of the youngest Keepers to hold sole power over a major Tower, but his proficiency was beyond question.

He reached out his hands and Dyannis placed hers on them, his palms cool under her fingertips. The physical touch catalyzed the mental contact. She needed no words of description, no explanation, no interpretation of what had happened. She poured forth the memory of her experience at the lake, knowing that he sensed every detail as vividly as if he had been there himself.

The sharing took only an instant. Raimon shivered as he broke the physical link.

"What you have seen is indeed of grave importance," he said aloud. "We must find out what is going on down there. I will reschedule tonight's work."

Dyannis nodded. The short distance from Tower to lake meant nothing to a full working circle under the guidance of a Keeper, particularly one as strong as Raimon. Together they had mined precious metals from deep within the earth and shifted cloud patterns in the skies above. Moreover, every one of them was familiar with the lake under normal conditions. Surely, their combined mental talents would unravel this puzzle.

That night, Raimon summoned the circle of Hali Tower. Halfway up the stairs leading from the common room, Dyannis swore gently under her breath. The hem of her robe had pulled loose again and she'd almost tripped and broken her fool head.

She bent to inspect the offending stitches. *After all this time, you'd think I could sew a decent seam,* she thought ruefully. She knew it was her own doing, that she would not take the trouble to learn properly. There was always something to do that was more interesting or important than sewing. Some of the older women in the Tower had maidservants to do such tasks, but Dyannis found their constant fussing an even greater burden. As she had so many times before, she simply tucked an extra fold under her belt and went on.

Dyannis had already forgotten the torn hem as she swept past the corridor that led to the Keepers' wing. Only one of the three suites was currently occupied, and since the death of Dougal DiAsturian, no one had the heart to even broach the subject of turning his rooms to other uses.

A narrow stair took her up two flights to the smallest and most heavily shielded workroom in the Tower. Through the open door, she heard the murmur of voices. She paused for a moment to collect herself. On her heels came little Ellimara, wearing a thick shawl over her long white monitor's robe. At thirteen, she was the youngest full member of Hali Tower, but she was of pure Aillard blood and strongly Gifted.

Raimon looked up as they entered. "Ah, there you are."

Dyannis shot Ellimara a quick smile. *Thanks to you, sweetling, I am not the last to arrive.* Her disregard for punctuality had long been the source of jokes.

Ellimara blushed prettily and went to take her place on the benches along the far wall. As monitor, she would remain apart from the circle itself. Immersed in the mental unity, the workers lost track of their own physiological functions. It was her responsibility to keep them healthy and their channels clear, free to pour all their concentration and power into the joining of minds. No tense muscle or stuttering heartbeat, no fall in oxygen or fluctuation in hormonal levels must interrupt that unity, lest the backlash endanger them all.

Dyannis slipped into her place around the oval table. In the center sat the matrix lattice, an array of linked starstones, which would focus and amplify their natural *laran*. It glittered as if lit from within, a crystalline fairywork of tiny starstones, linked and attuned to their purpose.

The circle was at full strength tonight, six workers plus Raimon as Keeper. Two more made up Hali's community, but a circle of nine was beyond his present skill, and they had not enough for two circles, even if they had a second Keeper. They often worked with only five, when others were needed for the relays or were barred from active work due to illness, exhaustion, or in the case of the women, the onset of their monthly cycles.

Hali is not the only Tower to be reduced to a single working circle, Dyannis reflected. Her glance met that of Alderic, who had lately come to Hali. He had ridden with King Carolin in his struggle to regain the throne, and in his thoughts, she sometimes heard the echoes of the dying minds of those *leronyn* who had fought on both sides.

Too many lost, and too many demands on those of us who are left. Hali had once housed a dozen or more young novices, as well as those *Comyn* youth in need of training beyond what their household *leronis* could provide. Now that Ellimara had finished her training, the novices' wing lay empty.

All things come and go in their season, her brother Varzil had said. *Nothing lasts forever, neither the good times nor the bad.*

Dyannis shuddered and as quickly, swept away any hint of gloom. Such vaporish maunderings were dangerous to bring to a working circle.

After a brief introduction, Dyannis repeated for the circle what had happened to her at the lake, both in words and telepathically. They were already in light rapport from their intense work together. As she spoke, she felt the individual members shift toward a working unity.

"Now, let us take a closer look at this thing," Raimon said. He gave the signal to begin.

Dyannis set her starstone before her, closed her eyes, and lowered her mental barriers. Already she felt Rorie's strength as a steady warmth, like the sun of high summer on the rocks by the river at Sweetwater, where she had lived as a girl. Raimon's mind brushed hers and she settled even deeper.

Drifting layers of color swept by her, blues fading into shades of green and then gold. It always felt this way when Raimon was weaving the individual members of the circle into a single whole. Once, she'd asked Lewis-Mikhail about the colors, only to be met with puzzlement.

"For me, it's like singing in a Nevarsin choir," he'd said, "many voices, some high, some low, all blending together until I can't hear them separately."

A hint of wildflowers shifted her awareness and she felt her shoulder muscles soften and her belly relax as she drew in a deeper breath. Ellimara was settling them all for a long session. Dyannis floated on the sensation of relief and contentment. She was no longer one solitary person facing the daunting mystery of the lake, but joined into a greater whole, with strength and wisdom beyond her own. At that moment, no challenge seemed beyond their combined abilities.

Raimon began his work, taking an imprint of the pattern in her mind and channeling it to the circle. Memories rose to the surface, the things she had felt and thought that day on the lake shore. This time they seemed distant, as if glimpsed through frosted glass. She felt him sifting, setting aside her own physiological reactions, her emotions, then refining and drawing out her direct perceptions.

A ripple passed around the circle and Dyannis knew that every one of them had shared those sensations, just as if they had all been there with her, put their own hands into the cloud-water, felt the jolt of electrical power.

A faint humming, little more than a vibration, swept through her. It was familiar, if artificial—the matrix lattice resonating to the pattern that Raimon fed through it. At this point, her entire work would be to concentrate on the lattice, to feed her own *laran* energy into it. Of them all, only the Keeper in centripolar position directed, controlled those energies.

When she first came to Hali, old Dougal DiAsturian had been Keeper, and most of what he did was a mystery to her. More than once, she'd been chastised for resisting his command. Raimon's touch was far more subtle, and his mind had a transparent, almost pellucid quality. She retained some degree of separate awareness as he established an anchor point here in the physical Tower and began to create a resonant bridge to the lake below.

There were many functions a Keeper performed that Dyannis understood and could well imagine herself doing, but not this. For such a spatial leap of consciousness to work accurately and safely, the Keeper must be supremely confident of his destination. He must hold the image in his mind as clearly as if he were looking at his own hand. Raimon never hesitated.

The next instant, she felt a gust of chill air, just as she had on that morning, although now it was night and her physical body was safely immured behind the Tower walls. Through the circle's power, she heard the soft splash of the waves and smelled the mingled odors of wet sand and river-weed.

Now, she floated above the lake, rocked by the movement of the waves. In a moment, she would feel their peculiar misty wetness. In one corner of her mind, she braced herself for the surge of eerie power—

But it never came. She remained suspended, untouched, just beyond the reach of the topmost crests. Following the stream of *laran* energy from her own mind through Raimon's and then the lattice, she touched a dense barrier at the surface of the water. Trying to move through it was like forcing her way through a thicket of interwoven reeds, resilient and yet impassable. Even the joined minds of the circle could not penetrate the energy layer. Clearly, whoever had created the artificial power source did not want anyone investigating it.

All the more reason to do so, she thought.

The direct way was blocked to them. Determination and curiosity flared up in Dyannis, despite Ellimara's soothing contact. She felt Raimon move to withdraw.

Just give up and go away? Not if I have anything to say about it!

Dyannis! Regain your focus! Do not break the unity!

With an effort, Dyannis stilled her thoughts and submerged her consciousness once more in the circle. Her emotions were not so easy to control, but she managed with an effort. She had years of experience in struggling with her unruly temper.

The resonance of the circle continued, unbroken. Her lapse had done no serious damage. For a long moment, the interwoven consciousness of the circle hovered above the lake surface. Then, with silken smoothness, Raimon lifted them into the Overworld.

Dyannis found herself standing on a plain of unbroken gray beneath an equally featureless sky. Around her rose the ghostly manifestation of Hali Tower, as insubstantial as if it had been made of water. Glancing down, she saw herself as she had appeared here many times before, in a body very like her own, clad in a soft gray robe that barely reached her ankles. Her hands hovered near those of her neighbors in the circle. Some of them looked younger or older— Ellimara appeared as a woman in her forties, and her robes were not the white of a monitor but rosy, as if the Keeper's crimson had seeped into them.

Raimon appeared as he always did, almost androgynous, glimmering like an ageless, nonhuman *chieri*. His eyes met hers, and his mouth curved in a smile.

With a movement of his mind, he called the lake to them. Here in the Overworld, distance and time lost their meaning, becoming mere products of the mind. Even the Tower around them had been shaped by the thoughts of the Hali workers over the centuries, simply because they were accustomed to working within walls and felt more comfortable with a familiar landmark.

The lake, too, retained much of its physical appearance, a depression filled with roiling mists. As Dyannis looked, it seemed not only greatly reduced in diameter, but much deeper. She could not see the bottom, even as Raimon turned the cloud-waters transparent, layer after layer. The strange creatures that lived in the lake waters, half fish and half bird, flashed by as brightly colored shapes and as quickly disappeared.

To casual inspection, the Overworld lake appeared as it always had. Under any other circumstances, Dyannis would have accepted it as normal and turned away. Now that very smoothness deepened her curiosity. Raimon brought the circle's focus closer.

A layer of psychic energy lay over the lake. It had been shaped to reflect the expectations of anyone approaching from the Overworld. A worker would see only what he thought *should* be there. It looked so normal that only someone with reason to be suspicious would be able to tell the difference.

Dyannis realized the mirrorlike pattern would also repulse any incoming energy. She'd studied devices like this before and had even constructed them. The barrier would use an attacker's own energy, so that the harder he pushed, the harder he was thrown back. Only a trained Tower circle could have created it.

Who? Who would do such a thing? And why?

Raimon, too, was no stranger to such a strategy. He shaped the circle's energy into a spear point, long and slender. Then, instead of aiming in a perpendicular manner at the barrier, he sent them skimming across it, dipping down at the narrowest angle. The tip of the point slipped beneath the outer edge. There was almost no resistance. He increased their angle of descent. A few minutes later, the barrier suddenly gave way. They had broken through.

The lake lay beneath them. Gathering the circle's forces, Raimon shifted the thought-stuff of the Overworld. Grays darkened, contrast intensified. The mists grew thicker, lapping the shores of the lake. At the same time, shapes appeared at the bottom. They were blurred and indistinct, yet present.

Dyannis felt a surge of elation. There *was* something there!

Wordlessly, Raimon drew upon them for more power. She gave it freely and felt the others do the same. They moved through the ethereal waters, deep and deeper.

Below, Dyannis glimpsed a vast jagged shape. Instinct recoiled, urging her to flee. She held fast. Though it took every particle of discipline she possessed, she forced herself to examine it.

It had no physical form, neither darkness nor light. With her *laran* senses, Dyannis felt it as a rending, a disruption in the continuity of time.

The thing drew her, repelled her. It reeked of *laran*.

7

After they had rested and replenished energies drained by the long session, Raimon brought the circle back together, this time in council. They must understand what they had seen, gather more information, and decide what to do next. The final decision belonged to Raimon, as Keeper, but nothing like this situation had come up within memory. They all were acutely aware of the importance of their next actions.

As they discussed what they had seen, Dyannis suddenly recognized an undercurrent of memory, like an itch at the back of her skull, which had been nagging her all day.

"I don't know if this has any relevance to our present situation," she said aloud, "but this isn't the first time I know of when something strange has happened at the lake. Years ago, my brother Varzil and I spent Midwinter season at the court of old King Felix in Hali."

In her mind, she returned to that time, and the others, still in light rapport after their long session together, followed her thoughts. She'd been very young, newly arrived at Hali Tower and in a state of constant over-excitement. Memory flooded through her, rippling through the circle, the texture of the stone wall she'd been concentrating on while practicing her breathing exercises, the jarring clatter from below, voices raised, people running. She'd rushed outside to see two men easing her brother's limp body from the back of a horse. Once the commotion had sorted itself out, the story emerged.

This is what had happened, she spoke to the circle with her mind.

The two men were Prince Carolin and his friend, Orain, and the drenched, bedraggled, half-drowned wretch was her own brother. The healers tended him for hours while Carolin paced the hallways, driving everyone else half-mad with his worry. At first, Dyannis assumed, as did everyone else, that Varzil had wandered into the depths of the lake and stayed too long. She'd been warned about the consequences as a novice.

But something happened to Varzil, she said, *something beyond exposure to cold and lack of air.* She'd known that the moment she saw him. There was a strangeness about his eyes that astonished her. This was her big brother Varzil, after all, who could hear Ya-men singing under the four moons and other things that sent her scurrying under the bedcovers just to hear of them.

Dyannis withdrew into the privacy of her own thoughts for a moment. Shortly after the incident at the lake, Varzil had tried to interfere with her first love affair, with a young *laranzu* from Arilinn. It had taken her a long time to forgive him.

Dyannis found it strange that she should think of Eduin now, for he had not crossed her mind in years, not since that disaster at Hestral Tower. She still believed that the entire story might never be known. One thing was certain, Eduin had been unfairly blamed. He had no powerful friends among the *Comyn* besides Carolin Hastur, and at that time, Carolin had been an exile, running for his life in the wild lands beyond the Kadarin.

The lake . . .

Dyannis turned her thoughts once more to the current problem.

"What exactly did Varzil find?" Raimon asked.

Varzil had not said so explicitly, Dyannis explained, but she believed he had stumbled upon some relic of the Cataclysm, that ancient disaster that had turned an ordinary lake into the eerie marvel of today. Perhaps the psychic residue of that event still lingered in the mists, perceptible only in the depths. Varzil with his extraordinary *laran* might have sensed what other men, even Tower-trained, missed.

The others glanced at one another with apprehensive expressions, and even Raimon looked somber. She couldn't blame them. Varzil was generally regarded as the most powerful *laranzu* of their day. How could they handle something that had almost overpowered him?

"Of course," Dyannis said aloud to reassure herself as well as the others, "Varzil was very young then. I don't think he'd been at Arilinn for a full year. He wasn't expecting what he found."

We'll be prepared, she added mentally, with a confidence she did not entirely feel.

Raimon caught her undertone of bravado. *We are not prepared yet. First we must gather information and resources. If this thing is connected to the Cataclysm event, it will be neither simple nor easy to deal with.*

There it was, Dyannis thought. He had put into unspoken words the fear that stirred within all of them.

"We must do two things," Raimon said temperately. "First, we must discover as much as we can about the energy source and, most particularly, whether it is causing the atmospheric disturbances, as we suspect."

"Anything that powerful cannot be left for anyone to use or misuse," Lewis-Mikhail said.

"Exactly so," Raimon said. "Therefore, the second thing is to find out who created the energy shield and for what purpose. We must go carefully here."

Raimon sent word that night through the relays of what they had discovered. He made plans to confer with King Carolin, for Hali Lake was within the Hastur realm. Whatever harm came to his people or lands from the presence of such a powerful and unregulated energy source was ultimately his responsibility. If another Tower were involved, this might well be a suitable occasion to extend the Compact.

Hali Tower had already sworn to abide by the Compact, that oath of honor that forbade the use of all weapons that killed at a distance. It might be one of the oldest Towers on Darkover, but it derived much of its prestige from the *rhu fead,* site of the ancient holy things, and its proximity to the royal seat. It had no power to compel any other Tower. In these uncertain times, with armed conflict ever a possibility, no Tower maintained true neutrality. The *Comyn* Council exerted great influence, but its meeting season was still some time off; like all institutions, it moved slowly.

A few days later, storm clouds gathered and poured down a spring torrent. Thunder crackled as waves of lightning bridged sky and earth. Only the fact that the rain had already drenched every tree and hut, house and field, prevented a rash of fires. The stone walls of Hali Tower vibrated with the ferocity of the winds.

When the rains eased and the great red sun appeared once more, the Tower community immediately noticed a great lessening of the electrical tension. Raimon decided to take advantage of the respite, for no one knew how long it might last. He sent Dyannis down to the lake, along with Rorie and Alderic, to take a closer look. The day was sunny and surprisingly mild for the season, as if spring had sent a perfumed herald to tease them. There were no clouds in the sky. Even so, she approached the cloud-water with some trepidation.

The three of them were in light rapport; linked in this way, the two men would search the lakebed while she would watch both of them, monitoring their breathing.

Dyannis found a place to sit on a tumble of weather-smoothed stones. She gathered her skirts around her and composed herself, using her deep breathing practice to settle her body. The sun warmed her face and made patterns through her closed eyelids. She smelled wet sand and the faintly pungent odor of river-weed. Behind her, small birds cheeped.

Her mind descended with the men, as if they were carrying her, silent and invisible, along with them. Mist, gossamer-white, swirled past her. Time itself seemed to slow. Light rained down in sheets of brilliance. Balls of color, like a patterning of bright yellow and orange-black stripes, darted across her vision. She exclaimed aloud, delighted by the strangely illuminated creatures that were neither bird nor fish. They clustered around the explorers, benign and beautiful, always beyond reach.

As the men went deeper, the colors shifted. Yellow gave way to tones of inky blue. The temperature dropped. Dyannis shivered in the sun, then found herself gasping for air.

Breathe—you must remember to breathe! she sent. She counted, *Inhale—two, three—exhale—two, three—inhale . . .* knowing that her friends below mirrored her discipline.

A time or two, momentarily blind, she lost touch with them. Each time, she strengthened the link with greater difficulty. It seemed that something more than distance separated them. The cloud-water, which once seemed to transmit psychic impressions, now acted as an increasingly resistant barrier.

Rorie? 'Deric? What's going on?

We've reached the bottom. Alderic's usually clear mental voice sounded blurred. *At least, we aren't going down any farther. I can't see far, but there doesn't seem to be much down here except rock and sand.*

Dyannis frowned. The jagged rent in the Overworld could look like anything—or nothing—to ordinary senses. *Keep searching,* she told them. *And remember to breathe.*

If we forget, we can trust you to remind us, said Rorie.

Laggard.

Pest, he retorted good-naturedly.

There's something ahead, Alderic broke in.

Dyannis glimpsed a pale shape emerging from the swirls of mist. The two men moved toward it with a slow, almost floating gait, half-suspended in the cloud-water. The outline remained infuriatingly indistinct, despite her attempts to concentrate. She became convinced the effect was not merely the distance or insulating cloud-water. It stemmed from some quality of the site itself.

What can you see? she asked.

Stones, Rorie responded. *Worked by tools, not natural. They're enormous, a sort of pillar, toppled and broken, but still more or less in line.*

Dyannis sensed Alderic running his hands over the curved surface. On one level, she felt the pitted hardness of the stone, the slipperiness of untold years of slime, the roughness where some creature had attached its shell and then perished with the passage of time. Another part of her mind shrieked in warning.

Strange discordant energies moved around them, *through* the stones. The cloud-water quickened, stirring the men's hair. Yet this was no ordinary current. She sensed a drawing, like a magnetic attraction.

Dyannis cast her thoughts wide as a fisherman's net, searching for the direction of the pull—

The Overworld!

Somehow the stones on the lakebed were linked to that gray realm of thought, and from there to some other destination. Clearly, immense power was moving from one place to another.

The only way to find out what was going on was to follow the energy flow. She stopped resisting the pull, allowing it to carry her along. Moments passed, and Dyannis found her awareness moving deeper into the lake, toward the row of fallen stones. The two men faded, leaving only the pale rock.

Nearer and nearer, the stream brought her, until she wondered if she would be drawn into the very substance of the stone. With the discipline of her years of Tower training, she suppressed panic.

Relax, she told herself. She was not solid in this place and could not be harmed. She must let it carry her along. . . .

In her mind, she felt the fine-grained hardness of the columns, the almost-obliterated traces of the tools that had shaped them beneath the layers of algae. In another moment, she would penetrate that hardness, even as she had done as part of a *laran* circle mining precious minerals deep within the earth.

With a jolt, she passed right through the fallen column and into the Overworld. For a moment, she did not recognize her surroundings. She did not stand upon the familiar, featureless gray plain, but floated in a pool of gently surging mists. The current lessened for an instant, and she saw something that astonished her. The cloud-water, or some astral equivalent, was draining from the bottom of the lake and into its Overworld counterpart. She was sure the Overworld lake, on the doorstep of Hali Tower, must have come into existence only recently. It had the feel of newness, none of the texture of shared envisioning.

Now Dyannis was moving again, caught once more in a steady pull. The Overworld lake waters were being siphoned off. She forced herself to relax and float along. For a moment, she felt nothing but the current. It reminded her of a tiny stream, where water ran swiftly between narrow banks. Here there were no eddies, no sandbars, no branches or tributaries, only a single relentless direction. Energies surged around her. She drew back a little at their raw power.

What could a Tower do with this energy source? Nearly anything! Every circle she had worked in had been limited by the amount of *laran* energy that could be generated. Here was a seemingly limitless supply. All that would be necessary would be a means to control it.

And for that, a Tower.

She stretched out her *laran* senses, casting ahead through the void. To receive the stream of energy, to shape and tap into it, a circle needed a presence here, an anchor point. Sometimes, a circle would recreate their own, familiar Tower, although the images changed with time and purpose. When hostilities between kingdoms extended to their respective Towers, warlike edifices took the place of homey, open buildings.

At first, Dyannis did not recognize the structure ahead. It resembled a water mill more than the Tower she expected. Energy poured through it, turning the enormous paddled wheel.

She let the current bring her as close as she dared. With a burst of concentration, she broke away from the cloud-water and took on the form she used in the Overworld. She knew that she looked very much as she did in the physical world, and she was most comfortable in a split riding skirt, laced boots, and open-necked shirt.

Now that she had an astral bodily form, sound rushed over her. The wheel creaked on its axle, the cloud-water surged and splashed. Within the gray walls, hidden machineries rumbled. She approached, searching for an entrance or any sign of human presence. There was nothing, which puzzled her for a moment. It was as if the mill and its apparatus had been constructed and then left to fulfill its purpose.

She stood beside the stream and considered. The mill, like any other structure in the Overworld, had been shaped from thought-stuff, yet the cloud-water appeared just as it did in the physical realm. Appeared . . . She knelt and dipped her fingertips into the curling mist. An electrical jolt stung her. Her arm jerked back reflexively, nerves tingling painfully.

Wiping her hands on her skirt, she turned back to the mill. She focused on the stone wall in front of her, shifting its solid appearance to transparency. At first it resisted her, then gave way like the rippling of a heat mirage. She stepped inside.

Shifting her mental focus, Dyannis was able to discern her surroundings more clearly. The machinery, like the cloud-water and the mill itself, was only a representation, a metaphor. It marked a gateway, an abbreviation of distance, a shortcut from the Overworld to the real one. To a Tower.

She felt rather than envisioned the circle at the other end of the energy stream. No flash of recognition rose to her mind; it was not a group she knew well. She waited, as each moment brought a new bit of information—a tinge of personality, the structure of a high-power matrix lattice, the texture of the Keeper's thoughts, the intricate braiding of power as it passed through the circle.

Dyannis sensed a faint acrid taste to the psychic atmosphere. Instinct recoiled from it, but she forced herself to remain passive, receptive. She might have only a short time before the Keeper sensed her presence.

It was not a true taste, for she had no true body, nor smell either. Her mind, she knew, suggested these senses for some primitive, elemental experience. The sensation shifted from repugnant to poisonous. Something coalesced, contained and shaped by the combined will of the circle.

They were making something. It must be a *laran* weapon. What? Nausea clawed at the back of her throat, but she held on. She must be sure.

Walls of energy shimmered, surrounding a heart of weakly glowing green.

Bonewater dust?

It was the most terrible of all known *laran* weapons, for it not only brought death to any who touched or breathed it, but it lingered for a generation or more, poisoning every living thing. There were still lands which no man dared pass through or eat any plant or animal grown there, left over from the Ages of Chaos. As far as Dyannis knew, no modern Tower possessed bonewater dust, or was willing to make it.

With an effort, Dyannis returned her focus to the weapon. Yes, it was very like bonewater dust in its vibrational pattern. But not exactly. This *felt* less virulent, but it also seemed to have a different physical configuration, more like granules or crystals than fine powdery particles. It would be more difficult to disperse, would fall to the earth instead of being carried by the wind.

A weapon, indeed. One that could be delivered more precisely, with less risk that an errant breeze might carry it back upon the attacking forces. That was said to have happened a generation ago at Drycreek, where the outlaw *laranzu* Rumail Deslucido had loosed bonewater dust upon the army of King Rafael Hastur, only to have it blown astray, condemning his own men as well. It was said that Rumail had perished in this way by his own hand, but his body had never been identified. Even now, no man who valued his own life dared venture into the wasteland that had been Drycreek.

She must tell Varzil. The *Comyn* Council must be alerted— Dyannis mastered the impulse to withdraw immediately. It would do them little good to know about the bonewater crystals if they did not also know who was making them. She forced herself to concentrate harder, to pierce the shifting, unearthly layers of the Overworld. She was a strong telepath, but the effort took every particle of her talent and training.

For an instant only, she glimpsed the room in which the circle met. The circle sat around a large oval table. Blue-white light from the artificial matrix at one end played across faces blank with absorption. The greater part of the table, however, was dominated by apparati—glass receptacles, distillators, separators, others so specialized she did not recognize them. Some were partly filled, their contents giving off a faint green luminescence. The room and its contours were unfamiliar, but a sudden surge in light brought the Keeper's features into stark relief.

She knew him, for he had begun his training at Hali and had still been there when she first came.

Francisco Gervais. Keeper of Cedestri Tower.

— ✦ —

Dyannis... Rorie's mental voice sounded hollow now, oddly distorted.

Zandru's curse! While she'd been off following her own impulses, she'd forgotten to monitor her friends. Without the normal air gases to trigger breathing, they had not noticed the fading of their own alertness. She reached out with her mind and instantly touched theirs. She could see them with her inner sight. Alderic had lowered himself to his knees, captured by the patterns of silt in the swirling waters. Lethargy weighted his arms and legs. A long, slender silvery shape undulated through the murky water, a tiny mote of luminescence hovering above its nose. He followed its motion dreamily.

Got to... get moving... Rorie said, but without conviction.

Just rest a while... so nice and warm...

Warm? The depths of the lake were *cold*—

Up, both of you! Breathe! Move! Dyannis shrieked silently.

Dyannis . . . don't fuss . . . we're fine . . .

Fine? Addle-witted, half-drowned—What's the use trying to reason with you? I'm on my way!

Dyannis bolted up from the rock to the water's edge. The cloud-water splashed over her boots, wetting the hem of her wide skirts. Damp mist curled around her legs, even through the layers of her garments. She gasped at the sudden chill.

Once I'm soaked through, these stupid skirts will weigh more than Durraman's donkey!

Dyannis halted where she was, waves knee-high, and reached for the ties of her overskirt. She offered silent blessings to Cassilda or whoever protected overdressed women, that she'd donned separate skirts and bodice over her ankle-length chemise this morning. She struggled out of the thick woolen overskirt by shoving it down around her ankles and then kicking it aside. The underskirt, meant for indoor wear, was lighter, but rapidly becoming drenched along its lower edge. She pulled off her jacket, tossed it back on to the sand, and applied herself to the skirt fastenings. She was already shivering, but at least, she'd be able to walk—or swim—as need be.

Dyannis! Stop—enough! We're coming! Rorie's thoughts were clear enough to convince her that he'd emerged partway from his lethargy.

Smiling, Dyannis waded back to shore and put her jacket back on. The overskirt was too wet to wear, but at least she would avoid the scandal of a Hali Tower *leronis* running around half-naked in public, even if it was a pleasant spring morning.

Rorie emerged first from the lake, supporting Alderic. Their clothes were damp and their hair hung in limp tendrils like river-weed. Alderic coughed and sputtered as his lungs drew in normal air. Dyannis handed them the dry cloaks they had brought, but it was a while before Alderic stopped shivering.

"The more we learn about what's going on down there," Rorie said as they made their way back to the Tower, "the more confusing it all is."

Dyannis shared his frustration, but felt it better not to say so aloud. They made their way back to the Tower, hot baths, and dry clothes.

Raimon listened gravely as they reported, both telepathically and aloud, what they had seen. He was particularly concerned with the discovery of a new type of bonewater dust.

That night, Raimon spoke directly with Cedestri Tower's Keeper over the relays. Francisco had firmly rebuffed Raimon's attempts at opening a discussion. Although Raimon was as composed as ever when he emerged from the relay chamber, Dyannis suspected that the response had not been as polite as he reported.

"What did they expect?" she said to Rorie in exasperation. They sat together in the common room, sipping hot, honey-laced wine as a restorative. "That they could exploit such an energy source right on our doorstep—and for such a purpose—and not be found out? Did they think we'd let it pass? Or are they waiting for Carolin to send an army to shut them down?"

Rorie shook his head. "Try to see things from Cedestri's point of view. They are not Carolin's subjects, as you know perfectly well, so they are hardly answerable to him. If the most recent reports are true, they will very shortly be at war."

Dyannis frowned. Cedestri was a legitimate Tower, but had flatly refused to sign the Compact. In fact, it had welcomed those workers who could not abide the restrictions. It was allied with the small kingdom of Isoldir. The reports to which Rorie referred described escalating hostilities with its neighbor, a branch of Aillard. Ellimara had reacted to the news that her family's enemies might have some more effective variant of bonewater dust with near-panic and was still unable to concentrate enough to work.

"They must be terrified that the entire clan of Aillard will be ranged against them," Rorie pressed on. "Given such a threat, would you not do everything possible to strengthen your position?"

"Including making crystalline bonewater?" she fumed. "Rorie, I cannot see *any* legitimate use for such a weapon, one that kills even little babes, and leaves the survivors so ill that death would come as a mercy."

"You talk as if you would take up the cause of your brother's Compact. I had not realized you were such a partisan."

Dyannis caught her breath. Hali Tower had signed the Compact soon after King Carolin and Varzil had formally presented it. The discussion had been brief, with little dissension. Hali was, after all, bound to Hastur.

She had not given the Compact deep thought, but had considered herself bound by the actions of her Keeper. But she was also acutely aware that she had only absorbed the opinions of those around her. She herself had never been tested. She had used her *laran* to heal the devastation brought by sword and *clingfire,* but she herself had never lain bleeding on a battlefield or felt the unquenchable caustic burn through her flesh and bone. Her childhood at Sweetwater had been filled with tales of war, but never the actuality.

Varzil, on the other hand, had known treachery and loss, had seen the people he loved under psychic bombardment, the very stones beneath them crumbling into powder, their minds reeling with madness. His dearest friend, Carolin Hastur, had fled into exile and had battled his way to victory at a terrible cost. During those years, when Hali had been commanded by Carolin's usurper cousin Rakhal, Dyannis had feared she might be called to war against her childhood friend, perhaps against her own kin.

"I do not know," she said slowly. A shiver passed over her as she realized that her own trials, whatever they might be, still lay before her.

8

Word reached Hali Tower that King Carolin, deeply concerned about the development of a new *laran* weapon, had asked Varzil Ridenow's help. Varzil, in turn, sent a message to Raimon that he would leave Neskaya for Hali as soon as possible.

At the news that Varzil was coming, relief akin to euphoria swept through Hali. Silently, Dyannis distrusted their confidence. To them, her brother had almost legendary status—the Keeper who had appeared mantled in the glory of Aldones during Hali's assault upon Hestral Tower, whose insight and persuasive powers had prevented a catastrophe of the magnitude of the destruction of Tramontana and Neskaya Towers only a generation ago.

Yet there were others who saw him as a weak, prattling peacemaker because he had not the strength to wage war. They suspected his motives and regarded the Compact as a ruse, a folly leading to ruin, a coward's gambit.

She knew her brother's temper, knew that it took far more courage to walk unarmed through the lands rent by hatred, as he had done and would do again, than to lead the safe and comfortable existence of an ordinary Keeper, behind the rebuilt walls of Neskaya.

He will come because we need him, because Carolin needs him, she thought. *He will not consider the risk.*

What, she wondered, would she do in his place?

— ◆ —

The next few tendays sped by while they awaited Varzil's arrival. Melting snows and spring rains made travel slow. He had to travel on horseback through the Hellers and down to Acosta, where Carolin would send an aircar. The treacherous wind currents made air navigation impossible in the mountains, even in the mildest seasons.

Meanwhile, Dyannis prepared to take her turn in the Overworld, keeping watch over the structure that Cedestri Tower had established there in order to harvest the energy from the lake floor rift. She had not encountered any human presence in any of her previous shifts, although Cedestri must know that it was being observed. Once or twice, she had caught a faint disturbance in the atmosphere, a swirl of invisible energy or a shadow fleeting at the very edge of her vision.

With a practiced breath, she cast her mind into the Overworld. During the first few moments, she sifted through the usual disorientation to find her bearings. Above her stretched the gray overcast, unchanging and featureless in all directions.

This is getting all too familiar, she told herself. *I've been spending too much time here.* The most difficult part was the continual discipline over her thoughts, for here in the Overworld, an imprudent impulse or moment of irritation could lead to dire consequences.

Once she felt stable, she formed a mental picture of the Cedestri water mill and waited for it to materialize. Usually, it condensed out of the amorphous colorless substance of the Overworld only a short distance away.

This time, nothing happened.

Dyannis turned in a complete circle, scanning the horizon. Perhaps she had formed an imperfect image, or the workers at Cedestri had altered their site beyond recognition. She tried again, searching for the power flow from the lake.

There it was, that twist of *wrongness.* As before, it bled into the Overworld, only this time there was no trace of the mill or any other device to harness its force. Instead, it spread out like a river over muddy flats, losing some of its impetus, but not entirely dissipating. The nerve-scouring tension was merely redistributed.

Although her skin prickled, Dyannis cast about again for any sign of Cedestri's water mill. She found fragmentary images in the central part of the power bed, where the current still flowed. Only broken outlines, like fractured glass, suggested the vanished structure.

Dyannis frowned. This was no mere erosion with time and disuse. Almost nothing remained of the sculpted thought-stuff of wheel and tower except this faint vibrational residue. Whoever had built it had gone to great pains to dismantle it.

There was nothing more to be gained by lingering here any longer. Dyannis dropped back into her physical body and went to inform her Keeper of what she had found.

— ✦ —

By the time Varzil reached Thendara, only the faintest traces of the stream and mill remained, and those were detectable only upon the closest examination. Perhaps, as Alderic suggested, Cedestri Tower feared they had been found out, or their enemies might use the Over-world route as a means of sabotage or sneak attack. Whatever the reason, the news was welcomed by everyone except Raimon, who pointed out that Cedestri already had a stockpile of crystalline bonewater, or possibly other weapons they knew nothing about, and had now been alerted to their discovery.

He said as much to Dyannis as they rode, along with Rorie and a couple of servants, to the King's castle at Thendara. Although the day was mild, for spring had taken hold in earnest, they rode cloaked and hooded. The road around the lake and past the city of Hali was dry and they made good time, but Dyannis felt the prickle of electrical charge in the air. After the brief respite, it had been increasing daily once more.

It had been some time since Dyannis had been to Thendara and now, with her nerves already scoured raw by the tension between sky and land, she wondered if there had been a coup, a second usurper to Carolin's throne, the city was so altered.

Unlike Hali, Thendara was a walled city, built for defense. In times past, she had entered through one or another of its gates with only a token greeting from the guards. The passages to the city itself had been open, the flow of travelers and merchants fluid and easy. Now there was actually a knot of people and pack animals waiting at the gate. Instead of the one or two guards in City colors, there were four, and they took their time questioning each person and inspecting each wagon and saddlebag.

Raimon nudged his horse to the front of the line. He and his party were above suspicion; there was no need for them to wait. Even if the guards did not recognize them personally, one glance would show them as *Comyn*.

"Halt there!" one of the guards called out, just as several travelers shouted, "Wait your turn!"

A man in common farmer's garb rushed forward to grab the reins of Raimon's mount. The horse, startled, threw his head up and danced sideways. Raimon kept his seat with an effort, for he was not a skilled horseman. The hood of his cloak slid off, revealing his bright red hair.

Laranzu! The thought shot through the crowd.

Rorie, who was a capable rider, shouted and pushed his horse forward, placing himself between the crowd and his Keeper. The farmer stumbled back, but not before Dyannis caught the twist of emotion. She read surprise, surely to be expected, but also—*hatred?*

Why? she wondered. *What harm have we done to common folk? We have never wished them ill. Perhaps it is the sickness of the times, the weariness of the soul that comes from pain too great to bear.*

Before she could react, however, the party surged forward. One of the guards quieted Raimon's horse, while another made room for them to pass.

Within minutes, they were ushered through the outlying markets along the broader avenues leading to Carolin's palace. Dyannis saw much that was familiar, but also changes everywhere. The winter had been a cruel one, and she had done her share of tending to the sick at Hali and sometimes Thendara. Some had fallen to the usual winter lung fevers, made worse by cold and hunger, but there had also been several waves of country folk from one area or another affected by war—farmers whose lands had been laid waste by ordinary battles, villagers scarred by *clingfire* burns, children who had strayed too close to lands still under the glowing poison of bonewater dust. Always, her efforts had been received with gratitude, even when she had been too late. She had never encountered such dark stares, such quickly-hidden fists.

Once, Dyannis overheard a bitter-laced, *"Sorcery! Witch-brood tyrants!"* What in the name of Aldones was going on?

"Raimon—" she began, but the Keeper silenced her with a gesture. Another escort, this time in Hastur blue and silver instead of the colors of the City Guard, had come to meet them. Dyannis had never liked being surrounded by head-blind strangers, but managed to keep silent as they passed into a gated courtyard. Stablemen took their horses, and a dignitary, most likely an assistant to the *coridom* or castle steward, greeted them with a deep, formal bow before ushering them inside.

Varzil and Carolin were waiting for them in the King's least formal chamber. Varzil rose from his chair as Dyannis entered. She felt his rush of joy at seeing her, his mind as clear as a mountain lake on a windless day. Physically, he looked thinner than she remembered, his face drawn and weather-roughened.

Dyannis slowed her pace, curtsying to Carolin. The years of exile and kingship had worn heavily upon him, the once sprightly youth now a man marked by the cares of his office. He greeted her with warmth and unaffected grace, putting her immediately at ease.

Glancing from Carolin to her brother, Dyannis sensed the harmony between them, the sympathy of mind. They were of a kind, she thought, although very different in appearance and temperament. Shared passion bound them together, each nourishing the other. She felt a little envious, for she had no such bosom friend. Ellimara came the closest, and even then, the difference in their ages made true intimacy difficult.

Raimon and the others from Hali showed Varzil so much deference that for an instant Dyannis wondered if she ought to bow to him also, before she decided that was a ridiculous idea. When he held out a hand to her, she brushed it aside, stepped into the circle of his arms and planted a kiss upon his cheek.

"Have I grown, brother, or have you shrunk?" she asked. "I must be nearly as tall as you!"

"As small, you mean," Varzil replied with a hint of his usual self-mockery.

"Not so small, I hope, that you cannot unravel this puzzle for us."

"I am glad to see you, too," Varzil said, ignoring the other Keeper's scandalized expression. "Also that size has never been the determining factor in *laran,* or there would be scant hope for either of us."

She laughed at that, happy to see that however much honor the world heaped upon him, Varzil had kept his sense of humor. With that same easy manner, he turned back to Raimon, and within a short time, everyone settled in their seats.

Carolin listened gravely as Raimon presented the latest information they had gathered. After Dyannis repeated her story, he sat for a long moment, elbow resting on the arm of his chair, chin cupped in his hand. His eyes looked dark and hooded like a hawk's. A core of strength, bright and hard as steel, shone through. Although Dyannis kept her *laran* shields respectfully raised, she sensed how deeply this news troubled him.

At last, Carolin said, "There is no hope for it. We must send a delegation to Cedestri Tower and convince them by whatever means necessary to sign the Compact. Although they are no longer draining the pool of energy, they have a stockpile of the new bonewater devilry and little reason for restraint."

Varzil nodded. He had often acted as Carolin's emissary in such matters, so that now most people thought the Compact solely his idea. "You are right, Carlo, but neither strategy nor diplomacy will solve the problem for the long term. Even if Cedestri agrees, there is nothing to stop another Tower, or an illegal circle for that matter, from doing the same thing."

"But surely now that Hali is alerted, such a thing is no longer possible," Carolin said.

Raimon shook his head. "That might be possible if only the *physical* lake were involved. In the Overworld, you cannot set a dog to guard a gate. Time and distance are quite different, and a trained *laranzu* can sculpt either with a thought. Even if we mounted a continuous watch upon the energy pool, it would never be secure, and that assumes we could spare the workers to do it."

No one disagreed with him, for Hali Tower, like so many others, had barely the numbers to do the work that came to them. Their Hastur King had forsworn the use of *laran* weapons, but could not guarantee a lasting peace. The next armed conflict would stretch their resources for healing and communications even thinner.

"We must act to eliminate the source of that power," Varzil said. "The longer we delay, I fear, the more psychic energy will drain through the rift into the Overworld and the more unstable it will become."

— ✦ —

Varzil took up residence at Hali Tower while he and Raimon studied the situation, both at the lake shore and from the Overworld. News quickly spread throughout Thendara as well as Hali of Varzil's presence. Groups of people, both city dwellers and travelers, assembled outside the castle, hoping for a sight of him, before being dispersed by Carolin's men.

The electrical storms got steadily worse, both in frequency and intensity. Several times, lightning struck buildings in Thendara and Hali.

Varzil's opinion was that the ruined columns were the remains of a massive *laran* device from the earliest Ages of Chaos. When he'd laid his bare hands on them so many years ago, he had received psychic impressions of its use—the device itself had acted as a magnet, drawing him back to the events that led to the Cataclysm. He'd caught only fragments of that story, two mighty Towers locked in mortal conflict, each drawing on powers far beyond any known today. Perhaps his own actions had created an opening between one time and another, between the ordinary physical world and the Overworld. Somehow, the workers at Cedestri Tower had discovered the pool of raw, unstable energy in the Overworld and had made what use they could of it.

"No one, least of all I, could have foreseen what would come from that one impulsive morning," he said. His eyes held a curious inward focus, as if he were seeing another time, other people. Dyannis sensed a sadness beyond speaking, but perhaps that was for the boy he once was, filled with hope and moony dreams.

We have all lost that innocence, she thought. It came to her, a flash of insight as quickly forgotten, that her own impetuousness might be an attempt to remain as she once was, young and brash and talented, with all the world before her and no tragedy as yet to darken her footsteps.

At last, Varzil and Raimon formulated their strategy. To seal off the seepage of power from the lake, they must repair the rift, the portal into the Overworld. In doing so, there was a good chance they might be able to repair the damage to the lake itself, to reverse the Cataclysm. Excitement surged through the Tower at this news. The lake, restored, would become a symbol of hope, of healing, even more potent than the rebuilding of Neskaya Tower had been.

Preparations were soon concluded and a circle assembled. Although *laran* work was usually done at night, to minimize the distraction of stray thoughts and psychic chatter, this circle would meet in daylight on the shore of the lake.

Dyannis rose early that morning, too excited to sleep. Along with Varzil, Rorie, and the others, she made her way along the lake shore. Varzil led the way, searching for a place that was flat enough for a comfortable site and at the same time provided a clear energy conduit through the currents of cloud-water to the lake bottom. At last, he halted them.

Varzil's plan was to begin the work as one united circle, with Raimon in the centripolar position as Keeper. Once a suitable resonance of mind was created, Varzil would descend into the lake with Alderic as his aide. Here he would establish a physical link with the columns and yet be able to draw upon the power and concentration of the circle.

Dyannis took her position, reaching out to Raimon on one side and Rorie on the other. She faced west, with the sun warm on the back of her jacket. There was only a little breeze, but it carried the scent of the tiny purple flowers that took root in the dunes. A few tendrils of hair had come loose from the butterfly clasp at the nape of her neck, brushing her cheek. Her spirits lifted. On such a day, in such a circle, she would be part of deeds that bards would sing of for an age.

For the past tenday, Thendara had crackled with escalating tension. The air reeked with unspent lightning. Eduin felt fear and suspicion building whenever he went into the streets. Mutterings of "Witchkings!" and "Damned sorcery!" filled him with elation. For the first time in more years than he could remember, he had hope—hope of justice, hope of revenge, hope of finally laying the ghost of his father to rest.

When Saravio spoke, using words they had carefully rehearsed together, the crowds grew larger and more restive. The numbers of sick people who made their way to the Tower at Hali dwindled, and those who attempted the journey now bore the strained look of desperation mingled with terror.

Day by day, as winter melted into spring, the city simmered. Eduin could feel it like a caged beast, drawing ever closer to the breaking point.

The electrical storms, after a brief respite, continued to increase in severity. Rumor had it that the circle at Hali Tower was working to control them, but Eduin cared nothing for that, beyond encouraging people to blame the Towers. If the strange weather distracted the *Hali'imyn* from the revolt brewing beneath their very noses, so much the better. The longer they kept to their own affairs, the angrier and more unstoppable the uprising. Yet nothing, not even his remarkable success in harnessing the simmering resentments of the populace, could have prepared Eduin for the next news.

One evening, Eduin and Saravio sat working out the next speeches in the back room of The White Feather. The evening was mild and they'd left the narrow window cracked open, admitting a thread of fresh air. The remains of a simple meal—wooden trenchers still damp with stew juices, crumbs of coarse nutbread, and an empty beaker—covered the battered table. A single lantern filled the room with tawny light.

A knock sounded at the door. Eduin's muscles tightened and he hesitated before calling, "Who is it?"

One of their most devoted followers, the farmer whose arm had been crippled by *clingfire,* stood outside. He bowed as if they were nobility.

Eduin gestured him in. Excitement brought a flush to the man's face and he stammered a little.

"Masters, I'm sorry to disturb you at this hour. I've been fretting all day since I heard this thing, and I wasn't sure if it had ought to wait, but then I says to myself, 'tis better to make a fool of myself than let it slip."

Eduin was about to snap out a reply, when Saravio said in his most soothing voice, "If you have come on Naotalba's business, friend, then you need have no fear. We are all her servants."

The man's eyes flashed white in the lantern light. "Don't know about

Naotalba, but I do know the wickedness of the Towers. It's on account of *them* I've come."

"Do you have word of some new doings of the Tower?" Eduin asked, his irritation fading into curiosity. "Tell us, man!"

"I just come from Moran's place—his sister's cousin knows one of the scullions up at the Tower—and he says the greatest sorcerer of them all—Varzil, him they call the Good—is to come to Hali. The whole Tower's agog with it. But he can't be good, can he, if he's one of them? None of them can be trusted!"

For a heartbeat, Eduin could not believe what he'd heard. Varzil, who he'd thought beyond his reach, coming here!

"Why does Varzil come here?" the words tumbled out of Eduin's mouth. "What does he mean to do? Is there any word of that?"

"Moran's sister's cousin says he's to meet with the other demon spawn at Hali to work some sorcery at the lake, I know not what. I've heard the very waters are bewitched." The farmer trembled visibly. "No decent folk go that way without cause."

"The Hali *leronyn* cannot do any greater damage to the lake than has already been done," Saravio said grimly, "not even with so strong a Keeper as Varzil."

"Are you sure—sure it was Varzil?" Eduin said. "And they are to work outside, at the lake?"

"Aye, I'm not mistaken in that. That's why I came to you, to see if there's aught we must do to prevent it. Who knows what they'll do next? Pull down the moons over our heads?"

"Not with Naotalba to protect you," Saravio said. "Of that, you may be certain. You have served her well in all things. Go now in peace."

The farmer left them, laden with praise that brought an even deeper flush to his cheeks.

Eduin lowered himself to the rickety bench, his mind reeling. Varzil, in the open, undefended by walls or the immensely powerful shielding of a matrix screen! Varzil—here!

It was not certain, of course—the farmer's sources could have been mistaken. Yet the mention of the lake granted it credibility. If the news were *true* . . .

Varzil, coming here? Within his reach—within the reach of the army of common folk he had been shaping into Naotalba's army!

Naotalba, bringing his enemy, unaware, to his doorstep . . .

A sensation bordering upon awe swept through Eduin. He had never considered himself a religious man, for what gods would permit the atrocities done to his family, the tragedy of his own exile? Aldones, the so-called *Lord of Light,* was a sop to the credulous, and the only thing Zandru had ever granted him was a temporary numbing of pain. He had thought Saravio's devotion to Naotalba a delusion, the workings of a mind diseased. The breath of Zandru's Bride now brushed his skin, trailing icy shivers that spread to the core of his bones.

"My friend, are you in distress?" Saravio asked. The question was politeness only, for although Eduin had long since established that Saravio could not receive telepathy, his empathic abilities were extraordinary. He could "read" a crowd better than the most highly trained Keeper.

Now Eduin roused himself. "Not distress, no. I am struck dumb by the glory of our goddess."

"Naotalba has again spoken to you?" Saravio's eyes flared with eagerness.

"Can you not see it? She has brought us together and placed us at the head of her army, ready to attack upon her command. And now she has brought her enemy within our reach. All is in readiness."

"Her enemy? Who would Naotalba have us strike down?"

"Who else have we been speaking of? None but that same Varzil Ridenow, Keeper of Neskaya and Lord of Hali." Eduin could not keep the bitterness from his voice and he did not try. "Betrayer, toady to the Hasturs, embodiment of all that is rotten among the *Comyn.*"

"Then, if it is the will of Naotalba, we shall triumph." Saravio's voice trembled on the border of laughter. "Even as they gather at the lake to do their unholy work, we will fall upon them. We will cleanse the earth of this accursed menace. With our triumph, people everywhere will rise up against the witch-kings. A new day will begin!"

Saravio continued on, but his words swept over Eduin, unheeded. Instead, Eduin was thinking that he would have to move carefully, keeping his *laran* barriers tighter than ever before. Varzil was a crafty one, and a strong telepath. Varzil must have no hint of warning, not even of Eduin's presence. Eduin had no plan to reveal himself. His army—Naotalba's faceless, irresistible army, led by the unsuspecting Saravio—they would do his work.

9

All night, the crowd had been building. Every few hours, Carolin's guards ordered their dispersal, but they reformed, like a multiheaded beast, in some other part of the city, each time more angry and adamant than before.

Eduin watched the scene from the rooftop of the house of a sympathizer. Along the twisting lanes and plazas, the open markets, he saw men carrying torches, streaks of brilliance against the inky night, but for every one that was visible, he knew there were dozens or more still hidden, shadow upon shadow, flowing and coalescing.

Since dusk, Saravio had worked tirelessly among them. He had gone hoarse repeating the phrases as Eduin had instructed him, until the words came back amplified a hundredfold by the simmering frustration of the gutter. Many of these people had been torn from their homes and families by Hastur wars, but far more of them simply scrabbled out their lives in unending, mindless despair. Now when they looked up at the shimmering palaces of the *Comyn,* the fairytale spires glowing with light and warmth, they saw the reason for their misery.

They idle while we starve . . . their sorcery has blighted our farms, rendered our beasts barren, crippled our sons, sent our babes deformed into the world . . .

The heavens cry out against their evil . . .

All the while, Saravio shaped their anger as a baker kneading a lump of dough, pushing it here, drawing it out there, leavening it with yeast and tears until at last its time had come.

With the rising of the sun, the gates to Thendara opened. Naotalba's army left the city in small groups. The appointed gathering place, a crossroads, was far enough beyond the Hali Gate to be beyond easy reach of Carolin's men. The City Guards made no move to stop them as they left. They wanted troublemakers out of the city.

Eduin followed, wrapping himself in the anonymity of the crowd. He'd slept little that night, and Saravio not at all, but this irritation was nothing compared to the bloodshot madness he saw in the eyes of the crowd. He felt their anger like tinder awaiting a spark.

"No more witch-kings!" they cried. The slanting dawn touched pitchforks, staves, wood-axes. A few had brought weapons, bows and arrows and knives, and looked as if they knew how to use them.

"An end to the Towers! Perversion of nature!"

Saravio stood on a little rise above the crossroads. As they'd planned, he wore a belted white robe with a hood. Eduin cast a faint glamour so that Saravio's form glittered as he raised his arms.

"Down with the devils of the Tower! No more tyrants!"

On their own, a handful of men had shaped a figure from dirty straw upon a pole and wrapped it in strips of red cloth. The bag around its head had been painted with a crude, almost obscene leer, and a chunk of broken glass hung from a cord around its neck.

Eduin recoiled. Saravio had succeeded beyond his expectations. He had shaped these people into a weapon as potent as any *clingfire*. Their minds, painted across the psychic space, surged in frantic patterns, veering toward madness. They had gone beyond rational thought. Nothing would stop them, not reasoned argument nor hunger nor physical wounds, for when one fell, ten would take his place. They would not stop until they had torn down the very stones of Hali Tower, not as long as they had life and breath.

For a moment, the men stood back from the mockery of a Keeper they had made. Eduin clenched his starstone for focus and used his *laran* to ignite the straw. Dry and powdery, it burst into flame. The mob cried out in an instant of terror. Then cheers rose, building to a word-less, mindless roar.

Several of the strongest men seized the pole and lifted it aloft, car-rying it forward. At Saravio's mental urging, they began crying out, "Hali! Down with Hali!"

Within moments, the entire throng rushed headlong down the road that led to the Tower. To get there, they would have to pass the lake where, if the latest reports were true, Varzil would be waiting.

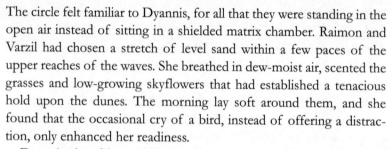

The circle felt familiar to Dyannis, for all that they were standing in the open air instead of sitting in a shielded matrix chamber. Raimon and Varzil had chosen a stretch of level sand within a few paces of the upper reaches of the waves. She breathed in dew-moist air, scented the grasses and low-growing skyflowers that had established a tenacious hold upon the dunes. The morning lay soft around them, and she found that the occasional cry of a bird, instead of offering a distrac-tion, only enhanced her readiness.

Dyannis closed her eyes to better focus her mind. Like the others, she wore her starstone unshielded, against her bare skin. Raimon gave the signal to begin. He wove them together with his cool, light mental touch. She quelled her excitement, reached out to the people she had worked with so long and so intimately, and dropped into rapport. Her breathing deepened. The physical world receded, so that she no longer knew whether she stood or sat, whether in day or night, winter or sum-mer, outdoors or cloistered within her Tower.

When Varzil and Alderic stepped away from the circle, only a ripple disturbed the unity. Raimon had bonded them in such a way that the physical separation might shift the tonal dynamics, but could not change the essential link. Dyannis stood on the lake shore, merged with the others of the circle, and at the same time, she journeyed with her brother and friend through the layers of cloud-water.

Dyannis felt herself floating, as if the universe held its breath. The only reality was the rhythm and texture of the circle's psychic pulse.

Through the lens of her Keeper's thoughts, she sensed the progress of the party below. Power shimmered through the web that joined them. So intense was her concentration that she lost all sense of time passing.

Varzil reached the columns and, through them, the energy rift. Dyannis felt it as a laceration, a tearing of the flesh of the world. The waters in their strangely altered form seemed like tears, as if Darkover itself wept for what had been done here.

We are here to heal that wound.

Hope rose in her, an unspoken prayer that such a healing would be possible, that she might be granted the power to do it. She yearned to see the lake sparkle with true water under the great ruby sun, and beyond it, Hali Tower soaring upward to unite earth and heaven.

It came to her in a moment of wordless understanding that this was the meaning of her *laran* Gift—to see the invisible, to grasp the immaterial, to repair the agonies of the world itself. The very word, *donas,* betokened something granted in a state of grace. Had not Hastur, son of the Lord of Light, from whom those gifts flowed, been both god and mortal?

The bond of the circle deepened as their joined minds focused through one Keeper and linked to the other Keeper below. As one being, they breathed in air and cloud-water. As one, life and time flowed through them. As one, they stretched across the gap of *wrongness* into a place beyond the Overworld.

Images drifted through their shared consciousness, pale as glass, fluid as water. Dyannis saw another circle bent over a matrix larger than anything that existed today, faces awash in eerie blue light. Layered over them, lightning danced over snowy peaks.

In the vision, waters rose, storm-whipped. Something dark moved beneath the surface. Dyannis shrank from looking closer, but had no power to withdraw, joined as she was to her circle at the most elemental level of her being. Granite determination swept through her and she recognized the touch of her brother's mind. With him, she descended further, not only through the physical lake, but into the visions of the past.

With only a moment's hesitation, Varzil approached the misshapen darkness.

Holy Mother, Blessed Cassilda, Aldones Lord of Light—be with him now!

Though Dyannis was not accustomed to formal prayer, the thought burst from her. She clung to it as a talisman against terror.

In the next heartbeat, the darkness closed around him. All sense of physical reality—the rocky floor, the pale shape of the fallen columns, the chill of the cloud-water—vanished.

She sensed utter, inhuman emptiness. Not even a pulse beat disturbed the void.

She floated through it, paralyzed, impotent.

Breathe . . . whispered through her mind, perhaps from the deepest recesses of her self or from the merged awareness of the circle. *Breathe for Varzil* . . .

The slightest hint of a shudder passed through the circle and in the next moment the darkness shifted, growing thinner. She moved through it and felt it draw apart, separating the darkness of this world and time from the darkness of another.

Breathe . . .

With each inhalation, the circle drew in energy and with each exhalation, divided the emptiness. How Varzil accomplished this, she could not tell, parting something as insubstantial and essential as darkness, each portion to its proper place.

Breathe . . .

The *wrongness* receded with each breath. The current of energy that had leaked into the Overworld dwindled to a trickle, a thread, and then nothing. The breach was sealed, the worlds once more separate.

They had done it. *He* had done it.

Yet Varzil made no move to withdraw. He held his position, listening and sensing. The circle became a fisher's net, gossamer thin and strong as spider's silk, spread wide to catch the waters themselves.

Elation sparked—he was going to change the waters back!

The net tensed as the pressure inside built. Mist churned, currents surging back upon themselves. Power, freely given, flowed from the circle and through the linked Keepers. Instead of froth, bubbles of transparency formed, taking on the clearness of natural water.

"Death! Death! Death!"

A jagged arc of pain shot through the circle, shattering the interwoven unity. The net frayed, severed strands of *laran* power whipping free. Hearts raced, stumbled. Lungs gasped for air.

Dyannis swayed on her feet. Light seared her—whitened sky, robed shapes she should know—twisting in a vision caught between psychic and material realms. Colors warped and shapes fused together—sand

and growing plants, the crimson of a Keeper's garments. Sound buffeted her, cries so distorted they seemed inhuman.

She caught a hint of trained *laran,* a flash of recognition, but only for an instant.

Eduin—how could it be—after all these years—

"Kill the demon-spawn!" "No more sorcery!" "Down with Hali!" Again came the rumble, like a drum roll—*"Death! Death! Death!"*— and overlaying it all, a looming shadow like a woman veiled in black. Eyes like shards of luminous ice glowed with pale, inhuman malice.

"Death! Death! Death!"

Dyannis whirled, staggering, to face a wall of men, faces red, eyes wild, clubs and sticks upraised. She had dropped her barriers completely, merged in the circle, and now her mind was utterly open. A boiling chaos of emotion overran her inner senses—the metallic heat of hatred run wild, smears of festering bitterness, curdled despair, the white, exhilarating shock of victory.

NA—O—TAL—BA! Death! Death! Death!

For a terrible moment, Dyannis was overwhelmed, swept away, torn into a hundred pieces. Each fragment was a thrum of agony and rage, the taste and smell of a separate life. She did not know these men, and yet in that instant, she *became* each of them. Most were a blur, a resonance of stories told or minds touched in her healing work or her childhood years at the ranch at Sweetwater. Some she had no reference for, they might have been Ya-men for their strangeness. For an instant, something flashed across her jumbled mind like the pure high note of a flute—*laran!*—trained like tempered steel—familiar, haunting—

Hold! Raimon's mental command shocked through the circle.

Hold? Hold what? she caught the dazed response.

Hands seized her. Fingers dug into her arm. Her muscles went powdery at the sudden physical contact, callused skin against her own.

She gasped. Air seared her throat.

Instinct took over. The *laran* coursing through her during the circle work erupted into coruscating energy. White-blue traceries shot across the exposed skin of her arm, held in the rough grasp of her assailant.

With a shriek, the man hurled himself backward, releasing her. In place of a hand, he clutched a blackened claw to his breast.

"Accursed witch!" someone screamed.

"Down with the sorcerers! Kill them all!"

The dark shadow of a woman bent over the mob, her cloak spread upon the wind to encompass them all.

Even as the crowd roared out their hatred, they hesitated. Glancing to each side, Dyannis saw that the Hali circle had reformed after a manner, this time facing outward. She stretched her hands to each side, creating a protective sphere of energy around herself and her friends. They were still joined in rapport, still partly in the psychic realm. But for the moment, they were safe.

Varzil was down in the lake, cut off from their anchoring support—

She sent out a mental call, though it meant shifting her focus from the angry faces and raised fists before her.

Get out of there!

Must—finish— His answer stumbled, distant, as if the very act of forming mental speech were barely possible.

Varzil had always had a stubborn streak, from her first girlhood memories of him. Once he had decided on a thing, not even their father's temper could dissuade him. What a fuss there had been about his training at Arilinn! Old *Dom* Felix had mounted such ferocious opposition that only Varzil's tenacious will could overcome it.

This time, he must listen! He must not risk himself. There would be another chance, a safer time—

Stones, some of them the size of fists, others handfuls of pebbles and clods of dirt, hailed down upon the circle. One hit Dyannis on the side of her forehead. She felt the impact as an instant of numbness, then the rush of heat as if she'd been struck by a flaming coal. Reaching up, her fingertips brushed a smear of wetness. An instant later, a second volley landed.

She felt the arrow pierce through the air even before the *thwap!* of its release from the bowstring. Pain exploded behind her eyes. She reeled, gasping. The mob rushed forward, all caution fled, even as a second flight of arrows fell upon the circle.

Instinct kept Dyannis on her feet, as the first crush of agony faded and she realized that she herself was not the one struck by the arrow.

Rorie!

Inner and outer vision leaped into a single focus. Rorie clutched the shaft still quivering from his upper chest. As if moving through honey, his legs bent, folding at hip and knee. Dyannis rushed to his side, faster than she had ever moved in her life, and caught him just as he hit the ground.

No, not Rorie!

His weight bore her down, but she managed to keep hold of him and land in a sitting position. In her arms, Rorie struggled for breath. With one hand, she brushed the bare skin of his throat. She felt the wound as if it were her own, the path of the arrowhead between the ribs, the punctured lung collapsing, the seepage of blood from severed vessels. There was no major artery cut, bless Cassilda—

Someone behind her cried out, so distorted that Dyannis could not tell which of her friends it was.

The mob surged forward. They scented victory. A miasma rose from them, reeking of blood lust and madness. Metal gleamed, the thin deadly crescent of a knife.

Another arrow *pong*ed into the earth beside Dyannis. Crimson flooded her sight, leaving an emptiness—Raimon! Without its Keeper, the circle fractured. Cold swept through her, as if the phantasmic figure generated by the crowd had touched them with Zandru's frozen breath.

Adrenaline sizzled through Dyannis. Outrage sharpened her vision. How dare they raise a hand against a circle battling to save their world? How dare they harm her friend, a *laranzu* whom they ought to revere? How dare they?

Zandru curse them all!

The sky loomed over her, the planet below her, and caught between them lay the residue of immense psychic power. Varzil might have cut off its source at the bottom of the lake, but enough of it remained for her purposes.

With a roar like a Hellers avalanche, the mob rushed forward. Dyannis threw her body across Rorie's to shield him. From the edge of her vision, she glimpsed Lewis-Mikhail grapple with a man wielding a wooden mallet. The others were down, or would be shortly. She could not feel Raimon's mind.

How dare they?

Dyannis curled her fingers around her starstone and reached out to the energy above her. In a spasm of fury, she drew upon images deep within her mind, the worst childhood nightmares she could remember. When she was four, her brother Harald had kept them all up with stories of hideous beasts, and she had awakened screaming each night for a month afterward.

Against the dark shadowy figure of the woman muffled in cloak and veil, she summoned a dragon out of legend—hugely reptilian, sinuous, and winged—and projected it into the minds of the mob. Her trained *laran* met with no resistance as she thrust aside their pitifully weak shields.

She added more details, each more vivid and horrific. From the dragon's tapered head, slit-pupiled eyes gleamed. Wings churned air into dust and a tail lashed the air with its barbed spines. From its fangs dripped beads of glowing poison.

As one, the mob halted their attack, drew back, eyes lifted, arms upraised. Their howls of anger turned to terror. From a single forward motion, some turned to bolt, others darted aimlessly, and still more fell to their knees or crouched with hands covering heads. Only a scattered few held their ground, but these men bore weapons. One or two notched their bows, aiming again at the circle.

Dyannis grasped the raw energy of their emotions—confusion and fear—and fed it into the nightmare image. The edges of the dragon sharpened. Its sinuous shape curved downward. She added sounds—the hiss of wing and talon through the air, the rattle of scales, rumbling thunder edged with brass.

Yammering in mindless panic, the mob broke. Pitchforks and bows clattered to the ground. Men shoved each other, scrambling over the fallen bodies of their comrades in their haste.

Dyannis sent the dragon harrying after them, spewing frozen sparks. She soared aloft with this monster of her own creation, looking down at the witless men. Vengeance, like Zandru's frozen whips, scored her heart.

Let them flee, the pathetic fools who thought to raise their hands against the leronyn of the Towers! See them grovel in the dust, scrabbling, stumbling, gibbering in fright. It was no more than they deserved!

She opened her dragon's mouth and breathed forth a stream of brightness, glowing white as if incandescent, but cold, cold as the breath of hell itself.

Those men who remained on their feet scattered, gibbering. Not a shred of the ghostly cloaked figure remained. Their thoughts, those who retained any vestige of rationality, were bent only upon escape. With another blast of malevolence, she let them go and turned her attention to those still on the ground. Some lay sprawled or tightly curled, knees drawn up and arms covering their faces. Other bodies jerked spasmodically.

Helpless prey, ripe for the taking.

Grim and exultant, she swooped toward them.

Dyannis! The name burst upon her mind, a sound so foreign she could not for a moment tell its meaning. A name—hers? And a voice she should know—

Dyannis, break it off! Now!

The words tore through her, as if she were suddenly thrust inside an enormous resonating bell. She paused in flight. A cacophony of horror and rage from the field below shocked through her. Through them she felt a silvery arrow of pain, metallic claws lancing deep into flesh—

—heart convulsing, chest gripped by an invisible vise, skin clammy with grave sweat—

Dark Lady, what have I done?

The dragon shape disintegrated as if it had never existed, leaving only a swath of unbroken sky.

Dyannis blinked, looking around her. Rorie sprawled unconscious across her lap. His breathing was slow, his skin cool, but not with deadly shock. She touched his mind, felt the stillness of healing trance. The bleeding had almost stopped. Lewis-Mikhail, untouched, was helping Raimon to rise. Blood matted the hair over the Keeper's temple, trickling down the side of his face, but his eyes were clear and focused. He'd been stunned, nothing worse, and she knew from her training as a monitor that scalp wounds bled freely. The other members of the circle looked unharmed.

All around, men, some in farmers' homespun, others in layers of stained, tattered rags, lay as if felled by a giant hand. She saw now that there were women among them, in garments as drab and ragged as the men's. One woman crouched beside a fallen white-haired figure, wailing.

Was this what war was like? Dyannis had never ridden to battle along with Carolin's armies. Her hands flew to her face and yet she could not cover her eyes or look away.

Everywhere, she saw bodies curled in agony or crumpled disjointedly like discarded toys. There was little blood, and only the occasional reek where some man had soiled himself. And yet a miasma, a mind stench, hung like an ashen veil over the lake shore. Underneath lay a terrible stillness, the silence after the final beating of the heart, the last shuddering breath.

I—I have done this thing.

10

Chill clawed at Dyannis, nausea shivering through her bones and numbing the skin around her mouth. If she did not act quickly, she would faint. She did not deserve that luxury, she whose anger had caused the devastation before her. Drawing upon her Tower training, she steadied her nerves. She sucked air deep into her lungs. Her pulse hammered in her skull, but her vision cleared.

Quickly she assessed the situation. There was nothing she needed to do for Rorie. He had already entered a state of lowered bodily function that would sustain him until proper care arrived. Raimon, his scalp wound still oozing, cupped his starstone between both hands, gazing into its depths, using his *laran* to contact Hali Tower for help.

And Varzil, beneath the turbulent cloud-water, cut off from them all—

I am well, little sister, came his mental voice, clear and strong. She realized it had been he who had called her back and broken her killing rage. *There is no time to waste. You must see to those who are hurt.*

Yes, there must be something she could do for these poor wretches. Their plight was all her doing. She rushed to the nearest and knelt down. From the twitching of his limbs, he was still alive. White ringed his eyes, but his pupils were equal, dilating as her shadow passed across his face. He was surprisingly young, yet weather-worn, his fingers marked by calluses cracked and gray with soil. She touched one hand, using the physical contact to reach his mind.

It is over, you are safe. Nothing can harm you.

After a long moment, the boy closed his eyes. His shudders eased and his hands relaxed. She thought he might slip into an exhausted sleep, but he braced himself into a sitting position. Shaking himself like a dog, he glanced around.

"*Dom'na,* I thank ye." When he spoke, he sounded even younger than before, with his light tenor voice and country accent.

Dyannis found she could not meet his eyes. "Are you well enough to help the others?"

"Sure and I've done my share of patchin' and dosin' on the farm, every time the King's men come through. M'brother, he went off for a soldier." Bitterness ran like a counterpoint through the boy's words. A soldier, his silence said, in some King's war, fallen under sword or spell or *clingfire,* and never come home.

With a clatter and a rush, a group of people from Hali came running, servants and novices and even pale-faced Ellimara. One of the men on the ground regained enough of his wits to snatch up a pitchfork and lunge at Lewis-Mikhail. The *laranzu* glared at the man, who fell to his knees, whimpering. Dyannis saw no more of the confrontation, for Ellimara darted up to her.

"We must find the dying and give them aid, quickly—the man with the heart seizure!" Steel rang in Ellimara's light, girlish voice.

Dyannis spotted the old man by his whitened hair. He was the one she'd spotted from aloft, with the woman bent over him already keening her grief. Everything looked so different now, as she wove through the toppled crowd. Voices rose about her, moaning, weeping, crying out names she did not know. Her mind was still open, and the tatters of their fear shivered through her thoughts.

As Dyannis approached, the woman straightened up, her expression unrecognizable, as if the horror of the day had burned away all human feeling. Lips, cracked and pale, moved for a moment before she forced out a sound.

"Demon-spawn—keep away—"

"I'm here to help," Dyannis said, moving past the woman to kneel beside the man.

"You—your lot have never—"

Beneath the coarse white beard, the old man's skin was chalky gray. Dyannis laid her fingertips along one wrist and felt the thready leap of a pulse. In that brief moment of contact, however, the flesh became dense and still. She grabbed her starstone with one hand, placed the other flat against the man's chest and focused her *laran* senses. Through the layers of coarsely woven cloth, past wasted muscle and arching rib, she dove, a mote of consciousness. There, in the lightless heat of his body, a heart struggled, muscle fibers stretching, tightening, like mice in the shadow of a hawk, each moving in its own disparate rhythm.

She knew enough to recognize what was happening, to know how little time she had to act. Like every other novice at Hali, she had first trained as monitor; over the years, she had served as healer many times, but never in a case so dire and complex as this. She could clear a blocked vessel, could ease the oxygen starvation of the tissues it fed, but it was beyond her power to do that and at the same time, restore the heart's normal rhythm. Either, untreated, would take his life.

Ellimara! she called out, hoping wildly that the younger woman was able to respond and not already sunk into a healing rapport with another victim. *Ellimara, help me!*

She cannot leave her patient, came Varzil's calm mental voice. *I will lend you what aid I can.*

Dyannis saw without looking up that although Varzil was only now climbing the sandy banks of the lake, in his mind he stood beside her in every way that mattered.

She dropped her barriers, so that he would see and sense everything she did.

We must stop his heart, Varzil said, *and start it afresh.*

Yes, that made sense. She gathered the psychic power running through her, even as she had gathered up the residue of electrical tension in the air, and sent it coursing through the old man's heart. The random jerk and twitch of the muscle fibers halted, minutely easing the dark blotch of the dying cells. She waited a moment, until she was sure that all motion had ceased, that the heart was completely at rest.

This way. Varzil's power lay lightly upon her, as if he gently rested his hands upon hers. She cast a bolt of energy through the old man's heart, starting at the upper pole, where normally the contraction would begin. Varzil came up and under her, sweeping through her, carrying her like one of the lake waves during a storm.

She waited for a long moment and then another, listening and hoping. Not a twitch, not a hint of motion answered her. She thrust her mind deeper, agonizingly aware that with each passing second, the man's life forces plummeted. With her inner vision, she saw the heart not as a solid object the size of her fist, muscle-red and tapered, but as a layering of light. Light that even now faded from her sight. Once or twice, she thought she saw the faint glimmer, like the trail of a shooting star, but never more than that.

Again! Varzil cried.

Though part of her wailed that the old man was already gone, that anything more was hopeless, she summoned her strength for another try. She could not have done it without Varzil's insistence, his surge of mental power. Even as his mind joined with hers, she felt his own desperation. For an instant, she seemed to be standing in the Overworld, watching the figure of a red-haired woman dwindle into the distance, longing to rush after her yet knowing she would never catch her, never reach her, never hold her.

With the second shock, a quiver ran through the aged body. Nerves and muscle fibers lit up in a tracery of fire. Dyannis heard a single beat of a drum, echoing deep and from a great distance, as if some other, hugely massive heart enclosed them all. Whether it was the last stroke of the old man's heart, she could never tell, but after that came a silence darker and deeper than she had ever imagined. She felt herself falling into it, welcoming it, becoming it . . .

As if a massive hand reached down and snatched her out, she came back to herself with a gasp. Brightness and noise battered her. A woman's hoarse voice howled, "He's gone! He's gone!"

"You did everything you could," said a familiar voice.

Dyannis squinted up into the face of her brother. He stood just beyond the dead man, his clothing sodden and trailing water-weeds, his face drawn, worn beyond his years. Compassion shone in his eyes.

Something inside her gave way. She collapsed over the old man's body. Guilt spasmed through her.

Everything I could? I caused this in the first place—death and torment! How can I ever put it right? Can I give this old man's life back to him or wipe the memories of this day from the minds of these people?

Nor was there any help for it—not in her Tower-trained *laran* that had caused so much harm to so many—not in empty words of comfort.

It is all my doing, mine! Mine!

"Dyannis Ridenow, one who is *leronis* and *Comynara* does not behave with such self-indulgent hysterics!" Her brother's voice lashed out, salt on her excoriated nerves. "There is work to be done and men who are not yet beyond our help!"

Stung, her cheeks flaming in shame, Dyannis straightened up. There was no need to reply, for anything she said in her defense would only condemn her further. She gathered herself and went to perform what small measure of restitution she could. Judgment would surely come, but for this hour, it would have to wait.

Dyannis lost all track of time, monitoring, assisting the healers, bandaging wounds, and offering what words of comfort she could dredge from her increasingly numb mind. More help arrived after what seemed an eon, men and carts from King Carolin. The King also sent his own household physicians and *leronyn*.

Varzil took charge of the operation, apportioning resources, conferring with the senior monitors as to which men and women were in direst need and must go to the Tower, which to return to the city, and which were well enough to go about their own business after a night's rest and a hot meal.

"You must warn them that for some time, they may have nightmares or see things that are not truly there," he told Dyannis and the others. "This was no simple mob, driven by hunger and injustice. These people have been overshadowed by some force beyond my understanding. I can sense a foreign *laran* behind their thoughts, as if some renegade *laranzu* had spurred them to this attack, but there is something more, some malevolent influence that I have never encountered before."

Dyannis noticed that he said nothing of her counterattack, of how she had abused her training and her Gift. At this point, she was too tired to care. She trudged back to the Tower, refusing the offer of a mount and biting back a retort when Lewis-Mikhail suggested she ride in a litter, as had Rorie. Varzil had already castigated her, and rightly so, for indulging in her own personal self-recrimination. She had no right to demand any special attention or consideration.

The next morning, although she had barely slept and forced down only a few morsels of food, she went down to the infirmary to work. Ellimara, who was in charge that morning, ordered her back to bed.

"What do you think you are doing?" the younger woman demanded. "How do you think you will serve anyone if you make yourself ill from inattention to the most elementary principles of care? And do not tell me your health is yours to abuse as you wish, Dyannis Ridenow, for we are all of us needed."

Mute and miserable, Dyannis did as she was told.

— ✦ —

Days blended into one another. Dyannis slept and ate, as she had been taught, escaping further censure from Ellimara, and awaited what came next.

During this time, she woke often from fragmented dreams, reliving the attack. Sometimes, she would be buried in an avalanche of howling, distorted faces, all crying out their accusations. She fell down corridors where every door gaped open and hordes of scorpion-demons rushed out, stabbing at her with pincer and stinger. Other times, she became the pursuer, seeking that flash of trained *laran* in the mass of fleeing minds. Once, as she strained to touch it, a breath beyond her reach, she found herself back in a real memory, lying in Eduin's arms at Midwinter Festival Night. She awoke trembling, confused, aroused. Had her mind, under the onslaught of recrimination and exhaustion, retreated for a moment to a happier time, or had Eduin been there, amidst the rabble?

Of Eduin, there was no trace. She must have imagined that moment of recognition. When she mentioned it to Varzil, he looked thoughtful but offered no comment.

Finally, the worst of the cases, the men and women who had withdrawn into nightmares within their own minds, whose bodies had been locked in catatonic spasm, had been judged well enough to go about their own lives again, or other provision had been made for those few who would never recover. The old man was one of three deaths. One woman jumped from a window high in the Tower, although it was never clear how she had gained access to it from the infirmary; a painfully thin young man, barely out of his teens, slipped away quietly in his sleep, his body riddled with tumors. It was a mystery how he had kept going so long.

I have done a wrong that can never be made right, Dyannis repeated to herself, and threw herself back into the oblivion of work.

She knew rationally that the boy's death was not her doing, but the three lives hung on her like leaden chains. She sat with each of them before they were taken away for burial, etching their features into her mind, the jaws slack and eyes sunken, the flesh so still in death, repeating to herself that this was the result of her willful defiance of all the rules of ethical *laran* use. Against all training, against all decency, she had used her powers over the minds of ordinary men and these deaths, with all the anguish the others had suffered, were the result.

I must never for an instant forget that these people paid the price for my own recklessness.

More than that, she had violated the Compact, to which every member of Hali Tower was sworn. She had used her Gift as a weapon to kill defenseless men at a distance, while she herself remained immune from any such counterattack.

When a servant came to her chamber with Raimon's summons, Dyannis knew the moment of judgment had come. She found herself strangely lightened by the thought that soon the waiting would be over. She would know the worst, would submit herself willingly to his punishment.

Raimon's voice was kind as he invited her inside. The sun was well past noon, and the chamber pleasantly light. A small fire flickered in the grate. Three chairs had been drawn up around the hearth. Raimon occupied his favorite, of wood so old it looked black. His pale hands rested on the arms.

Varzil, in the second chair, smiled in welcome. Dyannis lowered herself into the third, thinking the arrangement entirely too comfortable for such a serious hearing. Perhaps they meant to put her at her ease, to better receive her confession of guilt.

"*Chiya,* do not look so grim," Varzil said in an easy tone, after the usual civilities had been exchanged. "Are you still unwell after working so hard?"

Dyannis shook her head. She kept her *laran* shields tightly raised and used speech instead, just as she might if she were brought before the *cortes.*

"Please do not toy with me, *vai tenerézi.* I hope you will be merciful in this respect, although I do not deserve it in any other."

She felt the flicker as Varzil and Raimon exchanged a mental question. They must be aware that she had walled herself off from all telepathic contact. She had decided to do this very early after the disaster, when the full realization of her crimes was still fresh. She had abused her *laran* and therefore, must stand to judgment without any of its privilege, unworthy of her Gift.

Varzil's eyebrows lifted, and she wondered if he had caught the edge of her thought, even through her barriers. He was perhaps the most powerful telepath of his day, and certainly the most disconcerting. These days, he managed to divide the ruling *Comyn* into those who supported him with wild enthusiasm and those who wanted him dead. Now he settled in his chair and turned his attention to Raimon, as resident Keeper.

"Dyannis, we have no intention of tormenting you," Raimon said in his calm, quiet voice. There was a stillness about him, a clarity of spirit, that reminded Dyannis of the stories she had heard about his *chieri* blood. "As you have rightly assumed, we have asked you here to review the events of the attack at Lake Hali."

She drew in her breath, unconsciously bracing herself. "There is no need to elaborate the charges against me. I have lived with them every hour, waking or asleep, since then. I confess that I used my *laran* against my oath and every principle of Tower integrity, to invade and oppress the minds of ordinary men." She paused, gathering herself. "With the result that three people lost their lives and untold others suffered damage they will carry for the rest of their days."

"You condemn yourself, then?" Raimon said.

"I cannot see it otherwise." Though she wanted more than anything to hang her head in shame, she kept her gaze steady, unflinching. "Varzil, I gave only token agreement to your Compact before this.

Now that I see—I know—what I have done, what it means, I—" her voice broke, "I have betrayed our highest ideals. I—forgive me, I do not deserve—"

"That is quite enough," Raimon interrupted in a tone that reminded Dyannis of how Ellimara had scolded her. "Here is a unique situation, with the judge trying to persuade the accused of the possibility of her innocence. We understand you feel remorse for your actions. That is only natural, and it does you credit. A person of lower scruples would have brushed the incident aside, claiming all of the glory and none of the responsibility. It is equally wrong to do the reverse."

It took Dyannis a few moments to comprehend Raimon's meaning. Was he saying there was glory in what she had done? What, she thought bitterly, the glory of the berserker? The honor of the butcher? She would as well praise the heroism of a banshee on the hunt!

"What do you suppose would have happened if you had not acted as you did?" Raimon went on, unperturbed. "Defenseless, vulnerable, outnumbered, the circle had little chance of survival. Instead of three deaths, none of them deliberate, there would have been a dozen—" Here he paused, glancing at Varzil, meaning, *and one more, who is vital to Darkover's future.*

"I—I did not think—"

"Of course, you did not. How could you have, in the midst of the rabble's attack? Or if you had, by some superhuman feat, managed to reason it out, what else would you have done? Could it be that your instinct was true? That your quick action saved us all?"

Dyannis fell silent, although she softened her *laran* barriers to allow for mind-speech. *What you say may be true, but it cannot absolve my guilt.*

No, her Keeper responded in kind, *it cannot.* He said aloud, "Will you submit to my judgment?"

This was the moment Dyannis had been waiting for.

"Then hear my verdict, Dyannis Ridenow. You did indeed misuse your Gift, against your oath, the Compact, and the most fundamental principles of the Tower. You violated the minds of those people for your own ends, thereby inflicting great and lasting harm. You have betrayed your sacred trust."

Dyannis quivered, each word cutting deeper than a razored lash. Her cheeks burned and she wanted desperately to raise her hands to cover them, but held herself still. She had not anticipated the depth of her shame. It was one thing to enumerate her own wrongs within the privacy of her own mind, and quite another to hear them spoken aloud with such uncompromising bluntness. Yet it was no more than she deserved. Through the sting of tears, she kept her face lifted and lips pressed tightly together.

"Although you are guilty of this act," Raimon went on, "you also committed a heroic deed that saved many lives, and you have striven unstintingly to aid those very people who attacked you without provocation. Indeed, if your monitor has not exaggerated, you have come near to placing your own life and health at risk. It is my judgment as your Keeper that you have repaid your debt. You are free of any further obligation in this matter."

Dyannis stared at him through blurred eyes as his words sank in. She was sure she could not have heard rightly. How could he absolve her of such a thing? As for what she had done afterward, that was no more than any *leronis* of the Tower would do, and carried no special virtue.

Raimon must not have understood the enormity of her transgression. Perhaps the blow to his head had impaired him in some way. And yet he was her Keeper, the *laranzu* to whom she had given her oath. She had agreed to submit to his judgment, never thinking that it might be far more lenient than her own.

"Did you wish to respond to this sentence?" Raimon asked.

Dyannis was suddenly aware of how much time had slipped by. The tears that had brimmed her eyes were now drying upon her cheeks. She shook her head.

It is not enough, it will never be enough. But there is nothing I can do about it now.

"*Chiya,*" Varzil said. The tenderness in his voice scored her already raw nerves; she had forfeited all such consolation. "You judge yourself too harshly."

"I know what I have done," she replied. Her words came out low and hoarse, choked by the immensity of her emotions.

No, he replied telepathically, *I think you do not. Listen to me. There are forces at work here, powerful and hidden. Not all of them may be human. We who are Gifted with* laran *often err in believing ourselves elevated in foresight and understanding above ordinary men, but it is not so. There are destinies that shape our times and even the wisest of us cannot know them all. I certainly do not, and I know more of this story than any of us. But this much I do know. Many things were set in motion long ago and have not yet come to rest. The rift beneath the lake is only one of them, and its resolution is not yet complete, not while Cedestri Tower still possesses the terrible weapons it created with that power.*

She nodded. That much was true. Cedestri's bonewater dust must be dealt with.

We see the world as if through a keyhole, Varzil went on, *and even as we strain to make it out, it shifts before our eyes. We can only do our best with that small part we can see. Your story is not yet finished. Your penalty is to go on. Can you accept that?*

With an effort, she found her voice. "I will serve in any way I can." It would not be enough, but it was all she could do.

Varzil smiled, his expression echoed by Raimon. "Then when you have recovered a little more, you will ride with me to Cedestri, and there we will do our utmost to end this evil before it spreads any further."

11

Footsteps pounded by in the street, the heavy booted tread of the Thendara City Guard. Eduin flattened himself against the rough-cut stone wall of a side street, hardly daring to breathe. They were out in force, the Hastur scum, scouring the city for any trace of the lake shore rioters. He and Saravio had fled, along with the mob, from Hali all the long way back to Thendara, only to find themselves hunted here as well.

The echoes of the Guard died down and a sickly lassitude descended once more on the alley, a mixture of garbage and despair. Above, a window opened and a plain-faced woman in a dirty head scarf tossed a bucket of refuse into the alley. Eduin dodged in order to avoid the noxious splash, but not quickly enough. He was slowing, reflexes and *laran* worn thin by the day's catastrophe.

He had gone to the lake tightly barriered, lest one of the circle there—especially Varzil—recognize him. It was impossible to disguise Saravio's unusual *laran*, so Eduin hoped the psychic turbulence of the mob would mask any trace of individual personality. Saravio had been so overlain by the mental image of Naotalba that Eduin doubted he'd be recognizable as human, anyway.

Even now, when all his plans had come to nothing and he hid like a hunted rabbit-horn, Eduin remembered the rush of exhilaration when he heard of Varzil's coming. How he had counted the hours, numbered the heartbeats. Carefully, he had readied his forces. Individually, the poor beggars stood no chance against a Tower circle. But throw enough of them at the *leronyn,* distracted by their task, and even a circle of Keepers could be overrun.

He remembered thinking how he would trample Varzil beneath the thousand feet of Naotalba's army. He dreamed of gazing upon the smashed and bloody remains of the one man who stood between himself and freedom, the one man who had stolen his dreams, his happiness.

Deep within his belly, triumph, warm and liquid, had surged. The whisper in his mind had sung like silver.

Everything had gone according to plan. The mob had even improvised an effigy of a Keeper and set it ablaze. Howling, they rushed to the lakeside. Eduin, hanging back, caught only a glimpse of the Tower workers assembled there. How smug they were, how secure in their privilege. They had not even bothered to set a lookout, but had proceeded to their work. What arrogance to assume their work was so important and they themselves so revered, no one would dare disturb them!

When the concentration of the circle was broken, when the rabble's ingrained awe of Tower folk dissolved under the torrent of their rage, when victory was all but certain, only then had Eduin realized that Varzil was not on the shore.

Impossible! Eduin had thought. *He must have come down with the circle!*

Then Eduin had lowered his *laran* barriers, casting about for his prey. He had scented Varzil though the turbulence of the energy-charged cloud-water.

But how to reach him? Eduin had wondered. Would it be better to wait for Varzil to come to the aid of his fellows? Or should he risk descending into the lake after him? In that moment, he himself had become vulnerable to counterattack from the circle. He had judged there to be no real danger, disoriented as they were. At least two of them, including their Keeper, had been felled by the onslaught of stone and arrow. He was wrong.

Images had burst upon his mind, a dragon searingly vivid in color and brightness. The clash of its scales and the noxious reek of the poison dripping from its fangs filled the air. Instantly, he recognized it as a *laran*-driven hallucination. Its power and fury stole his breath. The mob, their minds weak and defenseless, gibbered in terror. They threw their weapons to the ground. Some collapsed in convulsions.

Eduin had slammed his psychic barriers tight. Some of the spell seeped through, like glowing patterns seen through closed eyelids. He had been long away from a Tower, but few telepaths in his memory could have created—and held—such a projection.

Then he had caught the unmistakable imprint of personality, the one mind he could never fully blockade himself against.

Dyannis Ridenow.

When they had been lovers so many years ago, she was only a novice. Talented beyond doubt, but unformed in the discipline necessary to bring those Gifts to fruition. At the time, he had not cared about her potential as a *leronis*. All that mattered was the heart-bond between them.

For as much as he had struggled against it, he had fallen in love with Dyannis Ridenow, younger sister to that very same Varzil the Good who was now counselor, defender, and support of his sworn enemies. He had met Dyannis at Midwinter Festival in Hali, where they were both guests of Carolin Hastur, then still a young prince. She had been very young, generous of heart, willful, and she had loved him without caring about his lack of lineage or powerful connections. Of all the people he had met during his time in the Towers, only she had offered such a pure and undemanding acceptance.

Even after a separation of years, Eduin remembered how hope rose within him, the vision of himself as something other than an instrument of his father's justice.

It had all come to naught, as it must. There was no room in his heart or life for anything beyond vengeance. In despair, he had prayed to have this love, this sweet, deadly, treacherous love, taken from him.

They had come together again, briefly, during his term at Hali, when he covertly searched the Hastur genealogies for any trace of the offspring of Queen Taniquel. Their encounter had been an uneasy mixture of old longing and new concealments. She had let him go his own way and he had not inquired into her own affairs. Clearly, in the interval, she had become a powerful *leronis,* the equal of any he had known, capable of blasting such a horrific image into the minds of so many.

The moment he had recognized her at the lake, he had withdrawn in near-panic, submerging himself in the roiling storm of ordinary emotions, desperately hoping that she would not notice him. If it were known, or even suspected, that the mob was led by a renegade *laranzu—*

No. Even to think such a thing was to court disaster. Far better to let them believe that years of poverty, the detritus of so much civil conflict, had driven ordinary men to riot. Meanwhile, he and Saravio must find a way out of the city. Soon, before the noose of searchers drew even tighter.

Once more, he is beyond my reach.

Gathering himself, Eduin made his way down the alley, across a narrow street, angling along a circuitous route. There were no wide avenues here, no direct passage from one end of the warrens to the other. This part of the city, even shabbier than that in which Saravio had once rented his room, had grown up like a diseased tumor, layer upon despondent layer.

Eduin found Saravio huddled around a garbage fire, along with a handful of strangers. Instead of his usual hooded cloak, Saravio wore a much-patched jacket and a knitted cap that covered his bright hair. He rocked back and forth, arms wrapped around himself, muttering beneath his breath. Since the day of the riot, he had spent hours each day like this, rousing only when Eduin forced him to some action. At least, his words made so little sense, being more babble than true speech, that there was little chance of betrayal.

The night air was dank and chilly. Men and women alike wore rags dark with filth, their faces reddened from exposure and drink. The smell, sweet and rank, stirred desires, but Eduin shoved them aside. He could hide, but he could not disappear. His newly-reawakened *laran* senses caught the flare of pleasure in their minds, the tang of Saravio's manipulations.

He does it without thinking, like a reflex, just because they are in pain, Eduin thought. *Just as I was. He doesn't consider the consequences.*

Saravio, holding his hands above the greasy flames, looked up. He moved aside from the fire's light and bent his head close to Eduin's.

"We must leave the city at dawn," Eduin said in a low voice. "The Traders' Gate is so thickly traveled at that time, few are questioned."

Saravio nodded and Eduin thought he understood. Their friends had given them what they could spare—a little money, food, a blanket or two. They'd go on foot, indistinguishable from any other refugees, limping back to wherever they'd come from after finding no hope in Thendara.

"Come," Eduin said. "We must be ready before dawn if we're to place ourselves in the midst of the throng."

He caught the edge of Saravio's half-formed thought. Thendara was lost, a barrenlands. Naotalba had forsaken her servants. Only the bond between the two prevented Saravio from surrendering utterly to despair. Eduin's own instinct for survival spurred him on, thinking to run and hide, wait for the hunt to die down, and most of all, to endure even when there was no hope.

But there was hope. Eduin could smell it in the air, even through the greasy smoke, the reek of garbage, and withered, ale-soaked flesh. It moved in the shadows beneath the moon in a half-remembered dream, the lift of his heart when he heard Varzil had come down from his Neskaya fortress.

He was almost within my grasp. And what has happened once may come again.

The scorpion in his mind rattled its pincers, *K–k–kill . . .* and Eduin shuddered.

An idea stirred. Eduin turned to Saravio, trudging by his side. "We did not prevail this time, but we have learned something vitally important to Naotalba's cause. Do you not want to know what it is?"

Saravio's chin lifted. "That men cannot be trusted."

"Nothing of the sort. These men would have died for her. Some did die, if the reports from Hali are truthful. No, we now know the identity of the chief of her enemies. The only one with the power to stand against her."

"Who is this man?" Saravio blinked, his expression blank. "I saw no one in that circle capable of such a thing." He seemed to have forgotten their previous discussion of Varzil.

Eduin wanted to shake Saravio. "Don't you remember?" he said through gritted teeth. "He was within the lake, using its arcane powers against us, drawing upon the power of Zandru himself, Naotalba's tormenter, to defy her."

Saravio gave a lurch, quickly catching his balance. He flattened himself against a shadowed niche between two dilapidated buildings and lowered his voice to a whisper. "Varzil the Good? It is true that some unholy force was raised against us. Does he serve the Lord of the Frozen Hells? I had thought him arrayed with Aldones."

Eduin now regretted bringing the gods into the conversation. "Appearances can lead all of us astray. Perhaps as we learn how to overcome this Varzil, we will learn more. For today, we must hold fast to our cause—victory for Naotalba and death to Varzil."

"Victory for Naotalba."

"And death to Varzil," Eduin pressed.

"As Naotalba wishes."

Eduin had to be content with that, for he got no more sense from Saravio that night.

The next morning, Eduin and Saravio slipped through the Traders' Gate, surrounded by laden pack animals, families in carts pulled by teams of antlered *chervines,* peddlers on foot, bent under the weight of their packs of trinkets and ribbons for country buyers, a dray wagon of empty ale barrels, a troupe of musicians in their gaily-painted caravan, and a scattering of children, some of them likely runaways.

The first few days, there was much company on the road. They traveled without a clear destination, their only object being to place themselves beyond Hastur's reach.

In talking with their fellow travelers, Eduin realized he had little need to disguise his interest in Varzil. The traders, who carried news as well as sale goods, had much to tell. Not all of it was accurate. Varzil had gone down to the lake at Hali, but not, Eduin thought, to wrestle with monsters from the depths. Nor had he summoned any, although the illusory dragon had indeed seemed to issue from Zandru's Seventh Hell. With a few retellings, the lake riot would be transformed into some other entirely different event. Varzil's mission now seemed to be to restore the lake and herald in a new age.

As they went on, the children began clustering around Saravio. Something in his gentle simplicity attracted them. The younger ones, in particular, were fascinated by his cap and teased him about what lay beneath. After that, Eduin shaved Saravio's scalp and buried the hair. It was only a temporary measure, but bought them less chance of discovery.

A company of mounted soldiers in Hastur blue and silver clattered by on the road. The travelers scrambled to make way for them. Eduin, in a moment of panic, dove into a hedgerow. He huddled there, shaking, until the hoofbeats died down. Only then did he notice the scratches over his arms and face, the rents in his already shabby clothing.

As he joined the others, Saravio stared at him, but said nothing. From the looks of his fellow travelers, they thought him a fugitive. His own instinct to hide had betrayed him. Fortunately, they turned back to their own business and asked no questions. They might well remember his behavior in the days to come, however, should there be any profit in it.

I have been in the city too long, Eduin thought. For the most part of his life, he had been cloistered in one Tower or another, or else scuttling through the back alleys of Thendara, keeping out of the light. *I must find a place to hide, at least until I can plan what comes next.*

It would not be safe to return to Thendara for a long time, and Hali was even chancier. Varzil would now be on guard and surrounded by *leronyn* dedicated to his protection.

Eduin had spent his childhood in a rough little village, little more than a few hovels along a mud road, near the Kadarin River, where his father had found safety and anonymity. Although he had been sent away to Arilinn Tower at a young age, he remembered enough of rural life to know how difficult it would be for two men to disappear in the countryside. They had no farming or herding skills; even their clothing would stand out beside the homespun garb of the country folk. After a few days on the road in the thinning traffic, it was all too plain that they could not reach any large city on their own.

They met a party of salt merchants coming in the opposite direction on the road, who had come through Robardin's Fort. Eduin remembered passing through it on his way to Hali Tower. It was a medium-sized town, little more than an overgrown market village with a headman but no *Comyn* lord or Tower, spacious open places, pens for livestock trading and fields for the wagons and tents of travelers. Two important roads crossed over the Greenstone River in a series of bridges, bringing a constant flow of people, their beasts, and goods. The two of them would surely find some kind of work, hauling water for horses, sweeping out taverns, scouring boat hulls. Best of all, in a place like that, no one would ask questions.

12

Carolin would not permit Varzil to travel outside the bounds of Hastur lands undefended, even on a diplomatic mission. Their party, therefore, was heavily armed. Varzil seemed to know all of the men within a few hours, quickly putting them at their ease. Clearly, he was no stranger to armies, adapting himself to their routine without complaint.

Dyannis, for her part, had traveled very little beyond the family estate of Sweetwater and Hali, so the journey to Cedestri offered an unexpected adventure. Despite her lingering moments of doubt, her spirits rose along with her curiosity once they were on the road. Even the necessity of a proper chaperone, a lady of unimpeachable rectitude from Carolin's own court, could not diminish her pleasure at seeing new territory. Everything, from the fields and hills to the tents and picket lines, presented a novelty. Barley and wheat rippled in the breeze. Dyannis passed orchards of nut trees and crabbed apple, spied rabbit-horns scurrying for shelter in the hedgerows. She passed low walls of tumbled stone, fish ponds, and streams. Here, under the protection of King Carolin, the land seemed to dream of its own riches. She caught Varzil's prayer that some day all of Darkover might know such peace.

From the first night on the road, she and Varzil dined together, sitting within the comfort of his tent and talking through the evening. In slow steps, they resumed the easy intimacy of their childhood. Watching him pause with his spoon in midair, eyes blank with some inner fancy, she recognized the odd, dreamy boy he had been, still hidden within the legendary Keeper. In his company, the guilt that had gnawed at her eased, and she found herself laughing at her own jokes. Lady Helaina looked up from where she sat, a proper distance removed, on her backless stool, her body as straight and poised as if a wooden rod had been placed through her spine, and smiled.

They went on in this manner for a tenday, as farms grew scarcer and pastures gave way to rocky slopes. Dyannis realized that Varzil was waiting for the right moment to bring up some serious topic. She sat with him in his tent, the flaps lifted to admit the evening breeze while, in the camp beyond them, men and horses settled down for the night.

Twilight still hung upon the air, a milky swath across the western horizon. Beyond the camp, hills rose like jagged teeth; tomorrow would bring a hard climb, but for this hour, they sat at ease, sipping the last of their measured wine. Lady Helaina had set aside her embroidery and clasped her hands tightly in her lap, her eyes fixed upon the horizon.

In the camp outside, horses nickered on the picket line, men joked with one another and someone began singing a ballad in a rumbly bass voice, accompanied by a reed flute.

Varzil had been wise to wait, Dyannis thought, and keep his thoughts from her. Any earlier, and she would have seized upon any hint of a serious conversation with a renewed spasm of self-recrimination. Now she sat back, feeling the leather straps of her camp chair flex under the movement, and gently asked what was troubling him.

Varzil smiled. "It is no trouble to me, little sister, although there are many who would find it exceedingly vexing."

"Oh, my!" She laughed despite herself at the image from his mind, a covey of old men and women, trying to hide their scandalized expressions and maintain their dignity.

Lady Helaina took the occasion to excuse herself. Picking up her stool, she withdrew to the edge of light cast from the tent lanterns.

"It is no secret," Varzil said, leaning toward Dyannis, "though many would like to keep it so. For the past five years, I have been quietly looking for a way to begin training women as Keepers."

"Oh, surely that's not possible!" burst from her lips.

"Yes, that's what I was taught, as were you. But why should it be so? With a little care to her cycles, a *leronis* may do any work as well as a *laranzu*. Is Ellimara not as competent a monitor as any man? Are you not as strong a telepath as Alderic or Lewis-Mikhail?"

"Certainly she is, and so am I," Dyannis protested in a furious whisper, "but Varzil, you're talking about becoming a Keeper!"

"How is that different from any other work if one is qualified for it?" he demanded. "I did not take on the mantle of godhood when I completed my training, nor did Raimon, nor any of us! It is a skill that any *Comyn,* man or woman, can learn if they have the aptitude and the dedication. For that matter, any one with the talent, regardless of lineage."

Dyannis downed the rest of her wine in a single gulp. "Now that is something that really will stir up the guardians of propriety—training commoners? Varzil, you will turn the entire world upon its head!"

"I mean to," he replied with the impish grin she remembered so well, "but not all at once. The time for new ideas is fast approaching— our Towers are at a fraction of their former strength and in another generation, many will stand empty if we cannot overcome our prejudices. You know as well as I that many a *nedestro* carries a full measure of talent. How can we afford to let that go to waste just because its bearer is never legitimated, or the bloodline forgotten for a generation? Never mind, let it go. The more pressing issue is one of replacing those Keepers who are aging or lost for other reasons."

She nodded, thinking of the empty Keepers' quarters at Hali. Only a generation ago, there had been three Keepers, with apprentices in training. After the death of Dougal DiAsturian, only Raimon remained. He was from a long-lived family and was relatively young. He might serve Hali for decades to come. But he was human, of mortal flesh and bone. He could have been killed in the riot like any other man. If the stone had struck his head just a fraction lower—

Varzil had caught her thought. "There is no under-Keeper to follow Raimon at Hali. And why is that?"

"Because—" she frowned, "because there is no one he deems suitable to teach."

"No man who is suitable."

Dyannis stared open-mouthed at her brother. The noises of the camp muted, suddenly distant. A chill wind whispered through the tent. When she found her voice, she said, "Are you saying that there is some woman at Hali whom he would train?"

"Not exactly." Varzil swirled the remains of his wine in his cup. "One of my reasons for coming to Hali was to discuss this very matter with him. While Raimon is sympathetic to the general concept, he is not yet ready to undertake the training himself. He will not, however, oppose my offer to bring a suitable woman candidate to Neskaya."

Lord of Light, does he mean me?

"You. Or Ellimara."

"Ellimara?"

"She is a powerful telepath, and young enough to endure the rigors of discipline. That is a factor against you, though you not only have the strength but the initiative and the self-reliance, as you so ably demonstrated at the lake shore riot—"

"Ellimara cannot possibly be a Keeper! She has hysterics—she's far too emotional, she—"

"She has never been given the chance to use her passions instead of being at their mercy," Varzil said, now darkly serious. "And you are evading the issue. Both Raimon and I believe you have the ability to become a Keeper. The work is not easy, but I do not believe anyone with the talent can be truly content with anything less. It would allow you to use all your abilities to their fullest, as well as serving Darkover in a way few others can. You would have to leave Hali and come to Neskaya. Will you consider it?"

"Varzil, you must be joking!" Dyannis scrambled to her feet, shaking with emotions she could not name. At the periphery of the tent lights, Lady Helaina looked up.

"All I ask at this time is that you consider it," Varzil said quietly. "Nothing need be decided quickly, certainly not at the end of a long day of travel. I ask only that you think about it in the privacy of your own conscience."

"You are completely demented!" Dyannis cried. Then she continued in a quieter voice, "Out of respect, I will think about what we have discussed before I tell you so again. My answer must remain the same. Meanwhile, I wish you good night, and dreams of sanity."

With that, Dyannis swept off to her own tent, Lady Helaina following with a puzzled expression and tightly closed lips.

"Go away," Dyannis cried. She could not bear the company of the other woman, so calm and sure of herself.

Helaina murmured that she would wait outside for a time, for the night was still mild, but would remain within hearing, should Dyannis need her.

Dyannis raged across the narrow space of the tent. Nameless emotions boiled up inside her, a tumult of jumbled thoughts.

Varzil was insane—the experience on the lake bed, contact with the *laran*-charged pillars, the turbulence of the day—must have warped his judgment. There was no other explanation. Training *nedestro* commoners was one thing—there had been a number of brilliant *leronyn* without proper family names in the past—and maybe—maybe some day, there might be a woman with the temper and strength to do a Keeper's work—

But herself? After what she had done?

She was exactly as worthy to direct a circle, holding the minds and sanity of its workers in her grasp, as she was to sit on Carolin's throne! She had no doubt of her own ability—the talent was there, she knew herself to be a powerful telepath, or she could never have controlled the minds of so many. Above all things, a Keeper needed self-restraint, judgment, discipline. She had never had those things in abundance— whenever she thought she had finally mastered herself, some wild impulse would seize her—she would go hawking, or run off to the lake—or in a moment of fury, heedless of the consequences, create the illusion of a dragon. . . .

No matter what Raimon said, she would never be free of the guilt of those three deaths, and the nightmares that haunted the survivors. She, she alone had done this thing. If her Keeper insisted she must continue to work, must go on this mission with Varzil, then in atonement, she would do her best. But she must never allow herself to be put in a position where she could do so much harm again.

— ◆ —

True to his word, Varzil did not bring up the subject of training women as Keepers again. Instead, they talked of their mission at Cedestri and what they knew of the folk there, what strategies might be used to enlist their cooperation. Varzil had never met any of them, but Dyannis knew the Keeper, Francisco Gervais, for he had begun his training at Hali and had still been there when she first came.

"I dare say I will remember him better than he remembers me," she said with a wry grin.

"Even then, you were hardly inconspicuous," he said.

She laughed at that, and the tension from their previous discussion lifted.

There was little enough to laugh about. Cedestri had surely been alerted to their coming, having withdrawn their Overworld edifice for draining the energy from the lake rift. They must be expecting some reaction. Varzil was not, strictly speaking, an emissary of Hali Tower, but of King Carolin. His objective was to convince Cedestri to sign the Compact or, at very least, refrain from using the bonewater and any other *laran* weapons they had created. Dyannis did not think Varzil's chance of success was very good, even with Francisco's old ties to Hali Tower. Varzil himself was unremittingly optimistic.

"If the Compact does not reach all of Darkover within my lifetime," he told her, "then others will take up the cause after me, and others after them, until there is no place from the farthest reaches of the Hellers to the shores of Temora, where an honorable man will use any weapon that does not bring him within equal risk."

He will not give up, she thought, *not until he is dead or we all are.*

Varzil's unswerving belief in the Compact brought Dyannis unexpected solace. The events of the riot had shaken her to her bones. It must never happen again. *Laran* was far too dangerous to be used, except in the most carefully controlled circumstances.

The more she thought about it, the more convinced she became that the Compact was necessary. Not only necessary, but a form of salvation. If she could not rely upon her own self-control, she could help to change the world so that such abuses would become impossible. At times, Varzil's patience exasperated her. He thought only in terms of weapons to be used in war—*clingfire* and bonewater dust, lungrot and root blight, which scoured the land sterile. He refused to see that any *laran* work carried the potential for harm. At times, she thought that even work in a monitored circle, under the supervision of a Keeper, was too risky.

They came down from the jagged hills toward the rolling countryside surrounding Cedestri Tower and, beyond it, the tiny kingdom of Isoldir. The land softened, as if weary of holding up the bowl of the sky. The hills were bare, bereft, and something in their treeless bareness struck a chord of sadness in Dyannis. She felt a kind of mourning, a destitution in the gray curling grasses and the sun-parched heights. A harsh land, she thought, and not one to foster any hopefulness of spirit. She hoped that the folk of Cedestri Tower were immune to its influence.

The road led them down from the hills and across a plain of hard-baked earth laced with cracks as deep as her forearm. There was no water beyond what they carried. The hooves of their horses stirred up dust as they slowed from a ground-eating trot to a walk. Once, they spotted a pair of *kyorebni* circling the heights.

Dyannis nudged her mount next to Varzil's. "I do not know the history of this place, but I fear something terrible happened here." *Or will happen.*

"Yes, I feel it, too."

For the past generation, Isoldir had been at war with a branch of the powerful Aillard family. Perhaps battles had been fought on the very terrain over which they now rode. Perhaps other, more terrible weapons had transformed lush pasture or grain fields into this near desert.

It must end. It must end now.

Varzil shifted his weight onto his stirrups, half-rising in his saddle, and pointed ahead. "Cedestri lies beyond. Another day or so should see us there."

Dyannis shaded her eyes with one hand, as if she could penetrate the dust that cloaked the horizon. She glanced aloft, searching for the huge carrion birds they spotted earlier. Two dots hovered in the brightness. She squinted, her eyes watering.

Varzil—

Dyannis unconsciously dropped into mind-speech. She felt her brother open his mind, reach out with his *laran* senses. The land stretched around them, sere and gray as ash, pierced by motes of radiance, the seeds that lay dormant even now, awaiting the return of rain. Above, the sweep of wind and sky brought the kiss of moisture, freshening.

The first two dots had grown visibly larger now, and they did not circle the way natural birds did. As Dyannis watched, a third joined them. She tasted metal, the concentrated heat of charged *laran* batteries and shielded human minds. Deep within them, layered in insulation and fragile glass vessels, pellets glowed unnatural green.

Crystalline bonewater!

Varzil signaled silent acknowledgment. *Aircars out of Isoldir. They must be bound for Aillard.*

We have come too late! she cried.

Varzil did not respond, and she felt his attention shift, leaping ahead to the pilot of the foremost craft. Dyannis had ridden in an aircar only once, for in these times, the cost of their manufacture and operation had become prohibitive except for military uses. The pilot, a trained *laranzu*, bent over his instruments, using his talent to guide the teardrop-shaped craft.

She sensed the pilot come alert, jarred from his concentration. In an instant, Varzil established rapport. Dyannis caught only the periphery of the link, a flash of the pilot's temperament, the desperation lashing at him.

We of Isoldir are poor and few. With each round, mighty Aillard harries us closer to ruin. The fields that grow our food, the rivers that meet our thirst, the trees that shield us against the winter's cold, they leave us nothing. Now even our children grow sick and die under their foul spells. We have only one chance, with surprise as our ally.

The aircars seemed to move faster as they approached. Dyannis had no doubt that the sentiments of the lead pilot were shared by all. In a short time, they would pass overhead and be beyond reach. If only Varzil could convince them in time!

Abruptly, and with a force that rocked Dyannis in her saddle, the pilot broke off the rapport with Varzil.

Spies! Enemy spies out of Aillard! The naked hatred of the man's mental scream gripped her heart for an awful moment. She gasped, and only the fact that she was already gripping the pommel of her saddle kept her from falling.

But we're not— She cut off the thought, realizing how their party must appear to the Isoldir pilots. Surrounded by armed men, deployed along the road in military fashion, what else could they be but a small, elite strike force, traveling swiftly to avoid detection?

The *leronyn* of Cedestri Tower might recognize Varzil or Dyannis, having exchanged messages by the telepathic relays, but to these pilots, they would be strangers. Varzil's overture, his attempt at a peaceful greeting, would be seen as a subterfuge to lower their guard.

The foremost aircar, almost upon them now, began descending. Dyannis clapped one hand over her mouth, her stomach roiling.

They do not mean to pass us by.

Beside her, Carolin's captain shouted out orders to his men. Quickly, they took up a defensive formation, lifting their shields overhead. What protection would that afford against bonewater, she wondered, which poisoned the very earth they stood upon?

For an instant, hope stirred. If the Isoldir aircars discharged their deadly burden, here upon their own lands, then none—or less, at any rate—would be left to reach Aillard. But she would not survive to see the result.

"Here it comes!" shouted one of the men.

In the blink of an eye, a handful of tiny glass spheres, no more than points of light at this distance, spilled from the belly of the nearest aircar.

Link with me! Varzil called. At the edge of her vision, she saw him, sitting erect in the saddle, reins loose upon his horse's neck, eyes closed, hands cupping his starstone. She shut out the visual world and launched herself into rapport with him, as if the two of them composed an entire circle.

Varzil seized upon their joined mental force and shaped it into a barrier like an invisible dome between the glittering spheres and the assembled men. Dyannis felt the first sphere break open upon contact, as if it were meant to hold together for only the briefest transit. Its contents splashed out, acrid and familiar.

Clingfire!

In her early years at Hali, Dyannis worked in a circle separating out each component element, combining and distilling the mixture, then pouring it into vessels of flawless glass, for it would eat through any lesser material. She knew its color, like clotted flame, its smell, the screams when a single droplet had spattered on the bare skin of a worker, a knife slicing through living flesh, cutting away every affected fiber, lest it continue burning through bone and sinew, nerve and organ, until nothing remained to be consumed.

She threw the full force of her *laran* into the shield, pouring forth every bit of psychic energy at her command. The torrent burned as it flooded her channels, at a speed and intensity she would once have considered suicidal. She gave no care to the pain, only to the utter determination to hold—hold—against the onslaught.

The first volley broke and splashed harmlessly to the barren earth. Men and horses escaped untouched. A wave of dismay and relief swept through her; unbarriered as she was, she caught the depth of their emotions.

Within her own body, nerves and *laran* channels ached with the strain. Varzil's mind was like a rock. She held on, afraid that if she loosened her focus for an instant, she would break like a twig in a spring flood.

She felt the first aircar veer off, a second come into position for its own attack. Varzil held the shield firm, as if he commanded an entire working circle. She could not imagine the scope of his talent, that he could do such a thing. She thought only of sending him strength and more strength, emptying herself into the psychic link between them. She must be his circle.

The second aircar discharged its cargo. This time, the angle of attack caused the *clingfire* to disperse in a different pattern. Most of the liquid particles followed the course of the first, but a few went wild. They landed upon the outer edge of one of the baggage carts. The woven fabric and leather burst into flame. Dyannis felt this much before her ordinary senses were jarred by the screams of a panicked horse and the shouting of the men. She could not tell if any of them had been touched by the caustic fire, only that the discipline that had held them all beneath the psychic shield had broken.

In the fraction of an instant in which her own concentration had wavered, the entire burden of the shield fell upon Varzil. Dyannis blinked, seeing the psychic and material worlds as overlapping images. Men rushed to put out the fire, some of them using their bare hands or cloaks, heedless of the danger, for the *clingfire* would spread to anything it could burn. A grizzled veteran struggled with a younger soldier, trying to force him away from the burning cart. Another clung to the reins of a rearing horse as it dragged him beyond the shelter of Varzil's shield. Beneath her, her own mount skittered, pulling at the bit. Only Varzil's horse remained still, though its eyes rolled nervously. His will held the beast under control.

With this second attack, his concentration was pressed to the brink.

Dyannis threw her head back to see the third aircar bearing down on them.

NO!

She trembled with the power coursing through her. Memory stirred, branded into the very core of her *laran*. A dragon, a creature of frozen unholy fire, bent over a crowd of lawless men and turned their resolution into groveling terror. The dragon was inside her—it was her—

It was their only chance. It was the one thing she swore she would never do again.

Oh, sweet mother, Blessed Cassilda—help me!

As if in answer to her prayer, Dyannis sensed her brother's steadfast presence, the strength and complexity of his trained talent, and something beyond him, a luminous pressure. For an instant out of time, her fear disappeared. She soared upon a current of purest light, utterly at peace.

Varzil dropped the shield.

13

No! Dyannis cried. *We will be defenseless*—

She cut herself off as the truth rose, inexorable as night. They were already defenseless. Varzil could hold the shield for only a few more moments, but not in the face of another attack. The men and animals were already scattering beyond the perimeter of safety. Even if the next round of *clingfire* failed to finish them, there was still the bone-water dust. . . .

Still in rapport with her brother, she caught no hint of fear or even resignation. Instead, he seized upon her first reaction.

We must reach the minds of those who commanded the aircars, yes, but not as some fearsome monster, striking terror and causing mayhem.

Varzil launched his consciousness as a fisher might cast a net. Dyannis fell into anchor position, feeding him power. The pilots reacted with surprise to the telepathic contact. Hands paused on the controlling mechanisms, but not from any imposed paralysis. Varzil had attracted their attention as perhaps no other living man could.

You must not continue on this mission. There is another way to peace. His words rang out like the deepest bell in Thendara. How could anyone, she wondered, doubt that he spoke the truth?

We have no choice—attack or die, kill or be killed.

And this is what you would do! Varzil's mental voice thundered, each syllable building, storm cloud layer upon layer until the very fabric of the psychic realm reverberated with its power. Then, through the lens of the most powerful Keeper on Darkover, Dyannis saw each man's private vision. She saw families, fathers, gray-bearded elders, children, lovers, mothers with babes in their arms, glimpses of firelit hearth and sweep of meadow, snatches of lullaby and rousing chorus, a hound's soulful eyes, felt the silken hide of a horse, tasted brambleberry ale and crusty bread.

Over all these myriad impressions a veil of dust drifted, each particle luminescing faintly green. It clung to leaf and rock and roof, washed into stream and barrel, a colorless film, a hint of shadow.

As Dyannis watched through three pairs of horrified eyes, the laughter of the children fell silent, the mothers' smiles turned to keening wails as they looked into the sunken faces and swollen bellies of their babes. The rich, ripe gold of wheat and barley faded to ash; leaves curled and fell from blackened branches. A horse stumbled, ribs gaunt in a coat covered with festering sores, fell to its knees beside the rat-gnawed carcass of a hound, and then lay still. A withered hag crouched before a cold and lifeless hearth, chewing on a scrap of leather, still wearing the bridal robes of a young girl. In the next heartbeat, she was no more than a pile of whitened bones, unburied and unmourned, beneath the sterile light of a single moon.

Behind the vision, Dyannis sensed yet a deeper shadow, one neither Varzil nor the Isoldir pilots had envisioned. A woman, her face no more than an ashen glimmer, hooded and robed in night, watched . . . waited . . . hungered . . .

In the echoing silence that followed, Varzil spoke, his words gentle and relentless, infinitely sad. *This is what you would bring, not only to Aillard, but also to Isoldir. To every land. I beg of you, let us pass. Return to your homes in peace. Do not spread this madness any further.*

For a long moment, there was no answer. The aircars continued in their formation, but seemed to slow their pace. Suddenly, the foremost broke off, circling back.

Even in Isoldir, we have heard tales of Varzil the Good, who preaches the Compact of King Carolin Hastur. We believed such a thing was folly, to surrender our only advantage and go disarmed among our enemies. But some things are more horrible than defeat, more final than death. I cannot speak for any other man, but I will not be a party to what you have shown us.

I am willing to die for my country, the second said, his mental words heavy with reluctance, *but I am not willing to bring that fate to any land, not even the Aillards.*

Dyannis covered her cheeks with her hands, feeling her tears hot and slick. Against all reason, against all hope, they were turning back! There was nothing to stop them from destroying this small force and continuing on their mission, and yet they had listened—they had believed!

Above, the lead aircar was already headed back to Isoldir, the second just beginning to turn. Lady Helaina burst into tears. The Hastur soldiers hugged each other and danced. Dyannis very nearly got down and joined them. She wanted to laugh, to shout. She looked toward her brother, thinking to share the triumph.

Varzil kept his gaze aloft, following the path of the third aircar, the one from which there was only silence. It continued on its deadly course, past them and on toward Aillard.

Rowland, are you crazy? Think what you are doing! came from the first aircar.

While I live, Isoldir still has one loyal son! was the reply.

Dyannis, watching the third aircar increase its speed, disappearing into the distance, cried out, "Can we do nothing to stop him?"

"Even if we could send word to the Aillards in their stronghold at Valeron to blast him out of the sky, I would not do it," Varzil replied in a low voice. "For to them, that would only prove the necessity of such weapons."

We will not betray our comrade, said the lead pilot.

I would not ask it of you, Varzil replied. *By your leave, I go now to speak with the folk at Cedestri Tower.*

We will return to prepare for your visit, the pilot said.

I thank you for your courtesy, Varzil replied.

May you walk in the grace of the gods, then, Varzil of Neskaya. And you, Dyannis of Hali.

May the Light of Aldones shine upon us all, she returned, for she felt certain they would all be in need of blessing in the days to come.

——✦——

They saw Cedestri Tower burning when they were yet an hour's journey away. It was late in the day, and all through that morning, Dyannis
had felt the psychic firmament shift and tremble. Although she reached
out with her *laran,* she could get no clear reading, nothing specific from
either Cedestri or the folk at the Aillard capital of Valeron. Only the
most gifted telepaths could transcend these distances, and then only
when making contact with someone they knew intimately, and that was
hardly the case with either Tower. She knew only that something terrible was happening, and one glance at Varzil's whitened face told her
that he sensed it, too. Neither could bring themselves to speak their
fears aloud. They pushed their horses for more speed, and their guards
kept pace.

They had come down over the last row of gently eroded hills where
flocks of goats grazed, between orchards of pear and false quince, and
farmsteads with barnfowl coops and plots of flowering herbs. The
land here was not so barren, the gardens, trees and neatly tended fences
indicating a level of prosperity. Clearly, the surrounding lands were well
able to support the Tower, and there were no signs of the poverty and
grinding despair of Thendara.

Before them stretched a wide valley dominated by an enormous out-
cropping of rock. From its size and configuration, Dyannis guessed it
must be some volcanic formation. She could not make out any means
of access to the heights, where a castle, apparently carved out of the
same rock, overlooked the surrounding fields. This must be the seat of
Isoldir. A short distance away, Cedestri Tower sat in the midst of a
sprawling village.

Charcoal smoke billowed upward from both the castle and the
Tower, mostly the latter.

Sweet Cassilda! Valeron must have counterattacked.

The nearest soldier shifted in his saddle, his face grave with concern.

"Captain, let us make haste," Varzil said. "Our help is needed at
Cedestri!"

They clattered through the outskirts of the village, their horses
blowing froth from the last frenzied gallop. Townspeople and soldiers
in Isoldir colors, gray banded by red and yellow, had formed brigades
to carry water from the cluster of wells. The thatched roofs of the village houses had already been thoroughly soaked.

Soot blackened the upper walls of Cedestri Tower, but the lower portions looked intact. It had been a graceful building, three stories of silvery, *laran*-crafted stone soaring above the low-walled gardens that now were little more than churned mud and trampled stalks. The main entrance was a tapered arch with a carved design of interlacing vines. Through it, two workers in charred robes struggled to drag a limp body. Other victims, some of them hideously burned, lay or sat huddled just beyond the garden walls. Those who could, looked up as the party from Hali drew to a halt, and cried out in alarm.

We are friends. Varzil sent out the telepathic message, so clear and strong that anyone with a scrap of *laran* could not have failed to understand him. He added, in a ringing voice, "We are here to help!"

At Varzil's signal, the Hastur captain barked out a string of commands to his men, sending them where they were most needed. Dyannis jumped down from her horse and rushed to the Tower doors. The two *laranzu'in* were still garbed for circle work, and the man they had clearly pulled from the wreckage above wore the crimson of a Keeper. Greasy smoke streaked their faces, and the arm of one hung limply, the yoke of his robe torn to reveal a laceration still oozing blood. His face was pasty with shock and he looked on the brink of collapse. Stumbling, they managed to drag their Keeper down the wide, shallow stair to the garden, where one of Carolin's soldiers picked up the Keeper as if he weighed no more than a child.

The wounded man swayed on his feet. His eyes rolled up in his skull and Dyannis managed to slip her shoulder under his armpit and catch him before he fell. His weight staggered her, but she somehow managed to keep him moving in the direction of the healers' area. His comrade followed, coughing and retching.

As soon as Dyannis touched the wounded man, she recognized him from the relays. His name was Earnan Gervais, kinsman to Francisco, Keeper of Cedestri Tower.

See to him, Earnan begged silently.

Dyannis lowered him to the ground and went to see to Francisco. One of Cedestri's monitors bent over him, her white robe torn and muddy. Blood clotted one temple, matting her coppery hair. She looked up as Dyannis crouched beside her. Freckles dusted cheeks pale as milk. She was very young. Dyannis thought she must have just finished her training as a monitor.

"Those Aillard monsters—they did this!" the girl's words tumbled out. "Can—can you help him?"

Poor child, Dyannis thought. *She's probably never seen a man so badly hurt.* The attack, horrible as it was, could have been much worse. The Valeron Aillards had retaliated with restraint, using only ordinary fire, or the Tower would still be in flames and all its workers dead. But it would do no good to say so aloud.

Dyannis closed her eyes and skimmed her hands over the Keeper's body. She drew upon her starstone to focus her *laran*. She sensed no broken bones—no internal bleeding—no disruption of spinal cord—

Ah! Smoke clogged the delicate tissues of the lungs. Starved of oxygen, nerves sputtered and failed. The Keeper's mind, with all its talent and trained strength, spiraled into darkness, beyond her reach.

You must help me, Dyannis cried, linking with the girl's mind.

After an instant of panic at the unexpected rapport, the girl's discipline held. Their two joined invisible hands through the body of the dying man. The thought-fingers elongated and meshed together, becoming a sieve to catch the particles of carbon and even smaller motes of toxic gases. By the blessing of the gods, the girl's telekinesis ability was strong, for Dyannis could not have done it alone. Together, they lifted smoke from lungs, bringing in fresh air with every gasping breath. At last, the Keeper's chest heaved and a fit of coughing racked his body.

Dyannis, breaking the linkage with the young monitor, rolled the Keeper onto his side. The strength of his spasms heartened her. From here, his body would be able to clear out the rest. She was only a little surprised when his eyes opened, gray and clear and focused.

Dyannis of Hali, rang in her mind, a tenor bell. *Your coming is most timely.*

She suppressed a tart reply about people who needed to be rescued from their own folly, making weapons like crystalline bonewater, setting up the mill in the Overworld to tap the Hali Lake energy rift, not to mention launching an attack against an enemy as powerful as Valeron. He was not, after all, her own Keeper, and she didn't want to risk Varzil's mission here by antagonizing him. Raimon had warned her often enough about her own imprudent behavior. Instead, she shaped a suitably polite response that she was happy to be of service, and went to see who else needed her help.

By the time the great Bloody Sun sank beneath the horizon, most of the smoke had cleared and the wounded were settled for the night, their most pressing injuries tended as well as might be. Even Lady Helaina had tucked up her skirts and worked as hard as any of them. The night was mild, so many of the Hastur soldiers, including their captain, camped beneath two of the four moons, leaving their tents for the wounded.

A soldier wearing Isoldir colors crossed by a bloodstained officer's sash approached Varzil as he met with the Hastur captain for their own sleeping arrangements. The Isoldir man bowed to his Hastur counterpart and began speaking of a council the next morning.

"I fear you've mistaken me," the Hastur captain said, his mouth quirking in a half-smile, "for I'm not the one who leads this party. I am under the command of *Dom* Varzil of Neskaya, who speaks for King Carolin." He gave a short bow in Varzil's direction.

"*Vai dom,* your pardon," the Isoldir man said, flushing in confusion, "I did not know—I was sent by my master, Lord Ronal of Isoldir, to find the Hastur lord who has aided us and bid him to council."

Varzil held his shoulders squarely, but Dyannis read the weariness in every fiber of his body. "I am no great lord, but a Keeper, and have come as emissary for Carolin Hastur. As you can see by the size of our company, we are here to parley and not to fight. This is my sister, Dyannis, a *leronis* of Hali Tower. By the grace of Aldones, we were in time to help the wounded. The day is late and there is still much to be done, but if the need is urgent, we will come."

We, Varzil? Dyannis asked silently.

Varzil took her aside and said in a low voice. "Valeron has just put a brutal ending to the dispute. Lord Ronal must be acutely aware of his helplessness, and such desperation breeds suspicion and rash actions. We are strangers, come without warning and just after the attack. What better way to convince him of our peaceful intentions than by your presence?"

"Varzil, don't tease. I'm hardly presentable at even a minor provincial court!" Dyannis gestured to her clothing, stained with travel dust, smoke, and blood. Her hair and face were equally filthy.

"Exactly."

"Meaning what?"

"Meaning that you, a well-born *leronis,* have been working side by side with his own people all day and under terrible conditions. Would an enemy do so?"

Dyannis sighed, knowing the futility of further argument, and followed the Isoldir messenger. She decided to leave Lady Helaina to her well-deserved rest and deal with the repercussions tomorrow.

As they approached Isoldir Castle, the last slanting light of the Bloody Sun cast an eerie tint over the cragged stone. The trail twisted along the cliffside to the summit. Dyannis, not daring to look down, let the reins lie slack on her horse's neck and trusted to the beast's surefootedness and familiarity with the route. It was not one she would want to try under any but the best circumstances.

The last part of the trail had been raised and the sides cut away so that only a narrow causeway remained, leading to the gates of the castle. A few men could easily defend it, for the attackers must come at them singly, with no room to maneuver in combat.

From what little Dyannis could see of the outer walls, the castle had suffered much less damage than had the Tower. Valeron had not meant to conquer them or to leave them defenseless against bandits and scavengers, only to prevent another such attack as the one Cedestri launched. The Tower had been all but destroyed, but Isoldir still retained its Lord and, so far as she could tell, the greater part of its fighting men. She wondered if Isoldir, made even more desperate by humiliation, would try again.

If they do so, they are greater fools than we thought, Varzil answered her. *They would lose all claim to a righteous cause. Their neighbors, small and great, will see them as the aggressors. If they wish to preserve what remains to them, they will not answer.*

They passed through massive double doors and into an entrance hall, where a handful of wary-eyed guards fell into step around them. Soot and dust streaked their clothing, and one had a nasty burn across one beardless cheek. A white-haired man in a courtier's long robes limped toward them. When the Isoldir messenger bowed and whispered, the old man's eyes widened.

"You come to Isoldir at a sad and perilous time, *vai tenerézu,*" he said in a hoarse voice. "My lord extends what welcome we can offer."

"I thank you, for in this, the intent is of greater worth than the deed," Varzil said, inclining his head in return. "There is too much to be done for those injured below for us to stand about exchanging courtesies. If your master would speak with us, bring us to him speedily."

A few moments later, Dyannis followed her brother into a smaller room, clearly a council chamber. Maps and lists covered a central table, along with a platter bearing the remains of a hasty meal. Some of the windows, which she guessed looked upon an inner courtyard, had been broken and the shattered glass still lay across the stone floor. Yet the wall tapestries, conventional scenes of battle and hunting, were of good quality if not new. Fresh torches burned steadily from their wall sconces.

At the far end of the table, a man of middle age, his belly just beginning to run to fat, straightened up from bending over the papers. His appearance betrayed little of his character, yet something in the lines of his face reminded Dyannis of Rakhal Hastur, Carolin's traitor cousin, when she met him so many years ago at Midwinter Festival at Hali. Then Rakhal had been a trusted aide to the ailing king, and no one guessed what treachery lay in his heart. She reminded herself that she must not judge this man on a superficial physical resemblance. She caught no hint of his thoughts, but his desperation battered her, his struggle to find a way to save his kingdom.

The elderly counselor performed the introductions. Ronal of Isoldir acknowledged Varzil with a slight bow, and then bid his servants bring chairs for his guests. Varzil refused food, but accepted *jaco* for both of them.

Dyannis settled into her seat as a mug of the steaming brew was brought to her. The kitchen must be functioning well enough to supply hot drinks. The *coridom* must be a marvel of efficiency.

After a brief exchange of courtesies, Ronal spoke. "Varzil of Neskaya, you say you came here as emissary of King Carolin Hastur. What is his interest here?"

"I cannot speak for him with regard to Aillard's attack upon you," Varzil replied with the same forthrightness, "nor of yours upon them. My mission concerns quite another matter, one which has been overtaken by these dreadful circumstances. I was sent to persuade Cedestri Tower and you, its Lord, to join us in a Compact of Honor, abandoning the use of *laran* in warfare. We know that Cedestri Tower developed a new variant of bonewater dust—"

Lord Ronal's mouth tightened, but he did not flinch.

"—and we sought to prevent its use, as well as the escalation of hostilities that must surely follow."

Most men spoken to in such a manner would respond with anger, Dyannis thought, but Ronal of Isoldir only nodded. Varzil had read him correctly.

"You came too late," Ronal said, his voice edged with weariness. "I doubt we would have listened then, when we were full of arrogance and pride. You may return to your master and say that our own folly has accomplished more than your words ever could. Here we sit, as you see, disarmed by those very events that we set into motion."

He knows that Aillard could have destroyed him utterly, and did not, Varzil spoke mentally to Dyannis. *For the moment, shock has humbled his pride, but it will return, and with it, a thirst for revenge. We must offer him something better.*

"By your leave," Varzil said, "my sister and I will remain here for a time. There are many injured folk both here and below at the Tower who need our skills. Cedestri must be rebuilt, at least until her relay screens and healing circles can function once more. No—" He broke off Ronal's interruption, "we ask no recompense for this. I offer it freely, without condition, for I am bound by my Keeper's oath to help my fellow *leronyn,* and by my conscience to sow healing instead of grief, so that hope and friendship may eventually replace enmity."

"By the gods," one of the counselors muttered under his breath, "have the Towers formed an alliance against us?"

"Hold your tongue," his fellow whispered, "the man is offering to help us. Without him, we have no chance of rebuilding Cedestri, not within our generation."

"Silence!" Lord Ronal snapped. "I most humbly beg your pardon for this ill conduct, *Dom* Varzil."

"That is not necessary," Varzil replied easily. "You have my pardon and anything else I can give that will allay your suspicion. I came to sue for an end to the most terrible weapons of war and that is still my mission, if not by prevention, then through reconstruction afterward.

Often we cannot choose how we may fulfill our purpose; we can only seize those chances the gods present to us."

A hint of color passed over the Isoldir lord's face, a lessening of the ashen gray of exhaustion. Again he welcomed Varzil and Dyannis, this time with genuine warmth. He offered them shelter for the night in more comfortable quarters than could be found below, but Varzil declined, saying there were still wounded who must not be left unattended.

Slowly, they made their way back down the trail. Dyannis, for all her adventurous spirit, would have quailed to attempt it by the uncertain light of moon and torches, but her little Isoldiran mare lowered her head and moved along surefootedly, never stumbling. She must, Dyannis thought, know the trail by heart.

Below them, fires still burned, marking the ruined Tower. She wondered if it would ever be functional again. The repair of the physical structure was easy enough, but the circle, if one survived, would be greatly reduced. She was not sure Francisco would live, even with their concentrated efforts.

"If I were Isoldir's Lord," she said so that only Varzil could hear, "I would fear being left bare to Valeron's sword."

"Ronal might seek protection from a more powerful king, but I cannot see him bending his knee as a vassal," he said. "Yet if he is the one to offer an alliance, he will retain his dignity. He need not accept whatever terms are offered, like stale leavings from last season's banquet."

"Why did Valeron leave him this much, then? Why not destroy him utterly and put a final end to the conflict?"

For a moment, Varzil did not answer. "Perhaps the Aillards understand, as others do not, how precarious is the balance between the powers of our world. Isoldir has never been mighty, yet her absence would leave a gaping wound, an opening for lawlessness that could spread like an unchecked forest fire."

"That's true enough," Dyannis agreed. "Better the adversary we know, whose temper is tried, than some outlaw king who understands neither honor nor restraint."

She felt his smile, although she could not see it in the darkness. "Best be careful, *chiya,* or you will become a formidable diplomat."

"The gods forbid!" she laughed.

In the next few days, several of the more seriously injured workers died, despite the best efforts of Dyannis and Varzil. By happenstance, the part of the Tower first struck had housed most of Cedestri's monitors. The young girl who had worked with Dyannis was their only surviving healer. The people of the village did what they could for the rest with herbs and soothing poultices.

Francisco mended slowly. It would be many tendays before he was well enough to resume any duties. The headman of the village insisted upon giving him his own bed, where the Keeper sat, propped up on pillows to ease his breathing, and discussed the Compact with Varzil.

Varzil's energy astonished Dyannis. During the day, they worked together, using their linked *laran* for healing, supervising the village folk and Carolin's men. Normally, *laran* work would have taken place after ordinary people were asleep, to minimize the psychic distractions, but with the loss or incapacity of so many of the Cedestri *leronyn,* they were heavily dependent upon the help of commoners.

When her day's work was done, an evening meal eaten and personal chores finished, Dyannis wanted nothing more than to crawl off to her own tent, one shared with several of the Cedestri women. Sometimes, she saw candles burning in the house where Francisco stayed and knew that Varzil was sitting with him. Other times, she sensed his mental signature from afar and found him sitting alone on the small rise beyond the barley field.

She went out to him during these times, fearing that something troubled his mind. He was the rock upon which they all rested. If he should fail, there was no hope for any of them. She knew he carried some secret grief; she saw it in the shadows of his eyes when he turned away into solitude. She felt it in the way he cupped the ring he wore on his right hand, one she did not recognize, one he never spoke of.

BOOK III

14

The town of Robardin's Fort lay on the edge of the vast Plains of Valeron. Here the Greenstone River crossed two major trade roads, linking the kingdom of the Aillards with Isoldir, as well as the Hastur Lowlands. It was an independent township, fiercely neutral, owing allegiance to neither realm.

The central part of the Fort lay behind stout palisades that had been buttressed and repaired over the years, some portions weathered into ghostly whiteness, others newly cut or glistening with oil.

On the day of their arrival, Eduin and Saravio shuffled along with a convoy of wool traders they had followed for the last part of the journey.

Eduin recognized the river with its bustling wharves, the bright pennons in the town's colors. When he had passed through Robardin's Fort many years earlier, he had been a privileged traveler, a *laranzu* trained at Arilinn. His belly had been full, his clothes rich and warm, and aside from a little trail dust, he had been as clean and well-groomed as any *Comyn* lord.

Now he wore tatters, stiff with grime, and he had not eaten in days. He carried a ragged pack, patched together from homespun and scraps of leather, to which he'd tied a water pouch and the blanket that had been his only warmth along the road. Their food was long gone and the last of their meager supply of coins spent. The pack was empty except for a shirt in even worse condition than the one he wore and a few oddments, a wooden cup and spoon of the cheapest sort, a stick for cleaning his teeth.

Saravio's health had deteriorated during their flight, although he made no complaint. With his *laran,* Eduin sensed the other man's withdrawal into himself, despair turning into mute endurance. Saravio did not suffer any fits along the road, at least none Eduin recognized, but he seemed to be slipping into a dream world. He ate when Eduin gave him food and lay down when it was time to rest, although he rarely slept in a normal way. Instead, he curled upon himself, eyes open, lips moving soundlessly.

Despite the added burden of caring for Saravio, Eduin refused to abandon him. If Saravio had exhausted himself in controlling the mob at Hali, it was at Eduin's instigation. Eduin was not unaccustomed to feeling responsible for another human being. He rationalized that Saravio was still useful to him. Even at times when Saravio seemed barely conscious of his surroundings, he would rouse at Eduin's urging and hum his special song. The relief was enough to keep Eduin's inner demons at bay. Although Eduin hated being dependent on Saravio, he also felt a strange pity for this poor addled soul, so racked with his own private torment. Perhaps when they found a place to live and work, perhaps Robardin's Fort, Saravio might recover some measure of sanity. Until then, Eduin determined to remain with him, caring for him as best he could.

Along the road, Eduin had listened for news from Hali, especially any hint that he might be hunted. He learned nothing of any significance. Because he and Saravio had left Thendara so quickly, never lingering in one place, they had outstripped the usual network of rumor. Occasionally, there would be some hint of a disturbance at Hali, but Eduin said nothing to his fellow travelers, pretending ignorance rather than risk betraying greater knowledge than an innocent man ought to have.

At the entrance to Robardin's Fort, Dry Towns *oudrakhi* lumbered amidst horses, mules and *chervines,* wagons and carts. Liveried footmen ran ahead of sedan chairs, crying for pedestrians to make way. A small company of soldiers, mercenaries by their battered armor and lack of any lord's colors, shoved their way through the crowd.

This late in the day, the great red sun cast long shadows across the dusty road and softened the worn, splintered palisade. They approached the gate. There was an inspection point, armed guards and a clerk of some kind, a weedy man who squinted down at his book as he inscribed the name and business of each man. He waved the wool traders through with a warning to unload their pack animals and have them out of the town before curfew.

He peered at Eduin and Saravio. "Names? Business?"

Eduin fabricated a couple of names. "We seek work."

"You and half the countryside," the clerk sniffed and rubbed his long, blade-thin nose. "I don't suppose you have the money for an inn either." He pointed with the end of his quill in the general direction of the motley sprawl outside the gates. "See those striped poles? You can offer yourselves as day labor tomorrow, starting an hour before dawn. If your employer requires you to enter the city, he'll give you a day token."

They headed for the livestock pens, since Eduin had often found work in Thendara at livery stables. He knew horses well enough and could manage *chervines*. It didn't take much skill to muck out stalls, just a strong back. This late in the day, however, the drovers had long since hired whatever casual labor they needed. By their sharp looks, Eduin knew that he and Saravio were not welcome to linger.

The light was fading fast, and with it, any hope of entrance to the town. Small cook fires dotted the clusters of hovels and marked where traders camped out with their wagons. By this time, Eduin was trembling with weariness and hunger, and Saravio had lapsed into silence. He moved only when Eduin pulled him along.

They approached several of the campfires, and each time they were turned away, sometimes with scowls, sometimes with an apology that there was nothing extra to share. When Eduin feared he might fall to his knees and beg, two grizzled men hunkered around a cook fire beside a shambling hovel offered them soup and bread. Eduin had seen their like a hundred times in Thendara. He knew the color of their skin, prematurely aged from exposure and hunger, knew the calculating look in their eyes. These were men he could bargain with.

The soup was barely more than grain boiled into thin gruel, with perhaps a little wild onion, but it warmed Eduin's stomach. He held the wooden bowl to Saravio's mouth for him to drink.

One of the men watched him break off pieces of bread and urge Saravio to eat. "Yesh, you got to look out for youse selves," the man said, the words distorted by the gaps in his teeth. His companion grunted and poked the fire with a stick.

"How do you find work here?" Eduin kept his tone casual.

As the two men explained the process of hiring and the best places to find various kinds of work, one of them drew out a leather flask. When he pulled out the stopper, Eduin caught a whiff of crude hard cider. The man took a swig and offered it around. Saravio gave no indication he'd seen it, but Eduin shook his head. One drink would surely lead to another, and he knew himself well enough to be certain he would find some way of getting thoroughly drunk and staying that way. His father's command throbbed between his temples, his empty belly cramped, and he recoiled at the smells of unwashed bodies and despair, the hard light in the eyes of the men.

"Can't hold it?" one of the men snickered, but the other narrowed his eyes.

"Ghostweed more to your liking, eh?"

Again, Eduin shook his head. Like most *laran*-Gifted, he had a horror of the mind-altering weed. "No, I just need to keep my wits about me."

"If you had youse wits about you," the second man said with a nasty grimace, "you wouldn't be here to begin with, eh?"

With that, the talk turned to life in the outlying encampments. The collection of tents and huts outside the walls of Robardin's Fort afforded shelter for a succession of travelers every summer. Most of these were wanderers like the two men, broken soldiers, farmers or herders displaced by war. Once there had been only a few vagrants, and then only in the mildest weather. They had been housed within the Fort. In recent years, however, their numbers had swelled to the point that there was not enough work or housing. Those who could, moved on. Others ended up facedown in the river.

"Eh, but you'll make it all right, soon as you get youse bearings," said the first man. "Here now, you bed down next to the fire and we'll go out tomorrow morning to the hiring place."

Weary past argument, Eduin unrolled his blanket and helped Saravio to do the same. Wrapped in the coarse wool, near enough to the dying embers to catch a glow of warmth, he fell asleep.

In his dreams, he swerved and darted down the mazework of alleyways. They should have been familiar, but he could not make out his way. He searched for landmarks, but found none, only unexpected dead ends, walls barring his way. The faster he ran, the greater his feeling of dread.

Kill! came his father's voice, no longer a whisper but a whip crack. *K–k–kill them all!*

Behind him, a dark shape like a woman in a hooded cape condensed from the cloud-choked sky. Eduin dared not take his eyes from the narrow lane ahead. He strained for more speed, dodging this way and that. With a hiss, a rope dropped across his shoulders. The next instant, it tightened around his neck. He jerked to a halt, clawing at the noose. He thrashed about, struggling for air—

Kill!

Eduin's eyes jolted open. A thin sharp edge of metal pressed into his throat. Any movement would drive it deeper into his flesh. By the dim light of a single moon, he glimpsed one of the men bending over him. Instinct froze him.

"There's nothing here," came the voice of the second man, and the muffled sound of a pack being shaken. "Not worth a single *reis*."

The first man cursed. He seemed not to realize Eduin was awake. "We'll have to finish them off, anyway."

Eduin gathered himself. He was no fighter, even if he had not been weakened by hunger on the long days on the road. But he was not defenseless; no one trained at Arilinn was. He focused his thoughts, *reaching* for the other man's mind, the nerves that would loosen his grip—

Kill!

Pain lashed at him, as if the skin had been flayed from his body and the oozing flesh rubbed in salt. His vision went white and the muscles of his chest locked in spasm, so that he could not draw a breath.

With a shriek, the man hurled himself backward. The knife went skittering into the dust. A short distance away, the other man howled like an animal.

Laran attack!

Saravio, perhaps roused by Eduin's nightmare, had lashed out with all the power of his Gift. The psychic projection of Rumail's compulsion spell—to kill—had blasted the tiny camp.

Eduin slammed his barriers into place, as hard and tight as he could. From the day he arrived at Arilinn, he had shielded his innermost thoughts from the most powerful *leronyn* on Darkover. The years of hiding in exile had only toughened his ability to create an unbreachable wall around his own mind.

The pain vanished instantly. He caught his breath. In the dim light of moon and embers from the fire, he saw Saravio sitting up, a look of mingled triumph and bewilderment on his face.

One of their assailants, the man with the knife, lay unconscious. The other had curled into a fetal ball, moaning.

In the name of all the gods, what had Saravio done?

Eduin knew well how *laran* could affect the vulnerable. During the siege of Hestral Tower, he had projected illusions into the minds of the enemy soldiers. Driven mad, each had fallen prey to horrific visions drawn from his own worst nightmares. Some, believing themselves possessed or attacked by Zandru's demons, had fallen on their swords or hacked off their own legs. For the first time, Eduin began to realize what he had done.

Tentatively, Eduin lowered his mental barriers. Saravio had broken off his attack. It should be safe enough to monitor the two victims. Eduin performed a quick scan of their bodies, looking for physical injury. As he expected, he found none. Saravio had not caused their hearts to stop or their internal organs to rupture.

Eduin searched for damage to their brains. There, in the deep primitive structures that governed primal emotions, he spotted ugly red auric fields streaked with black and purple.

Lord of Light, Lady of Darkness! Without meaning to, Eduin called upon Aldones and Avarra.

Saravio had blasted the pain centers of each man's brain with enough force to create a cataclysmic wrenching of their life energies. The tumult of raging colors enlarged, reaching toward other areas, the nerve centers for regulation of breath and heart beat, of sleeping and waking.

"What have you done?" Eduin cried.

"I—I don't know what you mean. Eduin, what is wrong with these men? Have they fallen sick from bad food? Or do they carry the plague?" Saravio sounded genuinely confused. His thoughts, what Eduin could sense of them, reflected only concern.

"Whatever you did to them, you must reverse it," Eduin said. "Now, before it is too late!"

Saravio shook his head, his face a pale shadow against the night. "What am I to do? This is beyond even a monitor's skill."

A white fireball edged with crimson flared up in the mind of the man with the knife and then collapsed upon itself. In the space between one heartbeat and the next, the man's mental energies fell away to silence. Not all the smiths in Zandru's Forge could bring him back.

Eduin watched numbly as a similar process consumed the brain of the second man. For long minutes, he sat beside the last dim embers of the cook fire. Saravio rocked back and forth, crooning under his breath. Eduin braced himself, but felt nothing from the other man, other than his fear and sadness. He could not look to Saravio for help. He must decide for both of them what was to be done.

The two would-be murderers were beyond anyone's help. Eduin did not think they would be missed, especially if they had waylaid other strangers. Certainly, no one in authority in the Fort would come looking for them. If they just disappeared, their neighbors, such as they were, might well assume they had moved on or chosen their next victims unwisely. Which was pretty much, he thought wryly, what had actually happened.

After a time, Saravio roused enough to help Eduin carry the bodies down to the river. The bank was sloped and muddy, laced with waterferns. The bodies slipped beneath the scummy surface. Even if some fisherman or river scavenger found them the next morning, Eduin thought, there was nothing to show how they had died. In the unlikely event he and Saravio were questioned, they could say that the two men had offered them gruel and a space to sleep, then disappeared in the night. Which was also, in its own way, the truth.

As they slipped and scrambled back up the riverbank, Eduin debated leaving before dawn, at least to another part of the shanty town. In the end, the advantages of the rude shelter and possessions the two men had left behind won out. The cook pot, although thin and battered, had been metal, too valuable to be abandoned.

The next morning, Eduin jerked awake, his nerves scoured raw, his eyes scratchy from lack of sleep, at the first sound of movement in the encampment. Eduin's fingers closed around the hilt of the knife that was now his. Haze swept the eastern sky, but people were already stirring. The smell of boiling onions came from the next hovel.

No one approached or disturbed them, nor did anyone take any notice of him and Saravio, beyond a stare and a nod, as they made their way to the striped poles in search of that day's work.

15

One afternoon, as spring wore into summer, Eduin finished his day's work and returned to the hovel that was now his home. He clenched half a loaf of bread wrapped in a scrap of cloth against his chest. His other hand made a stiff fist at his side, nails digging into the palms of his hands hard enough to draw blood. He welcomed the physical pain, clasped it to him. It alone was real, not the bone-weary fatigue nor the hunger nor the rows of tents and tumbledown hovels. Not the sour smells, the flat hard light in the eyes of passersby. Not the whispers in his head. Pain. Just pain.

He was almost there. Ahead, near the end of the ramshackle lane was the shed he and Saravio shared with a succession of tinkers and herders who could not afford anything better. The few coins or bits of food in rent eased their own situation, especially on the all-too-frequent days when Saravio could not leave his bed. Eduin concentrated on the familiar sagging contour, the central pole, the ragged panels. Saravio would be there. This night or the next, Eduin would reach that moment when he could not go on, when he had nothing left of will or endurance, and then he would ask Saravio to sing once more. At the thought, his belly quivered and his mouth filled with a sour, stale taste.

He had found refuge in this place, in the dregs and leavings of the trade that flowed along road and river. As one tenday blended into the next, he had sunk even deeper into its dust, until some days he could not remember why he was here and what he must hide from. He had nothing anyone would want, except these secret, shameful moments of pleasure.

That, and the relentless whisper in his mind.

Kill . . . kill them all . . .

Kill? He had no power to kill, not even himself. His only power was to hold on for one more day, and one more day after that.

Eduin was so tired of struggling against the whispers, so focused on covering the last distance, that he was almost to the hovel before he noticed the brightly-painted caravan drawn up in the field beyond. A slender youth was unhitching a dun cart horse whose sway back and frosted muzzle marked his age, but his coat was glossy and his mane was braided with colored ribbons. A line of Fort women and children, some of them well-dressed, watched the process.

Mingled with the jangle of bells, he caught a lilting melody and the sound of a fiddle. The onlookers moved apart and he saw what they were watching—two women performing an old ballad. The singer was quite young, although no beauty, but with a fresh, pleasant face. She wore a bright green bodice embroidered with straw lilies, open-necked blouse, and gaily striped skirt. A scarf fringed with little bells tied back her dark brown hair. Her sturdy body swayed to the fiddle accompaniment of her older companion, a withered crone in a black dress and shawl.

The music sank into Eduin's pores. It carried none of the soporific effect of Saravio's singing, being just an ordinary tune, sweetly sung and lively enough to send toes tapping. The children laughed and the smiles lightened the faces of the audience. If Eduin closed his eyes, he could almost see the common room at Arilinn, where he had first heard this ballad.

Instead of a shanty town and dusty field, walls of pale translucent stone arched gracefully around him. He remembered carpets beneath his feet, cushioned chairs arranged for comfort and intimacy before a massive fieldstone hearth. A girl with hair the color of flame sat on a low stool, her six-fingered hands moving across the strings of a *rryl,* her voice rising and falling. The weariness in his body fell away. He could almost smell the incense added to the fire.

Eduin startled back to the present. His eyes stung. The song ended with a flourish of the girl's skirts and a scattering of applause. Some of the women threw a coin or two at the feet of the performers. Laughing, the girl gathered them up and folded them into her sash. The old woman had already put away her fiddle and climbed up into the wagon.

"I'm going now, *Tia!*" The boy had finished unharnessing the horse. A muffled voice answered him from the wagon.

"Wait," the girl said. She leaned into the opened wagon door and drew out a gracefully tapering jar.

"Fill this, will you? And don't you dare use it for practice," the girl said, wagging one finger in warning. "Find something unbreakable until you learn to juggle properly."

Laughing, the boy led the horse toward the riverside. Eduin watched him go. He lingered, drawing out the memory of the music.

The two women began wrestling a folded tent from the back of the wagon. The poles were long and awkward, the tent itself too heavy for them. The old woman lost her grasp and it slid to the ground, throwing up dust.

Eduin set down the packet of food inside the shed and went over to them. Since his arrival at Robardin's Fort, he had set up many such tents, as well as whatever other work he could find.

"Let me help you."

Working together, the two women managed one side and he took the other. The other roustabouts had taught him the leverages to use, and regular hard work had strengthened his body. He was still thin, but his chest was broader and his shoulders and arms more muscular than ever before.

The tent was more pavilion than enclosure, having only a roof and one wall. It was faded and cleverly-patched, but had been designed with care. He recognized it as the backdrop for a stage. Next came a series of platforms ready for assembly, which would elevate the performers above their audience. He stepped back to admire the final arrangement, imagining a crowd of travelers and Fort folk.

"This is for your labor." The girl took out a small silver coin from her folded sash. Flushed with exertion, she was actually pretty.

Without thinking, Eduin shook his head. "I did not ask—"

"You earned it. Without you, we would be all evening putting up that wretched thing."

"I had nothing to give you for your song," he stumbled. "And I made no bargain for my help. I am no beggar."

"Well, that's the way it is," she said tartly, replacing the coin. Her gray eyes appraised him, taking in the worn clothes, the smeared dust. She turned back to the wagon, then paused, considering. "Would you take your wages in a hot meal?"

He lowered his eyes, knowing what she saw—a man who could not find a place among decent people, a drunkard, a wastrel, a man who had some good reason to hide.

"Think of it as a business proposition," she said. "That is, if you're interested. I'm Raynita, and it's my grandmother who runs this troupe. We've been short-handed since my father died two years ago, and we just lost our roustabout. *Tia* and Jorge and I, we can do well enough once we're set up, but we need another man for the road."

Work? And a way out of here . . . and music? Eduin wasn't sure he had understood, or if that nostalgic memory had befuddled his wits.

"Perhaps," Raynita went on, "you aren't interested in a job?"

"I take whatever work I can find," he admitted, "and a man can't live on song." *Though he can try.*

"A man can't live without it," she laughed.

"I—I have a friend. He goes where I do."

"Bring him along. With *Tia's* cooking, there's always enough for one more. No promises, though. Just a meal and talk. We may not suit each other." Clearly finished with the conversation, Raynita turned back to the wagon.

Through the long twilight, Eduin and Saravio sat around the cook fire of the musicians. At the edge of the firelight, the old horse dozed beside the wagon. Night birds called and then fell silent. In the distance, frogs chorused along the river.

The old woman, called *Tia* or Auntie, had simmered a concoction of roasted grain, summer greens, and onions. Eduin couldn't identify the seasonings; he thought some of the spices might have come from as far away as Ardcarran or Shainsa in the Dry Towns. The food was the sort of simple, nourishing fare that country people ate when meat was scarce, flavorful and nourishing compared to the swill he'd lived on in Thendara. Even the tisane, a delicate brew of herbs in boiled water, had a clean taste that left his stomach warm and his tongue satisfied.

Eduin said as little as possible about his own history, but Raynita freely answered his questions about the troupe. They had been performing in the countryside around Isoldir for the last year.

"We thought there would be a good welcome at Cedestri, where the Tower is, for we'd heard there was a great lord of the *Comyn* there, a *tenerézu* of renown, and that always means a need for music," she said.

Comyn . . . *a great Keeper* . . . Eduin masked a surge of excitement. Could it be true? Could he have stumbled upon a second piece of unbelievably good luck?

"Was it Varzil Ridenow, who's Keeper at Neskaya?" he asked.

"I know not. Before we drew near, the whole area was laid waste. Isoldir and the great lands of the Aillards have been at each other's throats ever since I can remember, but it has never been this bad."

Eduin nodded. Rumors spread like fleas through the shanty town when men had too much idle time on their hands.

"There was a great battle, with fire-bombings and desolation, and no money for entertainment. We played now and again for those poor folk, to lighten their hearts, but as the wise man said, joy fills no one's empty belly."

Eduin frowned. Varzil probably never went to Cedestri. It was dangerous to think such things. Better to believe that Varzil, like Carolin, was forever beyond his reach, that the life he knew was all there was.

You swore . . . whispered through his mind.

"As we traveled toward Valeron," Raynita went on, "we saw more of the war. Oh, it was terrible! An aircar had been blasted from the sky and there was blackened earth all around. You could see little pieces of it, even bits of metal."

"Accursed witchery," Saravio said.

At his outburst, Raynita paused and looked strangely at him. "Yes, that is what *Tia* said. She forbade us to go near, not even to harvest the metal."

The old woman rocked herself, sucking air through the gap between her teeth. "In such places, death hangs in the very air you breathe. You cannot see it or touch it, but it is there all the same."

"She frightened Liam, our roustabout, so badly that he took off one morning," Raynita told Eduin in a stage whisper.

After the meal, young Jorge, who had scarcely said a word, brought out a small, round-bellied lute from the wagon and began picking out a melody. Humming, Raynita tapped out a counterpoint on her lap. Within a few notes, Eduin recognized the song.

Oh, no, not now . . .

> *"Oh, the lark in the morning,*
> *She rises in the west . . ."*

Swaying gently, Saravio began to sing. There was nothing Eduin could say to stop him. Eduin braced himself for the underlying *laran* vibration that would signal the manipulation of his pleasure centers. Then he would be lost, trapped between sick oblivion and the rage of guilt and torment, without even the shelter of darkness to hide him. These people, Raynita and Jorge and *Tia*, whose black eyes missed very little, would see him for what he was. . . .

What should that matter? Those years in the Thendara streets, he had never spared a thought for the opinion of anyone else, only that they gave him as little notice as possible. The mob at the lake was but a means to an end, Naotalba's faceless army. Before that, at Arilinn, he valued his teachers for the learning that would buy his place, his chance. Varzil had been an obstacle, and Carolin . . .

Carolin had loved him as a brother, had taken his part, Carolin . . . Carolin must die, Carolin still must die . . . he must tear this weakness from his heart, now and forever. . . .

In a flash, Eduin relived that moment when Saravio pulled him from the Thendara gutter, that crack in the black armor of his aloneness. Carolin had first pierced it, and then Dyannis, and now the weakness lay within him, waiting for another such moment.

At any other time, he might have tried to block out Saravio's mental sendings, to maintain his barriers, but not tonight. Not with the insistent pressure building almost to the breaking point these last days. Not with the memory of Carolin's friendship so fresh in his thoughts.

"And comes home in the evening with the dew on her breast." Her voice clear as a silver bell, Raynita answered Saravio. She smiled, watching his face, but he gave no response, not even when she wove a descant harmony above his voice.

> "*. . . she whistles and she sings,*
> *And comes home in the evening*
> *With the dew on her wings.*"

Eduin braced himself, but no mental touch bore through him. No surge of ecstasy caught him up in its remorseless grip. There was only the music, sweet and simple, the girl's trained voice soaring above Saravio's, the boy strumming along, the old woman nodding in time to the beat.

Of course, he realized. These people harbored no deep pain to trigger Saravio's Gift, only warmth and easy affection. He himself had not asked, had masked his own need.

Jorge finished the song with a cascade of arpeggios. Raynita clapped her hands. "What do you think, *Tia?* Shall we take both of them? Eduin to haul around heavy things and Saravio to back me on a ballad or two?"

The old woman drew her shawl tighter about her shoulders, although the night was mild. "My granddaughter's taken with you," she spoke to the space between Eduin and Saravio. "She has all the haste of youth. It's true enough we need a pair of strong arms, and a second man's voice will not be a bad thing. But there's no need to rush into things. If you will, we can pay you by the day while we're here. Then when we're ready to move out, we'll talk again."

— ◆ —

All through the summer, the musicians remained at Robardin's Fort. Eduin hauled water and firewood, and Saravio sang with Raynita. They played for the Fort merchants and the succession of travelers and traders who passed through. *Tia* decided to cut their stay short and move on before the season turned, for Isoldir had closed its borders and there were fresh rumors of war. She would take her little company on to Valeron for the winter. The milder climate and the strength of the powerful Aillard clan would provide shelter against more than one kind of storm.

After Raynita invited both of them to come along, Saravio seemed singularly unenthusiastic. Eduin sat with him in their little hovel, which had become even shabbier and more confined as the summer wore on. Now every day spent outdoors, amidst laughter and music, left him less able to endure the squalor and isolation. The huts and tents were dismantled after the first snowfall, and Eduin did not think he could bear a winter immured behind the town walls, assuming by some miracle he could find a place for both of them there. The musicians' offer had come as a lifeline.

When he asked Saravio what his objections were, Saravio simply replied, "They are not Naotalba's own."

"What do you mean?" Eduin said, stung.

Saravio shrugged. He had been biddable enough since their flight from Thendara, but he could turn obstinate, particularly if he believed it was the will of Naotalba. Yet he had been more responsive and alert, sometimes almost joyful, since he began singing with Raynita. *Tia's* stews and tisanes had put some needed weight on him, and he'd smiled more than once at Jorge's antics.

"They are good people," Saravio said, "but they have nothing to do with Naotalba, or her with them. It matters not whether we go with them or remain here. But . . . but I cannot hear her voice or see her hand in this place. She cannot have forsaken us. She would not—she promised. We—we did not fail her, did we? Back at the lake? She would not turn away from us because of that?"

"No, no," Eduin replied, with all the reassurance he could muster. "Naotalba keeps faith when all others fall away. You know this, and that is why she chose you for her champion." The words sprang from his mouth unbidden, without intention or thought. He thought of the ease with which he and Saravio had joined up with the musicians, and for the first time it seemed more than a lucky chance.

Another thought came to him, and he seized upon it. "Perhaps there is something here that prevents us from feeling Naotalba's presence," he suggested. "She must have sent the musicians to us in order to bring us away from this place. Only when we are free of it can we know her will for us."

Saravio brightened. "Yes, that must be the way of it. Naotalba has many servants, and not all of them are sensible of her glory."

After that, Saravio bent to the preparation for the journey with a will. They left Robardin's Fort walking beside the wagon along with Raynita and young Jorge, while *Tia* rode, just as if they had always belonged together.

16

The troupe stopped on the side of the road in an open area between two ranges of hills to rest the aged cart horse. Clouds filmed the sky, diffusing the early afternoon light. Stones, some of them the size of the wagon, dotted the slopes, but the flat ground was mostly fine gravel. Hardy grasses had taken root and then dried to ashen curls. Jorge asked if there were any danger from flash flooding, but *Tia* said no, the river that once flowed here had dried up long ago.

The old woman soon had a small campfire lit and water boiling. She produced meals for everyone, including Eduin and Saravio, on some schedule of her own, sometimes serving hot meals in the morning and cold in the evening. Now she bent over her pot, stirring in slivers of wild green onion.

Raynita sauntered over to where Eduin stood. Her eyes followed Saravio, who had wandered off by himself. He stood, head thrown back, cap rucked forward over his brow, looking east along the river bed.

"He's a strange one," she said. "He stays right with me when we sing together, but the rest of the time I'm not sure he knows we exist."

Jorge came up to them, grinning. "I've found the perfect spot over there. It's wide enough, and almost sandy."

Raynita sighed. "Go on, then, and start warming up. I'll be along shortly." When Jorge trotted off happily, she turned to Eduin. "I was hoping Jorge would give his tumbling a rest, but he's bent on practicing whenever he can. He's right, of course. Back at the Fort, the performances were enough to keep him happy, but when we're traveling, he always wants to try something new."

Eduin confessed he knew nothing of acrobatics.

"Then come and learn. It would help if someone else could spot for him. I've felt so weary this last tenday, all I want to do is sleep." Yawning, Raynita headed for the wagon. She emerged a short time later in boy's breeches instead of her usual skirt.

Eduin watched for a distance as Jorge went through his preliminary exercises, stretching and rolling, flexing his muscles. Such feats of physical skill had never held much interest for Eduin. His years at Arilinn had left him convinced of the superiority of mental powers. He sensed Jorge's concentration as he settled into a handstand, straightened his legs and then parted them, wobbling so badly he almost fell, brought them together again and rolled forward. The boy bounded up without pausing and cartwheeled several times. He was clearly enjoying himself. Raynita followed him closely, laughing.

Raynita gestured as she commented on Jorge's technique. To Eduin's surprise, she then proceeded to repeat the same motions, only with a startling lightness and grace. Jorge groaned, "I just can't keep steady on the splits like you do."

"It will come," she answered. "Try it this way."

Eduin glanced back to the camp where he'd last seen Saravio, but the other man no longer stood there. What had he seen, gazing up along the riverbed? Another vision of Naotalba? A past impression of water flowing, perhaps a storm to come? Eduin reached up with his *laran,* beyond the covering clouds, sensing the air currents—

He heard a series of muffled thuds and then, Raynita screaming. Eduin whirled to see both performers lying in a tangle on the ground. He rushed to them. Raynita was struggling to rise, but Jorge lay motionless. Bright blood gleamed in the tangle of his hair.

"He just collapsed," Raynita stammered. "He must have put his hand wrong—I couldn't hold him—oh, gods, it's all my fault! I should have never—I was too tired—"

Eduin knelt to examine the boy. Old training took over. Without thinking, he lowered his barriers and began scanning, using his *laran* to trace the flow of nerve and blood, sensing the integrity of bone, the smooth arching vault of the cranium, the webwork of membranes cushioning the brain, the delicate pattern of blood vessels. The bleeding from the boy's scalp was superficial, the bone intact. But there— within the circle of interconnecting vessels at the base of the brain—

Jorge had not injured his head when he fell. He fell because of what was already within his head. Though Eduin was no monitor, he knew the basics. He could sense the integrity of muscle and sinew, blood vessel and energon channel, the nodes carrying life force and *laran,* the ganglia of nerves, the pulse and ebb of lymph, the slow secretions of glands. The *thing* within the boy's brain throbbed with its own arcane rhythm. Not a cancer, nor any abnormal formation of artery, but a kernel of unnatural blackness. Surrounding it, tissues fought and died, subsiding into a necrotic shell. It stank of *laran.*

Not only that, Eduin recognized the characteristic energy pattern of bonewater. He had never made the toxic dust, but every Tower-trained *laranzu* knew its signature. He'd never heard of a form like this, a single, relatively huge particle like a crystal, instead of motes of dust. The boy was still alive because the bonewater had not dispersed throughout his body, but it would nonetheless take his life.

Eduin pulled back, drawing the back of one hand across his mouth. Never in all his years of Tower training nor his exile had he encountered such a thing. He could not guess how it had been introduced into the boy's body, only that now it sapped vitality like a cancer, surrounding itself with a wasteland that spread ever outward with each passing day.

Then he remembered what Raynita had said about the battlefield they had passed: an aircar blasted from the sky . . . blackened earth all around . . . *Tia* forbidding the gathering of precious metal. The old woman herself had given a surprisingly accurate description of the lingering effects of bonewater.

"Death hangs in the very air you breathe. You cannot see it or touch it, but it is there all the same."

The aircar must have been carrying this new form of bonewater when it was attacked, and even though the musicians had not handled the wreckage, they might have been exposed. Jorge, with the impulsiveness of youth, might have ventured too close and a few crystals somehow made their way into his body.

As Eduin considered this, a wave of pain passed through the boy's barely conscious mind. Eduin saw it as a curtain of scintillating crimson, blanketing all else, yet when it touched his own thoughts, he recoiled.

The deadly particle pressed not only upon the boy's balance centers, but upon those areas of the brain that registered pain.

Eduin's body thrummed with a fine tremor, as if in response. It was no use. He could not penetrate the waves of agony to nullify the energy produced by the particle, even assuming that was possible.

With an effort, Eduin stilled the resonant echoes within his own body. His fingers moved automatically to his starstone folded into his belt. Grime stiffened the insulating silk pouch.

He hesitated. Fear, made reflexive by so many years of hiding, roused in him. The only safe course would be to shake his head and turn away, to let the natural course of the boy's injuries prevail. He owed these people nothing.

Yet something even deeper than fear spurred him on, the part of him that still held to the oath he had taken when he first opened his mind to a Tower circle at Arilinn. That part of him opened like a flower to the sun to the music and Raynita's easy friendship. That part of him could not leave Jorge to die along the trail.

A shadow fell upon him and then a figure knelt at the boy's other side. It was Saravio, his awkwardness transformed into supernal grace. Jorge's pain must have roused him to action. Saravio touched the boy's wrist with one hand and laid the other upon the bone-pale brow.

"Rest now, be easy," Saravio murmured. "No harm will come to you." The words were more sung than spoken, with a gentle calm that Eduin felt in his marrow.

"We will see to the boy," he told Raynita. "Go and prepare a bed for him in the wagon. Ask *Tia* to brew one of her tisanes." When she hesitated, he said with greater urgency and a nudge of his *laran,* "Leave us now. We must not be disturbed."

When he was sure Raynita could not see, Eduin took the starstone from its wrappings. He clenched it in his fist. It felt cool and then warm against his palm. He closed his eyes, looking inward.

Focusing his mind through his starstone, Eduin bent once more over the boy. Power surged through him, his own powerful *laran* amplified by the matrix crystal. As Saravio continued his hypnotic chant, the boy's pain lightened, soft as dawn. Though the *laran* particle still pulsed, now with an eerie luminescence, a sense of utter well-being suffused the boy's body. His mind drifted from agony to dreamy calm.

So this is what Saravio did for the dying girl back in Thendara, Eduin thought. Saravio could not save the innkeeper's daughter, but he could bring comfort to her passing. His Gift seemed to act like a mirror to each person's need.

The edge of euphoria brushed against Eduin's mind. His inner torment receded. Temptation soared, to drown himself in what Saravio offered. As much as he longed for it, he knew it for what it was, a trap more deadly than drink. He bent once more to the healing task.

The mote was small, and though there were several more in the boy's lungs, only this one had caused any degree of damage, and that only because of its location.

Eduin had never been taught how to neutralize bonewater, but he saw no reason it could not be done. What had been created by *laran* could as easily be uncreated. At Hestral Tower, Varzil and Loryn Ardais had dismantled the old supplies of *clingfire*, rather than turn them over to Rakhal Hastur.

It took a few moments to find the right vibrational signature. Under the onslaught of his trained mental probe, the crystal disintegrated. Within moments, the natural circulation of the tissues began removing cellular debris and draining excess fluid. Fortunately, there had been little permanent damage.

By the time Eduin had rooted out the remaining particles, the boy was already emerging from his daze.

"You see," Saravio murmured, "it is even as I told you. All is well with you, is it not?"

The boy sat up. His eyes were not quite focused, but the sudden lifting of his pain smoothed his features, giving him the aspect of a child awakened from a long-overdue sleep. "I fear I have practiced overmuch today. The heat . . . I must see *Tia* for one of her tisanes."

Eduin and Saravio helped him back to the camp. Eduin knew better than to try to discuss what had happened, though this was the most alert and responsive Saravio had been in a tenday. The red-haired man would only insist it was the will of Naotalba.

Several times, Raynita tried to talk with Eduin about what had happened. He brushed off her questions, saying that in their travels, he and Saravio had learned to treat simple injuries.

"I am not such a fool as that," she faced him, her gray eyes stormy. "I saw how he fell. I heard his head strike the ground. I saw the blood. I know it was not mere words and looks that healed him."

When Eduin started to protest, she rushed on. "No, do not spin me lies about *Jorge was not so badly hurt* or *You were too upset to see clearly*! I know Saravio worked some magic upon him. Tell me!"

"Jorge is well," Eduin said. "Can you not be content with that?"

"Ah!" she said at last. "I see you *will* not answer."

Eduin read the cost of his answer in Raynita's eyes. The easy, open friendship drained away. Something flat and gray took its place. She wanted answers, and he offered evasions. After a lifetime of keeping secrets, why should this one bother him now?

They traveled on between the hills, following a natural course over the dry riverbed. Gradually, the terrain shifted, growing less rocky. Copses of brush and groves of trees appeared. They passed a lake and fishing village, where they performed a few times, washed, and replenished their supplies of water and dried fish. From there, the road broadened. They saw other travelers, merchants with their laden wagons, a drove of sheep, an armed party escorting a covered carriage.

They camped in a grove of ancient oaks beside a stream. The site was just off the road and looked well used, for there were several stone circles for cook fires.

Raynita continued to watch Saravio. At twilight, Eduin spotted her behind the horse's picket line. She had cornered Saravio against a dead tree. Her voice was raised in pleading.

"It is only a small thing I ask, and not even for myself," she said. "After the way you healed Jorge . . ."

Eduin hesitated. They had not seen him yet. It was not too late to withdraw.

"Naotalba has said nothing to me concerning the blessing of

babes," Saravio said. Something of the girl's anxiety must have roused him, for he sounded unusually alert.

"It is early yet," the girl's voice sank. Eduin heard the fear naked in her voice.

He stepped forward, breaking the awkward silence between them. Raynita whirled and fled into the shadows of the massive trees. Her feet kicked up piles of withered leaves.

"No babes," Saravio mumbled. "Nothing for babes."

"Why not?" Eduin said. Saravio's refusal rankled unreasonably. "You had no problem helping the boy. Surely you can manage a blessing out of mercy."

As soon as Eduin uttered the words, he realized that *mercy* had nothing to do with Saravio's interventions. Had it been *mercy* to drive the Hali Lake mob into a killing frenzy or inflict lethal pain upon the two thieves? He stared at Saravio and wondered if this were the same man who had dragged him from the gutters of Thendara, fed him, befriended him, given him a glimpse of hope. Like Naotalba herself, Saravio seemed to have two faces. Eduin hoped he would never call upon the friend, only to be answered by the fanatic.

"Come, my friend," he said. "It is time for rest. We have a long way to go tomorrow. We must be rested to serve Naotalba."

"Rest," Saravio repeated. "Yes, rest is good."

Saravio dropped off to sleep as soon as he stretched out under his blanket beside the dying cook fire. Eduin sat gazing into the shifting orange embers, trying to still his thoughts. Sleep would not come.

Above, mauve Idriel and pale Mormallor spun their milky haloes across the sky in the opening between the inky shadows of the trees. The faint smell of river-weed and plashing of water came from the river. The echoes of Saravio's spell resonated faintly through Eduin. The pressure inside his head receded.

Nothing for babes, Saravio had said. Surely it would do no harm to make sure Raynita carried a healthy child. He could monitor her himself and then offer reassurance in Saravio's name. It was a small enough favor and would mean much to her. He wondered who the father was. Raynita had never shown any particular interest in a lover, but then, how should he know? If *Tia* did not object, it was hardly his place.

Strung on a cord between the wagon and a tree, Raynita's tent was barely wide enough for one sleeping person. He crouched beside it, for the coarse, patched cloth presented no barrier to his thoughts. Here in the shadows, he had no fear of discovery. He slipped out his starstone. A twist of pale blue fire flickered in its depths.

Raynita's mind wandered in dreams like those of a fever victim, casting an odd distortion over her energy channels.

As easily as sliding between layers of silk, Eduin reached through the girl's defenses. Though he probed through layers of muscle and connective tissue, he sensed no golden glow emanating from her womb. With a sickening jolt, he realized that Saravio had been right in his mutterings about Naotalba's silence on the subject of babes.

Raynita was not pregnant. Instead, she carried a pit of sickly green luminescence deep within her belly.

This particle was larger than the one in the boy's body, or perhaps there were several of them, aggregated together. They had lodged in one of the tubes leading to the womb, where a blood-filled sac had formed in grotesque mimicry of a true pregnancy. Very soon now, it would rupture, taking the girl's life with it.

Eduin did not pause to consider. He shaped his *laran* into a spear-point and thrust at the clump. Before, in Jorge's brain, the particles had flickered and gone inert. These turned molten for a terrifying moment before disintegrating into ash. Pain lanced like jagged lightning through Raynita's dreams. Dimly, he heard her shift toward a whimper. The flash of heat died, leaving a thickened scar. Eduin did not think he could open the blockage in such delicate tissues, and he was already feeling the quiver of exhaustion.

It was enough that the girl would live. He withdrew.

Sound jarred him back to the physical world, a rustle of the dry leaves, the crackle of a twig. A figure appeared, for an instant back-lit against the faint glow of the cook fire embers. Eduin made out the old woman's full skirts, back hunched under the weight of years. As he drew his feet under him to rise, he searched for a likely explanation for his presence here.

He cleared his throat, but she spoke first. "You are not such an evil man as you believe yourself to be, nor is your friend a simpleton. Keep your secrets; I care nothing for any man's past. Listen to me, Eduin . . . Isoldir has wizards aplenty and no need for your Gifts. Instead, I advise you to turn your path toward the Plains of Valeron and the city of Kirella, where the Lord's youngest daughter wanders within the prison of her own mad dreams and none can reach her. You could do worse than earn the gratitude of that family."

With those words, she retreated into the shadows.

Eduin sank back on the ground. Kirella was home to a small but powerful branch of the Aillard clan, and Aillard was Isoldir's sworn enemy. If he could gain the trust of the Lord there, he might well be able to use that great clan as his weapon against Varzil. Even if he failed, he still had Saravio. Together, they would find sanctuary at Kirella. That is, providing they were able to cure the daughter whose sickness had become such a well-known story.

17

Eduin and Saravio traveled with the musicians until they reached Carskadon, the next good-sized trading town. Only a ramshackle palisade defended the place, but crews of men worked at its repair and guards stood uneasily beside the gates. No collection of hovels marred the surrounding countryside. Cottages with neatly tended gardens and coops of barnfowl lined the road. The town itself had grown up around a central plaza, once an unpaved field where traders met to bargain, now bordered with wooden buildings, stables, inns, warehouses, craft halls. Upon their arrival, a boy driving a herd of fat *chervines* directed them to a place on the outskirts they might safely leave their wagon and find cheap feed for the horse.

The troupe gave performances in the market square and then moved on, but Eduin and Saravio remained. Eduin used their share of the takings for a room at one of the poorer inns. By then, he had formulated a plan.

"Naotalba has spoken to me again," he told Saravio. "She has commanded me to seek out those in need of her miraculous powers. Through us, she will restore them to joy."

"What must we do?"

"We must take on new names. We must turn away from anger and instead sow healing. Through us, Naotalba will cure the sick and make glad the hearts of all who heed her call."

Eduin then went about advertising Saravio as a divinely-inspired healer. Since there was no Tower nearby, few of the folk had access to any medicine beyond traditional herbs. Eduin clothed Saravio in robes of solid black, "as Naotalba's captain," and a tightly knitted cap of the same color. The unusual garb enhanced Saravio's charisma.

Saravio sang, while Eduin applied his *laran* skills. Together, they were able to deal with various disorders of both body and mind. After a few free treatments, they had enough work, between the townsfolk and the traders, to move to better lodgings. News of their success quickly spread throughout the surrounding countryside. People from outlying farms and villages traveled to the town with ailing loved ones, or sometimes just out of curiosity.

Soon it was time to move on, while the fair weather still held. They must not risk an early winter here. They had acquired enough coin to purchase decent clothing, two horses, and a pack animal.

From Carskadon, they descended onto the Plains of Valeron. Eduin had never seen anything so vast. The sky above the Plains was larger than he'd imagined possible. He had spent most of his life bounded by either mountains, the confines of a working Tower, or city walls. Something within him expanded, as if in response to the endless horizon. On rare occasions, he caught a glimpse of an aircar in the distance or *kyorebni* hovering on the thermal currents. Grasses bent their heavy heads in the wind, filling the air with musky sweetness. The horses snatched mouthfuls as they walked on.

Days merged into each other. At night, Saravio stared unblinking at the sky and carried on long dialogues with Naotalba, whose form he deciphered in the starry patterns.

Sometimes Eduin lay on his back, watching the moons spin their complex dances, each at its own pace, sometimes greeting one another but never touching, always apart. He felt a strange kinship with those orbs of colored light. His own life seemed to be a series of near-collisions—with Varzil, with Carolin. With Dyannis. And now with this poor benighted soul who was, for good or ill, the keeper of his sanity.

The Plains were neither entirely flat nor featureless. The Valeron

River cut through the expanse, providing lush forest on either bank. They spotted it from a distance as a line of dark green. Far to the west, the river widened into the marshy area where lay the city of Valeron and Castle Aillard. Valentina Aillard, who had served with Eduin at Arilinn so long ago, came from that region. He did not know what had happened to her, whether she still served in a Tower or whether her recurrent illnesses had overcome her at last, or her family had deemed her of greater value in an arranged marriage.

Turning south along the river, they came to the walled city of Kirella. As Eduin and Saravio approached, the road broadened through a series of sprawling villages that had grown up to house workers and supply goods to the citadel itself.

Kirella was much smaller than Thendara, but just as heavily fortified. Mounted soldiers drilled in formation on the one good flat stretch of land. They passed watchtowers, set within sight of one another in a perimeter. A deep channel cut from the river ran past walls pierced by slits for archers. As they approached, an aircar rose and then sped away in the direction of the city of Valeron.

Armed guards stopped them well before they reached the bridges and demanded their business. The guards eyed their clothing and laden pack animal, clearly reckoning their wealth and rank, and let them pass.

Once inside the city, they had no difficulty finding respectable lodging. Eduin spent several days walking the streets, familiarizing himself with its various districts, listening to the people's complaints, measuring the temper of the place. His years of hiding in Thendara had attuned him to the pulse and rhythm of the streets. With only the lightest use of his *laran,* he could sense the shadows of fear, the pinch of hunger, the belly-gnawing thirst. This was, he quickly concluded, a city on edge, but the people's concerns went beyond preparations for battle. Few had seen actual combat, and fewer feared an immediate assault upon their own city. The stresses lay right here within their own country, centered on the citadel.

Lord Brynon held his title as a courtesy, for in truth he was Regent to his only daughter. It was the late Lady Aillard whose lineage carried the rulership of the city and surrounding lands. Only a daughter could inherit, and it was she whom Eduin had come to heal.

The castle sat upon a little rise, the only hill in the entire area. In the brightness of the day, it seemed to draw in upon itself, gray-walled and unyielding. It was, Eduin thought, a place that gave nothing, that kept its secrets. He could not have wished for a better stage to play out his little drama.

First he must set the scene. A few judiciously placed inquiries brought him the information he needed. Instead of gathering a crowd in some public place, he sought a means of entry into the higher social circles. It was not long in coming. Tales of their healing miracles along the road reached had Kirella. With his strange manner and black robes, Saravio was unmistakable. Eduin soon obtained an introduction to a wealthy cloth merchant, recently widowed.

On the night Eduin and Saravio presented themselves at the merchant's residence, the wind blew chill and damp with the first intimations of autumn. Saravio as usual donned the black robes of Naotalba's servant. The house with its walled gardens sat within the protective sphere of the city, within sight of the residences of the nobility.

A *coridom* greeted them at the door, branched candelabrum held aloft, and led them to the room where his master waited. The place had a deeply funereal air, more tomb than presence chamber. The merchant looked up from his seat beside the empty hearth. A single candle sat upon a table of some darkly marbled stone. Deep vertical lines marked the man's face, as if tears had etched runnels there. Eduin sensed the man's grief as a dammed river, stagnant and festering.

The servant asked if he should bring more light. Eduin seized the opening. "On no account discommode yourself, worthy sir. It is we who are at *your* service."

"There is nothing you can do for me," the merchant said in a heavy voice. "Not unless you can raise the dead. I must have been mad to agree to this meeting."

"Sometimes our truest instincts speak through us in ways we least intend," Eduin replied. "I do not believe it is necessary to *raise the dead* to cross the abyss of parting."

"You speak nonsense." Despite his words, interest flared.

"If common sense can be seen on one side," Eduin said, holding out his right hand, palm up, "then the deepest desires of our hearts lie on the other." He raised his left hand and extended it toward the merchant.

"Deepest desires of the heart . . ." Pain welled.

Almost in reflex, Saravio responded. He stood behind Eduin, at the edge of the cone of light cast by the candle, where his black robes blended into the shadows. Eduin felt him *reach* into the merchant's mind.

The *coridom* departed, but his presence would have made no difference. There was nothing out of the ordinary to be seen, no incantations to be heard, no arcane rituals to be witnessed. Only someone gifted with *laran* and trained in its use could have detected what transpired.

As Saravio shifted energy currents within the merchant's brain, Eduin used his *laran* to reach behind the man's emotional barriers. The merchant had a touch of *laran,* but not enough to withstand a trained telepathic probe. Eduin found a tangle of regret, of petty unkindnesses, of hopes disappointed, of all the ordinary irritations of a long marriage. Interwoven with them were moments of tenderness, of trust, of wordless comfort. Caught between the good and the bad, the poor man could release neither.

Saravio's song evoked a rising sense of well-being in the merchant. It was just what Eduin needed to break through the despondency. Emotions surged forward—loss and love and even relief. Tears streamed down the merchant's cheeks. His body shook as he sobbed out his grief.

Now you are both at peace, Eduin spoke mentally while Saravio cast a euphoric veil over the pain. *Peace . . .*

Yes . . . the merchant repeated silently. *Peace . . .*

Eduin fed words into thoughts. *Let there be an end to mourning, to pain itself . . . embrace hope . . . return to health . . . joy . . . must tell the story . . . must . . . reach the ears of Lord Brynon . . . his daughter . . .*

They left the house some hours later with a filled purse. The merchant sang as he went to his bed, his head swimming with pastel visions and the promise to write the next morning to the castle steward who purchased his goods.

"The brothers Eduardo and Sandoval Hernandez," the herald called out the names that Eduin had presented, having devised them during their stay at Carskadon. The herald's voice filled the presence chamber of Lord Brynon Aillard. The room was long and low-ceilinged, its stone walls bare of tapestry, the floor rushes worn with many cleanings, yet some trick of construction rendered the acoustics superb. If the Lord whispered, everyone in the chamber could hear.

Lord Brynon slouched upon his heavy chair set upon a raised dais. The chair was draped with the gray-and-red feather pattern of Aillard. He braced one elbow upon the chair's arm, his chin resting upon his fist. Flanking him were a handful of somber, solid-looking men.

A lone woman, her chestnut hair coiled low on her neck in a style Eduin had never seen outside a Tower, stood a little apart from the others. From the simplicity of her dress and the telltale signature of *laran,* Eduin guessed she was the household *leronis.* He did not think she could penetrate his barriers, but he would have to be careful with any use of his powers lest she detect his trained *laran* at work.

The rest of the courtiers wore such dark colors that Eduin wondered if someone of importance had just died. They watched him with wary, almost haggard expressions.

Eduin stepped forward from the line of supplicants and bowed. At a murmur from the courtiers, he glanced back. Saravio did not bow but stood swaying. His black robe swirled around his angular frame as if caught in an invisible wind. Above it, his features shone with an unearthly pallor, his eyes burning in hollowed sockets.

"Uncover before His Lordship," a courtier hissed.

Eduin realized that although he had taken off his hat as he bowed, Saravio still wore the skull-clinging knitted cap of their journey. Before he could act, a guard stepped forward, hand outstretched to sweep it from Saravio's head. Eduin held his breath, for he had not shaved Saravio since their arrival in Kirella.

Saravio did not flinch as the strings that anchored the cap upon his head snapped. The guard stepped back with the offending garment in his hand. A murmur rippled through the assembly. Instead of treacherous red, a pure shimmering white covered Saravio's head. It was little more than a fuzz, but it gleamed in the light of a hundred torches.

Eduin caught the sudden flare of interest from the household *leronis,* as if she had sensed Saravio's mental powers. Eduin tensed. She was clearly the only one at court with any formal training, but his impression of her was one of a minor degree of talent, enough to teach children the rudiments of control, diagnose threshold sickness, ease a fever, or cast truthspell. And that, he thought with a trace of exultation, he need not fear.

Lord Brynon drew himself upright and for the first time, Eduin noticed the six fingers upon his hands. Many Aillards had that trait, said to be a product of their *chieri* blood. Certainly, this man did not resemble the half-mythical nonhumans in any other way. His hair, where it was not age-grizzled, was so darkly red as to appear almost black, and the shoulders beneath the rich mantle were broad and masculine. Even his face looked as if it had weathered years on the fields of war.

"So you are the healer half the city has been talking about," he rumbled. "A few hysterics claim to be cured, and everyone is amazed. I am not so easily fooled."

Eduin bowed again. "*Vai dom,* if you were, then you would be standing here and I in your place. Since it is otherwise, clearly you are no fool and I am but your poor servant."

The court fell silent, stunned. Faces turned from Eduin to the dais. Lord Brynon threw back his head and roared with laughter. "A man of wit as well as impudence! I like you already. But your companion there, the one they claim worked these miracles, can he not speak for himself?"

"He speaks but rarely, and then only to Naotalba or to me."

"Naotalba? The Bride of Zandru? I have never heard of such a thing. He must be mad."

"Some have said so," Eduin replied, "but it is that very madness that so often comes with the healing gift. Perhaps the rest of us, who do not speak with the gods, are not as often answered by them."

"Indeed. And is your friend one of those?"

"I am a simple man, *vai dom.* The gods do not concern themselves with the likes of me. Yet since Naotalba spoke to my brother, Sandoval the Blessed, I have seen men who were broken in body and mind returned to health when all else failed. If that is not a miracle, I do not know what is. You must judge whether he can do the same for anyone in this house."

"That remains to be seen," said the Aillard Lord, "Come, you will dine with us tonight, both of you."

The *coridom* who arranged the seating at dinner placed Eduin and

Saravio at the end of one of the long tables, well away from the Aillard Lord. The men who sat at the head table were important courtiers, signified by their rich robes and emblems of office. A few of them glanced curiously at the strangers, but most ignored the lower tables. They bent over their food, barely conversing with their neighbors.

Eduin accepted the situation without complaint, for he had accomplished his first goal. He was not so long from the gutters of Thendara to scorn a decent meal, but memories of his life before that came back to him. He remembered dining at Hali with Carolin, then yet a Prince, at the table of King Felix.

He had never seen such elegance as at the Hastur court, as if he had wandered into a dream. Memory burnished candlelight, the jewel-toned tapestries, the curve of a lady's arm, the brilliance of her glance.

Now, sitting in a smoky, crowded hall, crammed in among men he would have once scorned, Eduin remembered the smoothness of his borrowed silk shirt against his skin, smelled the fragrance of the green boughs and spicebread, heard the lilt of a superb singer, clasped the light, supple body of his dancing partner.

Dyannis.

He must, he knew, take care not to idealize her. She was human, as capable of folly as any other, and more than that, she was the sister of the man he must destroy. For all his wishing, Eduin could not tear away that luminous shimmer from her image. She had been the sweetest of young maidens, afire with life and joy, and immensely, unselfconsciously generous in spreading it to everyone she touched, at a time when his own heart was starved.

She existed only in the past, that radiant girl. The boy he had been no longer existed, except as nostalgic reminder, and the same must be true for her. He could not afford such sentimentality, especially here in the court of uncertain allies.

The next moment, he jerked awake from his reverie. Two of the Lord's dogs, huge rangy hounds, had lunged at the same time for a bone tossed from the table. The larger, a young male, caught the end of the joint between his jaws. The other was older, unused to challenge. Hackles raised, lips drawn back from yellowed teeth, he advanced growling upon the other. Eduin saw this much from his seat, halfway down the table.

The next instant, the two dogs erupted into a snarling, rolling mass. Someone shouted to stay back, another called for a bucket of water to throw over them. Several men rose to pull them apart. A lady shrieked. One of the young pages, a boy of six or seven, stood motionless, his mouth open and eyes frozen, as one dog drove the other, snapping and yelping, in his direction. Before any of them could react, the animals had knocked the boy down. His scream pierced the air.

Lord Brynon strode across the room, sweeping a table out of the way with one blow. He grabbed the nearer dog by the back of the neck and tore it away, in one movement hurling it against the next table. The other dog retreated, yipping in terror.

Eduin pushed through the onlookers. Lord Brynon knelt, his broad back cutting off sight of the fallen page. Blood soaked the floor rushes. Eduin could smell it. Adrenaline and shock rose like smoke from a wildfire. Around him, men drew back in silence. One of the women began sobbing, quickly hushed.

Yet the boy lived. Of all the swirling energies Eduin sensed, death was not among them. Not yet. Blood spurted from a deep, ragged gash along the side of his neck to soak the fabric of his tunic.

Eduin knew he'd be taking a desperate chance, using his powers in the presence of a *leronis* who, however minor her own talent, might well recognize his. She would ask why a Tower-trained *laranzu* was masquerading as the servant of an itinerant healer. But he might never have a better opportunity to gain Lord Brynon's confidence.

If he used Saravio's *laran* as a shield, he might yet escape detection. The *leronis* would see Saravio as a wild talent, trained but flawed and erratic. She might not think to look deeper. And if she did, then he would have to deal with her.

"*Vai dom,*" Eduin cried. "Is this not the reason you have kept us here, to help in such a case?"

Lord Brynon spun around, rising to his feet with the deadly speed of a swordsman. His face contorted for an instant, and Eduin realized that the page was not some youngest son of an insignificant distant cousin, but his own. *Nedestro* and unable to inherit, but deeply loved all the same. Even if Eduin had not possessed a scrap of *laran,* he would have been able to read the older man's thoughts, that for such a wound, there was no chance.

"Do—whatever you can—"

Eduin had no need to summon Saravio, for the other man had followed him like a shadow. He pushed Saravio toward the dying boy, aware that they had only moments in which to act. It was vital that Saravio be seen as the one who saved the child, and not Eduin.

Saravio responded instantly to the torrent of pain issuing from the boy. He threw himself to his knees, oblivious to the pooling blood, took the boy's hand, and began chanting loudly.

"Naotalba, we call upon you, save this boy—"

Eduin retreated to the shadows, confident that all eyes would be upon Saravio and the wounded boy. Slipping one hand between the folds of his belt, he grasped his starstone.

"Hear my plea, O great Naotalba, come to us now, heal him speedily—"

The court's attention now fixed firmly upon Saravio, whose voice rose in pitch and loudness. Reaching out with his peculiar *laran,* he propelled the boy into a state of pleasurable somnolence, damping all sensation of pain. The effect rippled through the audience.

Eduin plunged into the mass of energy currents, the outpouring of life force. He worked quickly, with all the skill of a *laranzu* trained at Darkover's finest Tower. The cut looked messy, the edges mangled by the dog's twisting bite. The artery, for all the profuse bleeding, had been only nicked, not severed.

With his mind, Eduin spanned the gap, creating a cuff of psychic force over the vessel. Nothing, not the droplets of liquid or the forces that bound them together, penetrated the barrier. The physical mending would take longer, but the boy's life was no longer measured in heartbeats.

Behind the temporary bandage, Eduin began weaving together the tiny fibrous threads that made up the wall of the blood vessel. Bits of clotted blood caught in the strands, matting them together. Eventually, the seal would resolve into a scar as the body itself completed the healing.

"I am here! All is well!" An elderly man in the robes of a physician rushed forward. His face paled visibly as he took in the extent of the bleeding. "My—my lord, you must prepare yourself, I—" He pointed at Saravio. "What is this man doing here? Clear the area! I must attend to my patient!"

"I believe you will find," Lord Brynon said darkly, "that this patient is no longer in need of your care."

"But—" The physician's glance darted from the bloodstained boy to his master. The boy, still under Saravio's influence, lay quietly. His breathing was soft, his face relaxed, lips gently smiling.

The physician's expression shifted from confusion to fear. He had enough sense, Eduin thought, to realize that something had happened beyond his medical skills.

The courtiers murmured. The *leronis* stood to one side, her *laran* barriers tight and pale face unreadable. Her gaze shifted from the physician to Saravio and back again, resting only for the briefest moment on Eduin.

Lord Brynon turned back to Saravio, but Saravio was already sinking into the stupor that often followed exertion of his powers.

Eduin moved swiftly between Saravio and Lord Brynon. Sandoval the Blessed, he said, using Saravio's alias, must rest after communing with the gods.

"Rest you shall have," Lord Brynon said, "and no farther than my own walls! Those outlaws at Cedestri may have Varzil the Good himself to aid them, but I doubt even he could have accomplished such a feat!"

Lord Brynon shouted for the *coridom* to arrange the finest guest chambers for them.

Varzil, truly at Cedestri Tower? This time, Eduin had no difficulty believing the news. *Varzil, within the walls of Aillard's bitter enemy!*

The scorpion whispers of his father's command died into silence. Hope rose, hot and singing, in his heart.

I will have you now! Eduin swore.

"You did well tonight," Eduin told Saravio once they were alone in their new quarters. The rooms, two bedchambers connected by a sitting room, were comfortable even compared to Hastur Castle. A small fire blazed in the sitting room grate. Feather comforters covered the beds, and basins of warm, scented water had been placed in each of the rooms.

"Naotalba was with us," Saravio sighed.

Eduin's first thought was that Naotalba had nothing to do with it. He was not accustomed to thinking of his own work as divine intervention. Yet he felt a kinship with the demigoddess, condemned as he himself was, to a fate not of her own choosing. What would have happened if he had not been born to his own father? What might he have become?

I should have been a Keeper. Over the years, he had worked with several of the most gifted *tenerézi* on Darkover, and he knew that what he had accomplished an hour ago would have been worthy of any of them. The thought filled him with an oddly sweet bitterness. He had never had a chance to use his potential. He had been fashioned into a weapon—his father's weapon—when he was too young to choose for himself. It had left him unfit for anything else.

As for Naotalba, whatever she had been, human legend or demigoddess, she was now the tool that would shape Saravio to his will and fulfill the destiny his father had laid upon him.

18

The next morning, a servant knocked at the door and carried in a breakfast tray with an assortment of pastries, an urn of steaming *jaco,* mounds of butter and soft cheese, and a bowl of stewed honeyed fruit. Eduin ate ravenously. The intense *laran* work of the night before had left him drained, yet he had feared that if he asked for this sort of rich, heavily sweetened food, he might draw undue attention to himself. Kirella might not be Thendara, where he was still hunted, but the old habit of hiding still ran like a current of darkness behind his thoughts.

Saravio had been sent a luxurious breakfast, suitable for a noble guest, in appreciation for his healing of the Lord's *nedestro* son, that was all. Only Eduin's ingrained paranoia questioned the gift. He would have to stop thinking this way, lest his very actions betray him. He must think—and act—like a man who had nothing to hide.

Despite Eduin's urging, Saravio only nibbled at the food. He had been awake for some hours, lost in his own thoughts, rocking and muttering unintelligible phrases. Only the name *Naotalba* was distinguishable, repeated over and over.

Hours passed and the great Bloody Sun, seen through the narrow windows, swung toward midday. Eduin, to calm his restlessness, practiced the basic monitoring drills he had been taught as a boy at Arilinn Tower. He took upon himself the discipline of single-minded concentration, tracing the energon channels in his own body as if nothing else existed.

He was considerably clearer in mind when a knock at the door brought yet another servant, this one a boy in the tabard of a page in Aillard colors of scarlet and gray, with the badge of Kirella. The child brought the summons Eduin had been waiting for. Lord Brynon wished to see both of them.

— ◆ —

The family's private chambers, although beautifully proportioned, seemed even gloomier than the presence hall. Heavy draperies blocked most of the natural light, casting the interior into shadows so deep that colors muted to shades of gray. Woven hangings and thick carpets muffled all sound. A small fire and torches set into wall sconces cast an uncertain light upon the faces of Lord Brynon and the girl on the divan. The household *leronis, Domna* Mhari, stood like a servant along the far wall.

Laran barriers tightly in place, Eduin bowed to each of them, taking care to include *Domna* Mhari. Her expression remained impassive, but he sensed her surprise. He guessed that she received little enough courtesy, barely that of a servant or common chaperone. She must have tried to cure whatever ailed the daughter, and failed. Thus, she had lost her previous status. Perhaps the physician had taken her place in the Lord's confidence. Eduin mused that if he handled the situation right, she might prove an ally.

Eduin turned his attention to Romilla Aillard, heiress of Kirella. At first, he thought her half a ghost, she sat so still. Her chest hardly moved beneath her layers of gauzy gown. She looked to be about sixteen, possibly younger. In the uncertain light and with her extreme thinness, it was difficult to tell. Her face, which would have been beautiful if it bore any hint of vitality, resembled alabaster. Her dark hair had been drawn back in a plain, severe style. Only her huge eyes revealed her awareness as Eduin and Saravio entered the room.

He lowered his *laran* barriers just enough to brush the outer edges of her mind. Unlike her father, whose talent was minimal, she possessed the full *Comyn* gift. In that instant, he saw her as a tangle of colored threads, a half-woven tapestry strained almost to the breaking point. She was not mad, not yet, but she wavered perilously close.

Eduin thought of her cousin, Valentina, who had been sent to Arilinn for the sake of her health and had, so far as he knew, never departed. There she had found a measure of balance in her life, as well as useful work, when she was well enough to do it. This girl should have had the benefit of such training. She was probably too old now, even if her father would allow it.

"My daughter, Romilla, wished to meet the man who performed such a remarkable deed last night," said Lord Brynon.

Eduin bowed again, this time directly to the girl. "My brother is most honored, *vai damisela*. As you can see, he is a man of few words."

Pale hands stirred, and Eduin saw the length of scarf that she twisted into a complicated pattern of knots around her wrists. She caught his notice and slipped her hands free. As she did so, the cuffs of her long sleeves fluttered back to reveal bandages on both wrists.

"I have heard," the girl said in a voice barely above a whisper, "that the greatest truths are those spoken in silence. Did not the poet say that, Papa?"

"Yes, my dear, or something very like it," said Lord Brynon.

With a visible effort, Romilla stood up and took a step toward Saravio. "*You* know what it is to crave that silence."

Eduin caught her next, unspoken words. *You know what it is to wish for nothing more than to sleep and never wake, that silence without end.*

Pain lanced through Eduin, piercing him to the core. His own despair rose up like an engulfing wave. Caught in its power, he could not speak, could not move. Her agony was his. An image flashed across his mind, the two of them lying on a bed of unblemished white, staring into each other's eyes with perfect understanding. Around them, the room grew hazy and dim. His heart beat more slowly and softly with each moment. No air stirred in his lungs. The only thing he could see or feel was the girl's gaze upon his. With a sense of fulfillment beyond anything he had known, he closed his eyes and saw nothing at all. In that moment, he knew he would give all he had, all he *was*, for that to happen.

With a jolt, he came back to himself. Lord Brynon had said something to him, but he had no idea what. Speechless, Eduin bowed again.

The movement helped unlock something within him. Perhaps Romilla's own despair had affected him so deeply because she touched some inner longing for oblivion, but the feelings that had come so close to overwhelming him were not entirely his. Anyone with a hint of *laran* must also be affected. The *leronis* had turned white and looked on the edge of fainting. The gloom of the castle was more than an accident of architecture and neglect.

Yet, his task was going to be easier than he had imagined. Saravio would surely lighten the girl's depression. She must come under their control and remain there. At the same time, the father and any important officials would experience a sense of hope, of well-being in their presence. From there, it would not be difficult to induce dependence, to convince Kirella to launch an attack against Cedestri Tower while Varzil was still there. It wouldn't take much. Varzil had created the opportunity by his own actions, and Eduin had a potent, persuasive weapon. He knew only too well the power of anything that took away such pain.

Eduin gestured for Saravio to come forward. The other man remained as he was, swaying on his feet, face slack and eyes unfocused, as if he were utterly unaware of what had just transpired. Eduin frowned. Surely Saravio had sensed the girl's agony. Why had he not responded, as he had to Jorge or the boy last night or even the fat old cloth merchant?

"What's the matter?" he spoke beneath his breath, but saw not even a flicker of recognition in the other's eyes.

Saravio! He caught himself in the useless mental cry. Useless and dangerous, for even if Lord Brynon had little *laran*, *Domna* Mhari certainly did, as did the girl. There might be others within the castle walls with the talent to hear him.

"I pray you, excuse us, *vai dom*," he said with yet another bow. "Sandoval the Blessed is, as you see, still drained from his exertions last night. How fares the boy?"

"He does well," Lord Brynon replied, with a noticeable lightening of his expression.

They talked on for several minutes about the boy's recovery, long enough for Eduin to achieve a graceful retreat and arrange a second audience the next day.

Only when they had reached their own quarters and Eduin had braced the door with a chair wedged beneath the latch, did he grasp Saravio by the shoulders. He shoved the other man into one of the bedchambers, closed that door also, and shook him.

"By Zandru's Seventh Frozen Hell, what happened to you? Have you lost your mind? Couldn't you feel her pain? Why didn't you *do* something about it?"

And how am I going to induce Lord Brynon into attacking Cedestri Tower while Varzil is still there unless you do your part?

Saravio sagged in Eduin's grasp, head rolling from side to side. His lips moved, he moaned, and then the words came clear.

"She is . . . Naotalba, come among us. I have stood in her presence. Ah, my friend, can you not feel her touch upon your soul? She has brought us to her at last. Here we will do her bidding and bring about her kingdom."

"What nonsense is this!" Eduin shouted, shaking Saravio even harder. "You blockhead! She's nothing more than a suicidal girl with more *laran* than is good for her! Can't you see, she's turned the whole castle into a tomb! We're here to help her, not join in her delusions!"

"Join her, yes! Join her . . . Join . . . Aaah!"

With an inarticulate cry, Saravio tore himself from Eduin's hold. Unsupported, he toppled to the floor, but not before the first convulsions shook his body. His spine arched, striking the back of his skull against the floor. The carpet muffled the impact. His breath came in ragged gasps between clenched teeth. Between half-narrowed lids, his eyes showed as crescents of white. For an instant, the fit relaxed and he howled out a single, unrecognizable syllable.

Eduin stood, breathing heavily, watching as his friend twitched on the carpet. He was so angry, he could not bring himself to place a cushion beneath Saravio's head.

Let the nine-fathered ombredin *thrash himself into bruises,* he thought furiously. *Just so long as he comes out of it and sees reason.*

But what if Saravio did not *come out of it?* What if he persisted in seeing poor Romilla as the incarnation of Naotalba? What if he obeyed her command to *join her?* What then?

Then, Eduin decided as he stormed out of the room, he himself would have to find a way to control the girl. But without Saravio's mediating influence, he would be once again naked against his old compulsions.

Ah, what was the use of it? He had spent the better part of his life trying to anticipate *what might happen next.* The old proverb rose to his thoughts.

When men make plans, the gods laugh.

Who was laughing now?

Eduin sank down against the far wall and covered his face with his hands. Of course, the gods were laughing at him. The truth he had been hiding from himself was that his control over Saravio was a joke, a figment. Saravio was daily slipping into his own delusional world, seeing only what he wanted to see. The man who had rescued Eduin from the Thendara gutters, who had once been a Tower-trained *laranzu,* was long gone. Once Eduin had reached Saravio in the depths of his madness by entering the other man's mind. He still flinched from the memory of that contact, the psychic storms, the nightmare visions, the first meeting with Naotalba. He never wanted to do it again and now the fear took root in his mind that in the end, he might have to enter Saravio's mind to restore him to enough sanity to control his talent.

Eduin was not yet ready to take that step. It might not be necessary, he told himself. Saravio might improve on his own in the safety and comfort of Kirella. Regular meals, a warm bed at night, rest—these might do much to heal an injured brain. And if not . . .

Eduin would deal with that necessity when the time came. The first time, he had been taken off guard, unprepared. Next time, if there were a next time, he'd know what to expect. He would be ready.

— ◆ —

Once the fit had passed, Saravio lapsed into a sleep so profound that he did not rouse even when Eduin lifted him gently onto the bed. Eduin paced the length of the chambers before settling down to his exercises again. He practiced a little on Saravio, monitoring his channels.

Saravio was still unconscious when, late in the afternoon, they had another visitor. At Eduin's call, the door swung open to admit the court physician. At his heels came a young servant carrying a large leather satchel, presumably medical supplies. A pair of guards stood just outside the door.

"Rodrigo Halloran, at your service," the physician said, inclining his head to show that he need not bow to any ordinary man, let alone some nameless ruffians the Lord had taken a momentary liking to.

"May I be of assistance?" Eduin asked.

"It is rather *I* who have been dispatched to render assistance to *you*. His Lordship is greatly concerned regarding the health of his guests, and it is by his order I am here to examine the patient. I understand your brother has not eaten or left his room all day."

There was no point in protest, not with the guards right there. Eduin stepped back, gesturing with one arm to the chamber where Saravio lay.

"He sleeps within. Pray, do not disturb his rest."

"I will determine what is best for the patient," the physician said.

Eduin stood in the doorway while the physician conducted his examination. For a man without Tower training, he was remarkably knowledgeable in the way he studied Saravio's breathing, rolled back his eyelids, tested the firmness of his skin and his reflexes, as well as his responses to stimulation. He even loosened the fastenings on Saravio's robe and placed one ear against his chest, then straightened up and felt for the pulses at his neck and wrist.

"Quite unwell," the physician muttered, shaking his head. To Eduin he said, "Your friend has unwisely exerted himself beyond his capacities. I suspect an apoplexy of the brain, although I cannot determine its extent until he regains consciousness. You must prepare yourself for a period of prolonged convalescence. The most prudent course is to bring him to my own quarters, where I may provide the best supervision." He turned toward the door, clearly meaning to summon the guards to carry Saravio away that very moment.

"He is very well where he is, I assure you," Eduin broke in. "I am perfectly capable of tending him, and I—"

"You cannot realize the seriousness of the situation! You have no medical training!"

You arrogant ignoramus! I was trained at Arilinn Tower!

With an effort, Eduin spoke calmly. "I have been his companion these many months and I am familiar with his condition. This is not the first such episode, nor will it be the last. A little rest will see him right again."

"I will not be responsible!"

"Of course, you are not, and I will be happy to inform His Lordship that you have done everything possible. We are grateful for your attentions, but really there is no need to trouble you further." Eduin moved to the door and opened it. He ushered the still-protesting physician and his assistant into the corridor.

Eduin waited until the footsteps of the guards had died away before returning to Saravio's chamber. He bent over the unconscious man and for a moment, could not recognize him as the same who had befriended him on the streets of Thendara. He wasn't sure Saravio's own mother would have known him, with the stubble of silver covering his skull, the deep hollows around his eyes, the gaunt lines of cheekbone and jaw, the bitten lips. And this was the man upon whose fragile sanity all depended.

What, by all the gods men knew and those they had forgotten, had he gotten himself into?

19

Saravio had still not awakened that evening. Eduin waited as long as he dared before venturing into the public areas. Luck was with him, for there was no formal dinner that night; Lord Brynon kept to his quarters.

The next morning, Eduin wandered down to the kitchen, just as he had in his years at Arilinn. Here he felt more at ease than at any moment since arriving at Kirella. The cook, a pleasant-faced woman with a Dalereuth accent, offered him freshly-brewed *jaco* and the last of the yesterday's bread with a little honey.

The cook bustled about, ordering the day's meals and supervising the scullery maids to be sure they chopped the onions finely enough and sanded the cookpots clean. Eduin sat in a corner, sipping the hot *jaco* and listening to the scullery maids talk. One girl spoke of her fears for two of her brothers, conscripted for foot-soldiers. Another replied with the story of border raids by Isoldir forces disguised as bandits, yet another of the broken betrothal between Romilla and the Isoldir heir, which the cook insisted had never happened and if it had, it had involved her grandmother, not the girl herself, and therefore could not be the cause of all this trouble, no matter what ignorant gossip said.

Eduin returned to his rooms with the added news that Lord Brynon would dine that night with a select few of the court, including the miraculous Sandoval.

The cook happily set aside a meal for Eduin to take up to Saravio, packets of meat pies and a ramekin of baked custard, still warm and fragrant.

"For as much as he's done, saving the young lad's life as we've heard, he deserves a rest. Half the busybodies in Kirella will be after a sight of him. And there's the young *damisela*," the woman's ruddy features turned somber and she bit down on her lower lip. "There, I've said too much already. You just take that pudding up to your friend and see he eats it up."

Eduin doubted that Saravio would be awake enough to eat the custard, and he was right. For the moment, Eduin let his friend rest, hoping that a period of quiet would restore him.

— ◆ —

Afternoon wore on, and still Saravio slept. The dinner hour loomed closer with each passing hour. Eduin became increasingly anxious. He dared not appear alone at Lord Brynon's table.

In the end, Eduin decided that he must brave Lord Brynon's displeasure, even appearing without Saravio. Trouble would certainly follow if he did not come at all. This evening, only a small group of courtiers dined with their lord. Eduin was placed at the main table, two seats down from Lord Brynon himself and opposite the court physician, who made little effort at a civil greeting. Romilla sat beside her father. She wore her customary white, the dress of a young noblewoman, funereal rather than spritely against the hollowness of her features. Only when her gaze met Eduin's did her expression take on a hint of animation. She laid one pale hand on her father's, and he bent to listen to her whisper.

"Where is your brother?" Lord Brynon asked, once the roast haunch of beef had been carved and the bread and stewed roots passed around. "I hope he is not taken ill. We had hoped to thank him properly for his services. My daughter, in particular, has a number of questions for him."

It could have been worse, Eduin thought. At least, Lord Brynon's tone was still cordial. He had not yet run out of patience. Best of all, the girl was clearly interested.

"Sandoval the Blessed would be exceedingly grateful for your concern, were he able to receive it," Eduin said. He kept his voice low and meek. "He has become aware of a terrible danger that even now draws nigh upon this fair land. He is communing with the gods, for without their intervention, great harm will soon be upon us."

Aillard's brow furrowed, darkening his eyes. He did not look like a man who would ordinarily give credence to *communing with the gods*. Yet his son would surely have died without Saravio's intervention. Aillard was enough of a soldier to know that no merely human medicine could have saved anyone with such an injury. Beside him, his advisers exchanged glances.

"It is just as I told you, is it not, Papa?" Romilla spoke up. "Last night, my dreams . . . The time of fire is coming, and soon it will engulf us all. Then darkness will stretch all across the land. What will happen then, I cannot foresee, but the very thought chills me to the soul."

"My dear child," Lord Brynon responded, placing his hand over hers, "your concern for the welfare of Kirella does you credit. These are desperate times indeed. The world is full of evil, and we have our share of enemies. Do not trouble yourself. War and statecraft are better left to . . . to those older and wiser, skilled in such matters."

Eduin noticed that he did not say, *left to men,* for in Aillard lands, women held full and equal rank. Someday, Romilla would make those decisions, if she lived that long. Aillard trod a delicate line between his responsibilities as Regent and the need to train his daughter to eventually assume them.

Romilla was clearly aware of this, for she lifted her chin. Her voice dropped in pitch so that she sounded like a mature woman, rather than an impetuous child. "Certainly, Kirella is in need of all the wise counsel that can be gathered. But some day this will be *my* kingdom. I have the right to hear this counsel and judge for myself."

Even as she finished, the court physician broke in. "*Damisela,* you must not excite your nerves with such worries! Perhaps when you are stronger, or the matters of state less onerous." He glanced at Lord Brynon. "Lady Romilla's health cannot withstand such unnecessary burdens. She will make herself even more ill if she continues on in this manner. She must retire without delay. Indeed, the most beneficial thing for her right now is a darkened room, as I have prescribed, and soft music to divert her mind from worrisome thoughts."

One of the courtiers sighed in relief and Lord Brynon looked troubled at this reminder of his daughter's frailty. Romilla herself sat like a statue, a whisper of color rising to her cheeks. Eduin felt a sudden desire to leap up and throttle the physician, or blast him with *laran*. He knew it was unwise and unreasonable, but his skin prickled and a pounding ache settled over his temples.

"I think *Dom* Rodrigo has the right of it, *chiya*," Aillard said. "We can manage for a time without you, and the sooner you regain your strength, the sooner you may return."

Slowly, the girl rose to her feet. "I will retire to my chambers if you think it best, Papa. But I do not want any more medicines. I do not need them. I—" she forced a smile, "—I will be better in a little while, truly. Especially if—if the Blessed Sandoval could come to me. Under *Domna* Mhari's supervision, of course."

So the girl was not a complete jelly, Eduin thought. She might be tormented to the brink of insanity, but she had backbone. If she survived to rule this small kingdom, she might become a force to be reckoned with.

"I will ask Sandoval to do so, as soon as may be," Lord Brynon replied. He glanced at Eduin with an expression that clearly said, *And that had better be soon.*

One of the ladies took Romilla by the arm and guided her from the room.

The meal concluded, a somberness broken by explosions of tension-laced laughter. Eduin could not eat any more. The food turned to stone in his belly. He felt a slithery tension over his skin, heard the distant, familiar whisper, *K–k–kill* . . .

He was acutely aware of the empty seat at Aillard's side and the opportunity that was, moment by moment, slipping away from him. As the assembly broke up, Lord Brynon summoned Eduin to his side.

"Walk with me apart from the others. I would hear more of this threat to which you alluded, this 'terrible danger' that requires your brother to—as you put it—'commune with the gods'."

They stepped into an alcove, well away from the nearest guard. Lord

Brynon was tall and powerfully built, his bearing that of a soldier. He grasped Eduin's shoulder in a demonstration of his physical strength. "Why are you here in Kirella? To warn me—or to worm your way into my council and then betray me?"

Eduin, spurred by a wordless instinct, dropped to his knees and held up his hands as might a faithful vassal to his sovereign.

"*Vai dom,* I swear to you I bring no harm to you or any person beneath your roof. May Zandru strike me dead if I lie!"

For a long moment, Lord Brynon peered into Eduin's face. Eduin felt only the normal scrutiny of a man used to dealing with uncertain allies in perilous times, no trace of a psychic probe. He felt confident that not even the Keeper of Arilinn Tower could read anything but sincerity in his thoughts.

"I believe you bear us no ill will," the Aillard Lord said. "But I also believe that no man acts except in his own best interest. Deal honestly with me and you will have your reward. Play me false and I'll have your guts for lute strings. Now, what is this danger you spoke of?"

Eduin clambered to his feet. "Why, he that you spoke of yourself— the Keeper of Neskaya Tower, Varzil Ridenow. For if it is true Varzil means to rebuild Cedestri Tower, it must be in order to bring it under his influence. Why else would he go to such trouble and use so much *laran* for the benefit of strangers? Isoldir alone is a small kingdom and no match for Kirella's might, but Isoldir allied with Hastur . . ."

"I see you have aspirations to become a councillor," Lord Brynon said, grinning.

Eduin bowed. "I am Your Lordship's servant—"

"You are nothing of the sort!"

Eduin paled, wondering what had given him away. Before he could sputter a reply, Lord Brynon went on.

"You are the keeper of the most extraordinary man I have ever met. I will not let either of you slip so easily through my fingers. If he can work a tenth of the miracle of the other night upon my daughter— well, we shall see. Meanwhile, do not trouble yourselves with imagined fears. The walls of Kirella are stout and well-defended. Winter will soon be upon us and that will put a pause to any immediate threat. Go now to your proper work and see that the Blessed Sandoval is ready to attend Lady Romilla as soon as possible."

Eduin, hearing the dismissal in Lord Brynon's words, withdrew. It mattered little that he had been cast off so lightly. He had planted a seed, which was all he wanted.

Now to create the garden in which that seed would ripen into a towering tree.

20

When Eduin dragged himself from sleep the next morning, bleary-eyed from restless awakenings and even more restless dreams, Saravio lay exactly as he had last seen him. Only the slow, shallow movements of his rib cage indicated he still lived.

Eduin washed, dressed, and sat down for what he prayed would not be a death watch. He did not know what he would say to Lord Brynon, and he suspected that he had run out of time and acceptable excuses. He wondered what he would do if Saravio continued on like this. Even if Saravio did not die in the immediate future, he could not go on for very much longer with any hope of reasonable recovery.

The time he had appointed to meet with Lord Brynon arrived. He knew he should bestir himself, but he could not summon the energy. He slumped to the floor beside Saravio's bed. His head dropped upon his folded arms, his face only a few inches from Saravio's. In that unguarded moment, he had no defense against the insidious despair emanating from Romilla's powerful but utterly undisciplined *laran*.

Thoughts rose unbidden to his mind. What was the use of going on? What was left for either of them but more hiding, futile struggle? More endless tormented dreams, broken by days of increasing exhaustion?

Why had he imagined a measure of security and purpose here? Misery and despair lurked in every corner. The brightness of the court with all its grandeur and comfort was but a mockery, an illusion. A shadow had fallen over Kirella and its inhabitants. They were doomed, all of them.

He knew the thoughts were not his, and yet he could not stop them. They rippled through his mind, drawing upon every memory of his own hopelessness.

Soon the lights would go out. Nothing could stand against the coming darkness. It would spread like a cancer across all the Aillard lands, all the Hundred Kingdoms from the Hellers to the Sea of Dalereuth. Only frozen ashes would remain.

Even the thought that Varzil, too, would perish brought only the faintest tinge of satisfaction. What did it matter? He himself would not be alive to see it.

Better, far better to surrender now, to find an end to the unremitting misery.

Eduin remembered his brief glimpses of the borderland in the Overworld between the living and the dead. Upon rare occasions, he had heard, a traveler might encounter the form of a dead person, usually a loved one, seen at a far distance. It was perilous to have anything to do with them.

In the Overworld, thought had the power to transport, to build, to destroy. Although he had not consciously willed it, Eduin now found himself standing on that vast, unbroken plain under the familiar sky of endless gray. The air, thick and still, seemed colder than he'd remembered it.

Turning slowly in a complete circuit, he saw nothing, only the colorless rim of the horizon. He glanced down and saw that, instead of being clothed in the robes of a *laranzu* of his rank as he had been each time before, he was naked.

This, then, must be death. Eternal grayness, eternal chill, eternal silence. Eternal solitude. It was neither the oblivion he craved, nor any semblance of peace, but it would do. He had only to wait here until his physical body, like an abandoned husk, perished from thirst and starvation.

He lowered himself to the ground and crossed his legs, placing his hands in an attitude of meditation. Time in the Overworld passed at a different rate than it did in the outer world, but he thought it would take a long while. His body might be discovered and attempts made to revive him. That charlatan physician might well be called in, to ply him with herbal concoctions. In the end, it would be of no avail. Deprived of animating spirit, flesh would fail. His escape would be complete.

The thought carried an unexpected lightening of despair. He had finally fled beyond pursuit. No one would find him here, or if they did, would not have the power to compel his return. He was, for the first time, safe.

Safe . . .

But not alone.

Eduin heard no footstep, felt no whisper of disturbed air, caught no scent. He felt the slight fall in temperature, a chill of the mind, not the body. It sank into his marrow and with it came a sickening jolt of recognition.

His father, Rumail Deslucido, appeared as large to him as when he had been a small boy. Eduin could make out only the faintest features, for the form was almost transparent. The face with its deeply incised lines was free of the snowy beard of his later years, and the body, what he could make out of it, appeared straight and strong. This was not the image of his father in death, but in the vigor of his prime.

Despite himself, Eduin shrank away from the pale fire of those eyes.

The ghostly mouth opened. No sound issued forth, nor any hint of breath. Lips curved, shaping words Eduin knew intimately as the palm of his own hand.

The evil of the Hasturs and their Ridenow defender goes unavenged . . . You swore . . . You swore . . .

Eduin willed himself to deafness. Yet he could not bring himself to turn away or lift an arm to cover his eyes.

As Rumail continued speaking, his features became sterner, more adamant. Eduin remembered those expressions all too painfully. His father had rarely seemed otherwise. It was not until he came to Arilinn that he knew adult men were capable of gentleness or encouragement. The first time his Keeper had spoken kindly to him, his response had been incredulity. Many seasons had passed before he realized that Auster spoke in that manner to all the young students, that he cared for them and wanted them to succeed.

Go away, old fool! Eduin thought angrily. *I've had enough of your criticism! You're dead now. You have no hold over me.*

No hold but the snare in his own mind . . .

But not for long!

Eduin hauled himself to his feet and turned his back on his father's ghost. The phantasm appeared in front of him. He dodged this way and that, spinning around. No matter which way he looked, the same visage confronted him, the mouth moved in silent phrases that echoed down the corridors of his memory.

Failed me . . . You swore . . . Revenge . . .

K–k–kill!

He felt a tug inside his own thought-body, like a tether at its length. In a moment of terror, he looked down at his hands, expecting to see pale unbreakable shackles linking him to the specter. It did not matter that they were invisible, even in this eerie realm of the mind.

I will never be free of him, and when I die, I will spend eternity like this.

"Curse you!" he screamed. The syllables resonated from one horizon to the other. "Curse you to Zandru's Seventh Frozen Hell for what you have done to me!"

Perhaps the mouth paused in its relentless litany, or the fierce light in the ghostly eyes abated. He still had some power, then, if not over the shade of his dead father, then over his own fate.

He would not die. He would refuse to remain here, chained forever to this specter of mindless vengeance. He would live, and out of that life, carve out his own triumph.

When Eduin opened his eyes again, the room was very much as he had last seen it. He might have hovered in the twilight of the Overworld for a day, an hour, a heartbeat. Hunger cramped his belly. The smell of freshly baked bread hung in the air. Tracing it, he found that a tray with a simple breakfast, still warm to the touch, had been left in the central sitting room.

The bread was fine and soft, the cheese creamy, the *jaco* pleasantly bitter. Eduin ate it all, using bits of bread to mop up the traces of cheese from the plate. Gazing into the *jaco* dregs, he considered his next step.

Try as he might, he saw no way of continuing on here at Kirella without Saravio. He had failed to kill Varzil at Hali Lake. This time, he would not depend upon the vagaries of chance and an enraged mob. He needed solid resources—trained soldiers, aircars, *laran* weaponry. What Kirella lacked, Valeron, the seat of the entire clan, would supply.

He needed a way to insinuate himself into Lord Brynon's confidence. For that, he needed control over the heir, Romilla.

And for that, Saravio.

There was no help for it. He knew what he must do next, and though the idea repelled him, he steeled himself to it.

He must enter into Saravio's sleeping mind, establish control, and drag him back into the waking world.

Eduin's first telepathic rapport with Saravio had been unintentional. He had meant only to shock the other man out of his seizure, not to penetrate into the inner depths of his consciousness. Certainly, he had had no idea of the extent of Saravio's insanity or possession, whatever it was. Now the situation was different. He was no longer ignorant. He knew what he faced.

He settled himself on the bed beside Saravio and reached out to touch the other man's hand. Physical contact was necessary for the depth of rapport he needed. Eduin steeled himself, repeating that he had no choice but to violate the most fundamental ethic of Tower work—never to enter unbidden into the mind of another person. It was all nonsense and pretension. Tower circles broke the rule every time they went onto the battlefield. Even the casting of a simple truth-spell involved a certain amount of coercion.

Even as he justified his actions to himself, Eduin knew that what he was doing was different. He was not shaping the thoughts of a madman back to sanity for any altruistic purpose. On the contrary, he needed Saravio's obedience, and he meant to get it any way he could. Why else would the gods have given him *laran,* if not for such a purpose?

He skimmed the surface of Saravio's thoughts, finding only a howling emptiness that reminded him of a storm-swept plain. There were no images of everyday things, of light and food, the places he had passed through, the people he had spoken to. The very texture of the mental landscape felt barren, abandoned. Saravio had indeed withdrawn from life.

Eduin pressed deeper. He wandered through a house that had stood vacant too long. The impressions left behind by all the activities of daily living had faded and the unique stamp of personality all but vanished.

He had touched the minds of dying men. He knew the taste and weight of that severing. Saravio still lived, but had withdrawn to a level that mimicked death. Eduin had expected to find, somewhere within the tangled web of Saravio's unconsciousness, some core of the man he knew. He had thought he would be able to manipulate the form of Saravio's thoughts as he had done before, to enter into the other man's delusions and dominate them to his own advantage.

But there was nothing here—no black-robed woman with burning eyes and a face like ice. No Tower racked by lightning. No multitudes pleading for salvation, for release from suffering.

Saravio had said that Romilla Aillard appeared to him as the incarnation of Naotalba. Was that why the Bride of Zandru was now absent from his mind? Had Saravio decided his own purpose was fulfilled, that he had no reason to continue living?

I still have a purpose for him, Eduin thought savagely. *I cannot let him slip away.*

If he could not track down the kernel of personality that was Saravio by means of the delusion they had once shared, then he must use something else. Eduin paused and gathered himself, turning inward for anything, any resonant imprint that he could use.

He remembered Saravio's gentle voice saying, "I brought you in from the storm." Saravio speaking of the innkeeper's daughter and how he had sung her free from her pain. Saravio bending over the fallen musician, murmuring, "Rest now, be easy, no harm will come to you."

Something inside Eduin, some tremulous childhood memory, breathed in the words like balm across his ravaged heart. Saravio, for all his divine insanity, had offered him simple kindness, generosity. Love. He had freely given these things not only to Eduin, the man he had dragged, a pathetic sodden wreck, from the gutters of Thendara, but others. The dispossessed, the hopeless. The injured.

And now, the daughter of this house. But only if Eduin could drag Saravio back to life.

Using Saravio's own compassion to control him seemed like the only hope, and yet Eduin shrank from it. That moment of kindness shone out from all the years of filth and degradation. Now it seemed he must twist it, use it for his own ends.

He told himself that Romilla Aillard was in need, was not unworthy. He told himself Saravio would do these things anyway, that he would never know the difference, that he would give his consent if he could.

For a long, heart-chilling moment, Eduin hovered in indecision. None of these arguments changed what he meant to do. Saravio might cure the girl and lift the miasma of despair from the entire city. All the Aillard lands, not just Kirella but Valeron itself, might bow before him. All these actions, no matter how good they seemed, would forever be tainted. The work of Saravio's remarkable ability would no longer be a freely bestowed gift.

Nothing in the world remained pure, as Lord Brynon had said. No man acted except in his own best interest. Not Saravio, not he himself, not Carolin Hastur on his high throne, or even Varzil the Good. In the end, what drove men was selfishness. Yet even as Eduin thrust the thoughts from him, he felt a flicker of shame for what he was about to do.

He found what he sought, a kernel of tightly interwoven mental energy, an ember of personality consumed and fallen in upon itself. It reminded him of an immense, congested energon node, one of the structures that channeled and stored *laran* in the human body. He used his own thoughts to shape a net around the kernel.

At first, Eduin met no resistance. As he tightened the strands and began to draw them toward himself, awareness sparked. There were no coherent thoughts, only a stirring, an expansion. Slowly, and then with escalating speed, Saravio's mental faculties returned.

Quickly, before Saravio had regained enough awareness, Eduin struck. He did not reason through what he was doing. He only knew that this chance might never come again. Now, while Saravio was still confused and only fragmentally aware, before his sense of self-preservation had returned, he was still vulnerable.

Eduin speaks with the voice of Naotalba. Follow his commands as you would hers.

Naotalba . . .

Images drifted, ghostly and distorted, through the firmament of Saravio's mind. Eduin made out the superimposed figures of two women—Naotalba as he had first seen her, beautiful and tragic, yet with a kind of nobility—and Romilla. For a moment, they seemed not at all alike. Then Eduin understood why Saravio had confused them. The sense of utter hopelessness, of doom, linked them. But for his plan to work, Romilla must have a future and the courage to meet it.

With all the skill at his command, Eduin began separating the two figures. Naotalba he drained of color, so she shimmered like a statue of ice, a true bride for the Lord of the Seven Frozen Hells. He brushed Romilla with brightness, envisioned her lifting her head, cheeks flushing, lips rosy. Then he had Romilla fall to her knees before Naotalba.

Surprise rippled through Saravio's dreaming mind as Eduin raised Romilla's hands in supplication.

Heal me, O great Naotalba. Give me strength! Give me hope!

Without Eduin's conscious direction, the demigoddess responded. She placed one hand on the girl's dark hair and smiled. Eduin flinched at that smile, for it was only partly in blessing. Underneath the benign surface ran an undercurrent of ruthlessness. There would be a price to pay for such healing and he did not think it would be an easy one. He nudged the figure of Romilla to her feet and watched as she dwindled in the distance. The test of whether he had successfully detached the girl from Naotalba in Saravio's mind would come the next time they saw her.

Eduin waited as Saravio rose toward waking. Saravio's thoughts strengthened and his mind once more took on its complex, familiar patterns. Eduin recognized the areas of damage, like burned patches of a forest after a fire has passed. He knew better than to try to speak telepathically. Instead, he placed his hands upon Saravio's shoulders and shook gently.

"Saravio. It is time to wake up."

Saravio's eyes shifted behind closed lids. His chest heaved, lungs drawing in air. He stretched his legs. The joints of his spine crackled.

"Eduin." Saravio's voice was hoarse, his words slurred. "I feel so strange. I must have slept too long."

"Indeed you have," Eduin replied with a smile. He helped Saravio to sit up. "I will call for food and a bath. You must regain your strength."

"Have I been ill? What has happened?" There was something almost pathetically childlike in Saravio's questions.

"There is much work for you to do."

"Yes . . ." Saravio tilted his head in an attitude of listening. "I can sense it—so many people in pain."

"It is Naotalba's wish that you help them. I will guide you in this."

Saravio's expression turned eager. "Tell me, then, what I am to do."

"After you have fed and washed, we will arrange an audience with *Damisela* Romilla . . ."

Eduin watched Saravio for any reaction, but the other man's expression continued as eager and innocent as before.

Good, Eduin thought. *Now we can get to work.*

21

The whole castle buzzed with daily reports of Romilla Aillard's decline. The girl had been unable to eat or sleep, becoming agitated whenever anyone approached her. By the time Lord Brynon sent a second, desperate plea for the intercession of Sandoval the Blessed, Saravio had recovered sufficiently.

Lord Brynon led the way into his daughter's chamber, followed by Mhari, the household *leronis,* Lady Romilla's nurse, and the physician. *Dom* Rodrigo insinuated his stout form as close to his Lord as was seemly, effectively placing himself as a barrier between Lord Brynon and Eduin and Saravio. He directed his attention entirely toward his noble patron. In unguarded moments, however, the lines around his mouth deepened. Mhari spoke little, although her gaze followed each of the others as they entered the chamber of her young charge.

Eduin took in the scene in an instant. The room was smaller than he'd expected for a young woman of Romilla's rank. Perhaps it had been hers as a child. It was richly furnished, overly so. The ornately carved furniture seemed to overpower the delicacy of the chamber's proportions. It might have been a pleasant room, if it were less crowded and if the curtains had been drawn back from the beautiful mullioned windows. As it was, he glimpsed those windows, with their garden view, only when Lord Brynon ordered a servant to open the curtains.

"No, no!" Romilla shrieked, her voice like the cry of a stricken dove. She thrashed on her bed.

Dom Rodrigo rushed to her side, and Eduin saw that the girl's arms and body had been tied to the bed with lengths of white cloth. The physician checked and tightened the bonds. "She must have rest—complete rest! Why were these restraints loosened? I gave no orders to that effect!"

"The light—I am burning!" Romilla cried. "The fire is coming! It will destroy us all!"

"Close the drapes! Quickly, man!" shouted Lord Brynon, even as the servant hurried to obey.

Eduin halted inside the door. Indeed, there was almost no room for the addition of any other person, with servants, physician, nurse, *leronis,* and father all rushing about. He could scarcely see Romilla.

He touched Saravio's arm and felt the instant response. "Go. She needs you."

Somehow Saravio managed to steal his way to the bedside. No one paid attention to him and he had long ago developed the ability to move unobtrusively through a crowd. To Eduin's relief, Saravio gave no sign he'd ever mistaken the girl for Naotalba.

Through the raised voices, Eduin caught the low, familiar murmur. "Be not troubled, sweet lady, for help is at hand. Soon all will be well. Rest easy, as I am here with you. There is nothing to fear."

Eduin moved a step or two into the room, close enough to see Saravio crouch beside the bed. The girl's slender white fingers lay in Saravio's larger hand. Her face turned toward him, rapt.

Yes, that is good, Eduin thought, although Saravio could not hear him. *Establish physical contact.*

There was no need to encourage Saravio further. He was doing what he did instinctively, perhaps what he had been born to do.

Romilla's distraught features relaxed. Eduin, his *laran* sense focused on the scene before him, knew the moment Saravio touched her mind. Eduin sensed a shifting of invisible colors, a spreading warmth. Pleasure surged through him and with it, the sudden lifting of pain, of sorrow, of struggle. He allowed himself to soar on the moment, knowing it would not last, but lacking the strength of will to break it off.

Romilla's eyes opened with a look of incredulous relief.

"Get away from her, you barbarian! How dare you lay hands upon the lady!" *Dom* Rodrigo grabbed the nape of Saravio's black robe and attempted to pull him away.

Saravio gave the physician not the slightest heed. His attention remained focused on the girl. Their gazes locked, unself-conscious bliss mirrored on their faces.

I knew you had come to save me. Her lips shaped the words, inaudible above the din and clatter, but readily discernible to Eduin's *laran*.

"Guards! Summon the guards!" With a prodigious heave, *Dom* Rodrigo yanked Saravio off balance.

Her concentration shattered, the girl began screaming again. Lord Brynon, who had been supervising the drawing of the curtains, moved toward them. Eduin leaped into action. He cut through the crowded room, angling to intercept the lord.

"*Vai dom,*" Eduin cried. "I appeal to you, put a stop to this interference. Did you not ask for our help? Then let the Blessed Sandoval do his work!"

At these words, the physician spun around. Dusky blood suffused his features. He looked ready to strike Eduin, but for the nearness of his master.

"The *damisela* is under my professional care," *Dom* Rodrigo said with stiff dignity. "I need not remind you that her continued recovery is due to *my* ministrations! She is too fragile for this kind of—of overstimulation, this—melodrama. It is highly detrimental to her progress. In fact, I classify it as outright abuse!"

"We see how well she has prospered with you!" Eduin flamed. "What are you afraid of, that someone else may succeed where you have failed?"

"Stop it!" Romilla wailed. "I want Sandoval!"

"Enough!" Lord Brynon bellowed. "Stand down, both of you! I will not tolerate such behavior! It belongs on the practice fields, not in my daughter's bedchamber! Stand down, I say, or I will have both of you taken away in chains!"

Eduin instantly regretted his rash words. His self-control was not what it should be, or such an officious, prattling fool would never have caused him to lose his temper.

"I cannot believe you are seriously considering these charlatans from who knows where!" *Dom* Rodrigo said. "They are no more qualified in these matters than Durraman's donkey!"

"Yet they—or rather *Dom* Sandoval—were able to help little Kevan when the dog slashed his throat." Mhari glided to stand at the right hand of her Lord. Though her expression remained neutral, her eyes flickered over Rodrigo's face.

Now Eduin was certain of the rivalry between *leronis* and physician. Clearly, Rodrigo had stepped in when Mhari failed to resolve Romilla's depression and had usurped her position of influence with Lord Brynon. Mhari was not a woman to easily forget or forgive.

"A happy accident!" Rodrigo shot back. "The boy must have been less badly hurt than it first appeared. Blood flows freely from certain kinds of superficial wounds, giving them the appearance of greater severity. Clearly, that was the case. He would have recovered just as well with the attentions of—of a stable hand!"

Mhari's voice remained serene, a counterpoint to the physician's rising frenzy. "There have been other stories of Sandoval's abilities—cures for the mind and spirit beyond the power of any ordinary medicine. They cannot *all* be accidents."

"Mere rumors! I have heard them, too, down in the village. Tales to prey upon the credulous have no place in educated society. I will not be responsible for the consequences of the slightest disruption in Lady Romilla's treatment regimen! I demand that these men be removed immediately and—"

"Papa, please! Make them stop!" Romilla sobbed. "The noise, it hurts my head!"

"That will be enough," Lord Brynon said in a deadly quiet voice. He beckoned to the guards stationed just inside the door.

Before the physician could protest further, the guards each took one of his arms in a joint lock and escorted him, white-faced, from the room. Eduin permitted himself a moment to watch, although he was careful not to allow any hint of exultation to leak through his psychic barriers.

Mhari, he noticed, refrained from pressing her own advantage. Instead, she drew up a low bench and, helping Saravio to rise, placed him upon it. In her very action, she reasserted her own position; she was no lowly servant, easily dismissed. She might serve the Lord and his family, but her status as a trained *leronis* gave her the dignity of rank.

"My little love," Mhari murmured, "here is *Dom* Sandoval to tend you, just as you asked."

"*Vai dom,* I beg your forgiveness for my outburst," Eduin bowed to the Aillard Lord. "I spoke only from my concern for Lady Romilla, although it was not my place in this great company to do so."

Lord Brynon pardoned the breach with a slight inclination of his head. His attention returned to his daughter, for Saravio had once more taken her hand.

Murmuring in his soft, hypnotic tones, Saravio reestablished contact with the pleasure centers of her brain. Eduin felt the pulse of receding despair, as if a wave of living light flooded through the dark corridors of her mind. This time, however, he steeled himself against his own response. He had to move quickly, think clearly, act rationally. He could not afford to indulge in even a moment's peace. That fool of a physician had almost ruined everything. Eduin swore to himself he would never be caught off-guard again. If he were ever to achieve his goal, his eventual release from his father's compulsion spell, then he must set aside all immediate personal gratification. He must become an instrument of his own will.

Mhari stood behind Saravio's bench, swaying slightly, almost close enough for her skirts to brush his shoulder. She had closed her eyes, her lips curving in a half-smile. Saravio's talent was strong enough to overwhelm her defenses.

Of course, Eduin thought. With her *laran* sensitivity, she could not help being affected, too. In addition, she had recently fallen from favor, perhaps had even been publicly humiliated. On a daily basis, she would see the evidence of her failure, both in the person of her ailing mistress and the bombastic exultation of her rival. The burst of pleasure must be balm to her shredded nerves.

After a time, Eduin spoke to Lord Brynon. They must not overtax Sandoval's strength. It would be advisable to schedule another treatment. Perhaps that afternoon? Was there a solarium or some other bright, cheerful room? Would Lady Mhari be available as companion and chaperone, since she knew the young *damisela* well?

Lord Brynon replied that was an excellent idea. One look at Mhari's dreamy expression told Eduin that she would be a pliant and enthusiastic ally.

The solarium had once been Lady Aillard's favorite room, facing south and east to receive the morning sun. The windows were thick and almost flawless, a marvel of glassmaker's art, and set between ribs of fine-grained white stone carved with stylized flowers. The room had been little used in the last few years, so Eduin, acting in Saravio's name, ordered new plants to be brought in to replace the yellowed, elderly specimens. Fresh cushions brought new life to chairs and divan.

The first time Romilla entered the rejuvenated chamber, she clapped her hands and exclaimed in surprise. Even Mhari colored and smiled.

Romilla still bore her cadaverous paleness, and the hollows around her eyes told of yet another night of tortured dreams. For the first time, Eduin wondered if Saravio's song alone would be enough to lift her desolation. He dared not leave the outcome to chance. He must act, and pray that he would not be discovered. The soporific effect of Saravio's singing would, he hoped, mask his own efforts.

Eduin placed the ladies to either side of Saravio, having arranged the seating so that Saravio occupied a position apart and slightly elevated above the others.

"Do not speak of Naotalba," Eduin had cautioned Saravio. "They must first become attuned to her wisdom."

Saravio had no difficulty with this logic. He took his place on the divan, apparently oblivious to the luxury around him. Eduin had placed a low bench on a front diagonal.

Eduin gestured to a servant to bring in the warmed wine and cakes. The cook had prepared both to his specifications. An herb with mildly soporific qualities had been added to the wine, its taste masked by the extra dose of honey.

"Ladies, we have a special delight for you today," Eduin said, bowing low. "Sandoval the Blessed will sing for you. If you, *damisela,* will accompany him on the *rryl?*"

"With pleasure," Romilla replied, "although I do not play at all well."

"Together, you will make beautiful music," Eduin said.

Romilla accepted the instrument from Eduin and moved from her chair to the low stool. She plucked a few chords, her six fingers moving with some hesitation over the strings.

Saravio began singing the same lullaby he had used with the innkeeper's dying daughter back in Thendara. After a few wrong notes, Romilla settled into the simple chord sequence.

Eduin let his eyes drift out of focus and softened his psychic shields. Saravio's voice, weaving through the sweet notes of the lap harp, evoked a sense of deep relaxation. Though he knew it was risky in the presence of the *leronis,* Eduin opened his *laran* senses. He had an idea how he might lift Romilla's depression, which involved imprinting her with the imagery that Saravio's vision had once evoked in his own mind.

The colors of the room shifted subtly, as if a thick, warm mist settled there. The music lingered in the air, huge round gobbets of soporific sound. Eduin swayed with it. The faint, remembered thrill spread through his body. He felt the pressure of Saravio's talent, manipulating, stimulating.

Eduin's vision blurred. The diffuse golden light of the solarium turned gray and then silvery. Trees, slender and graceful, rose from the mist. In the distance, growing closer with each heartbeat, came the bell-clear voices. He drifted toward them. Figures moved within the mist, weaving among the trees, passing one another, joining hands . . .

He reached out to them, sensed their response, and at the same time reached out to Romilla's mind. She was open, almost expectant, yet robed in shadow. Only her face shone, a pale mask. No wonder Saravio had mistaken her for Naotalba. She reached slender fingers toward Eduin, inviting him to join her in the growing darkness.

Come instead into the light, he urged.

He clasped her hand and drew her closer. The shadows fell away and she stood beside him. Around them stretched the forest, moon-touched and old beyond reckoning. The voices were nearer now, rising and falling, sweet and sad. Silvery hair glinted, tapering, six-fingered hands gestured in welcome. A fragrance rose from their bodies, of morning, of hope, of endless seasons beneath the stars . . .

He let the moment linger and then slowly dissolve.

In the real solarium, color had risen to the girl's cheeks and throat. Her lips parted, breath deepening, head tilted back, and eyes half-closed.

Mhari leaned back in her chair, hands loose in her lap. Her gaze met Eduin's. Her expression revealed only dreamy contentment. Behind her, the young court ladies of Romilla's retinue swayed in time to the music.

Saravio finished the song and proceeded to another and then a third, all slow and rhythmic, melodies designed to calm a fretful babe. When he reached the end of the last one, no one stirred. By their slow, measured breathing, the women might have been asleep, or deep in trance. By the time they opened their eyes, one by one, Eduin's head was clear.

Romilla got to her feet, stretched, and took a couple of dancelike steps. "I remember how much my mother loved this room. It's so full of light! I feel so peaceful here, I—I could almost be happy. Sandoval, will you sing to me tomorrow?"

"Yes, indeed, *damisela,*" Eduin replied, "if that is your wish."

"Come now, little love," said Mhari, "it is time to rest."

As Romilla and her ladies prepared to depart, Mhari drew Eduin aside.

"Your friend is very—" she paused momentarily, "—talented."

Eduin kept his face impassive, the polite mask of a subordinate to a person of her modest rank.

"As are you," she added.

"You are perceptive," he responded. "Your own training does you credit."

"Alas, I have not been able to accomplish what your—" again that faint hesitation, this time accompanied by a whisper-light contact of *laran,* "—brother has done so well."

So Mhari had seen through their disguise, but had made no move to expose them. She had been waiting and watching to see how events unfolded.

"You have restored my young mistress to health, or will surely do so with time," she went on. "Do not believe me envious or wishing you ill because of it. Believe instead there are those who do not share my joy at her recovery. Others who would rather keep her in darkness, than see another succeed."

She lifted one eyebrow. *Do you take my meaning?*

"A warning?" he asked, keeping his tone light. *The physician is a buffoon, not to be taken seriously.*

Mhari's smile faded. "I might have done as well for her, if I had been allowed to work without interference. I would not have your friend's good beginning meet the same fate as my own efforts. Even a buffoon is capable of intrigue."

Eduin bowed again, for the little procession had formed and Romilla had finished her leave-taking of Saravio. Mhari followed in her proper place without a backward glance.

— ✦ —

Saravio and Eduin attended Romilla in the solarium every day. Each time, the girl's vitality improved. She laughed and played her *ryll* with a new level of enthusiasm and obvious regular practice. She grew less thin and the bruised look around her eyes disappeared. Eduin knew without asking that she now slept soundly, dreaming only a young woman's normal dreams.

Despite the shortening days and gray skies of oncoming winter, the entire castle seemed to come alive. The kitchen buzzed with stories of romances and the smells of festive meals. Servants sang as they went about their duties.

Lord Brynon showered Eduin and Saravio with favors. When he feasted with his court, they were often seated on his right side. He presented them with fine horses, fur-lined cloaks, and knives set with jeweled hilts. Eduin accepted these honors on Saravio's behalf, repeating that seeing Lady Romilla restored to health was all the reward they craved.

"Your brother Sandoval has done far more," Lord Brynon said. "He has given Kirella back her hope."

— ✦ —

As one tenday melted into the next, the weather turned chill with the first intimations of the turning of the seasons.

The cook, who supplied Eduin with the specialized food he and Saravio needed for intense *laran* work, also presented him with the latest rumors. By the pattern of migrating birds and the roughness of the dogs' coats, it would be a long winter. The old smith, not Jake but his father, retired now these twenty years or more and took up bad in his joints, *he* said the roads would be closed within the month. Eduin replied that he was not going anywhere.

"Some years, they all gather at Valeron for Midwinter Festival, His Lordship and all the kin," the cook said as she laid out a tray for Eduin to take with him. "And a grand time it is, to hear tell of it, with all the high *Comyn* lords. Happen you two would go along. Everyone's talking of all the good your brother's done for the young mistress."

"They won't go this year, I don't imagine," Eduin said absently.

Perhaps the weather would, as the cook had indicated, turn foul enough to prevent the journey. If not, they might risk it. This did not alarm Eduin as much as it might. With Romilla's improvement, his confidence in his disguise increased.

"There now!" the cook said as she finished assembling the meal.

She'd saved the best of the sweet pastries and a small savory pie, meat laced with nuts and dried fruits, simmered in wine, then baked under a flaky crust, and had wrapped it, still warm, in a thick cloth. There was also a half-round of bread and a pot of clotted cream, along with the usual beaker of watered wine. It smelled wonderful. Eduin had not eaten so well since his days at Arilinn. His belt was beginning to grow snug. He thanked her with genuine warmth and picked up the tray.

While they were speaking, *Dom* Rodrigo entered the kitchen. He wore his usual formal robes, his mouth pulled down in an expression of perpetual disapproval.

When Rodrigo noticed him, Eduin rose and bowed slightly. Since he had not grown up in court, he lacked the precise nuances that would turn the salutation into an insult. Meticulous politeness was quite sufficient. Despite Saravio's success with Romilla, suspicion and jealousy still existed.

Rodrigo inclined his head in return, the insolent acknowledgment of an inferior. Perhaps, Eduin thought, the man was so sure of his position that he was simply waiting for the usurpers to be found out and summarily expelled. If so, let him think that, let him dream of his own reinstatement.

The cook wiped her hands on her apron and asked what the good doctor would have. Eduin gathered from the slight rise in pitch of her voice that this visit was unusual.

Oh, he needed nothing for himself. He had come to inquire after some feverbane, which was required for a patient. There was, Eduin reflected, no shortage of rheumatics and colic in the world.

Dom Rodrigo bent over the bundle of dried herbs. He made his selection, wrapped it in a packet of oiled cloth, and took his leave.

The cook turned back to the hearth, where a pot hung from a hook over the banked embers. When she lifted the wooden lid, savory-smelling steam curled upward. The mingled aromas of meat, onions, and herbs evoked a sense of nostalgic comfort. Eduin paused with the tray still in his hands. A wave of something he could not name passed over his skin.

With a long-handled wooden spoon, the cook stirred the contents of the pot and, blowing across the surface, tasted it. She stood poised over the spoon, brow furrowed in concentration. Then she dipped it once more and offered it to Eduin.

He set down the tray and sipped the broth. It was rich and meaty, with a hint of sweetness from the browned onions. Yet the taste was subtly lacking.

"Needs rosmarin, don't you think?" the cook asked, tilting her head to one side.

Eduin shrugged. He would have said salt, for that was the one cooking ingredient he could recognize. He had never prepared even the simplest dishes for himself, neither at any of the Towers he'd served at, nor in the slums of Thendara.

She bustled over to the open shelves where rows of stoppered pottery jars and glass vials stood in neat rows and selected one. Opening it, she peered in. Her nose wrinkled. "Ugh! Moths!"

She called out in the direction of the scullery, "Here, you! Liam!"

A half-grown boy appeared in the doorway, scrubbing brush in hand. His eyes grew round at the sight of Eduin.

"Ask *Dom* Rodrigo for the key to the still room and bring it back, quick as you can. He was here but a moment ago, so you can catch him on the stairs. Go on, now."

The boy departed without a word. Eduin said thoughtfully, "How is it that the physician has a key to the still room and you do not?"

"Most of the time, it's of little enough matter. I have my own supplies of whatever's needful for cooking and simple remedies. Needlewort for burns, a sprig or two of feverfew, golden-eye for women's troubles. Things we common folk can do for ourselves. *Dom* Rodrigo, he tends to the court. Mixes his own potions, all kinds of outlandish things. Powdered banshee beaks and elixir of dragonsblood, I'll wager." She laughed. "I don't touch those things. I only take what I know, like the rosmarin."

Two young girls, the strings of their aprons wound three times around their slender bodies, dragged in an enormous basket of sweet gourds and a smaller one of tiny green apples. The cook set them immediately to sorting and washing the baskets' contents.

"*Domna* Mhari still has her key, I think," the cook went on amiably as she picked over the apples. "Many an evening she'd be down there brewing up her own concoctions for when the young *damisela* was first took sick."

"Yes? And when was that?"

"Oh, two or three years back, when my lady first grew out of being a little girl."

Eduin remembered his own months of disorientation and nausea during adolescence. So Romilla, like so many others of her caste, had suffered threshold sickness. Perhaps her depression was a lingering effect, triggered by the intense hormonal and psychic upheaval. Mhari, as a trained *leronis,* would know how to distill *kirian* to ease the transition. The raw materials, dried *kireseth* blossoms, were psychoactive, and too dangerous to be handled by anyone untrained in the proper precautions. Locking the workroom made sense, and Eduin supposed it was also appropriate for a physician, who had his own preparations to make, to have a key.

Eduin frowned. Many things that could cure in one dosage could also kill. He wondered if Romilla's illness could possibly have been made worse in that way, but he had never seen any sign of an external cause.

"Sweet thing she was then, I always said," the cook chattered on. "It's a pity things went so badly for her. But that has all changed now that your brother— Will you look at this!" She held up an apple, covered in black spots. "Ah well, no one has ever died from want of a second slice of apple tart, though there's a few who'll be wanting even the first before the spring comes again, I'll wager."

The scullery boy came back with the key. From his reddened cheeks and hanging head, Eduin guessed that the physician had not been gracious in lending it. The cook patted the boy's shoulder, gave him an encouraging word, and bustled off to the still room.

Eduin carried the tray back to his chambers. Saravio was resting, just as he had left him. Saravio had the faintly absent expression that followed a long session. Eduin handed Saravio a plate of food and urged him to eat. Saravio picked at the pastry of the meat pie. Gauntness still clung to him.

"You must replenish the energy you put out," Eduin insisted. When Saravio still hesitated, he said in a firmer voice, "It is the will of Naotalba."

He sensed rather than saw the shiver pass over Saravio's thin shoulders. Then the other man bent to his meal with concentrated determination.

22

Within the space of a tenday, winter clenched its fist around Kirella. Winds whipped across the open fields and tore the last few dry leaves from the hedgerows. Nighttime temperatures plummeted. Frozen rain fell like flights of arrows. The roads went from mud to ice. The little open market in the village lay deserted, although once or twice a farmer drove a cart to the castle to offer an extra barrel of apple cider or a slab of smoked meat in exchange for salt or metal needles, things he could not provide for himself. The shops and cottages seemed to shrink in upon themselves, hoarding the fruits of their harvest and waiting for the first deep snow. Suddenly, the winds fell away, leaving the air cold and still, expectant.

Romilla went out riding a few times with her father and returned rosy-cheeked and excited. Even when it was too cold to venture out, the solarium remained bright and warm. Half the castle ladies crowded in to hear their lady's "special music." More than once, Eduin overheard Romilla prattling about the possible journey to Valeron for Midwinter Festival, with all the delights of dancing and music, handsome young men and entertainments.

During this brief respite in the weather, a messenger arrived from

Valeron. Within hours, the entire castle learned of his coming. Eduin, as usual, got a few additional details from the cook. She'd had it from the stableman who'd taken care of the horse that the beast had been pushed hard, nothing more.

Valeron. Eduin turned the name over in his mind. He knew it was the principal seat of the Aillards and that, following family custom, it was ruled by a woman. The cook happily informed Eduin that the Lady was a force to be reckoned with, and her firstborn daughter, her heir, had inherited her temperament along with her rank. Lady Julianna Aillard ruled Valeron with an iron hand, enforced by her brother, Marzan, who was reputed to be a seasoned and ruthless general.

"Mark my words," the cook said as she sent Eduin on his way with the usual tray of provender for Saravio, "there will be war come spring."

With rest, good food, and the comfort of the palace, Saravio seemed to be strengthening. Slowly, he became less gaunt, and the hollows beneath his cheeks began to fill in. His eyes seemed more focused, his expression often one of interest instead of apathy. He spoke little and only to Eduin.

The day after the messenger arrived, Lord Brynon had still not made any official announcement. He remained secluded with his most trusted advisers. *Domna* Mhari was summoned to his private chambers for a time. Rumors thickened, each more dire than the one it followed.

Eduin kept his ears sharp for any hint of war with Isoldir or any mention of Varzil Ridenow. He contrived a few words with Mhari after a session in the solarium. Saravio had retreated to his chambers, as he usually did after a session.

She looked grave as she said, "My lord required me to cast truth-spell, but what was said thereafter, I have given my oath as a *leronis* not to reveal."

Eduin bowed, a gesture of respect. If he pressured her, it would only damage their fragile alliance. She clearly had regained much of her status.

"I would not presume to question matters that are none of my affair," Eduin said, "but I would seek your counsel. I am not privy to Lord Brynon's deliberations, nor do I have his ear. My brother . . ." He lowered his eyes and let his words trail off. "He is not exactly like other men."

"Yes," she responded with an indulgent nod that faded into a dreamy smile, "I had noticed that."

"In addition to his other . . . abilities, he has the power to dream things that come to pass. I have seen this many times. In fact, it was one such dream that led us here to this very household. I knew he could help the young *damisela* because he had seen himself doing so in a dream. But perhaps you will think me foolish to believe so."

"No, not foolish. Eduardo, or whatever your name is, you may be able to pass yourself off to everyone else as an insignificant commoner, but you cannot hide your true nature from me. I have trained in a Tower. I know you have *laran*. Why you seek to disguise yourselves is perhaps none of *my* business . . . but perhaps it is," she paused, narrowing her lips, "if you intend ill to any person under this roof."

Eduin lowered his barriers enough to emphasize his words with mind-touch. "Have we harmed a single person here? Have we not brought good—to the boy, to your mistress. To *you?*"

Her long eyelids fluttered. "Your coming has been like the ending of night. This much I cannot deny. Keep your secrets, as I will, for whatever you have done in the past, you have shown yourself Kirella's true friend. As for your friend's dreams, these are untrustworthy omens. If I were you, I would not risk the position I have for the very uncertain possibility of greater influence. Do not seek to put yourself forward beyond your abilities. Be content with what you have."

And do nothing to undermine my position at Lord Brynon's court!

It was exactly what Auster, Eduin's first Keeper at Arilinn, would have said. *Be content. Stay in your place. Do not seek to advance yourself. Wait for someone else to decide the course of your life.*

It seemed to Eduin that his entire life had been determined by someone else's judgment—Auster at Arilinn, Loryn Ardais at Hestral Tower, Lord Brynon and his pet *leronis* . . . his father.

Anger boiled up in him, but he kept it contained behind a smile polished to seamless perfection over the years. His father, who should have guided him, supported him, nourished his talents . . . his father had wedded his soul to his own fanatic quest for vengeance.

I will find a way to rid myself of it. I will live my life on my own terms, or I will end it.

"Of course," Eduin said to Mhari with a gesture at a bow, "I would never do anything to distress His Lordship. I wish only to serve, and spoke in that capacity. Nothing more."

With an imperious nod, she returned to her own business. Eduin remained in the solarium, shaking with suppressed emotion.

I will live my life on my own terms, or I will end it.

He had found a refuge here at Kirella, but he had found no peace. Everywhere he turned, some new prison waited for him—the subservient position he was forced to play, the ever-present seduction of Saravio's singing, the schemes and intrigues of the courtiers, Mhari's veiled warnings, and hovering like a canopy above it all, permeating everything, the image of a woman in black, her eyes like pits of darkness.

Naotalba.

For the time being, Eduin saw no way out. Mhari was right. Here he had comfort, and as much safety as could be found in these times. Certainly, no bounty hunters would find him here. He was in Aillard territory, and after Romilla's astonishing recovery, he did not think Lord Brynon would surrender him, even to Carolin Hastur himself.

Comfort and safety. He told himself no man could expect more. Then why did he feel like a prisoner with the walls of his cell closing in ever more tightly?

A shiver passed through him. To shake off his dark mood, he headed for the kitchen. After fetching the tray the cook had laid out, he might linger in the uncomplicated warmth and companionship. He had never found it odd for a Tower-trained *laranzu* to take comfort in such humble surroundings. Perhaps it felt like the home he could barely remember.

With these thoughts, Eduin pushed open the door. It swung easily at his touch, as if the latch had not been completely engaged. The aroma of herb-laced stew mingled with the fading smell of this morning's bread. There was a flurry of movement and *Dom* Rodrigo hurried across the room, fumbling with the opening of his fluttering robes. By a trick of the light, Eduin caught a glimpse of the object in the physician's hand, a round-bellied vial about the length of his hand. It was a distinctive shade of blue-green. The next instant, it vanished into an inner pocket.

Dom Rodrigo pushed past with the barest nod of recognition, so that Eduin was forced to give way.

If he knew who I really was, he would not dare . . . No, he must not think that way. For all the years since the siege of Hestral Tower, he had schooled himself to be invisible, unnoticeable. Now something surged up from the forgotten depths of his mind, pride perhaps or hunger too long denied, and he found it terrifying.

The kitchen was empty except for the haze of sunlight through the far windows. A huge pot, the source of the appetizing aromas, hung above the cooking fire. Pottery pans, deep and wide, lined with pastry dough, sat in a row on the central worktable, waiting to be filled.

A moment later, the cook bustled in through the far pantry door, carrying a jar of honey. "It was in the back—"

She paused, seeing the kitchen empty except for Eduin. Her face twisted in exasperation. "Will you look at that? His Medical Mightiness says he must have spiced honey, it cannot be wildflower or rosmarin, and he must have it now—now, in the middle of making meat pies! Of course, it is on the very farthest shelf, for there's little enough call for it, outside of Midwinter Festival. So to oblige him, I leave my work, drag out the tallest step stool, find a jar—and covered with dust and cobwebs it was, too—and what do you think? He cannot even wait!" She set the jar down in the cupboard in a row of other ingredients and went to wash her hands in the basin. "Well, I'll not go trotting after him like some servant. If he wants it that badly, he can come back for it himself!"

Having expressed herself, the kindly woman turned back to Eduin with a smile. "I've some *jaco* and a spiral bun or two I saved for you."

Eduin shook his head. Any other time, he would have relished both the treat and the companionship. Something niggled at the back of his thoughts, some unformed restlessness. He went over to the table where Saravio's tray sat in its accustomed place and straightened the cloth that covered it.

"Well, then," the cook said after he had made his excuses, "I know you have important work, the two of you." Her voice held no trace of resentment or even disappointment, only gentle encouragement.

As Eduin carried the tray back to their quarters, his sense of unease increased. He felt as if there were pieces of a puzzle scattered about in his mind and he could not quite make out the pattern.

Dom Rodrigo had been alone in the kitchen, the cook dispatched on a needless errand. And the cloth, which she had always placed with such meticulous care, as if it were devotional, had been askew.

The bottle. The blue-green bottle.

He was a fool not to have seen it immediately. In a moment of carelessness or perhaps haste, the physician had not properly hidden the container before leaving the kitchen.

Eduin halted before the door, staring down at the tray, and its tantalizing aromas now seemed like poisonous lures. Many medicines could kill or cripple as well as cure, and *Dom* Rodrigo had every reason to wish Saravio out of the way. In her own fashion, Mhari had warned him.

In their chamber, Saravio looked pale, his cheeks pinched. His lips curved and he sighed as he reached for the tray.

"No!" Eduin burst out. What could he say? He could not be sure of Saravio's reaction, but he could not leave him in ignorance. There might well be another attempt. He drew back, removing the tray from Saravio's reach, half-closed his eyes, and began swaying.

"Yes . . . yes, I understand," Eduin moaned. "O great Naotalba, I will do as you command!"

When he halted and opened his eyes, Saravio was staring at him with exactly the expression Eduin had hoped for.

"She has spoken to you?" Saravio said breathlessly.

"She has *warned* me," Eduin replied, "of danger in this place, of a hidden enemy." Pointedly, he looked down at the tray. "Who seeks to destroy those who serve her. With poison."

Saravio's features hardened. "Truly, there are many who have not heard her call . . . or who do not wish to. They might well seek to silence her messenger. They must not prevail." He looked down at the tray in horror.

"They shall not," Eduin responded. "Naotalba will protect you. She will reveal the villains. Meanwhile, we must let them believe they have won. You must stay hidden, as if you had been taken ill. I will take away this tainted food and prepare some that is safe."

Eduin rushed back to the kitchen, staying well away from the corridors that the courtiers, including *Dom* Rodrigo, used. The cook was putting the final decorative touches, vines and leaves of pastry dough, on the filled pies. She looked puzzled as he spun out a story of Saravio receiving a vision commanding him to abstain from meat, but put together a meal of bread, cheese, and stewed vegetables. She balked when Eduin asked her to safeguard the first tray.

"Why, what is wrong with my cooking?"

Eduin gave an ingenuous shrug, as if he, too, was confounded by the whims of the great healer. "Perhaps he will want it later. It is a simple thing to set it aside where it will not be touched by anyone else, is it not?"

"Aye, 'tis no problem at all. Many's the time our young mistress has sent back some dish, saying she could not abide it, and then changed her mind. I've a shelf in the back pantry where it's nice and cool. Mind you, the stew won't stay good forever."

— ✦ —

That evening, *Dom* Rodrigo approached Eduin and inquired after Saravio's health. The physician's guilt hung about him like a psychic fog.

Eduin assumed an anxious expression. "The Blessed Sandoval is not able to leave his quarters."

"Is he ill? Shall I attend him?" the physician asked. "We would not want such an important personage to go wanting."

"No, no, it is a temporary indisposition," Eduin said, raising the pitch of his voice so that he would sound worried. "He will be better shortly. I am sure of that. If you will excuse me, I must go now to consult with *Domna* Mhari."

As Eduin turned away, he caught the edge of Rodrigo's thought, *Yes, go seek the counsel of the little witch. She cannot help you, or even herself, in matters of the court. And as for what ails your friend, it is already too late.*

Eduin thought with dark amusement that it was not Saravio for whom it was too late.

23

"**Y**es, I still have my key." Mhari looked surprised when, after breakfast the next morning, Eduin asked if she could show him the still room. "I have not used it for some time, not since I was last called upon to attend a patient. I thought I might need some of the things stored there for my own use, since there is now no one in the castle at risk for threshold sickness."

Eduin did not ask for the loan of the key. He wanted Mhari to remain an unimpeachable witness to what he suspected they would find there. She might be only recently back in favor, but as the household *leronis,* her word was above question.

The still room lay some short distance from the root cellars, a little stone-walled chamber perfect for storing various medicines. Bunches of dried flowers and herbs hung from the rafters, and bottles, vials and oiled packets sat in neat rows on the shelves. Eduin paused, inhaling the mixture of scents, some familiar and reassuring, others odd. He recognized the distinctive, but very faint, tang of raw *kireseth.*

What can cure, can kill. Or drive a man mad.

Only someone properly trained could handle the dried blossoms safely, for the unrefined pollen was a potent hallucinogen. From it, a variety of extracts could be prepared for the treatment of threshold sickness and other ailments related to *laran.*

Eduin approached the nearest cabinet, scanning the contents. The doors were unglassed, but tightly-meshed and locked.

"Are you looking for anything in particular?" Mhari asked.

With a surge of elation, he pointed to a shelf. The vial looked very much as he remembered it in *Dom* Rodrigo's hand. "What is in that container?"

Frowning, Mhari bent to look. "That's odd, it's not in its usual place. Look, the dust has been disturbed." She straightened up, eyes narrowing. "What is it you aren't telling me? Why are you so interested?"

"First, tell me what it is."

"*Shallavan.*" She practically spat the word at him.

Eduin felt sick. *Shallavan* was one of the more treacherous distillations known to the Towers. Auster, Keeper of Arilinn, had banned its use as too dangerous. In diluted quantities, it could quell the upheavals of newly-aroused *laran.* More concentrated, it could cripple a *laranzu's* mind, leaving him senseless and paralyzed. An even greater dose . . .

Dom Rodrigo, who was no fool, must have guessed Saravio had *laran,* that Saravio used his mental gifts to cure Romilla.

"Take it out," Eduin said. "Tell me who last handled it."

The cabinet unlocked with a little key attached to the main key. Mhari removed the vial and cupped it in both hands. Eduin felt her mind scanning the surface of the glass for the lingering imprint of personality. After several long moments, she drew in a hissing breath. When she spoke, her voice rang like steel.

"How did you know—"

"I saw *Dom* Rodrigo pour some of it into a meal intended for Saravio."

Too late, he realized he had used Saravio's true name, not the alias of the Blessed Sandoval. Mhari seemed not to notice, or perhaps she too was distracted, focused on the puzzle that was even now resolving itself.

Eduin felt her surge of elation, saw her fingers curl white-knuckled around the vial. He had, he knew, just handed her an instrument of revenge against the man who had tried to usurp her place. She was not a woman capable of easy forgiveness.

"And your friend?" she asked.

"Tasted nothing of the dish."

"What happened to the food?"

"I asked the cook to keep it in a hidden place."

"Show me where."

Mhari carefully locked the cabinet, retaining the blue-green vial, and escorted Eduin from the still room. The cook was, for once, not busy with some preparation, but sitting comfortably with two of her young helpers, stirring honey into mugs of *jaco*. They rose as the *leronis* entered, the girls flushed with alarm. The cook disappeared into the back reaches of the pantry and emerged a moment later with the tray. She had been as good as her word, for not even the cloth cover had been disturbed. It was exactly as Eduin had left it, askew and with a triangular rumple in one corner.

Cook held it out to *Domna* Mhari as if it contained a nest of venomous serpents.

"Put it down," Mhari said, gesturing at the end of the worktable, which had been cleared and scrubbed clean. She bent over the tray, her nostrils flaring very slightly, corners of her mouth tight, and brought out her starstone. She carried it in a silken pouch on a long braided cord around her neck. "Now remove the covering."

The woman did so, holding the cloth by the edge of one corner. Eduin suspected the offending item would mostly likely end up in the fire rather than the laundry.

Fingers spread wide, Mhari passed her free hand over the covered dishes. She half-closed her eyes, searching with her *laran* for psychic residues. Eduin did not need to follow her with his own thoughts to know what she would find.

I have him now! Triumph flared within her mind, filtered through a veil of simmering resentment.

Mhari would do his work for him, and no one, not even Lord Brynon, need ever know that it was Eduin and not she who had discovered the poison attempt. Let her keep all the credit for herself; he wanted no fame. All she would have to say was, *I have learned that someone has tried to murder Sandoval*—the Blessed Sandoval, the savior of the heiress of Kirella—*and I wish to examine the suspect under truthspell.*

Her eyes gleaming, Mhari commanded the cook to safeguard the evidence and then swept from the kitchen.

"Well!" the cook exclaimed, when she returned from replacing the tray in its hiding place. "What do you suppose that was about?"

"I don't know," Eduin lied, "but I expect we will soon find out."

They did not have to wait for long. Within the hour, Lord Aillard commanded the cook to produce the tray, and the Blessed Sandoval, along with his assistant, to attend him directly in his presence chamber. Saravio followed Eduin without comment, uninterested in the happening.

The chamber was already filled with every person of importance in the castle, so that the atmosphere, laced with tension, was thick and close. Even without *laran,* Eduin would have recoiled from the jangle of nervous energy.

Lord Brynon sat in his accustomed place, with Romilla on a smaller throne at his side. The girl's face was as set and pale as the first day Eduin had seen her, but her expression was grim and her eyes alight with inner fire. *Domna* Mhari stood a little to the side, her hands cupped between her breasts.

As Eduin and Saravio entered, a courtier came forward and escorted them to two chairs near the front of the room. As they took their places, the crowd fell silent except for the occasional nervous cough or rustle of a lady's skirts.

Lord Brynon gestured to the captain of his guard and a moment later, two armed men brought out the physician. One held each elbow. They halted before Lord Brynon. *Dom* Rodrigo delivered a formal bow with the same ease as if he were a welcome guest and not a prisoner. Even so, fear rose like a dark mist from his mind.

"*Vai dom!*" the physician cried. "I beg of you, tell me why I have been brought before you in such an unseemly manner. I am no common thief, to be thus surrounded by armed men." Shrugging his robes into place, he jerked away from his guards. "If some malcontent has laid a complaint against me, let me hear it from his own lips, that I may refute the scoundrel!"

"Silence!" Lord Brynon's voice rang out above the rumbling of the court. "Let there be not a single word spoken until all is prepared," he nodded to *Domna* Mhari, "and let us speedily reach the heart of this matter, for the very thought of such treachery is abhorrent to me."

Mhari turned her palms upward. The blue-white fire of her starstone flashed in her cupped hands. She bent her face over the gem, as if breathing in its power.

Eduin braced himself for the first stirrings of the truthspell, although he had no reason to fear it. He had done nothing to injure any person within these walls.

Old habits of secrecy died hard, and he had carried secrets for as long as he could remember—his true identity as the son of the outlaw *laranzu,* Rumail Deslucido, his unsuccessful attempts to assassinate Prince Carolin Hastur, he who was now king, his successful murder of Felicia Leynier, the circle he had illegally gathered to defend Hestral Tower, his role in the riot at Hali Lake . . . Depending upon how the questions were phrased, it might become apparent that he was hiding something. There was so much to hide. If pressed, he could draw upon the Deslucido Gift, as he had in the past. That was the greatest and most terrible secret of all.

The *leronis* began the ritual phrases that would establish the spell. "By the fire of this jewel, let the truth lighten this room in which we stand."

Eduin had seen the setting of truthspell a number of times, and had been trained to do it himself; he knew that he alone possessed the ability to nullify it, and yet the process stirred him on some deep and wordless level. From the small blue jewel in Mhari's hands, a glow began, slowly suffusing her features. It filled the room, creeping slowly from face to face as if it were a living thing with an intelligence of its own. He felt it shimmer across his skin, cool as polished glass, saw it bathe Saravio in a twilit glow.

The blue light touched each according to his nature, heightening the essence of the person. Romilla looked as if she had been carven from alabaster, her father a cragged bird of prey. *Dom* Rodrigo's features turned blotched, the folds and lines of his face becoming crevices of darkness.

Mhari lifted her head. In that moment, she seemed taller, worthy of her own pride. "It is done, my lord. While this light endures, the truth alone may be spoken here."

"Now, we will have the truth of this business." Lord Brynon's voice deepened, like distant thunder. Hearing it, Eduin remembered the unnatural storms over Thendara, the crackle of unspent lightning, the taste of power in the air.

"*Dom* Rodrigo Halloran, stand forth."

Visibly gathering himself, the physician stepped away from his guards. He licked his lips and bowed deeply to his lord. "I am here, and ready to serve to the full capacity of my skill and training." He paused, then added with a trace of his old arrogance and a sidelong glance at Saravio, "As I always have."

"You say you have always served this house?" Lord Brynon asked.

"I have ever sought the health and welfare of every member of the ruling family." The blue light remained, clear and steady, on Rodrigo's features.

"And all who dwell within these walls?"

The physician hesitated before replying, "That I cannot swear for certain, my lord, for I do not know all of them. I am bound by the oaths of my profession to harm no one, regardless of my personal feelings."

"So there are none whom you dislike here in this company?"

Dom Rodrigo remained silent.

"Make him answer!" Romilla cried, half-rising. "He must not hide behind silence!"

"None whom you wished any ill? What about Sandoval, who saved young Kevan's life? Who succeeded in restoring Lady Romilla to sound mind when you had failed?"

"My lord, I cannot—" Rodrigo lifted his arms in a piteous gesture. His hands shook.

Lord Brynon rose slowly to his feet and pointed to Saravio. *"Did you attempt to harm that man?"*

Dom Rodrigo fell to his knees. The only sound that emerged from his mouth was an incoherent stammer. "I—I—" The blue light on his face wavered and then went out.

For a moment, stunned silence hung over the room. Eduin jumped to his feet. "My lord, I ask you—on behalf of the Blessed Sandoval— permit me a question or two before you pronounce judgment."

Romilla touched her father's arm. "Yes, let him speak. Let us know the will of Sandoval in this affair, for it is *he* to whom I am indebted and *he* who has been injured by this treacherous villain."

Eduin bent over until his mouth was beside Saravio's ear. "Attend carefully to what I say, and watch this man's reactions. Remember that it is Naotalba's will that all men love her and rejoice in her service, and also that they suffer in the presence of her enemies."

Saravio nodded.

Taking a step toward the cowering physician, Eduin pitched his voice so that the entire assembly could hear him clearly. "*Dom* Rodrigo, for the moment let us set aside the matter of whether you acted alone or at the orders of some other party. Instead, I ask this on behalf of the man you would have harmed: What do you know of Naotalba?"

In an instant, *Dom* Rodrigo's expression went from guilt to confusion. The blue light of truthspell flickered across his features once more. "Naotalba? I—I know nothing—have nothing to do with her. Why should I? She does not even exist, except as a tale to frighten foolish maidens."

Eduin bent over Saravio again, giving the appearance of consulting about the next question. "Do you hear? He denies even her existence."

Saravio's eyes glinted in response. The muscles of his jaw clenched.

"But he is no leader," Eduin went on. "We must find out whom he serves."

Eduin straightened and asked, in the same tone of voice. "What about Varzil Ridenow? Do you also know nothing of him?"

"Of course, I do! I am no ignorant simpleton!" Regaining a measure of composure, *Dom* Rodrigo heaved himself to one foot and then the other, standing. Now the blue glow steadied. "Varzil of Neskaya was first trained at Arilinn Tower and is perhaps the most notable Keeper of our time."

"So you approve of him? Believe in him?" As he spoke the words, Eduin felt a lash of fear and anger from Saravio. Romilla flinched visibly. Mhari paled within the aura of blue light.

"What kind of questions are these? Unlike the mythological figure you previously cited, this man is real and so are his accomplishments. Together with Carolin Hastur, he rebuilt Neskaya Tower. Now he is emissary to that same King Carolin and his name is often praised as a force for peace and justice. Many call him Varzil the Good."

"And you? Do *you* admire him also?" Eduin pressed.

"He is honored wherever he goes."

Again Saravio's mind sent forth an intimation of fury, stronger this

time, like caustic over raw skin. The courtiers murmured, restive. Several voices rose above the others.

"Traitor!"

"He sold us out!"

"The Hasturs? Could *they* be behind this?"

One of the chief councillors, an older man with a dignified bearing, stepped forward. "*Vai dom,* must this continue? The prisoner has failed the test of truthspell."

Lord Brynon stirred in his great chair. Truthspell turned his features stark and grim. "I do not understand this line of inquiry. What is your point?"

"He has not yet told us who sent him here to destroy Kirella's hope for the future," Eduin said. "We must have the entire truth."

"Varzil Ridenow?" the old councillor said, astonished. "Why would he concern himself with Aillard business? You cannot seriously—"

"Silence!" Lord Brynon cut him off. Drawing himself up like a predator about to strike, he said, "*Dom* Rodrigo Halloran, did you place poison in the food of Sandoval?"

The physician stood like a beast at bay. With an odd dignity, he raised his head so that all might see the truthspell. "I did add a substance to a meal intended for this charlatan. It was no poison, and would have brought no harm to any ordinary man. But I did not believe him ordinary. How could any normal man presume to intervene with the treatment of the young mistress? Since the moment of his arrival, I suspected this Sandoval as being a wild *laran* talent, untrained, lacking even the rudiments of discipline, erratic and unpredictable, in short, dangerous in the extreme. How else could he have suborned Lady Mhari, a legitimate *leronis,* and recruited her to be his ally? How else could he have cast his net of seduction over this entire court, especially young Lady Romilla, who in her illness and confusion, fell victim to his wiles? I sought only to reveal his true nature—"

"You admit it, then?" Romilla cried out, her voice sharp and harsh like the scream of a hunting falcon. "You admit you tried to poison him? Or at the very least incapacitate the one man who could bring light into my darkness?"

"You know not what you speak, *damisela,*" *Dom* Rodrigo returned, his voice now soothing. "Sandoval might have seemed at first to help, but in the end, his lack of training would surely have brought you even greater illness. What his purposes are, I cannot say, beyond his own advancement in this court through illicit control over your susceptible mind. I, on the other hand, have always been your true physician, desiring nothing more than your happiness and well-being, and have ever sought to use my knowledge and skill in your service."

Throughout the physician's oration, the light of truthspell remained on his face. He truly believed what he spoke. Pompous and self-important he might be, but not deceitful. He had indeed served the court of Kirella for long years.

Dom Rodrigo's speech, so measured and reasonable, spread like balm over the restive crowd. Eduin saw in their faces that many believed him and even now were thinking that what he had done was not so very terrible. Many in the courtly audience had benefited from his skill. Sandoval, as they called him, was an outsider whose aloofness had earned him little friendship outside of Romilla's circle. A few more minutes, and some might even begin to wonder if it might be simpler to dismiss Sandoval and let the physician continue in his former place.

"My Lord!" Knowing he had to act quickly, Eduin spoke up. "This man stands convicted by his own words, but he has not yet revealed the extent of this conspiracy. We must discover who sent him, what power lies behind this dastardly plot. For Romilla's sake, for the sake of all Kirella, we must *know.*"

"What is this nonsense?" Regaining his confidence, *Dom* Rodrigo whirled on Eduin. "Who said anything about a plot? I acted in the defense of Kirella and its young mistress, nothing more!"

"But you admit that you admire Varzil Ridenow, that insidious agent of the Hasturs?" Eduin continued. "Can you then deny that you seek to spread his influence here in Aillard lands and bring us under the rule of King Carolin?"

"This is outrageous! Preposterous!"

His words were cut off as, under a renewed burst of pain and anger from Saravio, Romilla screamed, "The fire! The fire! Sandoval, save us!"

Lord Brynon watched with a horrified expression as his daughter, whom he thought cured, shrieked and trembled.

The audience surged like a wild beast straining against a cage. Lord

Brynon, his face suffused with darkness, leaped to his feet, shouting out orders. His guards shoved the crowd back. Steel clashed. A woman shrieked. *Domna* Mhari wavered and collapsed in a faint. The pale blue light of truthspell vanished.

Eduin took Saravio by the shoulders and forced the other man to meet his gaze. "You must calm them. Call upon Naotalba in this place and bring her peace to them. Only then can we defeat her enemy."

Although he could barely hear his own words above the uproar, Eduin saw the light of recognition in Saravio's face. Saravio got to his feet and stepped into the middle of the chamber. The milling crowd parted for him. Guards lowered their weapons. Courtiers fell back. *Dom* Rodrigo, who had been struggling in the grip of a guard on one side and a young lordling on the other, abruptly stopped his resistance.

Saravio raised his arms and began to sing.

> *"Oh, lady of the starless night,*
> *Bring us into your shadow.*
> *We give ourselves to you.*
> *Take us now, take us speedily now—"*

For an instant, Eduin's vision went white as the familiar wash of pleasure swept over him. It was too much, he thought, and then he could not think at all.

He stood once more in the gray forest, where willowy trees lifted their pale branches to the sky. Music chimed, soft and distant, awakening a resonant vibration in his bones. *Chieri* moved through the grove in the serene complexity of dance. They encircled him, embracing him with their luminous eyes, brushing him with their fingertips or the strands of their long, loose hair. He moved through their midst, caught in the ebb and flow of movement. Time itself seemed suspended. The sadness and beauty of the song pierced him with sweetness. A figure stood in the very center of the interweaving dancers, muffled in a cloak the color of shadow.

When he opened his eyes, he saw order emerging from chaos. Weapons were lowered. Some had sunk to the floor, heads thrown back. Romilla had thrown herself at Saravio's feet, sobbing. Mhari got to her feet and went to her mistress, helping her to rise.

Lord Brynon ordered *Dom* Rodrigo to be taken away and kept under close guard. The chamber quickly emptied. Eduin knew that within the hour, the story of what had happened here would not only spread throughout the castle and surrounding villages, but be well on its way to Valeron.

As he turned to go, Lord Brynon gestured to Eduin and Saravio. "Attend me privately, both of you."

A few minutes later, they stood before him in a small sitting chamber, more suitable to an intimate family gathering than the grim business at hand. A small fire gave off faint warmth. A servant hastily added more wood, lit a range of candles, and retreated.

"After what I have seen and heard," Lord Brynon said thoughtfully, "I now have cause to suspect that the physician's perfidy is not his alone. Despite his denials, I cannot believe he acted by himself. His might be the hand that wielded the poison, but not the will. He thought he was doing nothing more than his duty to this house. Someone must have used his loyalty to their own ends."

Eduin waited for a moment, then said, "I believe we can say who that was."

Frowning, Lord Brynon strode over to the chair beside the fireplace and lowered himself into it. "You were the one to bring up the names of Varzil Ridenow and King Carolin Hastur. Until today's events, I would have said they had nothing to do with us. Now, I wonder. Why did you speak of them? What else do you know?"

"Varzil the Accursed has long opposed the will of Naotalba," Saravio said.

"What he means," Eduin said, "is that together these two men seek to alter the balance of power with their talk of a Compact, persuading king and lord alike to surrender their most powerful means of defense. What purpose can they have, except to plot the eventual domination of all Darkover?"

As Eduin spoke, Lord Brynon nodded, eyes hooded and thoughtful. "The realm of Hastur has indeed grown powerful. Now that Carolin has his throne back, and there is none to stand against him . . ."

"As you say, my lord, without anyone to stand against him, how long can even the best king remain free from ambition? Carolin may have begun his reign with noble intentions, but even he must succumb to the temptations of power and conquest. He has the most powerful *laranzu* on Darkover, the great *tenerézu* Varzil Ridenow, to do his bidding. Together, they will disarm any who might oppose him. If we do not act soon, it will be too late for any mortal power to withstand him. Darkover will be united under one king and that will be Carolin Hastur!"

Lord Brynon's frown deepened. "If what you say is true . . . I cannot decide these issues alone, for Kirella is but a small part of Aillard. As soon as may be, we must confer with the Lady of Valeron and the wise councillors there. I expect—I *ask*—that you and the Blessed Sandoval make ready to accompany me."

BOOK IV

24

Dyannis Ridenow did not leave Cedestri Tower until almost the following spring. At first, there was too much work yet to do, tending the immediate injuries of matrix workers and villagers alike. Some were so badly burned, the reconstructive healing required many sessions. Over and over, she thanked whatever god might be listening that the Aillards had used ordinary fire-bombs and not *clingfire*. In addition, a supply of bonewater crystals had been returned to the Tower after Varzil convinced the pilots to abort their mission. Some of the storage containers had been shattered in the attack. Each particle had to be sought out and destroyed, a meticulous and exhausting task. Dyannis thought it ironic that Cedestri's experiment proved to be a greater danger to itself than to its enemies.

Then came the work of rebuilding the matrix screens, particularly the relays. Few travelers had visited Cedestri since the fire-bombing, so the Tower was cut off from news. The main road seemed to be blocked, but it was not until Varzil, working with a partly-constructed screen and his own starstone, was able to reach Hali Tower, that they learned why. The single aircar that had continued on, refusing to be dissuaded by Varzil's argument, had been attacked by forces from Valeron and its deadly contents scattered. The road and the surrounding countryside were contaminated, and no one knew how long the poison would persist. If it behaved like the bonewater dust it resembled, that might be a generation or more. Varzil sent out word for any who traveled there to seek help at a Tower.

"I do not have much hope that we will be able to reach all of them," he told Dyannis, "for with war between Aillard and Isoldir brewing yet again, people flee, seeking safety wherever they imagine it lies. The pity of it all is that in such a conflict, there *is* no safety."

When he said this, they had been standing together at the window of the largest house in the village, the headman's own dwelling, given over to their use until the Tower could be rebuilt. From its balcony, a simple wooden railing, they could see the tumbled walls of a once-graceful Tower. The rising sun cast a rusty glow over the scene as if it, too, bled.

Dyannis thought of the lives that had slipped through her grasp, broken in body or spirit.

How many of those deaths are my fault? How many would still be alive if I had chosen differently?

"*Chiya.*" Varzil touched her gently with his fingertips across the back of one wrist. "You must not take that burden upon yourself. In the past, you have acted rashly, but your instincts have always been sound."

"Perhaps, but not my discipline. If only—"

"How long are you going to carry that single lapse like a stone-filled sack upon your back? You have been judged by your own Keeper, and *he* is satisfied."

"You make light of my crime, calling it a 'single lapse.' Yet I almost repeated it along the road."

She left the brightness of the window and retreated into the room. This early in the day, the only light came naturally through the opened shutters. Candle wax and *laran* were in far too short supply to be wasted in illuminating rooms for people who were not working.

Varzil was trying to hearten her, she thought, to assuage the guilt that rumbled like distant thunder in her mind. He was so good, so true and loving, that he could not see the shortcomings in others. Nothing he said erased the memory of those dying minds, the hearts and souls that her own impetuousness had destroyed.

I will never be free from what I have done.

"Now you *are* being willful and self-indulgent," he said in a sterner voice.

Stung, Dyannis turned back. Something in Varzil's voice, or perhaps a trick of lighting or glimmer of *laran* power, made him seem taller. He was no longer merely her big brother, but the most powerful Keeper on Darkover.

"If you truly wish to make restitution," he went on, "consider your *present* actions. The past is behind us, and nothing you can do will change it; the future cannot be known. If you truly feel indentured to those you injured, you have no right to cripple yourself with idle self-recrimination. Your talents do not belong to you alone, but to the people you serve. You say you accept responsibility, yet when it comes to honoring that obligation, you behave no better than a spoiled child!"

Heat rose to her cheeks; the last time she felt like this was when they had clashed over her first love affair. Then she had thought Varzil was opinionated, domineering, and interfering. He had no right to command her against her own desires. She had done as she pleased, as her heart bade her. Now, he was not only her brother, but the Keeper of Cedestri Tower, and for the time being, *her* Keeper. He had every right to upbraid her.

Dyannis wanted to lash out at him, to shout back that he should mind his own business, but in doing so, she would only prove the rightness of his accusation. A spoiled child, indeed! Part of her atonement must therefore be acceptance of whatever censure he saw fit to inflict upon her. She gathered the shreds of her dignity around her. "I will do so no more."

"That is a fair reply," he said.

Working together with the townspeople, Dyannis and Varzil, along with those Cedestri *leronyn* who were able, cleared away the worst of the rubble. Large sections of the walls, both outside and interior, remained, although some of the stones had been cracked by the intense heat and must be replaced. Francisco was not yet able to do this energy-draining work.

Standing in the shadow of the Tower one afternoon, Dyannis gazed upward, her eyes following the broken outline, the streaks of black still marring the beautiful stone. Her first impression of the physical structure had been one of grace, shattered, and she had never lost that feeling. Cedestri Tower reflected the world in all its imperfect grandeur.

The other members of their improvised circle assembled, two men and a woman from the original Tower. Two other women, including the young monitor Dyannis met when they first arrived, stayed in the town for the continued healing of the most severely wounded.

"A fair day to you," Earnan said, nodding. He was the youngest of the three Cedestri workers, sweet-faced and eager to try new things.

She smiled at him, and also at Niall and Bianca, although she didn't like either of them personally. Niall hated authority and had to be flattered into his best efforts, and Bianca, although sobered by the Aillard attack, was no better, being fonder of resentment than patience. They nodded back at Dyannis, reserved but impeccably polite.

Today they were going to raise the largest stones to complete a chamber suitable for a matrix laboratory. It would be a long, exhausting session, with little energy to spare for petty irritations.

Cedestri Tower had long had a tradition of joining hands when forming a circle. Dyannis found the physical contact a little distracting at first, but accommodated herself to it. These people had been traumatized enough; it was a simple enough thing for the comfort of familiarity. Varzil, as the circle's Keeper, didn't seem to mind, one way or another.

Dyannis closed her eyes, focusing inwardly upon an image of an open sky. She knew from long experience that this was the best way to set aside petty irritations that might form a barrier to the circle. Instead, she imaged herself a falcon, wings spread wide to catch the faintest air currents.

The wind caught her, sustained her, carried her upward . . .

Her heart leaped in her throat at the sheer pleasure of soaring. From one pulse beat to the next, she felt herself drop into rapport with the rest of the circle under Varzil's infallible mental control.

A sense of rightness and order suffused her. If she became a Keeper, this is how it would be.

If.

She felt Varzil gather the combined *laran* power of the circle, shaping it subtly, deftly, felt the rough granularity of the first stone, the lingering hum and chisel of its fashioning, the intrinsic taste and weight.

Air . . . stone . . . breathe . . . in and out and up . . . It was as natural as the rhythm of her own body. She poured her strength into the psychic linkage.

Slowly, the stone rose. Her mind sensed it as a series of overlapping images, of tiny motes of substance spinning through emptiness, of spheres of shimmering power forming and reforming within the larger field of *laran.* She held the stone and guided it to rest in its precise position. It took no effort at all. Weight and size no longer mattered, only the power streaming through her mind. In that moment, she felt as strong as a Hellers peak, her touch as steady, and yet as fluid as clear water.

Air . . . stone . . . fire . . . water . . . Each element complemented and balanced the rest, parts of a perfect whole. Air and stone might change places, like dancers moving through a complex figure, but it was all the same. Nothing was added or taken away, nothing burdened or strained. Everything was as it should be.

The next stone rose at her unvoiced command. She lost all sense of the passage of time, floating between sky and earth, shaping the link between them. An hour might have passed, or an eon. There seemed no end to the joyous energy.

There came a time, however, when she felt the final stone slip into place. The entire building hummed like a *rryl* coming to life in the hands of an expert musician. The Tower had originally been built by *laran,* and its energy imprint remained. The physical and the psychic resonated in harmony.

Enough. Break now.

The words echoed through her mind in a voice not her own. She shivered, suddenly aware of her individual separateness, the shell of fragile, human flesh. Around her, the unity of the circle dissolved.

Dyannis caught her breath, blinking her eyes open. Her fingers felt stiff from holding Varzil's hand on one side and Earnan's on the other. When she lifted her gaze, she saw the completed roof of the Tower, the soaring arch of her vision.

Earnan let out a whoop of joy. Varzil turned to Dyannis, a smile lighting his gray eyes. The world blurred around the edges. She bent over, fearing she might disgrace herself by fainting. Someone hurried up with a plate of food, a confection of nuts, dried peaches, and honey. She stuffed a piece into her mouth and let the concentrated sweetness dissolve on her tongue. Her vision steadied and nausea receded.

"We all need food and rest," Varzil said, "for today we have accomplished a great feat. Soon we will begin moving the Cedestri folk back into their home."

Dyannis emerged from sleep to a sound like pebbles cascading over the roof. She shared the second-story room in the headman's village house with two of the Cedestri *leroni,* the three sleeping together in the master's own bed, for there was little room to bring in even a pallet; the house was roofed with fired-clay tiles instead of thatch. Pale light sifted in through the single window across the room. She shivered, drawing the bedcovers around her shoulders as she sat up.

Bianca pushed the door open with one elbow and sidled in, carrying a tray. She wore a thick shawl crossed over her chest and then tucked under her belt. She set the tray down on the bed, rummaged in the pile of clothing on the single straight-backed chair, and handed another shawl to Dyannis.

"It's hailing outside, can you believe? The storm came out of nowhere last night." From her tone, she thought some vengeful Tower had sent it expressly to annoy her.

"It's late in the season for hail," Dyannis said. She looked at the tray, a little puzzled that it seemed to be intended for her. Bianca had always acted as if her *laran* Gifts placed her above the work of a servant.

"That is as it may be," the other woman replied. "If you don't eat your breakfast, it'll get cold, that much is certain."

Dyannis took a piece of honey-smeared nutbread and wished *laran* work did not require so many sweet foods. Just yesterday she'd eaten more than she would in a month. One bite led to another, as if her body still craved the concentrated energy. She finished off three pieces before she turned to the pots of cheese curds and preserved fruit.

Dyannis had never been one to lie abed once she was awake, although for a fleeting second, she understood the allure of indolence. As soon as her appetite was satisfied, she pulled on a thick wool underdress and began her stretching exercises. Her body felt as stiff as if she'd slept for a tenday. Eventually, the rhythmic movements loosened her muscles. She finished dressing and went out to see what the day had to bring.

She found Varzil in conference with Francisco, sitting together in the single chamber of the Tower that had been largely untouched by the fire-bombing. It was on the ground floor, a small snug room once used for teaching but now the heart of the Tower community. Maps and diagrams covered the central table.

Varzil smiled as she entered. "You have anticipated our summoning you."

"Good morning to you, brother," she answered, feeling a bit impish. "*Dom* Francisco, I am glad to see you well."

"It is some hours into the afternoon, and you have slept for two days," Varzil said. "We have already inspected the repairs and laid out plans for the interior restoration."

"Two days! No wonder I was so hungry." Dyannis sat down. "I will have to step merrily to catch up with you. What's the work for today?"

Francisco paused for a moment before replying. The sunlight streaming through the windows accentuated the deep lines in his face, the jutting projection of jaw and cheekbone. The near destruction of his Tower and his own injuries had weathered him beyond his years. When he spoke, however, his voice was firm.

"It is said that what the gods grant, they also take away," he said, "and I believe the reverse must be true. Before this catastrophe, we at Cedestri and our masters in Isoldir lived in a constant state of desperation. How could we defend ourselves against the might of Valeron, which seemed to threaten our very existence? Not by force of ordinary arms, that much was sure.

"As you know," he went on with a slight inclination of his head toward Varzil, "we have never accepted the imposition of any outside restrictions upon our actions. In recent years, we were approached by disaffected workers from other Towers, who could not in conscience abide by King Carolin's Compact. They saw us as an honorable and legitimate alternative and we welcomed their skills, although perhaps we were overhasty in several cases. Sometimes there were other reasons why a *laranzu* found himself unwelcome in his former community.

"Be that as it may," Francisco continued, "when we discovered a previously unknown, untapped power source of immense magnitude, we rejoiced. By ourselves, we had insufficient *laran* to produce the kinds of weapons Isoldir needed to balance its lesser force against Valeron. By harnessing this power stream, our single circle became the equivalent of three or four."

Dyannis sensed his memory of that discovery, the surge of triumph. It frightened her as much as the idea of a novice loose in a laboratory of twelfth-order matrices. Given Isoldir's desperation, all considerations of safety, all fear of consequences would be swept aside in the passion of hope. She knew where it had led. She had seen the mill Cedestri had constructed in the Overworld, had stood beneath the Isoldir aircars on their way to rain poison upon Aillard lands. She had watched Cedestri burn.

Beside Francisco, Varzil sat quietly, letting the other man find his way through the story.

"When Aillard retaliated, I saw how vain our pride had been." Francisco's voice dropped a tone. "I cursed them, and I cursed you, too, Varzil, for having interfered with our attack. I thought—" and here he gave a bark of laughter, "—that if only we had succeeded, there would have been an end to it. There would have been no retaliation, no fire raining from the Aillard aircars. Valeron would have been a wasteland until our children's children's time. Instead, we would have achieved enduring security for Isoldir, for who else would dare to menace us, when we were thus armed?

"How wrong I was! I think I must have had a brain fever to make me think that way. Now I see there could have been only one result of our actions. Even if by some miracle we had triumphed, it would have brought us only a temporary peace. Sooner or later, some other kingdom, driven by that same desperate fear, would have launched an attack against us, or we would have found a new enemy. This time, our enemy might not be as merciful as Valeron. Yes, I call this merciful."

He gestured to the partly-restored Tower around them. "Merciful because they used ordinary fire instead of *clingfire;* we had something left to rebuild, and some few precious lives spared. And . . ." his voice cracked, ". . . and we had help beyond any right or expectation."

"We did only what any people of good will would have done," Varzil said mildly.

Now who is being overly modest? Dyannis shot at him.

"If you had come to us earlier with fine speeches and asked us to sign your Compact, I would have sent you away and then laughed at you behind your back," Francisco said. "I would have thought you fools and cowards."

Varzil gave a wry smile. "It has happened before, and will again. That is not a reason to stop trying."

"Ah, but in this case, your deeds preceded your words and gave them substance. You put into practice your doctrine of fellowship and compassion. I know perfectly well that King Carolin Hastur has nothing to gain from my gratitude. I, on the other hand, have seen the price of continuing as we are. My masters of Isoldir agree, though it can be said they have little choice, without a single functioning Tower to defend them. They would not even have what little we can offer, were it not for your assistance." His gaze took in Dyannis as well as Varzil.

She started to say that there had been no question of refusing aid. What did allegiances matter, when her fellow *leronyn* were suffering? The loss of one Tower diminished them all. The words that sprang to her mind seemed but pale echoes of her brother's. She held her tongue.

"Therefore, at our urging, Isoldir has agreed to abide by the Compact. A messenger brought formal word this morning, and Varzil is to carry the signed oath back to Thendara." Francisco's joy radiated like an aureole of light around his weary features.

Caught up in Varzil's own jubilation, Dyannis felt her heart give a little lurch. *So you see,* she could almost hear Varzil say, *what seemed like a disaster has in the end brought good not only to this poor land but to all Darkover.*

"This is all very well," Dyannis said, her thoughts spinning in a more practical direction, "but if you are to return to Thendara, Varzil, how will we continue our work here?"

"The physical rebuilding of the Tower is largely complete," Francisco answered her. "Isoldir will send masons and carpenters to help with the interior. Thanks to your efforts, I am strong enough now to resume limited duties."

Dyannis restrained herself from pointing out that Varzil's departure would deprive the Cedestri circle not only of its temporary Keeper, but of his extraordinary *laran*.

"We will indeed be diminished in strength, with many tasks ahead of us," Francisco said gently.

Dyannis flushed, realizing that he must have picked up her unvoiced thought. "Please forgive me, *vai tenerézu*. Truly, I meant no insult to you."

"I have taken none, *vai leronis*," he replied with a playful echo of the honorific. "Indeed, I and all of Cedestri would be deeply in your debt if you remain with us for a time, for you are the strongest of the remaining *leronyn* and the only one capable of acting as under-Keeper."

A—what?

She blinked. "Forgive me, I believe I have just suffered a momentary lapse in consciousness. I must be more fatigued than I realized. I thought you referred to me as an under-Keeper, but that is impossible. I have no such training."

My dear sister, you have been functioning as my under-Keeper for this past tenday. Varzil's mental voice bore a touch of amusement.

Dyannis remembered the way she seemed to lift the stones that formed the very same walls that now surrounded them. At the time, she had been lost in the floating bliss of the circle. Now she realized that instead of being one strand in an interwoven whole, *she* had been the one to channel and guide the combined mental energies of the circle. Somehow, with a touch so smooth as to be unnoticeable, Varzil had eased her into the centripolar position.

If you do not cease gaping at me as if I were a three-headed rabbit-horn, Varzil said, *you will surely disgrace us both.*

She closed her mouth, promising herself that at the first opportunity, she would make Varzil regret he'd done such a thing without her permission. To Francisco she said, with all the dignity she could muster, "If my Keeper at Hali allows it, I will remain as long as there is need of my services."

25

Dyannis followed Varzil from the little chamber. Varzil stopped to speak with Earnan, who was supervising a crew of laborers from the town. They were sorting through a pile of rubble for salvageable bits of metal and starstone. She waited patiently, pretending to be interested. News of Isoldir's adoption of the Compact had already spread through the Tower community, and probably to the town as well. Earnan's eyes shone and he looked as if he wanted to kiss Varzil's feet.

"Some of the others, they are still suspicious, but we all agree that we cannot go on as we have before. You have brought us great good, *Dom* Varzil, and I most fervently believe this Compact will, even more so."

Varzil excused himself as quickly as he could without being rude. He hurried up the road toward the town before anyone else could approach him on the subject. Dyannis caught his discomfort, his reluctance to accept personal credit for something that went so far beyond any one man's creation. Her own outrage seemed petty and fleeting by comparison.

But, she fumed, she had been maneuvered into a role for which she felt so unworthy. As soon as they were out of hearing from the Tower, she turned on Varzil. "How dare you! How dare you do that to me!"

"And how dare you act like a spiteful child, holding back your Gift when it is so sorely needed?" he shot back. "You cannot say that you are incapable or untrustworthy, for you have already demonstrated otherwise."

"Without my knowledge!"

"You know it now," he said, refusing to be drawn in.

"You tricked me!"

Varzil smiled. "In no way did I violate my Keeper's oath. I merely exercised a Keeper's prerogative, which was to shape the circle in the manner I deemed best. If you object to the truth that was then revealed, you had best examine your own motives."

"You would have me undertake a Keeper's training, whether I will it or not—whether I am fit or not!"

"On the contrary. I would have you make a free choice, with reasoned judgment instead of misguided guilt."

Dyannis fell silent, her next retort dying on her tongue. She felt like a petulant child, hurling one angry accusation after another. His responses had been unfailingly kind.

She bowed her head. "Forgive me. I have been perverse and bad-tempered. I beg you, do not press me further, at least until I know my own heart. Let us not mar all the good work we have done together by quarreling."

To her surprise, he smiled. "When we first came to Cedestri, you would never have accepted my censure with such grace. You have learned much about self-control through your work here."

"I have had little choice," she retorted. Then, as if a wall within her gave way suddenly, she went on. "I have never had to work so hard in my life, not even when I was a novice at Hali. Everything came too easily for me then. Even when I gave way to this accursed temper of mine, I escaped with only the lightest punishments because I had also accomplished something brilliant."

She remembered how she'd discovered the power source at the bottom of the lake, and she flushed at how reckless, how undisciplined she had been. "Brilliance has its limits," she added wryly.

"Yes, I think so, too." He gave a little chuckle. "On the other hand, when pushed to it, you accepted the consequences of your actions, as well as obedience to your Keeper. This has led to greater maturity on your part."

"Don't mock me," she said. "I know what I am."

"Do you?" His gaze bore down on her. He repeated in a softer, even more penetrating tone. *"Do you?"*

In a flash, she saw the direction of his thoughts.

Perhaps when we first came here to Cedestri, you were too impulsive, too rash to be considered for Keeper training. The people around you have always indulged your fits of rebellion and, as you said, success came too easily to you. Rebuilding Cedestri required you to dig more deeply into yourself, and you have proven yourself capable of humility as well as initiative.

She lowered her eyes. *I know my limits.*

Exactly. The training of a Keeper requires just that kind of honesty. You already knew how to act, how to rely upon your own resources. Here you have also learned to control those impulses for a greater good. I tell you, there is no better proof of your fitness as a Keeper candidate. Will you not reconsider?

For a long moment, she stared at him, letting the full import of his thoughts sink into her mind. All her life, there had been some important piece missing, like a stew without salt. Without realizing it, she had thrown herself headlong into each new possibility, as if she were searching for something. Always, she had come up short, dissatisfied without being able to say why. The only real challenge had been to escape the inevitable consequences of her recklessness.

Was that the problem? That she had never found any task too difficult, too daunting? Was she meant to be a Keeper, with all the discipline and demands of the post?

"I will consider it," she said, bowing her head.

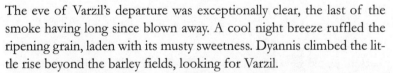

The eve of Varzil's departure was exceptionally clear, the last of the smoke having long since blown away. A cool night breeze ruffled the ripening grain, laden with its musty sweetness. Dyannis climbed the little rise beyond the barley fields, looking for Varzil.

She found him sitting cross-legged upon a folded cloak. The light of three moons and the milky sweep of stars limned his features in silver. His hands lay loosely upon his thighs, one cradling a ring. The stone glimmered as if lit from within. It reminded her of a starstone, but of unusual size and shape, lacking the characteristic blue tint. He held the ring as if it were a living thing, precious and yet not to be grasped too tightly, an odd way to treat a thing of metal and crystal.

He turned his head slightly as she lowered herself beside him, at once her familiar elder brother and a stranger. From his stillness, she knew he had been meditating.

"I'm sorry to disturb you. There's little enough peace for any of us these days," she said.

He said nothing, only covered the ring with his other hand. Its light remained like an after-image. Sensitized as she was from overlong hours of *laran* work, Dyannis slipped into rapport with him. She realized he was lonely, that he welcomed her company, a familiar presence to ease some unspoken heartache.

A shiver ran through him, of spirit rather than body.

"Did you ever meet Felicia Leynier?" he asked her, his voice roughened with hidden emotion. "She worked for a time at Arilinn before going Hestral Tower." A pause followed, like the stillness between one heartbeat and the next. "She trained there as under-Keeper."

Dyannis sat very still. There was more beneath her brother's words than his scheme to train women as Keepers. Listening to the resonance of his voice, she heard love—and loss.

"I knew of her," she said gently.

"She was at Hestral Tower when Rakhal Hastur attacked. When he ordered Hali to destroy them."

And she died there, Dyannis thought, carefully shielding. "You could not save her, as you saved Harald when he was captured by the catmen so long ago, as you saved so many others." She laid her fingertips on the back of his wrist in the fashion of one telepath to another.

Bredu, she spoke telepathically, *I did not take part in that battle, although I was at Hali then.*

"I would not blame you if you had," he said aloud. "I blame no man—or woman—for following the lawful orders of his king. Felicia herself would never want that. She—she would have been pleased to see Hali Tower as it is today, bound in honor by the Compact. She believed in it. She—"

He broke off, clenching the ring. Dyannis laid her hand over his fist, thinking to ease the knot of anguish. His hand opened beneath hers and she brushed the smooth faceted surface of the crystal. To her surprise, it was warm, warmer than it should have been from mere contact with Varzil's skin. And alive—a sweet fragrance like sun on wildflowers . . .

She jerked her hand back. "What—what is it?"

"Felicia placed her consciousness, her personality into this stone. At least, I feel her presence there from time to time."

"How is that possible?" Dyannis asked. "A starstone focuses and amplifies the *laran* of its owner, but has no power of its own."

"During the Ages of Chaos, there was some research in using psychoactive crystals to preserve a personality separate from the fleshly body. Perhaps this stone is a relic from those early experiments, waiting to be imprinted by a dying mind."

Dyannis shivered. Images rose unbidden to her mind, for she had seen the desperation of power-mad men—Rakhal the Usurper and, before her time, the outlaw *laranzu,* Rumail Deslucido. What if some Keeper, crazed by fear of his impending death, found a way to place his consciousness— and his psychic power—into a starstone? What if he found a way to control others—direct a circle—overshadow vulnerable minds—

Calm your fears. Varzil sent a wave of reassurance. *I know of no such abomination, and those times are behind us now.* "As for Felicia," he continued aloud, "she would gladly have chosen oblivion rather than use her Gift to harm anyone. What I feel from the ring is comfort and memory." He shrugged, straightened his shoulders, put the ring back on.

"You loved her very much," Dyannis said.

"I never thought to find another human being who was so much the other half of my soul. Dyannis—I have held back from saying something to you, because of your . . . feelings. Now I am to leave Cedestri, and I do not know when we will see one another again. I would not leave it unsaid."

"We are brother and sister, fellow *leronyn,*" she said with an assurance she did not feel. Something was coming, she knew not what, and she trembled inside. "Surely, we should have no secrets from one another."

"Very well, then. Felicia's death was not the result of Hali's attack. She was already mortally wounded, preserved only in a *laran* stasis field. I am afraid—no, I am *certain* the person responsible for that attack was Eduin MacEarn."

Dyannis flinched. No, it could not be, not her Eduin. Not the sweet boy who had won her heart that Midwinter Festival when she was newly come to Hali. Misguided, rejected—even outlawed after his flagrant disobedience to his Keeper during the Hestral battles—

And yet—years ago, before Hestral fell, he had come to Hali Tower for a short time, and he had been strange, withdrawn, secretive. *Changed.*

A conspirator, perhaps. An outcast, certainly. But a *murderer?* She could not believe it.

Varzil lifted one hand, as if to forestall her objections. "I would never have brought this up if he had not been present that day at Hali Lake." His mind brushed against hers. *As you yourself know full well.*

"Dyannis." He turned to face her squarely, taking her hands in his, a gesture that was practically a confrontation among telepaths, shocking in its directness. "There is a link between the Hali Lake riot and Felicia's death. I don't know what it is, I don't even know how to proceed in finding out. I just know it is there."

Dyannis found her voice. "You say this only because you dislike Eduin, as you have from the very beginning!"

"I tried not to hate him when we were boys at Arilinn," Varzil said in a low voice. "I tried hard. Carolin always took his part, because Eduin was poor and talented and had no other friends. I could always see the better part of other people, but not Eduin. I never understood why. I suspected him, rightly or wrongly I will never know, of intending harm to Carolin."

"Harm Carolin?" Dyannis asked, startled. "How?"

Varzil swept his hair back from his face with one hand. "There were a number of . . . accidents during those years, before Carolin came to the throne. He refused to take them seriously, saying he couldn't live in a silken cage. One incident, though, was an outright attempt at assassination. We were on our way to Blue Lake for a holiday." He paused as images flashed across his mind.

Dyannis, in light rapport with her brother, watched two youths ride carefree through a sunlit forest—

—a sliver of deadly metal burst from the underbrush to streak through the air—

—Varzil twisting it within the muffling folds of his cloak—

—Carolin struggling with a bearded man on the muddy banks of a river—

—a voice ringing through her mind, raw with urgency—*"Death to Hastur! We will be avenged!"*

"What does it mean?" she wondered aloud. "Who will be avenged?

Surely this proves there is some other agent at work, some festering resentment responsible for your conspiracy, if in fact that exists. Even a king who is loved must make enemies. None of this proves anything against Eduin."

"The whole story makes no sense unless you know who Felicia is— was," Varzil said. "Although she did her best to keep it secret, she was the *nedestra* daughter of Taniquel Hastur-Acosta and therefore, kin to Carolin."

"How would Eduin have known that?" she snapped.

How, indeed? She was shaking inside, remembering how Eduin had searched the archives at Hali Tower, especially the genealogy records, how he had startled as if guilty when she found him there . . . She'd assumed he pursued some task for the Keepers. Was he using legitimate work to mask a personal search of the Hastur bloodlines?

Something hovered at the edge of her memory, dark as *kyorebni* wings.

Irritably, she said, "You're just looking for an excuse to blame Eduin for things that have nothing to do with him."

"You're not thinking clearly," Varzil said with exasperating patience. "Felicia was Hastur; Eduin tried to kill her—did kill her. Eduin tried to kill Carolin, another Hastur, and failed, for which he probably hates me even more. What the Blue Lake assassin has to do with Eduin, I don't know. But when Eduin shows up with an armed mob in Hali, in the heart of Hastur territory, I am suspicious. I am very suspicious."

"You are very *wrong!*" Dyannis cried. "You have some boyhood grudge against Eduin and you've concocted a pack of wild guesses to convince yourself he's guilty! Isn't the world difficult enough without creating imaginary conspiracies and blaming those less fortunate?"

With an effort, she reined her tongue under control. They were both exhausted, mentally as well as physically. He had been working for days without a rest, giving unstintingly of himself. Any other man would have stayed at Neskaya, safe and comfortable behind its rebuilt walls. If old insecurities preyed upon him, he might be forgiven.

"I am sorry I said those things," she said. "I always did have a temper. This won't be the first time I've rattled off without thinking things through. But I do believe you speak without any proof in the matter.

Eduin's life was broken at Hestral. I don't know where he is now or how he fares, but it cannot be well. He deserves your compassion, not your censure."

"That is true enough," Varzil said after a pause. "Some things we will never know, and that is as it should be. For now, a path lies clear before me, the quest to which I have already sworn myself. I thank you for your help, and I wish each of us—even your poor Eduin—peace in our souls when all is done."

With that, he rose and left her, striding back toward the Tower, preparing the way for the night's work. Dyannis watched him go, feeling regret and admiration. He had suffered far more in his life than she had, and yet he took on the mantle of his duty with a quiet clarity of mind she could not help but envy.

A shiver ran through her. *I am a better person when I am with him.*

She would simply have to take what he had taught her and urge herself to improvement, just as if she were her own Keeper. The thought frightened her.

— ◆ —

Winter came and left, with only the briefest interruption of the work. The Isoldir Lord sent the promised masons and carpenters, along with wagons of supplies to help the Tower and its townspeople through the long dark months.

By Midwinter Festival, it was clear that Francisco would never recover sufficiently to resume full duties as Keeper. He could manage small circles of two or three, enough for simple tasks. Several of the workers had died of their lingering injuries. Dyannis knew she had not the training to take over the entire circle of five on a permanent basis, and Francisco did not ask it of her.

With the spring thaw, travel became possible once again. With some trepidation, Dyannis made plans to return to Hali. The contingent of soldiers who had accompanied her and Varzil had departed when he did, providing for Carolin's emissary. It was unthinkable for Dyannis to travel unescorted, even with Lady Helaina as chaperone. The Lord of Isoldir offered to take her to Arilinn for the meeting of the *Comyn* Council, and from there she could travel to Hali along with Carolin

Hastur's contingent. The meeting, she noticed, would not be held until that autumn. She suspected Isoldir's generosity was tempered by his desire to retain her services for as long as possible.

Did she want to stay that long? Francisco had recovered as much as he was going to; already he was increasing the pressure upon her to function as a Keeper. With her strong telepathic abilities, she had no problem linking with another *leronis* and attuning their joined minds to the particular task. Gradually, one became two and two extended into three. She learned to submerge her personal antipathies, finding ways to appreciate and make the most of the particular strengths of each worker.

Varzil had been right. She had both the strength and the aptitude to do a Keeper's work. But whether she *ought* to assume that responsibility was another matter. Her thoughts again bent toward the incident at Hali Lake, the monstrous dragon she had inflicted upon the unprotected minds of the mob, the deaths that had resulted. Varzil had insisted her debt was discharged, her restitution for that rash act complete. Even her own Keeper, Raimon of Hali, said so. As Varzil had pointed out, she had restrained herself from a similar spell when they encountered the Cedestri aircars.

What, then? What? Night after night, after her work in the circle was done, she paced the confines of the Tower room that had been given over, newly refurbished, to her use. Instinct told her that once she proved biddable, the Isoldir Lords would find an excuse to hold her here. Until she was clear in her own mind whether she could fulfill a Keeper's responsibilities, it was dangerous to remain under such conditions.

If Isoldir would not provide a timely escort, then she must apply to Hali. Surely Carolin would, at Raimon's request, spare a handful of men to bring her home. Though it was near dawn and the night's chill lay thick and heavy upon the stone walls, she threw a shawl over her working robes and made her way to the relay chamber.

Dyannis seated herself on the bench in front of the screen and composed herself. She herself had repaired much of the damage to the matrix device. The lattice of starstones brightened, humming in resonance. She closed her eyes and the familiar, floating sensation engulfed her. Every Gifted worker experienced relay communication in a different way; since she preferred visual imagery, she saw the psychic firmament as a vast, misty void, like the sky before dawn.

Hali . . . she thought, and watched as the pale light shifted and condensed into a pinpoint of light.

Hali is here—Dyannis, is it you? Rorie's mental voice sounded strong and clear.

Dyannis felt an absurd rush of gladness.

Quickly, he shifted. *Is something amiss? Some new trouble at Cedestri? Are you well?*

Yes, I am quite well, she answered quickly. *Cedestri continues with its recovery and there have been no new signs of war. In fact, things are going so well here that I fear they do not want to let me go.*

She felt his grin. *That's because you're still on your best behavior, imp.*

Pest. Seriously, Rorie, I'm either going to grow roots here or steal a horse in the dead of night. Since I'm trying to observe some minimal propriety, would you be so kind as to ask Raimon to arrange an escort for me?

With pleasure. Life here is much too dull without you. You are wise not to travel without armed escort.

Why, is there some new trouble? Dyannis asked.

Not in Thendara, but in Asturias—do you know of it?

Dyannis felt her heart give a little flutter. The small kingdom of Asturias had long threatened Ridenow lands and she had heard of their ruthless new general, the Kilghard Wolf.

Carolin wishes an end to hostilities, Rorie said, *so I do not think he will be easily drawn in as a combatant.*

They talked for a while longer of other, less important news such as the comings and goings of Tower workers. Ellimara Aillard had gone to Neskaya to be trained as under-Keeper.

I wish her joy, Dyannis replied, with an odd shiver. She did not know if it came from regret or jealousy or relief that Varzil had found some other woman willing to take on the responsibility. Ellimara was younger, more flexible. It was better this way.

A tenday later, word came from Hali that an escort had been arranged, and within a month, a company of soldiers, clad in Hastur blue and silver, arrived to take Dyannis home. If Francisco and the Isoldir Lord were sorry to see her go, they gave no sign, but heaped her with expressions of gratitude and what small gifts could be spared. She returned the copper coins and jewelry, saying that as a *leronis,* she had little use for riches. As for herself, she did not take a truly free breath until she could no longer see the Isoldir promontory on the horizon behind her.

26

Returning to Hali, Dyannis felt like a stranger, though she had lived there for most of her adult life. When she had first come to the Tower, she had been fourteen, barely a woman. She had but lately recovered from a bout of the threshold sickness that had claimed the lives of her older brother and sister. She had seen the fear in her father's eyes that she, too, would die in convulsive madness. To this day, she did not know what would have happened had Varzil not gained admittance to Arilinn Tower, and thereby opened her father's mind to the possibility. As soon as it was safe for her to travel, she had been bundled on her way.

Hali Tower had been a world like none other. The *leronyn* had welcomed her for her Gifts, even undeveloped, but more than that, they had treated her like an adult woman, capable of managing her own life and taking responsibility for her own actions. How proud she had been of her psychic strength, how eager to practice her new skills. Everywhere she looked, some wondrous new vista opened before her—life as a *leronis* of one of the most prestigious Towers on Darkover, the *rhu fead* with its mysteries and ancient holy things, the lake with its cloudwater, the city, the glittering court . . . the knowledge that she belonged here and had a part in it all.

Varzil had come to the Hastur court for that first Midwinter Festival, along with Carolin, who was returning from his own season of training at Arilinn . . . and Eduin.

Dyannis turned her vision inward, toward memory. Her body moved to the easy gait of her mount as she rode, surrounded by King Carolin's escort, along the length of Hali Lake to the Tower.

Eduin.

When they had danced, he had held her in his arms as if she were the most precious thing in the world. She had no previous experience with the feelings that arose in her, each wave more tender and tempestuous than the one before. Something in him touched her heart of hearts, perhaps the vulnerability she sensed beneath his borrowed finery. It was not until Varzil had forbidden her to have anything more to do with Eduin that she fell in love.

Would I have done so without Varzil's interference? She could not be sure. In all honesty, she knew her own reaction to being ordered about by anyone. Regardless of the instigation, she had ended up in Eduin's bed, and it was a good thing the monitors at Hali had already taught her how to prevent conception, for she had come away without any permanent entanglements.

In due time, Eduin had returned to Arilinn and she to her life at Hali. She had studied and mastered and worked. And loved, but never with that feverish intensity of her time with Eduin.

It is a good thing that first love comes but once, or none of us would get anything done. So her first Keeper, Dougal DiAsturian, had said.

Before her, Hali Tower rose like glimmering alabaster reaching for the sky above the shifting currents of the lake. Its beauty caught at her heart. Her vision blurred. She knew every room, every stair, every window ledge, every corner of the kitchens, every viewpoint, and yet now she stood outside.

It was all nonsense, of course. Hali was her home. They were waiting for her. She had missed Midwinter, but that was of no great matter.

What was she waiting for? Why the odd thoughts, the hesitation? There was plenty of work to be done.

The riot at the lake had taken its toll in more ways than one. She had changed, and never again could she stand beside the lake or walk the halls, sit in a matrix laboratory or bend her mind to the relay screens, as if nothing had happened. Events had brought her to a crisis in her own mind, and brought Eduin back into her life.

Eduin had come to Hali some years back, before he went to Hestral Tower. Before Felicia Leynier had died under mysterious circumstances, and before he had led an unlawful circle in a brutal counterattack against Rakhal's besieging army. She set that thought aside and returned to their brief reunion.

He had been distant, almost cold. She might have sworn he had never loved her, except for the memories. He had come to Hali, he said, to serve as archivist and do genealogical research. She had assumed it was either for Dougal or Barak, who was Keeper at Arilinn. It had never occurred to her that he might have been searching for some reason of his own.

What had he been looking for in the Hastur lineages? Had he found it—acted upon it?

That way, Dyannis told herself sternly, lay madness. The past was beyond amendment, and Varzil was right in that there were some things she might never know.

Let it alone.

They rode up the last stretch of road, almost to the Tower gates. Rorie and Alderic came out to greet her. She urged her weary horse forward.

I am home, Dyannis thought, but she did not truly believe it.

Dyannis settled back into her old quarters, unpacked her belongings and sent her travel clothing to be cleaned. She spent the evening gossiping with her old friends and then soaking in a steaming tub, something she had not enjoyed since leaving Hali. Certainly, Cedestri had not been able to offer such luxuries, and she had grown weary of bathing with a sponge and a basin of cold water.

Raimon suggested that she rest a while before resuming her usual duties, but Dyannis would not hear of it. She insisted on joining the circle that very evening. "I am not some pampered plaything who cannot travel a few leagues without collapsing for a tenday," she told him with more tartness than she intended.

That sounds like our Dyannis, he replied mentally. Aloud, he said, "We are most heartily glad to have you back among us."

She composed herself upon her usual bench in the laboratory that was as familiar as her own chamber. The task tonight was straightforward, making medicines for the muscle fever ravaging the lake district. It struck children, and those it did not kill were left crippled, sometimes mute as well. The circle at Neskaya had devised a method of using *laran* to enhance the potency of herbal remedies, and Carolin had asked Hali to produce a supply.

Dyannis glanced across the table, spread with flasks and beakers of tinctures. Once this chamber, like so many others, had seen the manufacture of *clingfire* and worse, but now was given over to the making of medicine to heal children.

Without thinking, she reached out her hands to either side, then quickly drew them back. The circle at Hali did not make physical contact. After the initial feeling of strangeness, she had become accustomed to it at Cedestri.

Dyannis lowered her barriers, focusing on the matrix lattice in the center of the table. Deftly, Raimon wove their minds together. The process felt at once familiar and strange. She found herself out of step, resisting his control.

I have become accustomed to having my own way, she thought.

It is of no great matter, Raimon answered her with unexpected kindness. *We will accommodate one another. Varzil told us you had been working as under-Keeper at Cedestri.*

Varzil again!

Come now, it is hardly a state secret. He also said you wished to return to ordinary circle work. I was merely observing that giving up a Keeper's autonomy is just as difficult as acquiring it.

Indeed, she agreed ruefully. *Not all the smiths in Zandru's Forge can put that chick back into its egg.*

Dyannis bent her will to submerging her thoughts in the unity of the circle. Being unfamiliar with the method, she took the plan from Raimon's mind and concentrated on each step. Although the work was not difficult, she approached it with care. The ingredients, herbal tinctures, distilled wine, honey, extracts of flowers and powdered bone, felt fresh and clean, still bearing the energetic signatures of living things. The work refreshed rather than drained her.

Dyannis was surprised when Raimon dissolved the bonds of the circle. She realized from the stiffness of her joints that some hours had passed, and yet she felt little fatigue. Knowing better than to trust her sense of well-being, she went with the others to eat and rest.

"Aldones, you've grown strong!" Rorie commented when she spoke her thought aloud. "What have you been doing, drinking banshee milk?"

She shook her head. "Building stone walls."

"That'll do it every time." He eased himself into a chair and she realized that he was still favoring the shoulder that had been shot by an arrow at the lake shore riot. How easy it was to forget events when she did not have to live with their consequences.

Seeing her pensive, he reached out and touched her lightly across the back of her hand, tracing a line from wrist to fingertip. "It is good to have you back."

She knew then that he meant it for himself, and not just as a member of the community.

Blessed Cassilda! She cut off the thought and, as gracefully as she could, hurried away toward the women's quarters. Only when she was within the confines of her own room did she let herself finish the thought. *He is in love with me. How could I not have known?*

Dyannis lowered herself to the edge of her bed. Perhaps Rorie himself had not known until now. Sometimes when people met again after an absence, they saw each another differently.

When and *how* were fruitless questions whose answers changed nothing. Of far greater importance was how *she* felt about *him.* A dozen images rose to her mind . . . Rorie laughing at some joke, teasing her, calling her *Pest,* rushing to meet her . . . his mind like fine-grained steel, strong and flexible, welcoming her mental touch—

Overlapping each of these memories came a series of far more disturbing thoughts.

Eduin looking up from the scroll he had been examining in the Hali archives . . .

She'd sought him out in the end, for he had avoided her. He had gestured to the pile of scrolls, some of them in such fragile condition that they would not survive more than another winter or two. "The work—"

"Has lain here for longer than Durraman owned that old donkey of his, and is not about to sprout legs or go anywhere," she'd said, adding, "you must please yourself." When he started to turn away, she pulled up a stool so that, short of unspeakable rudeness, he had no choice but to sit with her. "What have you been excavating?"

"Genealogy records."

That much was obvious. "Whose?"

"Obscure branches of the Hasturs," he'd answered and then added that he was researching lethal recessive genetic traits from the Ages of Chaos.

Dyannis shuddered, for like most modern young people, she found the thought of inbreeding to manipulate *laran* traits utterly repugnant. "I think we are living in an age of progress. You should hear my brother talk! He's full of new ideas."

Varzil had last visited Hali some time ago, for a funeral. At the time, Dyannis had little interest in it, small and private. She was saddened to hear of the death of Queen Taniquel Hastur-Acosta, of whom so many ballads were sung, but she had never known the legendary heroine. Queen Taniquel had ridden at the side of her uncle, Rafael Hastur II, he who held the throne at Thendara before it passed to Carolin's uncle, and even defied the might of the assembled *Comyn* Council. If half the stories were true, Taniquel had been instrumental in Hastur's victory over the power-mad tyrant, Damian Deslucido. Without her determination, the present world would have taken a very different shape. There would be no Hastur ascendancy, no bloody wars of succession, no King Carolin, no rebuilding of Neskaya and Tramontana Towers . . . no Compact.

After the funeral, Dyannis had been pleased to see her brother again, and intrigued by his unvoiced but obvious love for Arilinn's new *leronis,* Felicia, newly come from Nevarsin Tower.

How young they had all been then, Dyannis thought with a trace of nostalgia. She had eagerly picked up Varzil's unguarded emotions and spun them into a tale of romance. He had no intention of being indiscreet, of course, but their closeness of blood and sympathy granted her an exceptional sensitivity to his thoughts. When she realized that the woman he was so smitten with, this Felicia of Arilinn, was actually the *nedestra* daughter of that same legendary Queen Taniquel, she thought it the most wonderful thing imaginable.

But Felicia had died in the wreckage of Hestral Tower, and Dyannis could not help wondering if some part of Varzil's heart had died with her. She was still naive enough to think that such love, such passion came only once in a lifetime.

And so, he carries her memory in his heart. And so, he looks to blame Eduin, his old adversary.

That explanation, although reasonable, brought little comfort. If it were true, why did the suggestion of Eduin's guilt gnaw away at her like some dreadful cancer? Why could she not set it aside and let the past rest? She could not shake the feeling that she had forgotten something crucial.

She would have no future here at Hali, nor any chance of resolving her feelings for Rorie, until she discovered the truth.

— ✦ —

Raimon had directed the circle to rest for several days, although various members had other tasks. Dyannis pleaded continuing fatigue from her journey, and went to that part of the Tower devoted to the storage of ancient records. She found the room in which she had spoken to Eduin without any difficulty. It was one of several set aside for the study and copying of manuscripts.

She lowered herself on the bench drawn up at a reading desk beside a tall window. It was early in the afternoon, for she had slept long and fitfully. The bar of brightness across the desk glowed, strong enough to read or write by. She placed her hands in it as if conjuring a spell that would burn away all falsehood, all confusion, leaving only the starkness of truth.

She closed her eyes and the image of brilliance remained for a time behind her eyes. Memory answered her. The light had been grayer then, the sky outside overcast. Perhaps she remembered it that way because then her life had been painted in such vivid colors, the heat of her impetuosity, her innocence, her unshakable self-confidence.

What had Varzil said, when he told her that he believed Eduin had a part in Felicia's death? That Felicia had died because she was a Hastur, and Carolin had almost died for that very same reason.

Death to Hastur! We will be avenged! Those were the dying thoughts of the assassin who had waylaid Carolin and Varzil on their way to Blue Lake so many years ago.

So someone held a death grudge against the Hasturs, one that spanned a generation. Carolin was an obvious target, the heir to the throne. But why Felicia? No one beyond a few intimates knew of her lineage, and why would that matter? She had no pretensions to power, but had sought only to use her Gifts in the service of the Towers. Felicia was also the first woman to openly train as a Keeper.

Did that have anything to do with her death? Was someone so incensed that a woman would defy all tradition to wear the crimson? Was Ellimara Aillard in danger also? Was she, herself?

Sighing, Dyannis rose from the desk and began to pace. Her movement stirred fine eddies of dust. These scrolls were very old, reaching back into the Age of Chaos, and she doubted they'd been dusted in the last century. What marvels of matrix technology might be found there, she wondered, and what horrors?

She ran her fingertips along the stitched bindings of several scrolls, studying the labels. The parchments felt brittle to the touch, as if they might disintegrate at the first attempt to open them.

I will find no answers here, she thought. *I do not believe Eduin did either.*

She conjured a memory of Eduin startling as she came toward him. Yes . . . details fell into place. A scroll had been spread across this very table. It could not have been very old, then. She had no memory of curling, age-darkened edges or the crackle of parchment as he thrust it aside. The scroll had been supple, although a shade darker than the creamy white of one newly made.

Newer records, then . . .

She widened the scope of her pacing, as if in that way, she might pick up some faint trace of his presence, his intentions. Her movements took her down the ranges of shelves, back toward the central corridor. The records here were more recent. When she searched with her *laran,* she caught the traces of the craftsmen who had prepared the parchment and casings, the scribes who had dipped quill into ink, the archivist who had arranged them in such meticulous order. Whoever had been in charge when this time period was recorded had unusually tidy standards. Every scroll was placed in exact alignment with its neighbors.

No, one was slightly askew, as if it had been taken out and then hastily shoved back.

Dyannis brushed her fingertips across the scroll. Mentally she probed it, sinking down through the protective sleeve. The coiled parchment still bore faint traces of the living animal whose skin it had been. Interwoven with it, she sensed a great seriousness, a shadow, a weight, and knew it for the mind of the scribe. He was Gifted, of that she was sure, and he had left behind, like the film of fingerprints, some measure of his emotions as he wrote out.

On impulse, Dyannis slid the scroll from its place and took it back to the desk. She imagined Eduin doing the very same thing on that day, perhaps this very same scroll. He would have carried it thus, placed it thus upon the surface.

Dyannis sensed an answering resonance as she removed the sleeve. It was so faint that had she not been thinking specifically of him, she would have missed it. He *had* handled the scroll.

She settled herself in the hard-backed chair and carefully opened the scroll. It was a historical chronicle, but as she read line after line of painfully precise calligraphy, she could not escape the feeling that much more had happened than was recorded. There were too many vague phrases, too many gaps. Something had been deliberately left unsaid. Suppressed? she wondered. Hidden?

On its surface, the scroll documented the events of a generation ago, sometimes called the Hastur Rebellion or the Hastur Wars, because then-King Rafael II had defied the will of the *Comyn* Council, taken the part of his niece, Taniquel Hastur-Acosta and single-handedly opposed Damian Deslucido of Ambervale. Dyannis struggled through the convoluted political rationale for the conflict. Deslucido had apparently laid claim to certain Hastur lands on the basis of a marriage between his son and Queen Taniquel. Rafael, speaking on her behalf, denied the validity of the marriage, saying that Taniquel, newly widowed by Deslucido's bloody conquest of Acosta, had refused consent.

She wouldn't be the first woman of rank to be forced into such a marriage, Dyannis thought furiously. *And unless she accepted her fate and pleased her new lord, as soon as the first son he'd sired on her was born and his claim to the throne secure, she would quietly disappear.*

The Council still held considerable sway, and even King Carolin had to obtain their approval before marrying Lady Maura Elhalyn, but Dyannis had never heard of them forcing an abhorrent match.

The two kings had clashed at Drycreek, which even now was unsafe for man or beast to approach, thanks to the bonewater dust Deslucido's sorcerer brother, Rumail, had unleashed. In the end, however, King Rafael had been victorious.

"... *and the terrible scourge eliminated forever* ..."

What an odd way to describe a military victory, Dyannis thought. She'd assumed Deslucido and his son had either been killed in battle, or else gone into exile. The brother, an outlaw *laranzu,* was presumed dead by his own villainy, for no trace of him was ever found. Vanquished Kings, like widowed Queens, tended to disappear with no one the sadder.

Dyannis brought her thoughts back to the present, rerolled the scroll, placed it in its sleeve and returned it to the storage rack. Whatever it was the historian had been at such pains to conceal must remain buried. She'd learn no more from these records.

The scroll clearly had nothing to do with *ancient Hastur lineages.* The only explanation for Eduin's interest was that he had been tracing the lives of King Rafael or Queen Taniquel.

Which meant Varzil might have been right, Eduin had some reason to hate Carolin Hastur, even when they were teenagers together at Arilinn. Had Eduin really attempted to kill Carolin? Dyannis did not entirely believe this, for she had sensed Eduin's love for Carolin, but decided to accept the premise to see where it led.

If Carolin, then why Felicia? To all appearances, she and Eduin had worked together in perfect amity at Hestral Tower.

Eduin couldn't have known she was a Hastur. Varzil said how carefully she guarded her secret. Eduin had no way of finding out—

Or had he?

The room went suddenly cold. Dyannis swayed upon her feet, and had to catch hold of a post of one of the storage racks to keep from falling. Like some monstrous volcanic eruption, the truth came boiling, hot and caustic, out of her memory.

He knew. He knew because I told him.

Dyannis lowered herself to the floor, heedless of the dust. Her heart beat like a wild thing against the prison of her ribcage. Acid rose in her throat and she swallowed hard to keep from retching.

"An insignificant Tower for a nobody pretender," that's what Eduin had said when she told him that Hestral Tower was going to train Felicia as under-Keeper. And then . . .

I told him.

Varzil would never have betrayed Felicia's secret. Varzil would have let the insult slide, but she in her pride had blurted it out.

It didn't matter that she had no reason to distrust Eduin. It didn't matter that he had secrets of his own, those parts of his mind that deflected any overture like polished steel.

In one moment of willful carelessness, she had destroyed the life of one of the most brilliant and courageous *leroni* of her generation, and her brother's beloved.

It was my fault, mine!

On some level, somewhere in the depths of her heart of hearts, she had always known what she had done. It was not her rash actions at the lake riot that spurred her to such tenacious guilt, but this far deeper transgression.

For what I have done, I cannot become a Keeper. I do not even deserve to live.

Slowly, Dyannis returned to herself. How long she had lain there, curled in a tortured ball on the floor of the archives, she could only guess. The slanting bar of light was gone, and outside the window lay a darkening sky. She trembled as she got to her feet, although the room was not cold. The chill came from deep within her. Her muscles shook as if she had worked without a break for a tenday, and her belly cramped.

Varzil would have railed at her for such emotional hysterics, such overdramatized, extravagant self-indulgence. He was right. Whether or not she was to blame for Felicia's death, she had no right to wallow in self-hatred. Or, she added ruefully, to leave her corpse for some poor novice to find.

I always do things the hard way.

With difficulty she moved toward the door. Her body needed water and food and rest. Her mind needed calmness in which to reason out her next step. Her spirit . . .

The disease that afflicted her spirit lay beyond the healing of any monitor or physician. She was not especially religious. The shrines of Cassilda or Dark Avarra offered her no solace. There was only one place where she might find a measure of respite, of quiet in which to decide what she must do next. She had scarcely thought of it for many long years.

I cannot leave without telling them. Raimon, as her Keeper, and Rorie, at least, deserved some word of where she was going, if not why.

As she made her way, slowly and painfully, back toward the living areas of Hali Tower, Dyannis gathered herself together. She did not want to encounter any of her colleagues, who would surely sense, even before they saw her face, that she had been through a terrible ordeal.

She stopped instead at the kitchen, where the cooks assumed she had just come from some especially draining *laran* work and showered her with dishes known to be restorative. At least they did not ask questions, though they hovered and clucked over her as she struggled with one mouthful after another of the rich food. At last, she felt her energy rise enough to make her way back to her own chambers, where she fell across her bed in a dreamless sleep.

Waking again was easier. Her body, with the resilience of youth, had mended itself. If she had no remedy for the anguish that gripped her soul, at least she had a plan. She washed in the basin of petal-scented water that had been laid out for her, pulled on a loose gown of green and gold, the Ridenow colors, and went to seek a last audience with her Keeper.

Raimon had clearly sensed her inner turmoil. He looked thoughtful, but made no attempt to reach her mind with his own. She had deliberately chosen to formally voice her request aloud as an expression of her separation from the Tower.

Dyannis refused his offer of a chair, preferring to stand. "I wish permission to return to my home," she said after the usual greetings had been exchanged.

"Are you also asking to be released from service here?" he asked.

She hesitated. One part of her mind said, *Yes,* and another said, *No, I would not close that door until I am sure,* and yet a third argued that although technically Raimon as her Keeper could free her from her oath, in practicality he would not do so without conferring with King Carolin, and she did not want to face her brother's dearest friend.

"That can be decided later," Raimon said smoothly. "Let us consider this a visit only. All of us need to return to our homes and families. You have not done so before, and perhaps it is time."

She lowered her head, grateful for his undemanding acceptance. There was far more to being a Keeper than simply organizing a group of Gifted minds into a circle.

"I will send to the city for a suitable escort as soon as it can be arranged," he went on. "Until then, you are excused from work in the circle, and if you wish, you may take your meals in your room. I will speak with the others on your behalf, so you need not be troubled."

It was too easy. For all her feeling of relief, she found an odd disappointment in the absence of a heated confrontation.

"I am not so disinterested as it seems," Raimon said as he rose in signal that their audience was over. "I only wish to speed your return. Clearly, there are matters which you must decide for yourself. No one can choose for you."

He thinks that after a time, I will hunger for my life here and my work as leronis. *But I can never return to what I was.*

27

Dyannis and her escort crested the last ridge and halted, letting their horses breathe. Below lay Sweetwater Valley, a cup of emerald velvet. It was just past noon in early spring, for they had stopped at an inn the afternoon before. Dyannis herself had insisted upon the rest, arguing that it was better to delay a day than to arrive late and exhausted.

She was not so sure about her own motivations. At first, she had been desperate to leave Hali. If she had lost the Tower and everyone who belonged to that life, it was better to depart at once, rather than linger on. Having set herself upon a course of action, she could not bear idleness.

As the days and leagues passed, however, the thoughts of what she was leaving behind, with all the pain and joy, the fellowship, the deeply satisfying work, receded. She was left to contemplate what lay before her.

Sweetwater. Home.

She had not given a great deal of consideration to what she would do when she got there. She had grown up on a country estate, not in a King's palace. Everyone worked, from the Lord himself to the lowliest pot boy. Even as a child, she had chores. She had only a small measure of the Ridenow Gift, empathy with nonhumans, but as a trained *leronis,* surely there would be some use for her talents.

Did she have the right to use them, after what she had done?

Do I have the right to throw all my training away?

Ah, that was a question Varzil would have asked.

Varzil... Try as she might to keep him from her thoughts, she could not escape the hard truth that she had, in some measure, caused the death of his beloved. She had injured him beyond reparation, beyond hope of forgiveness.

Dyannis nudged her horse with her heels and they started down the hill. The manor house below, the barns and storage sheds, the livestock corrals, the pond with its willow trees, were all very much as she had last seen them. In this world of horses and cattle, of age-weathered wood and tall grass rippling in the wind, the wars of men and Towers seemed very far away.

She reminded herself that, despite the appearance of pastoral tranquillity, Sweetwater was as much a part of the larger world as Hali. When her father had died, some years back, neither she nor Varzil had been able to return home because the roads were too dangerous. Now all the Ridenow lands stood poised on the brink of bloody conflict with their neighbors. The new Asturias general, nicknamed the Kilghard Wolf, was building a reputation for ruthless daring.

At least, Asturias does not have clingfire *to rain down upon us,* she thought. *At least, not yet.*

They were spotted before they had descended very far, and a handful of horsemen rode out to greet them. Dyannis recognized Black Eiric, now more gray than dark. Many of the men she had known as a child, old Raul the horseman and Eiric's own son Kevan, were gone, some to old age and others killed in raids by outlaws during the unsettled times of King Carolin's exile. The household *leronis* who had been the source of her first *laran* training had died of the same lung fever that carried off her father.

Black Eiric beamed at her. "Ah, it's the lass come back to us again. Lord Harald's out with the horse herd, for we did not look for you for a tenday yet."

Dyannis found herself smiling and returning his banter. "What, am

I now some Lowland lady who cannot travel a league from her door, but that she must stop and rest for three days?"

Black Eiric rolled his eyes and winked. *She has changed but little, our Dyannis.*

Dyannis started to reply, then realized that she was not intended to hear his thought. Black Eiric was a Ridenow cousin, with a good measure of the family Gift with animals, but no interest in formal training. He had made his decision long ago, to work here as paxman, first to old *Dom* Felix and now to his son, Harald.

The horses picked up the pace as they neared the stable yards. Black Eiric set about arranging for the care of their animals and lodging for the men.

Dyannis went up to the house. Broad wooden steps led to a wide porch where she remembered playing with dolls and toy soldiers on the long summer evenings. She paused for a moment in the outer chamber. Here, boots and outer gear, drenched or caked with mud, would be exchanged for indoor clothing. This had been at her mother's insistence, and it looked as if Harald still kept the custom. Dyannis felt the sting of tears, utterly unexpected. She could barely remember her mother, for she was the youngest of the children.

What would she think of me, of Varzil, of these times we live in?

Dyannis took a breath and pushed open the inner door. Harald's wife, Rohanne, who was now lady of Sweetwater, rushed forward to meet her amid exclamations and kisses. Dyannis, whose nerves were already scoured raw, recoiled against the effusive display of affection. The years spent at Hali among telepaths, for whom even a casual physical touch might feel like a violation, had left her with few defenses against such well-meaning intrusion. It took an act of discipline not to push the woman away. Dyannis resorted to pleading fatigue.

"But of course, my dear, you must be absolutely drained! So many days with no company but those rude men." Rohanne did not add, although she thought it so loudly that Dyannis could not help but hear, *Your hair! Your complexion! Your attire!* Dyannis had worn a comfortable, loose-fitted jacket, boots, and split skirt suitable for riding astride, instead of a proper lady's gown.

At last, Dyannis escaped into her old room. It seemed to have shrunk in size since she was a child, for only a few strides took her from one corner to the other. White-flowered ivy had grown up around the window, filtering the light. She sat on the bed and patted the old quilt. The patches had been worn to flannel softness.

Once I could not wait to get away from this place and go to Hali, and then I could not wait to leave there and return home. Now . . . now she was sure of nothing, except that she no longer belonged in either place.

Sighing, she curled on her side. The bed creaked softly under her weight. Someone had folded a sachet of dried blossoms under the pillow. The scent stirred memories of a tall woman with long blonde hair, strong arms, and soft breasts, of being rocked gently, of the uncomplicated comfort of this very same bed. Something deep within her loosened. Sighing, she closed her eyes. All she needed was a little rest . . .

Dyannis startled awake to the sound of commotion below. Only a dim light came through the ivied window and the wisp of breeze had turned cold. She rubbed the sleep from her eyes.

I must be careful of this place or I will start reacting like the girl I was. Given the slightest encouragement, Rohanne would fuss over her like a mother barnfowl over her wayward chick.

Someone had entered the room while she slept. Her baggage had been unpacked, her gowns laid neatly in the chest. Arrayed on the table, her hairbrushes sat in a neat row beside the small carved box that contained her hair clasps and a few pieces of jewelry. A basin, ewer of water, towel, and a small cake of soap had also been laid out.

She straightened her rumpled riding skirt, smoothed her hair, checked the result in the tiny, badly scratched mirror on the table, and went downstairs.

Harald had always been an active man, and the years had solidified him. The golden beard was now silvered bronze, the waist thickened but not slack, the skin of his face weathered. He shouted out commands and questions in a voice more suited to the open fields than the confines of a great house.

They had never been playfellows, for he was the oldest of five siblings, and she the youngest. He was already a stripling youth when she was born, and she could not remember a time when he had been anything but her overbearing older brother. It had been a long time since any man besides her Keeper had the right to command her.

"You are most welcome home, *breda*," he said with genuine pleasure. "It has been too long since we last saw you."

"I thank you for your hospitality," she replied. "I am truly sorry that my duties have prevented an earlier visit."

"Yes, but now we are together again as one family," he said. "We will feast tonight in honor of your return. Rohanne!"

The lady had already glided silently to his side. "What is it, my husband?"

"Does my sister have everything she needs?"

"I am quite comfortably settled into my old room," Dyannis answered for herself.

"That will not do—a child's chamber for a grown lady. We must find something more suitable for her. And what about—" Harald gestured with his hands, "—gowns and all the things a woman needs."

Dyannis broke out laughing, quickly smothered at Rohanne's shocked expression. "I am sorry if my traveling attire offends you, brother. At the Tower, we pay little attention to such things when we are working. As for my room, I would be offended if it were *not* my old familiar quarters. If I wanted a suite of fine chambers and servants everywhere, I would have gone to Thendara and visited Carolin!"

Harald huffed and said that was all very well, but as *Comynara* and Ridenow, she deserved the best.

My poor brother, he does not know what to make of me!

Dyannis slipped her arm through her sister-in-law's. "Then I must look especially elegant tonight, or my brother will think we are all savages at Hali. Will you help me to choose a gown for dinner?"

Rohanne looked doubtful, but came along. She regained her composure as Dyannis brought out the single good gown she had brought, simply cut in exquisitely soft gray-green wool. The neckline was perhaps a little low for country manners; she had worn it, crossed by a tartan in the Ridenow colors of gold and green, to informal affairs at Carolin's court. Rohanne made cooing sounds over the workmanship, the fineness of the weaving, the elegant geometric embroidery along the sleeves, the drape of the skirts.

"I will send my own maid to arrange your hair," Rohanne told Dyannis, brushing back a stray tendril from her forehead. "And do not say you can do it on your own, for I cannot believe that even sorcery can manage these curls. You have pretty hair, though it is hardly at its best after such a long journey. Once we have settled you with a maid of your own, she will put it to rights."

"I am not accustomed to needing help with either my clothing or my hair." Dyannis did not want to offend Rohanne, just when the emotional atmosphere between them was softening. If she had a maidservant hovering about, she might never know a moment's peace.

Rohanne gave her a look. "Now that you are here, you must take your rightful place as a Ridenow *Comynara,* even as Harald said. I suppose it may be difficult to adjust to the responsibilities as well as the privileges, as you leave behind your life in the Tower."

"I—I am not sure we understand one another," Dyannis said. Rohanne had a manner of speaking that, for all its superficial politeness, she found intrusive to the point of rudeness. "You speak as if I am to remain here permanently."

Rohanne arched her perfectly groomed eyebrows. "That is not for me to decide. You had best speak to *Dom* Harald of such matters, as he is the head of the family."

Dyannis frowned. If she did not know her own intentions, how could she talk to her brother? How could she begin to explain all the things she had experienced, from the day she first took her place in a working circle, to the dragon she had summoned at Hali Lake, to the rebuilding of Cedestri Tower? The surge of *laran* power, the bliss of submerging her consciousness in a circle, the shock of a dying mind in hers? How could anyone outside a Tower truly understand her dilemma?

As for Harald, he might have only minimal *laran* and no formal training, but surely he would respect whatever decision she came to. He had seen for himself what *laran* could accomplish when Varzil had done the impossible, negotiating psychically with the catmen who held Harald captive.

I will tell him when the time comes, Dyannis decided. Meanwhile, it was best not to say anything further.

Shortly thereafter, Rohanne excused herself. Dyannis set about washing her face and hands. The soap was as fine as any she had ever seen, and left a faint clean scent on her skin. She wished she could so easily wash away her own indecision. The truth, she grudgingly admitted to herself, was that she had no idea how long she intended to remain. She had fled Hali, giving no thought to anything beyond her own desperate guilt. Was Sweetwater a haven or an exile? Only time would reveal the answer.

She sat on the edge of the bed and freed her hair from the simple wooden clasp. Beginning at the ends, she attacked the tangles that had so offended Rohanne. This was the one part of traveling she did not enjoy. By the time camp was ready or dinner at the inn finished, the last thing she wanted was to spend an hour wrestling with her curls. She winced as the tines of the comb caught on a particularly tight knot.

A quick, light knock sounded on the door. At her invitation, a woman about her own age, wearing a neat apron and cap over a gray dress, entered. She set down her covered basket just inside the door and curtsied.

"Rella!" Dyannis exclaimed. "I had no idea Rohanne meant you!"

"It's been that long, *Domna* Dyannis," Rella said, beaming. "I didn't think you'd remember me after so long, and you off to such fine places as Hali and Thendara." Her eyes shone and Dyannis caught her eager curiosity.

"Hali is indeed fine, but I've seen little of Thendara, beyond the few times Carolin invited us to his court. Mostly, I work hard, and almost entirely at night. Matrix work may sound glamorous, but much of it is tedious."

Except, she reflected, *when people are rushing at you with axes and arrows, bent on killing you. Or you find yourself in the middle of a burning Tower.*

"You have met King Carolin! Is he handsome?"

"Yes, very, but I do not know him well. He and Varzil—you remember my brother?—became close friends when they were at Arilinn together. Surely you have heard how they rebuilt Neskaya Tower, where Varzil is now Keeper?"

"Oh, yes! The minstrels sing of it!"

Dyannis reflected that ballad and reality were often not at all the same. "So you are to arrange my hair? Can you make any order from this?"

Rella placed Dyannis on a stool in the middle of the room, remarking that she needed a proper dressing table, and began combing her hair with such a deft, light strokes that Dyannis scarcely felt a tug. She plaited the hair and coiled it low on the neck, then added a coronet of braided ribbons and tiny silver bells.

"There now, you are as beautiful as Queen Maura!" Rella exclaimed, standing back to admire her handiwork.

"Oh, hardly that." Dyannis studied herself in the mirror. The scratched reflection seemed younger and more innocent. She had worn bells in her hair like this on that fateful Midwinter Festival Ball, when she had first met Eduin.

"Don't you like it?" Rella asked. "Perhaps a different color ribbon—"

"Leave it." Dyannis made a dismissive gesture, which seemed to only increase Rella's agitation.

"I am to dress you as well, and I have brought rouge and powder."

Sighing, Dyannis allowed Rella to help her into the green gown. She had chosen the style because there were no laces or buttons up the back that required another pair of hands, but she would not have the girl return to her mistress with her tasks undone. She drew the line at painting her face.

"I am as the gods made me," she told the maid, "and if that does not please my brother's wife, she must take her complaints to them."

Harald beamed when he saw Dyannis. He wore his own finery, including the heavy silver chain that had been old *Dom* Felix's prized possession. His children, two boys and a girl, came out to greet Dyannis.

The oldest boy would reach puberty soon, and Dyannis sensed the stirrings of his *laran*. She must speak to Harald about the proper precautions, should the boy be prone to threshold sickness. Nausea and disorientation, sometimes with irritability and visual disturbances, could lead, if untreated, to life-threatening convulsions. Before she was born, her own older brother and sister, twins, had died during the psychic upheavals of adolescence. She had heard the story a hundred times, mostly as a warning when she had been naughty. Varzil, who had more *laran* than the entire family put together, had passed so smoothly through his own youth that for a time, their father had difficulty believing in the strength of his talent.

Either the family dined far more elegantly than Dyannis remembered from her childhood, or else the cook had outdone herself in preparing a feast on such short notice. There was so much meat, and

Harald pressed her so earnestly to take more, that she ate far more than she normally would. Hali's cook tended to be sparing with meat. Some *leronyn* refused to eat any animal flesh whatsoever, and others restricted themselves to fish, claiming that meat dampened their powers. Dyannis had never noticed any difference.

Not that I will have any need of laran *out here,* Dyannis thought as she accepted a third helping of beef swimming in its own rich juices.

"So you have at last grown weary of life in the Tower?" Harald said. "I never expected you to endure this long, for you were ever a lively, strong-willed lass. To think of you, cloistered away like some *cristoforo* monk! But they did not send you packing, in the end." His voice held a hint of a question.

"No, coming home was my own choice. No matter what you have heard, we are hardly *cloistered,*" Dyannis replied, thinking of the freedom with which the Tower women took lovers, earned their own money, and made decisions about their lives, things that would have been scandalous anywhere else. "Ever since my first day as a novice at Hali, I have loved the work."

"Even being under the command of your Keeper?" Harald raised one eyebrow in disbelief.

"Yes," she replied, smiling. "Even that. If you had known Dougal or Raimon, you would not need to ask. Oh, I complained as much as any novice, but in the end, I gladly accepted the discipline, just as you submitted yourself to Father when he taught you to use a sword." She paused, choosing her next words with care. "Even the most rewarding work becomes a burden when mind and spirit are stretched too far. After Isoldir, I needed a rest."

Dyannis went on to briefly relate the events at Cedestri, for her family had heard little of it.

"I simply cannot not believe it, that you traveled through such dangerous country, and in the middle of a war!" Rohanne exclaimed. "What was Varzil thinking, to bring you into such peril? Were you not terrified?"

Dyannis found herself smiling gently. "Sister-in-law, I was too *busy* to be frightened. We reached Cedestri Tower right after the firebombing, and there were many wounded to attend to. After the worst of them were mending, Varzil and I, along with those *leronyn* who could still work, set about repairing the relay screens and rebuilding the walls with our *laran*. Otherwise, it might have taken a generation or more."

Rohanne's brows drew together. "It is not seemly to send gently-born women into such situations. It is the natural instinct of men to protect them instead of attending to their own duties."

"I am no hothouse flower, but a trained *leronis*," Dyannis replied patiently. "I assure you, I worked as hard as any of the men."

"All that is behind you now," Rohanne said. "We are glad to have you here amongst us, where you are safe."

"I am happy to hear that you have so far been spared the horrors of warfare," Dyannis said. "May it be ever so. If Carolin and Varzil succeed in persuading others to forswear their most terrible *laran* weapons, your children may indeed see a new and glorious era of peace."

"What do you know of such things?" Harald meant the question as rhetorical, and looked startled when Dyannis answered him seriously.

"Hali Tower now abides by the Compact, and has pledged to make no *laran* weapons and take no part in any fight," she said. "But during the reign of Rakhal the Usurper, my fellow *leronyn* took to the battlefield. I helped to make *clingfire*, and was lucky enough to come through that ordeal unscarred."

Dyannis shuddered, for she had once had to cut away the burning flesh of a Hali worker when one of the glass vessels shattered during the distillation of the caustic stuff. She thought, too, of the devastation she had seen at Cedestri, the charred, blood-stained bodies, of the frenzied mob at the lake, of Rorie with an arrow in his chest . . .

No, she would not speak of these memories.

Rohanne had been staring at her, open-mouthed and, for once, speechless. Harald glanced at his wife, his concern for her clear in the set of his jaw, the furrow between his brows. "Women should not have to think of such things as *laran* weapons."

"*No one* should!" Seeing his sharp look, Dyannis wished she had held her tongue. He was her host as well as her eldest brother, and it was ungracious of her to provoke him with talk of politics. More gently, she added, "If it be the will of the gods, we will see that dream become reality. Surely that is something all people of good will desire."

Visibly relieved, he raised his goblet and called for another round of wine. "Let us drink to that day."

28

On her journey from Hali, Dyannis had become accustomed to rising early. Despite the heavy dinner and wine of the night before, she came downstairs as the household servants began their day's work. She found breakfast laid out. The dishes of boiled eggs, sausages, and freshly-baked bread were still warm.

She helped herself to spiced apples, a slice of fragrant bread, and a smear of soft cheese. Just as she sat down at the table, one of the maids, a fresh-faced girl she didn't recognize, trotted in with a pitcher of *jaco*.

"Is my brother about?"

The girl dropped a curtsy. "Yes, *damisela*. He's already left with the men and won't be back till dinner."

"Yes, of course." There was no point asking what he'd be doing, for the maid's tone made it clear this was "men's work," and of no proper concern to ladies.

"And Lady Rohanne?"

"She takes her breakfast upstairs." The girl dimpled with a trace of mischief. "Much later."

"Oh, I see." Such languor was fashionable among ladies at Carolin's court. Dyannis wondered if Rohanne expected her to do the same. She left the fruit, smeared the cheese on the bread, and went out to the yard.

The stables were empty except for a sedate white mare, probably Rohanne's mount. In the corral, a few rough-coated horses, working stock, watched Dyannis with curious eyes. She thought of taking a hawk from the mews, but there was no need for extra meat, and like all the empathic Ridenow, she disliked killing things, even small birds, without good cause.

Having no other demands upon her time, Dyannis went in search of her niece and nephews. The two younger ones were occupied in the nursery, but she found Lerrys, the older boy, in one of her own favorite childhood haunts, the loft above the tack room. The familiar smell of oiled leather, hay, and horses brought a smile to her lips.

"May I join you?" she called, one foot on the ladder.

"You want to come up *here?*" His voice cracked a little.

Dyannis laughed and climbed up. Except for the makeshift table, the place looked exactly as it had when she used to hide here so many years ago. She picked up a wooden horse and examined its belly. The paint had been worn away, leaving the pale-gold wood, but she found her initials where she had scratched them with a knife stolen from the kitchen.

"What do you call him?" she asked, setting the horse back beside the other wooden animals, deer and *chervines,* two other horses that had obviously been repainted, and a Dry Towns *oudrakhi* with only three legs.

"Pacer."

"Oh?" Dyannis settled herself on one of the tattered pillows, tucking her skirts under her. That had been Varzil's name when the toy had first been made for him. They'd almost come to blows when she tried to rename it "Sunshine." She wondered if the boy might have picked up some psychic residue from the horse. Varzil had powerful *laran* even as a child, enough to leave an invisible trace for anyone sensitive enough to read it.

Lerrys looked away, flushing.

"It's as good a name as any," she said carelessly. "Come, tell me what the others are doing. You've arranged them in such an interesting way. It looks as if they are speaking to one another."

In response, he began stuffing the toys into a canvas sack. The last one, the *oudrakhi,* he held for a moment, as if weighing it. His eyes flickered to her, then he shoved it in with the others.

Even as Varzil did, he has learned to hide his feelings, especially those his father cannot understand.

"I used to play with those very same animals when I was a girl, did you know?" She underscored the overture with a gentle psychic nudge.

He shrugged. "I guessed they belonged to somebody, my father or Uncle Varzil."

"Oh, yes, he had them before me, but everything he had, I wanted, do you see? So even before he left for Arilinn, I'd sneak up here and play with them."

"My sister is like that, too," Lerrys said, brightening. "She'd be up here right now, except Mother wants her to act like a little lady."

Dyannis made a face. "Poor thing, do you suppose she's inflicting embroidery practice on her? I hated needlework, always have. Sticking little pointy things where they don't belong, ugh! I'd much rather be up here or on a horse. Do you ever go out to those caves beyond the sheep pastures?"

"Where Uncle Varzil rescued Father?" The boy's eyes widened. "Father would *kill* me if I went out there!"

"Let me tell you, *my* father wasn't too happy about it, either." *But I went, anyway.*

"You *did?*"

She nodded, suppressing a surge of excitement. He'd heard her unspoken thought and responded, in an unguarded moment. "Lerrys, may I touch you?"

He looked puzzled, but held out a grubby hand for her. She took it between her own, a perfect contact, and reached out with her *laran* . . .

When Dyannis closed her eyes, the pattern of nodes and channels of the boy's energetic body glowed like a constellation of brightly-colored spheres joined by white-gold cords. She searched further, looking for congestion, the shift toward reds and muddy browns, disruption of flow. Yes, down along the pathways leading to the lower body, she spied the warning signs. As she watched, the colors darkened, pulsing.

The boy's hand trembled between her own. As she released him, he

blushed again. She caught a surge of embarrassment, of sexual awareness. Here he was, alone with his young and pretty aunt, *holding hands.*

"Lerrys, how old are you?"

"Fourteen."

"Hmmm." She would have guessed twelve from his size, but Varzil,
too, had always been slender. "I can't keep track of who was born
when."

"It's all right."

"Are you ever sick to your stomach for no good reason? Or out of
sorts, quick of temper? Or do your eyes play tricks on you?"

"What do you think I am, crazy?" He drew back, and she knew from
the vehemence of his denial how deeply troubled he had been by these
symptoms.

She shook her head. "I am a *leronis,* trained at Hali. I do not ask these
questions lightly, or as an insult." How much did the boy know? Did he
realize the risk? "Do you have a starstone? Might I see it?"

If Lerrys kept it at the bottom of a chest of toys, or some other separate location, then his *laran* might be as yet unawakened. He fumbled
at his waist, beneath his shirt, where he wore a strip of cloth folded to
make a sash. He drew out a small bluish crystal and held it up. The interior was as yet dim, untouched by inner fire.

"Here." Without warning, he tossed it in her direction.

By reflex, Dyannis caught the crystal, and then in horror realized
what she had done. She thrust the stone back into his hands and folded
his fingers around it.

"Never do that again!" Although she was not skilled in the use of the
commanding Voice, as Varzil was, Dyannis was powerful enough to re-
inforce her words telepathically. The boy flinched visibly.

"You may think this is only a pretty toy, a trinket," she plunged on,
"but once you have attuned it to your mind, it is your very life. Do you
understand me? No one else must *ever* be allowed to handle it, except a
Keeper."

Except a Keeper.

The world fell away beneath her.

"You don't understand," Lerrys said, clearly unhappy. "I *can't* have
laran. Oh, enough so Father can present me to the Council. But anything more only brings trouble."

Dyannis pulled herself back to the present. "We are as the gods made us, *chiyu,* and not as our fathers," *or brothers,* "would have us. If you have been given the talent, nothing anyone says will change that. It's no surprise, considering how many of your relatives have strong *laran.*"

He looked unhappy. "Aunt Dyannis, I know you mean well, but truly, it would be best not to say anything to Father. You don't know how he gets when his mind is set."

"Your grandfather, *Dom* Felix, was the same way. Harald is very like him." At first, their father had flatly refused to allow Varzil to train at Arilinn. Dyannis hoped Lerrys wouldn't have the same difficulties. If necessary, she could appeal to Varzil. After all, Harald owed him his life.

— ✦ —

Harald did not return that night until well after the rest of the family had dined. From Rohanne's lack of concern, Dyannis gathered this was the rule during the working seasons. The dinner honoring her return had been a special occasion.

She retreated to her room, rather than be left alone with Rohanne. Although she tried to meditate, her mind would not be calmed. When she rose to pace, the sensation of suffocation only intensified. The closeness of the walls, the constant reminders of a time when she was small and subject to the orders of older men, pressed in on her like the bars of a dungeon.

Gods, how had she ever stood it? How had *Varzil,* with his powerful Gift awakening in him so young, ever stood it?

She remembered standing before her father, *Dom* Felix, half-crazed with anticipation of leaving. A change had come over him ever since he had given his blessing for Varzil to enter training at Arilinn Tower. Before that, he would never have agreed to let her go, not even when the household *leronis* pleaded with him.

"Dyannis is at grave risk if she remains here, and you know it."

Dyannis, then about the same age as Lerrys was now, had felt the passionate words of the old *leronis* even here, in her own room. They seemed to hang upon the air even now, so many years later.

"The danger comes not from the threshold sickness that carried off Anndra and Sylvie, but from the very power of her Gift. I tell you, if you keep her caged like a

songbird, or marry her off to some head-blind oaf who will get one brat after another upon her, or try to thrash that indomitable spirit out of her, you might as well slit her throat now and be done with it!"

She had crept down the hall to hear the rumble of his answer.

"I have lost too many I love. My wife, two of my babes, and now Varzil gone."

Gently came the woman's response: *"It is your only hope of getting her back, to let her go."*

And so, Dyannis thought, *I have come full circle of my own accord.*

Sensitized as she was, she felt Harald's return. It seemed she was retracing the past in more ways than one, making her way down that same corridor to the chamber that had once been her father's and now belonged to her eldest brother. She tapped on the door and heard his invitation to enter.

Stepping inside, she could not shake off the sensation of moving into the past. The outer chamber still had the same heavy, dark-polished wooden chairs, the table with its bowl of sugar-dusted nuts, the grate in the patchstone fireplace. Harald stood sideways, stirring the kindling. For an instant, she saw—not him, but their father. Then he moved and the illusion vanished.

She gathered herself like the skilled *leronis* she was and seated herself near the fire. "I must speak to you about Lerrys. He is very near the time when his *laran* will awaken, and I believe it will be strong. You should take precautions, should he develop threshold sickness."

"Surely, he's too young, and we have had no such problems in a long while."

"He is *not* too young," she said flatly. "I have seen this before, at Hali, where a delayed puberty produces exceptionally powerful upheavals in both sexual energy and *laran*. Believe me, he is—"

"Silence! Enough!" Harald rounded on her. "You may be my sister, but I will not permit any woman in my house to speak such filth."

Dyannis was so stunned, she could only stare at him. In the Tower, physiology and health, even sexuality, were discussed frankly, without any hint of shame.

"You are not to mention such things again! It is not seemly, nor is it modest, as becomes a decent woman."

She got to her feet. "I am speaking of your son's health, perhaps even his life. What could be more decent than that?"

"There is no problem. He is a strong, healthy boy."

"Yes, but he will soon become a man and therein lies the danger. Have you forgotten what happened to Anndra and Sylvie?"

"Better than you!" For an instant, he looked as if he might strike her, but then he softened his tone. "He is my son and heir. I will not send him away from Sweetwater." *As Varzil was sent, and then lost to us. He could not even return home when Father died.*

Her heart ached for him. "Perhaps that will not be necessary. You are not without resources. I trained first as a monitor at Hali and I know how to handle many aspects of threshold sickness. If you will permit it, I will do what I can."

Harald inclined his head. "It is said, *Bare is brotherless back.* In these perilous times, we must all of us, sisters as well as brother, stand together."

Dyannis nodded, already planning what she would need. "Do you have a supply of *kirian,* perhaps stored with the other medicinals?"

"I doubt it," Harald replied, scratching his head. "That is, unless there's some left over from your time. There's been no need since you left."

There would be little call for the psychoactive distillate outside a Tower, except for the treatment of threshold sickness. Dyannis knew a dozen other uses for it, but only for *laran*-associated disorders.

She sat down again and drummed her fingers on the wooden arm of the chair. "Unless it's been wax-sealed and undisturbed all these years, it will have lost its potency. I'd better make some fresh." She glanced out the window, where clouds, wind-driven, scudded across the sky. Her body remembered the rhythm of the seasons here; spring had hardly begun, and there would still be snow on the heights, and more storms to come.

"It will be another month, I think, before I can gather the *kireseth,*" she commented.

Harald scowled.

"Don't look at me like that," Dyannis said lightly. "I've done this before. Everyone at Hali is trained in the preparation of something as necessary as *kirian.*"

"I do not doubt your competence," he said. "It is your business as a *leronis* to know such things. But there is no *kireseth* within a day's ride. You will have to travel high into the hills and that is too dangerous."

"Harald, I am a Ridenow. I learned to ride before I could walk, even as you did."

He shook his head. "But not to wield a sword. Asturias grows more belligerent with each passing season, and all the lands between us are rife with displaced and lawless men. So far, Sweetwater has remained unmolested, but with the end of winter, I cannot tell how long the peace will hold. As head of this family, I am responsible for your welfare. The only way I will permit you to go that far is with an armed escort."

"I do not think that wise," Dyannis said. The pollen of the bell-shaped flowers could produce dangerous, unpredictable hallucinations in both men and beasts. "I am trained to handle the *kireseth* pollen, but I do not want the responsibility for anyone else. Swords cannot protect ordinary men against an inadvertent exposure."

She did not want to provoke a quarrel in which Lerrys would be the real loser. Harald was only thinking of her welfare, as both her brother and lord of Sweetwater. She reminded herself that none of the men here were strangers to natural dangers. Some of them might have weathered a Ghost Wind, an unseasonable release of *kireseth* pollen.

"I will respect your wishes in this," she said, "so long as *I* may use my best judgment regarding the other risks."

Harald consented, although he was clearly unhappy about letting her go so far from the main house. Soon after, Dyannis took her leave. She knew she should be satisfied, for his concession was more gracious than she expected, but she could not shake off the feeling there was something important she had missed.

— ◆ —

As spring settled on the land in earnest, the days grew longer, the air milder, the smells of budding trees and moist earth more pungent. Dyannis awoke, fully alert and rested, two hours before dawn. Pushing the bedcovers aside, she rose and went to the window. Her body ached from inactivity. She had been at Sweetwater for a full month now, and had not had the opportunity to ride much beyond the yard. Her escort had returned to Thendara after a few days' rest. After the first flurry of welcome, the estate continued about its business. Rohanne repeatedly urged her to sit and embroider, which Dyannis had so far found one excuse after another to decline. The rest of the time, she had been left to her own entertainment with the constant assurance that she need not bestir herself.

Bestir myself? Drive myself mad!

Outside, the gardens and yard were washed in pastel, multihued light. Craning her neck, she saw three of the four moons spread like gemstones across the sky. She could almost hear them calling to her.

On impulse, she pulled on her boots and traveling clothes. Downstairs, servants were already about their work, and the smell of baking bread rose from the kitchen.

In the stables, men mucked out stalls and carried in fodder and buckets of water. Horses moved restlessly in their stalls. Dyannis, not wanting to explain herself, slipped into the tack room, took up a bridle, and went out to the corral where the working horses pawed the last of their morning's ration of hay. These were hard, rough-broken mounts, not the docile mare Rohanne used. They snorted and jumped as she entered the enclosure.

Dyannis reached out with her *laran,* soothing the nervous beasts. They watched her with wary, curious eyes and allowed her to move among them. She chose a small, sturdy roan gelding, one she could mount bareback without too much difficulty.

Will you carry me, little brother? she asked, stroking the coarse gray mane.

In response, the horse bent his head and nuzzled her shoulder. He stood quietly as she slipped the bit into his mouth and tucked the strap behind his ears. Speaking softly, she led him from the corral. One of the stable hands called out to her, but she waved at him and sent a mental suggestion that all was as it should be, and he turned back to his work.

Once beyond the yard, she slipped the reins over the horse's head, took a double handful of mane, and managed to scramble on to his back. His spine was bonier than she expected and she'd be sore the next day, but she didn't care. She clucked to the horse and tapped him with her heels, turning him in the direction of the hilly pastures. He went off willingly and once they were well clear of the house grounds, moved from a walk to a bone-jarring trot and then into a rocking canter.

Dyannis laced her hands in the horse's mane, feeling the animal's muscles bunch and surge between her legs. Wind brushed her cheeks and ruffled her hair. She inhaled the horse smell, the sweetness of the grass, and the cool moistness of the coming dawn.

The horse, sensing her mood, bounded forward. For that instant, she felt nothing but the rushing air and the muscled strength beneath her, saw only the milky skies above, the rising gray-green hills. She and the horse became a single creature, plunging between earth and heaven. Together they inhaled fire and breathed it out again, straining at the bounds of flesh. She felt sun and wind, grass and stone, the thrust of bone and muscle.

Run away . . . run far away . . . pounded through her mind to the rhythm of the horse's galloping hooves.

She bent low over his neck, as if she could merge with the beast, leaving behind all human thoughts, all memory, all desire. Above her, beyond the brightening sky, the moons swung through a field of stars. Distant creatures fought and mated, swam and danced, howled out their lonely anguish to those same stars. . . .

Dyannis jerked free from her reverie so sharply the horse shied, stung by the abrupt rupture of their bond. The roan plunged sideways, lowering his head as if to buck.

She had heard, no—*felt* something. Only a mind attuned to the natural world could have picked up the faint, far harmonic.

The Ya-men wailing beneath the moons. Varzil had described hearing them as a boy, but no one believed him then. Their father had thought him fanciful, deluded, and certainly devoid of any respectable *laran*. Varzil had turned out to be the most powerful Keeper on Darkover. Perhaps his story had been true.

By the time she slowed her panting, sweating horse, the great red sun stood above the horizon. The roan pulled at the bit, clearly wanting to keep running. Heat radiated from his body.

Dyannis glanced back the way they had come. They were well up in the hills, beyond the sight of the house. Something inside her relaxed, unfolded. For the first time in longer than she could remember, she was alone, truly alone. She opened her mind and sensed only the simple emotions of beasts—the horse beneath her, rabbit-horns with their new babies hiding in their burrows, a hawk circling, mice and birds, the distant contentment of sheep beyond the ridge of hills. And there, hidden in their fastnesses, the Ya-men and their song.

And she had the *laran* to hear them.

She could not outrun what she was, any more than she could bury herself in the consciousness of a racing horse. Sweetwater was a respite, not a destination.

29

Dyannis went to gather the *kireseth* for the preparation of *kirian,* accompanied by Harald's escort. She found the clusters of bell-shaped blossoms, laden with pollen, high in the hills. At her insistence, the men remained at a safe distance. The harvest went without incident, for the day was still, almost windless, and the pollen lay like golden dust upon the petals. She wrapped the flowers carefully, stowed them in a sealed leather satchel, and carried them to the stone-walled still house.

She moved about the room she'd set up as a laboratory, rinsing, measuring, preparing for distilling. With her sleeves rolled up, hair covered with an old scarf, and an apron tied around her waist, she felt like a working *leronis* and not some pampered and useless lady. The work settled her, reminded her of the skills she had trained so hard to acquire.

Dyannis found herself singing, but the tune turned sad, shot through with loss. The more time went by, one tenday melting into the next, the greater was her longing for the life of the Tower. She wished Varzil were there, or Ellimara, or even Rorie, so that she would have someone to talk to and reason things out with. Harald would not understand, and there was no hope for a serious conversation on any topic with Rohanne. Besides, Harald had all the cares of running a large estate to contend with. Dyannis decided it was best to keep her own counsel.

She had only enough pollen for a single bottle of *kirian,* but that would be more than enough to see Lerrys through the worst. Perhaps the boy would have a smooth transition, or need only a little care. Some adolescents learned to manage the milder symptoms of threshold sickness with simple meditation techniques. Dyannis had already begun working with Lerrys, teaching him elementary concentration exercises, when he would permit it. It wasn't easy to hold his interest; many times, she had to break off a session they'd barely begun when Harald sent for the boy for some chore or other. Lerrys was old enough to be learning the management of the estate that would one day be his.

"I know there's little for you to do here at the house," Harald said to Dyannis with unexpected insight. "If you want to do something useful, the wife of one of my tenant farmers, Braulio, is near her time to give birth. Perhaps you could help her, as we have no midwife at this time."

Dyannis agreed with some hesitation. If she weren't careful, Harald would plan out her future for her, maybe even marry her off before she was too old.

After a suitable introduction to the husband, she rode out on her favorite roan gelding to meet the pregnant woman. She found Annalise to be an active, pleasant women, her belly hugely rounded with her second child. Their home, a large cottage with three rooms, looked well made, the plot of vegetables bountiful. Annalise looked up from gathering a basket of early summer greens. A sturdy, golden-haired boy of three or four ran after her, laughing.

When Dyannis offered to assist at the birth, the woman blushed and stammered, "Oh, but you're a grand lady, a *leronis* of Hali. 'Tis not for the likes of me—I mean—"

"I have often tended ordinary people, even beggars, when there was need," Dyannis told her.

"Old Kyra was still with us when my first babe came," Annalise said, kicking off her garden clogs as she stepped across the threshold and gestured for Dyannis to enter. "I didn't think he'd ever be born, he took so long. Now that I know the way of it, I'm not so afeared." She moved awkwardly about the kitchen area, setting the vegetables in a pan of water.

Dyannis thought of King Carolin's first wife, who had died in child-birth with their third baby. One successful pregnancy did not guaran-tee the next, and a laboring woman's life was always at some risk, but it would be insensitive to say so. Perhaps confidence in her own abilities was a woman's greatest strength.

She said, "I'd still be happy to keep you company during your time, even if you don't need me. It's women's work, don't you think?"

At this point, Annalise giggled, "Aye, and best to keep the menfolk well out of it. Old Kyra had to order my Braulio clear out of the house!"

Dyannis sat at the clean-scrubbed table, sipping last fall's apple cider and watching the toddler play with a stack of beautifully carved wooden blocks. *This is all any woman should want,* she thought. *A good hus-band, a healthy son, a house of her own, a garden to tend.*

Then, as if to answer herself: *I am not any woman. I am Dyannis of Hali.*

— ◆ —

About a tenday later, Braulio rushed up to the manor house in the mid-dle of the night. Annalise had gone into labor. Dyannis pulled on an old gown of Rella's, one she would not mind getting soiled, and rode out to the cottage. The first thing she did upon arrival was to order Braulio out of the house.

"Chop wood," she told him, "boil water, and bring me a lantern. And clean rags! Lots of clean rags!"

Annalise cried out in relief when Dyannis entered the bedroom. The laboring woman was breathing hard and sweating. The night was unusually warm, even for early summer. She'd thrown back her shift and lay half-naked on the bed on a folded, much-patched old quilt. Using both her hands and her *laran,* Dyannis checked the position of the baby. As far as she could tell, for she had assisted at only a couple of births, the baby's head was almost at the birth canal.

"It won't be long now," she told Annalise. "A fine strong daughter." That much she had been able to easily determine.

"Oh!" Annalise's body tensed and for a time, she could not talk. "So soon?"

"Yes, it is often so, after the first," Dyannis said. "Here, let me wipe your face. You must hold my hand when your pains come." Immediately, Annalise gripped her hand. "Breathe now," Dyannis urged, "that's a good girl."

"I—I want to push!"

Dyannis sensed the shift in energy of the woman's body, the demanding need to bear down. She held Annalise's hand and reached out with her *laran* to the baby. The position was good, as best she could tell through the intense pressure of the birth passage. Then, at the peak of the labor pain, Dyannis sensed a ripple, a stutter. It disappeared as the pain eased, as if it had never been. She was sure she had not imagined it. A moment later, Annalise bore down again, straining and holding her breath. Dyannis managed to get both her hands free so she could cradle the taut belly. She used the direct physical contact to reach the baby—

—and felt the heartbeat slow . . . pause . . .

—and speed up, a light pitter-patter, as the tense muscles softened and the laboring mother drew breath.

Even with her *laran* enhanced by touch, Dyannis could not clearly read the baby's condition. Nothing like this had happened in the births she had attended. Under her hands, the woman's body tightened.

"Push!" Dyannis cried, trusting to her own instinct to get the baby out as soon as possible. "Push now!"

Behind her, Braulio knocked on the door. "I've got the hot water—"

"Later!" Dyannis shouted. "Come on, Annalise, push!"

With a strange, smothered cry, the laboring woman curled forward, grabbing her knees, chin tucked, face congested with effort. She made no further sound for a long moment, but every fiber in her body quivered. Dyannis felt the baby move with agonizing slowness.

"Ah!" Annalise cried. Her head fell back on the bed. Dyannis reached around just in time to cradle the wet little head as it emerged. A heartbeat later, one shoulder followed the other and the newborn slid into her hands. The umbilical cord was wrapped tightly around the baby's neck. Dyannis pulled it free. The baby lay there, hot and still.

Oh, Blessed Cassilda!

Braulio, who had moved silently into the room, shoved a folded rag at Dyannis. Not knowing what else to do, she rubbed the coarse fabric over the tiny form. Suddenly, the baby gave a convulsive twitch and began to cry. Dyannis felt the sting of tears as she wrapped the little girl in a second cloth and handed her to her mother. Then she stepped back as Braulio embraced his wife and new daughter.

She waited until she was sure both mother and child were doing well. There was little for her to do, besides clean things up. Annalise confidently put the baby to nurse and shortly afterward, both fell asleep.

Braulio thanked Dyannis effusively, as if she had done something wondrous. Dyannis thought the only wonder had been the natural process of birth. In truth, any other woman with a modicum of experience or common sense could have done as well, and Dyannis would not have known what to do had something gone truly wrong.

Dyannis rode back to the manor house, somber and thoughtful. Her horse bobbed its head, knowing the way. He belonged here, as she did not. She could send a relay message across hundreds of leagues, rebuild a stone wall with her mind, conjure a dragon out of thought, or walk the Overworld. Yet now she felt humbled by the birth, by the rolling hills, the distant heights, the solid animal sureness of her mount.

I must be what I am—a leronis of Hali. She would set aside what she had done as under-Keeper. Let some other, more worthy, take that place. There was work enough in the circle where her strength and experience were needed.

As she considered her return to the Tower and the community of Gifted workers, an invisible weight lifted from her shoulders. She arched her back and stretched, inhaling the moist night air. The horse picked up his pace, as if to hurry her on her way.

By the time Dyannis reached the house, she knew she'd made the right decision. She would stay at Sweetwater a little longer, until Lerrys passed the awakening of his *laran*. It would surely be soon, from his increasing irritability. Then she would make the trip back to Hali, perhaps even in time for Midsummer.

Greatly contented, she rode into the yard, stripped the tack from the horse and turned him loose in the paddock. Then she went into the quiet house for a well-earned rest.

Midsummer came and still Lerrys hovered on the edge of maturity. The Festival itself was subdued that year. Each family member seemed to Dyannis to be harboring some grievance. Lerrys, like many of the adolescents she'd known at Hali, alternated between sulky withdrawal and fits of temper, sometimes outright defiance of his parents. Rohanne had never given up trying to induce Dyannis to join her in embroidery and gossip, two things Dyannis loathed. When Dyannis politely but firmly declined, this seemed to irritate her sister-in-law.

Harald's temper fared no better. The day before Midsummer's Eve, word had come from Serrais, the Ridenow capital. *Dom* Eiric Ridenow, having determined that an offensive strike against Asturias was necessary, had ordered Harald to send another twenty men and horses. Harald could scarcely afford to spare them, and Dyannis saw how it pained him to be sending men he had known all their lives into battle. So, although the central hall was bedecked with flower garlands and the tables were laden with platters of roast lamb and barnfowl and summer gourds, pots of honeyed fruit and baskets overflowing with the braided egg buns, a shadow hung in the air.

During the festive dinner, Harald and Lerrys almost came to blows when the boy declared his intention of joining the war party. Harald, red-faced in his holiday finery, retorted that it was out of the question.

Lerrys glared back at his father. "Siann's going, and he's only a year older than me! Besides, he's riding Socks!" The old chestnut, marked by three white socks and a blaze on its forehead, had been his favorite horse as a child.

Rohanne cried, "You must not say such things, Lerrys! Harald, tell him no! He's just a child!"

"He is almost a man," Harald replied, "but he is heir to Sweetwater, and I will not have him risk himself needlessly."

"Aunt Dyannis!" Lerrys turned to Dyannis, his eyes bright and pleading. "Tell him I can do it—I've been practicing—I'm ready!"

Dyannis shook her head with a little shiver of sadness. "Lord Harald is right to forbid you, *chiyu*. Would that none of us—not you, not your friend Siann, not myself—face such horrors. Ordinary battle is terrible enough, but once *clingfire* and other *laran* weapons are brought in, there is no honor or glory, only death." Her throat closed up and she could not go on. She wondered if the lucky ones were those slain in the first fighting. She thought of Francisco and the other Cedestri folk, of the refugee farmers and soldiers she'd tended at Hali. No one, she thought, should live with such memories as she'd seen in the minds of the survivors.

"You're all against me!" Lerrys cried, and bolted from the table. Rohanne started to rise, but Harald stopped her with a gesture, saying, "Let him be. He will get over it, once his friend and the others are well away."

Rohanne glared at Dyannis as if the boy's rebellion were all her doing.

Harald sighed. "In the end, we may have little choice, once the war is upon us. *Dom* Eiric has taken his own sons into battle, and we must all be prepared to defend our homes."

After that, the heart went out of the festivities. No one wanted to dance. Harald and Rohanne retired early so that those servants who cared to might continue their own celebrations unconstrained.

Dyannis, deciding that a suitable cooling-off time had passed, sought out Lerrys. His room was down the hall from her own. When she knocked, she heard the sounds of scuffling, the clink of metal and the lid of a chest slammed shut. Pausing with her fist poised to knock again, she smiled and shook her head. The boy had a good dose of youthful Varzil in him.

Lerrys opened the door a crack. A single candle set on a ledge on the far wall lit the room.

"It won't work, you know," she said.

Lerrys drew his brows together, very much as his father did when confronted. Although she hadn't used her *laran* to sense the borrowed sword, the rain cloak, and other gear at the bottom of the chest, she caught his unguarded thought, *She's read my mind!*

"Are you going to give me away?" he said.

"No, I don't see the point in it. But I'd like to talk."

"You mean *you* talk and *I* listen." With an aggrieved sigh, he stepped back for her to enter.

She sat on the bed, pushing herself back so her feet swung free. "And *I* try to convince *you* to mind your father, like a good aunt should, is that what you mean? It doesn't sound like very much fun, but if you insist, I'll try." She chuckled until she noticed his outraged expression.

"What's so funny?"

Ah, youth. Had she been so deathly serious at his age? "I wasn't laughing at *you*, but at all of us Ridenow. We never seem to do things the easy way, do we? I'm too young to remember whatever Harald did, but Varzil—oh, my! When he wanted to go to Arilinn Tower and Father refused, what a fuss!"

The boy's mood lightened minutely. He took a step closer, although his posture remained one of mistrust.

"Varzil ran away just after he'd been presented to the *Comyn* Council," Dyannis continued, "and Father went berserk, not knowing where he was. I suppose Harald told you all this?"

Lerrys sat down beside her, listening now. "Father told me once, but Mother said he wasn't to mention it again. She thought it would give me ideas."

"Oh, yes! Varzil's been giving people *ideas* all his life!" Dyannis laughed again, and this time, Lerrys laughed with her. "It was bad enough that Varzil tried to get admitted to Arilinn Tower on his own, but we weren't yet on good terms with the Hasturs, and the Keepers there wouldn't take Varzil without his father's permission. Too politically dangerous, you know. So what did you think he did?"

Dark eyes flashed. "He found a way to get in anyway." *Obviously.*

"No, he didn't." She shook her head. "What you must understand about Varzil is that all his life, he had been different. It would have killed him to stay here, herding cattle and horses, running Sweetwater along with Harald. His *laran* set him apart. He was born to be a Keeper, and he felt it in his bones. He wanted to train at a Tower more than anything else. Anything else, except honor."

"Is there a point to all this?"

She watched him, the soft candlelight making him seem even younger. He was no child, nor was he completely a man. Yet he now faced a man's difficult choices.

"You see," she went on, "if he went against Father's wishes and snuck off to some place like Cedestri, where they'd take him no matter what, he'd be turning his whole life into a lie, instead of keeping faith with who he was."

Lerrys looked uncertain. He was old enough to understand the importance of integrity, but clearly had not thought that staying home and obeying his father's wishes might be an honorable course. Gently, she said, "It was the hardest thing for Varzil to do—to give in, to leave Arilinn with Father, but he did it. I think that decision helped make him who he is today, a man who shapes our times. He didn't just do whatever he wanted, he did the right thing."

Lerrys wasn't ready to give up. "But he *did* go back to Arilinn. He found a way."

"Only after Father agreed. Actually, it was Harald who changed Father's mind, after the incident with the catmen. Harald isn't as hidebound and unreasonable as you think. It's the natural course for all sons to challenge their fathers. But he loves you. He wants you to grow strong and wise, to rule Sweetwater after him. How can you do that if you cannot even rule yourself?"

Lerrys glanced away. His chest rose and fell; she could almost hear the pounding of his heart. His desires—for adventure and glory, for his father's approval, for honor—roiled in his breast.

"It isn't easy, is it?" she said in a low voice.

He shook his head. "What should I do? I can't just give in."

She touched the back of his hand, brushing his mind with her *laran*. "Just go about your chosen course. I doubt Harald will say anything. Your mother will fuss, but then, she would do that no matter what you decided."

He grinned, and she knew he'd truly understood. Two days later, the men left to join *Dom* Eiric's attack on Asturias.

30

A tenday later, returning from her early morning ride, Dyannis knew something was wrong as she rounded the last curve of hill back to Sweetwater. Harald still wasn't happy about her going out on her own, but as long as she returned by midmorning, he kept his objections to himself. It was one of many things they tacitly agreed not to discuss.

As usual, she rode the roan gelding. Given an easy rein, he set a brisk pace back to his familiar corral and breakfast. He showed no particular sign of alarm, yet even before the house and stables came into view, something shrieked like a burst of acid fire along her nerves. She caught a visual image of colors smeared together like a child's painting, overlaid with the hot silvery shiver of terror.

Lerrys!

She dug her heels into her horse's sides. The beast snorted in surprise, then moved into a bone-jarring trot. They pounded down the steepest part of the trail. The horse lost his footing on a patch of loose rock, forefeet skidding. The next instant, he turned sideways and arched his back, and shifted his weight to his hindquarters. Snorting and blowing, the roan gelding came to a halt. Dyannis nudged him to continue downhill, but he flattened his ears and hunched his back menacingly.

Without warning, the sense of urgency returned. Colored lights twisted and melded behind her eyes. Her stomach rebelled; bile rose to her throat. She retched, swaying in the saddle. Around her, the horizon smeared into a sickening jumble of earth and sky. She took hold of the reins, dug her knees into the horse's sides and yanked his head around, facing downhill. The horse took one step and then another, picking his way. His tail lashed in protest.

Without thinking, she blasted out a psychic command with all the power of her trained *laran* and her special Ridenow Gift: *GO!*

The horse bounded down the last slope. Dyannis clung to his neck, using all her remembered skills to hang on. He clattered into the yard and she jumped off, even before he came to a halt. One of the stable hands ran toward her, hands raised to catch the dangling reins. The beast shied and the man ran after him.

"Lerrys! Where is he?" she gasped.

The stable hand was too busy cursing under his breath at idiots who ran a horse like that and then turned him loose without walking him cool—

"*WHERE IS HE?*" The commanding Voice came roaring out from her throat, reverberating through the yard. Every animal turned in her direction, eyes and ears focused solely upon her.

The stable man whirled, his jaw dropping. "In—in the house. *Damisela*—"

Dyannis sprinted from the yard. Her breath rasped like fire through her lungs. Her feet pounded up the wooden stairs. She shoved aside the great heavy door as if it were paper.

Lerrys! A silent howl answered her.

Once inside the shadowed entrance, Dyannis knew exactly where he was. She burst into the central hall at a dead run, her riding skirt flapping about her legs. The servants in the hall jumped aside, except for one maid carrying a pitcher on a tray. Dyannis swerved, but not soon enough. She brushed the girl's shoulder. Tray and pitcher crashed to the floor, splattering steaming *jaco* in all directions. Rohanne, pausing halfway down the staircase, shrieked.

Dyannis crossed the hall just as Rohanne drew breath for a second scream. She took the stairs one, two at a time, slipping and scrambling.

The boy's mind went silent.

The hallway sped by in a blur. Behind her, Dyannis heard shouting. She yanked open the solarium door. Instantly, she spotted the overturned chair and the tightly-curled body on the carpet beside it. The chair still vibrated with the force of his first convulsion. The air reeked with surging, chaotic *laran*. Dyannis threw herself to her knees beside Lerrys. She knew even before she touched his shoulder that he had stopped breathing.

Lerrys! She drew upon her years of training at Hali, shaping her thought to penetrate the psychic turmoil. Taking his hands in hers to amplify the contact, she dropped below the level of thought.

As a novice and later as a working *leronis*, Dyannis had monitored many others, both her colleagues and commoners. Never had she done it under such pressure for speed. Lerrys had stopped breathing a minute or two before she arrived. His heart had already begun to falter and his energy channels were so congested, they looked almost black.

With a practiced movement, she opened the locket containing her starstone. It flared into brilliance at her touch. As she had so many times, she used the gem to amplify and direct her natural *laran*.

Breathe! Lerrys, breathe!

She sensed the clogged *laran*-carrying nodes just below his diaphragm, pressing on his solar plexus, pulsing with dark energy. It would take time to drain off the blockage, but Lerrys did not have time. Each passing moment further depleted his vitality. Working with critically-injured patients at Hali and then at Cedestri, Dyannis had learned to temporarily sustain life processes. At her command, muscles tightened and ribs lifted. Air rushed along breathing passages. Darkness eased. She felt the life spark brighten.

Dyannis poured strength into the boy's heart, stimulating the contracting fibers. The heart responded, beating once, twice, each time more strongly.

"What are you doing?" shrieked a woman's voice, barely recognizable as Rohanne's. "Get away from him!"

Dyannis turned her head to glimpse her sister-in-law's livid face. Beyond her, servants hovered, and the same maid Dyannis had knocked over stood wringing her hands.

"I need *kirian!*" Dyannis cried. "The blue bottle—still house—near the rosmarin. *NOW!*"

A sudden shift in the boy's energy riveted her attention once more. She dimly heard receding footsteps and the chatter of feminine voices. Lerrys still breathed and his heart still beat, but deep within his psychic form, another upheaval was building. It would burst forth into a physical convulsion in a matter of moments. His muscles would lock in spasm, his heart would falter, and the very cells of his brain might burn out from the overload. What was she to do? There was no one to turn to, no one else to act.

Dyannis could think of only one course of action, so desperate that had the boy's very life not been at risk, she would never have considered it. She must take his starstone into her own hands. The risk was extreme; from her very first days as a novice, she had been warned of the dire consequences of even casual contact with another person's starstone. It might throw him into the very crisis she hoped to prevent. Yet if, by the physical connection, she could somehow reach his mind, she might have a chance of saving him.

Lerrys had curled into a tight ball, his muscles quivering. Dyannis let her starstone locket swing free on its chain. She needed both hands to loosen the boy's shirt around his waist. Bless all the gods, he still wore the strip of fabric as a sash beneath his clothing. She felt a lump within its folds. Her fingers trembled as she tugged at the folds. For an infuriating moment, it resisted her. Everything she did tangled it further.

The matrix crystal, afire with inner light, dropped into the palm of her hand. She sensed the answering rush of energy as a burst of heat from her own stone. Closing her eyes, she felt herself suspended in an ocean of brilliance. Like twin suns, the two starstones filled the psychic firmament. Rays of blue-white clashed and fractured. They warred with one another in overlapping patterns. She became a mote within the storm, torn by invisible gales of radiance, at any moment on the verge of being ripped loose from her moorings. If she gave in, if she failed to hold fast, then Lerrys would surely perish, and she along with him.

In a flash of understanding, she saw the light not as two separate sources but a single entity out of phase with itself. Using the power of her mind, amplified through both starstones, she began to shift the light within them, to guide and reshape it. Slowly, order emerged. Color attuned into harmony. Overlapping images resolved into a single, stellate focus.

Carefully, Dyannis allowed the two patterns to separate. One remained as she had always known it, the faceted brilliance that was her own starstone. The second, belonging to Lerrys, immediately began to drift, dimming and assuming a darker shade of blue. The configuration was more a twist of muted color than the star-shaped a energy pattern of her own matrix. This was a crucial moment, she knew, for once freed of the order imposed by her own stone, his might revert to chaos. But it did not. Not yet, anyway.

Dyannis shifted her awareness now to the boy's body. He was breathing slowly but regularly. His heart beat steadily, blood circulating and organs functioning normally. The dusky red of congested *laran* nodes had lightened. Flow returned to his channels.

His mind, however . . . how had it fared?

Lerrys . . .

An answer came like the clangor of a distant bell, fading quickly. This time, the silence carried no deadly emptiness. Dyannis sensed, rather, the boy had slipped beyond her hearing. With each passing moment, his starstone grew darker and more muted. In some ways, it resembled an unkeyed stone, one that had never been in resonance with a Gifted mind.

How was that possible? Lerrys had keyed into his starstone so strongly that the same storms of light and power had raged through its crystalline structure and the fabric of his own mind. Dyannis had little experience with such things, but she wondered if the convulsions had damaged the *laran* centers of his brain. Raimon, back at Hali, would be able to tell.

She opened her eyes and studied the stone in her hand. It looked subdued, almost quenched, with only a glimmer of blue light in its core. She did not trust that quietness, not until she proved to herself no invisible storm still lurked within its faceted confines, a mirror to the boy's mind.

Trembling rippled through her, bone-deep weariness and hunger. She had not felt this depleted since she had raised the stones to rebuild Cedestri Tower.

Someone cried, "He's awake! He lives!"

"Oh, my baby!" Rohanne sobbed.

"No, my lady, leave them be. See, he rouses."

Lerrys moaned, opening his eyes. Dyannis steadied herself enough to lift his head.

Someone, the same servant who had restrained Rohanne, thrust the glass bottle of *kirian* into her hands. Dyannis yanked out the stopper and held the bottle to the boy's lips. The faint lemony tang of the psychoactive distillation filled her head. Her own body revived, drawing nourishment from the aroma.

Lerrys swallowed the two mouthfuls she provided. He sighed, murmured something, and fell into a deep, natural sleep. Dyannis caught an image from his mind of a young man, face flushed with excitement, galloping away on a chestnut horse with three white legs.

"Take him," Dyannis said, lifting her head to the circle of worried faces. Hands reached down to lift him. "Take him to his bed. The best thing for him now is rest. I will check on him in a short while. I must—"

She meant to say, *I must speak with his father,* but got no further, for as she attempted to rise, another wave of weariness swept through her. The brief surge of energy from the *kirian* had vanished, leaving her even more drained than before.

"*Vai domna.*" It was the servant who had handed her the *kirian,* an old woman with a face carved from granite. Dyannis remembered her from her childhood, although Nialla had worked in the kitchen then. She'd run into Nialla a few times since her return. Now they were alone in the solarium. Lerrys had been carried away by his mother in a flurry of exclamations. "How may I serve you?"

By not asking me to stand up, Dyannis thought. She accepted the old woman's surprisingly powerful support, enough to seat herself in a chair. She felt the urge to simply fall asleep where she was. Then nausea clutched her belly. Years of experience had taught her that was a sign of how dangerously depleted she was. "Bring me something sweet—candy or dried fruit or spiral buns. And a goblet of honeyed water, not wine."

I'll just . . . close my eyes.

Dyannis startled awake as the old woman set a plate of sugared nuts, spicebread smeared with apple compote, and dried honey-glazed pears on her lap. Despite her aversion, Dyannis forced herself to eat. The food was delicious enough to tempt even a recalcitrant appetite, and her trembling subsided as it replenished her spent energies.

"It was ever so with Master Varzil," Nialla said, nodding. "Always wanting sweets after he'd been out dreaming."

Dyannis nodded, unexpectedly moved. Intense *laran* work sometimes left her feeling emotional, but this was something more, this kind-hearted woman who remembered her brother as a child.

Dyannis felt the uproar of Harald's arrival even before she heard his booming voice, calling out for his son. Although she still ached with weariness in every joint and muscle, the food had restored her enough to speak with him.

"You sit there, m'lady," the old woman said. "Let *him* come to you."

Harald burst into the solarium a short time later. His spurs jangled as he strode across the room. He smelled of horse sweat, wild herbs, and leather. His fear filled the room, a rank undertone.

"Lerrys—"

"He's all right," Dyannis cut him off. *For the time being.* "Even as I feared, he suffered a threshold crisis, an intense initial episode of *laran*-awakened sickness. I don't know what precipitated it, but it was by Cassilda's own mercy I was nearby. Otherwise, I do not think he would have survived."

She paused to let her words sink in. Harald paled as the realization shook him. He ran one hand over his reddened, sweating face. "I—I am grateful, sister."

Dyannis brushed his words aside. She had warned Harald and urged him to send Lerrys to Hali, but had she really done everything in her power? Had she failed because she was preoccupied with her own unanswered questions? She felt as if a mist had lifted from her eyes with her own decision. Yes, she had contributed to the boy's danger by not acting upon her best judgment. And yes, he ought to have had proper training before this, but in all truth, that might not have averted the crisis.

"He is stable enough for the moment," she said. "I will examine him while he sleeps, and again when he is awake. Meanwhile, we must make preparations for his further care."

"I thought you said—he was all right."

"I meant that he is alive. I do not know if his mind and body have taken any permanent damage. How his *laran* centers fared, I cannot tell yet, either. And he may suffer another episode, as bad or worse."

"Holy Aldones, Lord of Light, have mercy on us!" In a couple of long strides, Harald flung himself into a chair. "What am I to do?"

Dyannis sensed Harald's memories of Anndra and Sylvie, who had died at the same age, despite the best efforts of the household *leronis.* It was said that during the heights of the Ages of Chaos, when the great houses enforced selective inbreeding programs to fix genetic traits for *laran,* such deaths were common.

What if such a thing had happened to Varzil as a child? she wondered. *Or Raimon, or herself?* The fate of their world turned upon such a fragile axis.

Lerrys remained unconscious for two days. Rohanne fussed and wrung her hands and Harald looked taut and anxious. Dyannis, once she had rested, examined the boy several more times, and was able to offer the reassurance that for the time being, he appeared to be out of danger.

Lerrys had always been an active, healthy boy. He was soon well enough to get out of bed. His appetite returned and he quickly grew restless in the house. His *laran* remained clouded, his starstone infused with dull blue light. Dyannis judged it unsafe to try any psychic contact for the present, except within the safety of a Tower.

Dyannis thought of urging Harald again to send Lerrys to Hali. The boy would soon be fit to travel. She herself would be returning to the Tower, although she had not yet found the time or a way to tell her family. At first, she was too weary, and Harald clearly too distressed to discuss anything as emotional as sending the boy away. She decided to wait until they were both rested and clear of thought.

Just when Dyannis was about to broach the subject to Harald, a rider arrived from Serrais, his horse lathered to exhaustion. He remained closeted with Harald for half a day. Then Harald gathered the entire household and the leaders of his men, both on the home estate and outlying farms.

"Evil tidings have come from Asturias," he announced. "That *nedestro* offspring of King Rafael, may Zandru scourge him with scorpions, whom men call the Kilghard Wolf, has taken to the field. Serrais is thrown back, the entire army in disarray, and *Dom* Eiric now lies in the Asturias dungeon."

"No!" one of the men cried, and a ripple of dismay passed through the assembly. "The scoundrels! How dare they!" "Witchery, it must have been, damnable witchery!"

Rohanne gave a little shriek and looked as if she were going to faint. Lerrys, standing beside Dyannis, flinched.

"When did this come to pass?" Dyannis raised her voice. When Harald told her, her heart clenched. It was the exact time Lerrys had suffered his attack. She turned to him and saw the echoes of a horror too great for his young mind to bear. With his awakening *laran,* he had somehow linked to his friend Siann, the one who'd gone with the Serrais levies. This had been no ordinary battle. She caught fragmentary images from the boy's mind— Men and horses thrashing in pools of blood . . . the stench of *clingfire* . . . spell-cast terror shredding men's minds . . . swords . . . arrows . . .

Dyannis saw the Ridenow army lying cut to pieces, the remnant fleeing in confusion; the heart had gone out of them with the first charge, slashing through their rear guard. *Clingfire* shells burst into flame, stampeding the horses. Men blazed, their flesh on fire, and died screaming. Then it was all over but the slaughter and the final surrender. The armed men inside the castle covered their foes with bowmen from the walls, and at the end, the Asturias *leronyn* spread terror among the Ridenow army, so they fled shrieking as if all the demons in all of Zandru's frozen hells were after them.

Through the boy's mind, Dyannis felt each death, each scream, each drop of molten fire. These were her own people, her kinsmen and their vassals, now scattered on the blood-drenched field as the *kyorebni* circled silently overhead. Horses lay among them, some thrashing in agony, others still. Because she saw through the mental eyes of Lerrys, she recognized the chestnut horse with three white socks that had been his favorite, now a lump of inert, gore-encrusted flesh. Beneath the horse lay the trampled form of a man in Ridenow colors crossed by the insignia of Sweetwater. Lerrys, linked through his awakening telepathic Gift, had felt them both die.

Varzil was right. The madness must stop.

No wonder Lerrys had gone half mad. This was no simple case of threshold sickness, to be treated with *kirian* and a little basic training. The boy desperately needed skilled help. If he were not to be scarred in mind and spirit by what he had seen, he must make his peace with it. She knew of no place he could find that solace and healing except in a Tower.

She could no longer delay her departure. She must return to Hali as soon as Lerrys was strong enough, there to take up her place as *leronis* and work to fulfill Varzil's dream.

31

Since late spring, messengers had been racing between Sweetwater and the other major Ridenow estates, and also Thendara. Now not a day passed without some news. Having escaped back to Serrais, the sons of *Dom* Eiric waited anxiously for word from Asturias, a ransom demand or news of his execution. Emissaries also went forth to King Carolin and other powerful rulers, to see whether an alliance might be made.

For the time being, however, there was a lull in the fighting. Even victors, Dyannis thought wryly, must take time to lick their wounds.

One evening, shortly after the news of the defeat at Asturias, Dyannis arranged a meeting with Harald in the private chamber he used as the estate office and library. The room was small and a little gloomy with its empty hearth and darkened windows. Summer was nearly over, but the evenings were not yet cold enough for a fire. The chill, Dyannis thought, was of the spirit. She felt some regret that at such a time, she must leave her family, but she had already delayed too long.

Harald eased himself into the wooden chair beside the table that served as his desk. He'd been up since before dawn, for it was high summer. Come harvest time, Sweetwater would feel the loss of so many men, but for now, they could manage. Lerrys grew stronger every day and Dyannis often rode with the others out to the pastures. She had changed into a house gown for dinner, mostly to please Rohanne, but Harald still wore his working clothes.

He offered her wine and a plate of tiny fruit pastries dusted with crystallized honey. It was a childhood treat, perhaps a reminder of their shared past. She declined both, for unless she was doing *laran* work, she did not care for sweets. She settled herself in the second chair, with the table between them, while he filled a goblet for himself.

After a few inconsequential comments on the day's work and the weather, which had been very fine, Dyannis began the conversation in earnest. "The roads are safe enough for the time being, at least between here and Thendara. We cannot know how long the peace will last, so we must not delay. Lerrys must come with me to Hali while we still can."

"Surely there is no reason for Lerrys to go all the way to Hali," he said. "The boy's getting stronger every day, and besides, he is needed here at Sweetwater."

"He is not well, and you know it. Harald, he barely survived his threshold crisis, and although he has not had another such episode, we cannot be sure this is the end of it. If he has another one, it might kill him." She leaned forward, trying to put the complex interactions of mind and body into simple terms. "His *laran* was just awakening when he linked to his friend at the battle at Asturias Castle. I think his empathy with the horse, his Ridenow Gift, made that bond strong enough so that he experienced the slaughter, the pain and terror and death, up here," she brushed her temple, "just as if he had been there himself."

Harald listened, his eyes hooded and unreadable. Dyannis sensed his love for his son, and his fear.

"It is possible the experience burned out his *laran,* or damaged it so badly that he will never be able to use it," she said. "But that is only a part of the problem. You know that even grown men who live through such a tragedy are changed. Sometimes they can never go back to their homes and families. They wander the roads or turn outlaw. I have seen them in Thendara, drunkards and beggars. I do not want that to happen to Lerrys, who was so young and unprepared."

Harald nodded. "I understand the danger, but Lerrys seems to be fine. He has said nothing of this to me."

"I do not think he will speak of it, if he even remembers. But it is still in his mind, of that I am sure, and it will prey upon him like some putrefying abscess, if it is not drained. Although he *seems* fine, he does not *feel* fine, not to my mind. Harald, I am a trained *leronis*. I know a great deal, and I tell you, this is beyond my ability to deal with by myself. If Lerrys were an ordinary man, without *laran,* I could treat him well enough. But with his Gift, and what he has been through, he needs a protected environment, and skilled care, which I cannot give him here at home."

Harald had shuddered visibly at her words. He spoke in a voice thick with emotion. "And the *leronyn* at Hali Tower can help him? You are sure of this?"

Dyannis nodded. "I have seen men and women come through worse nightmares, and become whole." She did not add that some were as a result of her own impulsive behavior, that she herself had worked to undo the harm she had caused. Raimon had been right; she had made her amends. Now she was in a position to use what she had learned to help her nephew.

"Rohanne will fret, but I think you are right," Harald said after a pause. "We must do whatever is necessary for my son's recovery. You and I and Lerrys must journey together to the Hastur lands. We will leave as soon as preparations can be made."

Dyannis sat back in her chair with a little sigh. The talk had gone far more easily than she had hoped. She had expected resistance, and instead had found cooperation. Harald was not *Dom* Felix, and he truly loved his son.

"I have another reason for traveling to Thendara," Harald said with a faintly pleased expression, "and that concerns you. I am glad you arranged this conversation, or I would have had to."

"What did you want to talk about?" she asked.

"Your future. After Lerrys has been to Hali, he will no longer need you. You are a grown woman, and should have a household of your own. More than that, these are desperate times. Ridenow needs powerful friends. Blood ties are the strongest of all, but marriage is still a potent way to make allies."

Her stomach gave a lurch. She did not at all like this new direction to the conversation. "What—what do you mean?"

"I have arranged your betrothal to *Dom* Tiavan Harryl, and the ceremony will take place in Thendara—"

"*What!*" The word burst out like the cry of a stricken deer. She could hardly breathe.

"It is a good match, *breda*. From all accounts, *Dom* Tiavan is a courteous, honorable man. He is a kinsman of the young woman lately married to Geremy Hastur, son of Lord Istvan of Carcosa, and therefore kin to King Carolin himself. Moreover, *Dom* Geremy has been named Regent for the exiled heir to Asturias."

Dyannis felt as if she had been plunged into someone else's life. This could not be happening. Her own brother could not have done this to her.

Although her mind reeled, Dyannis also grasped the political implications of her brother's words. Harald was well within his rights to use her marriage for an alliance. Such arrangements were common. Most women of the *Comyn* never expected anything else, and if the gods smiled upon them, their husbands would treat them with courtesy and perhaps, over time, love. If not, there was always the consolation of children, of rank, and of the knowledge they had served their families in the only way most women could.

I am not most women. I am Dyannis of Hali!

"He has no objection to your age," Harald went on, oblivious to her reaction. "You are not too old to bear him sons, but in the event you do not, his lands will revert to the Hasturs, who are overlords to the Harryl clan, so in the end, everyone is satisfied. You will have a good marriage and become mistress of a household of your own, instead of lingering on here as a dependent spinster, and your family will gain great advantage from the match."

"I—" Dyannis opened her mouth and then shut it. *I cannot turn aside from the destiny that the gods laid upon me.* She did not see how she could possibly become anyone's wife and still do the work she loved, using the Gift she was born with. She must put a stop to the conversation, before Harald took her silence for consent.

"I thank you for your efforts on my behalf, brother," she said, "but what you propose is impossible. I wish you had consulted me before entering into any such arrangement."

Harald's brows drew together and the muscles of his shoulders tightened. "Are you pledged to some other? If so, why did you keep it secret? Or is there some reason this marriage is not pleasing to you?"

"I have absolutely no desire to marry anyone! I proposed accompanying Lerrys to Hali in order to resume my duties as *leronis* at Hali Tower."

The ruddy color drained from Harald's face. "What do you mean? You have been here all these months since the beginning of spring, and never once mentioned you wished to return to the Tower. I thought you had given that up. You said so little of your former life, I assumed the subject was painful to you. What else was I to think? As head of this household, I became responsible for making some other arrangement for you. I believed you would be unhappy and frustrated living under the same roof as Rohanne, with no real place of your own. I saw the chance to benefit our family and at the same time secure your happiness."

"You should have asked me first!"

Harald got up and started pacing. "If only I'd had the slightest idea . . . Why didn't you say something?"

What a fool she'd been, so preoccupied with her personal problems that she never noticed what was going on around her. A dozen clues rose to her mind, phrases casually dropped by either Harald or Rohanne.

"We must all of us, sisters as well as brothers, stand together" . . . *"As you leave behind your life in the Tower"* . . . *"All that is behind you now"* . . .

"I came home for a visit only," she said. "I should have made that clear. Not only that, I have not been released from my oath, and until my Keeper grants that request, I am not technically free to accept any proposal of marriage. There are so few trained telepaths . . ."

Harald strode to his chair and grasped the high back. "This does create a difficulty. The offer has been made in the name of Ridenow, and has been accepted. We are committed. We cannot go back on our word or withdraw with honor."

Dyannis felt a sudden chill go all through her. She bowed her head, overcome. *Blessed Cassilda, grant me grace. Show me what I must do.*

There was only one possible answer, and Dyannis did not want to face it.

"How can any of us know what we are capable of, until we are put to the test?" she said aloud.

Harald looked at her curiously, as if he had not expected this answer.

"Varzil has been trying to persuade me to train as a Keeper for some time now," she said, "but I did not think myself worthy until Lerrys went into threshold crisis. I do not know what fate the gods have set down for me. I only know that I cannot discover it by insisting upon my own will. My talent—and Varzil is right, I *could* be a Keeper—urges me in one direction, but my obedience to you and to the welfare of our family lies in another."

"Varzil—"

"No, please, let me finish, or I may never again find the courage. All my life, I have done what I pleased, submitting to discipline and authority only as a means to get what I wanted. I thought my talents were mine alone to use and direct. Instead, I now see that it is the other way around, that it is I who have been given to them, even as I have been given to my family. For what purpose, I do not know. I only know that whatever action I take—or fail to take—must be with honor."

For a long moment, neither said anything. She felt the turmoil of Harald's emotions, determination and anger, fear and yes, love. He was her brother, blood of her blood and bone of her bone, and he believed utterly in the rightness of his actions. He saw their land beset by enemies, and her marriage a hope for their survival.

"So be it," he said. "I know this is not what you would freely choose for yourself. I wish we had some other choice."

"As do I," she answered with a little smile, "but what is done is done. I will not bring dishonor to you or our family. Too many times in my life, I have acted on selfish impulse and then regretted the consequences. I have done things that brought great sorrow and pain to others. I will not knowingly do so again. Therefore, I will go with you to Hali, I will ask Raimon to release me from my oath, and I will fulfill the pledge you have made in my name."

32

Under other circumstances, Dyannis would have enjoyed the journey to Thendara. The roads were dry, the weather clear. She rode the same sturdy roan that had been her favorite at Sweetwater, and everyone was in high spirits. In the company of her kinsmen, she required no chaperone other than a maid, and for this purpose Rella had been appointed. Dyannis would have preferred Nialla, but she was too old to make the journey.

To Lerrys, the trip was clearly an adventure. He had been to Serrais before, but never beyond Ridenow lands. As for Harald, he seemed to be doing everything he could to make the journey pleasant. He paid special attention to Dyannis and often asked about her comfort, until she grew irritable with him. She suspected that he was trying to make up for his actions out of guilt. He didn't see that, in the end, she had freely chosen to honor her obligation to her family. She understood that he had only been doing what he thought was right.

They met a caravan of traders from the Marenji border who were taking advantage of the lull in hostilities to do their business, and shared a pleasant meal together. Harald had clearly given thought to where they would stop, at the most comfortable inns, and had sent messages as far as Thendara. Dyannis remembered how she and Varzil had traveled to Cedestri, how they'd camped along the road and eaten when there was time, how their work had come before everything else. She told Harald he was making a great deal of fuss over soft beds and hot meals.

"I suppose I might get used to it, for such is likely to be my lot once I am *Dom* Tiavan's wife," she added ruefully.

"Fear not, you will never become like Rohanne," he said, "with nothing more important to occupy her time than fretting over gowns and hair. All may yet turn out for the best."

Now that she was reconciled to her decision, Dyannis felt a subtle lightening of spirit as they came down the last gently rolling stretch of the Venza Hills and into the Lowlands. They rode through pastures where the afternoon sun hung like a veil of honey and cattle lifted their heads to blink sleepily at the travelers, beside orchards already heavy with apple and pear, and past villages with snug cottages, neatly thatched, and well-mended pens.

"I grew up in a village very much like these," Rella commented.

Children pointed to the strangers, exclaiming over the unfamiliar colors of green and gold, before their mothers hushed them. "They're Ridenow, and no enemy of ours," one woman chided her child within earshot. "Varzil the Good is the King's own *bredu,* did you not know?"

"That's Uncle Varzil they're talking about," Lerrys said to his father. They were riding close enough for Dyannis to overhear.

Dyannis knew the history of the enmity between the two great houses of Ridenow and Hastur, but Harald was old enough to have grown up with it. Even long after the Peace of Allart Hastur, which had put an end to the worst of the feuding, suspicions lingered. Now, with the abiding friendship between Varzil and King Carolin, even those gave way to new hope.

New hope, she thought, but not new peace. Ridenow and Asturias were now bitter enemies. Just before they left Sweetwater, one of Harald's messengers brought word that Varzil had returned from the Asturias capital as Carolin's representative to convince the other claimants to sign the Compact. Carolin had even offered to recognize the claim of *Dom* Rafael, brother of the last legitimate king, if he would refrain from using *laran* weapons in war.

So whether he wills it or not, Carolin is involved in this conflict. Hastur might be linked with Ridenow against Asturias, but Asturias also had powerful connections. *And if we are drawn into open warfare, each side calling upon its allies, will the whole world go up in flames?*

And where would she be? Not in a circle, not rebuilding a Tower or healing broken bodies and shattered minds, but locked away, kept safe and idle, perhaps pregnant with *Dom* Tiavan's heir, unable to use the talents she had trained so hard to master. . . .

An image flashed across her mind—a Tower illuminated by fire, lightning bolts slashing down from the sky, human bodies blazing like living torches . . . the stench of charred flesh . . . screams . . .

She blinked, and the vision faded. Before her, just beyond the base of the hills, Thendara glittered in the afternoon sunlight. Lerrys exclaimed and pointed, but they were as yet too far to make out any individual buildings, even the King's great castle.

Hali lay beyond the next ridge, the city where she had first met Prince Carolin, the Tower that had been her home for so long, and the lake with its heart of shadows. Raimon waited for her with pleasure and Rorie with hope. Alderic, who had also been her friend, had finished his time there and gone to his marriage with Romilly MacAran, as she would shortly to *Dom* Tiavan.

At the gates of Thendara, guards in Hastur blue and silver politely but firmly asked their reason for entering the city. Harald answered, "Our business is with the king. We have his leave to travel here, and that is all you need to know."

"No offense, good *mestre*," the guard said, without the slightest touch of servility, "but it's my business to make sure that no one but a friend to Hastur passes through here."

An older guard, who had been standing a little distance away, walked over to investigate. Dyannis recognized him, and saw in his eyes that he knew her, too. He bowed and then said, a little gruffly, to his fellow, "D'ye not know the Lady Dyannis of Hali? Gods, man, what are you thinking, to question a *leronis* of the Tower as if she were common rabble?"

Harald's eyes widened, but Dyannis could not read his expression. With this many people around, she had raised her *laran* barriers. Lerrys turned in the saddle to stare at her. The guards bowed as they passed through.

Dyannis found Thendara very much as she remembered when she'd left it half a year ago, a great walled city with palaces and towers, marketplaces and mansions. Here the *Comyn* had ruled for unimaginable centuries, since before the Ages of Chaos.

They rode past shops and inns, tables set out upon the cobblestones, between carts laden with rolled Ardcarran carpets, carriages, riders on horses and antlered *chervines,* and curtained sedan chairs trailing perfume. The noise and mingled smells surrounded Dyannis. They came almost to a standstill while several enormous wagons laden with furniture negotiated a difficult turning.

At last they reached the gates of Castle Hastur, a fortress within a fortress. The guards here wore the badge of the King's household, and if any of them recognized Dyannis, they gave no sign. They searched the entire party for weapons, except for Dyannis herself. It would have been unthinkable for any commoner to lay hands upon a *Comynara,* even if she were not also a *leronis.* Unasked, Dyannis handed over the small eating knife that she carried in her boot. Then she accompanied Harald and Lerrys inside, leaving their attendants to tend to the animals in the courtyard.

It had been Harald's plan that they arrange for an audience with King Carolin, as befitted their rank as *Comyn,* and then obtain lodging in an inn of suitable respectability. While they were waiting in the outer foyer where other petitioners had gathered, a courtier appeared and immediately ushered them into Carolin's presence chamber.

Dyannis remembered being presented to old King Felix in a similar chamber shortly after she had arrived at Hali. Prince Carolin had just returned from Arilinn, along with Varzil and Eduin. Felix Hastur, over a century old, occupied the throne, attended solicitously by his nephew, Rakhal.

The world had gone on, through Felix's dotage and his death, Rakhal's treason, and Carolin's exile and restoration. This chamber was very much like its fellow at Hali, with its rich furnishings and courtiers like extravagantly feathered birds in their costly robes and ornaments of copper and gold.

They halted where the courtier bid them, to be announced. Carolin, smiling warmly, gestured them to come forward.

"*Dom* Harald, I am delighted to welcome the brother of my friend Varzil to Thendara. Lady Dyannis, it is good to see you again."

"The pleasure is all mine, Your Majesty," she replied.

"And who is this fine lad?" Carolin asked.

Harald bowed, stiffly but with dignity, and introduced Lerrys. He had anticipated a wait of hours or days before being presented formally to the great king, and certainly not with trail dust clinging to his boots. Lerrys held himself well, although his awe and delight were obvious.

Carolin, with his characteristic graciousness, said, "All three of you must dine with us tonight. Maura will be pleased to see you again. Meanwhile, be at your ease in Castle Hastur. My *coridom* will find suitable chambers for you and your people, and stabling for your animals. Once you have settled in, *Dom* Harald, I will send word to Varzil of your arrival. I believe he has been waiting to see you."

"*Para servirte, vai dom,*" Harald replied in formal *casta*.

A middle-aged man in the garb of a highly-ranking *coridom* stepped forward and made a deep reverence. Dyannis recognized him from years before, although he had held a far lesser rank then. After receiving orders from Carolin, the *coridom* led the party from the presence chamber.

"*Mestre* Ruival, isn't it?" Dyannis asked as they followed the *coridom* down the long corridors laid with runners of wine-colored carpet. "How fares your family?"

"Very well, *vai leronis*. Thank you for your kind inquiry."

She laughed. "The kindness was all yours once, for I think we would all have starved without you, that first Midwinter season."

"If you will follow me to your chambers, I pray you will find them appropriate." Without waiting for a reply, he led them to a suite of luxurious rooms.

The furniture was comfortable but not overly ornate, the wood oiled to a satiny sheen, the air freshened with bowls of rosalys and lilias. Thick carpets cushioned their steps. A central sitting room gave way to several interconnecting bedchambers. Harald and Lerrys proceeded to their own.

The one indicated for Dyannis clearly was meant for a lady with attendant maids. Rella was already laying out the contents of the clothes chest. The girl's face flushed with excitement. The journey to Thendara

had been more adventure than she'd known in her short life, and she
had never dreamed of staying in the royal castle.

Dyannis closed the door and lowered herself into the cushioned
chair beside the fireplace. It had not yet been lit, but the room was
warm enough. She could hear the faint rumble of Harald's voice from
across the suite. She had not realized until now, when she was to leave
him forever, how much she would miss her brother. Even the thought
of seeing Varzil again only increased her sadness, for she must disap-
point all his hopes for her. They would never join their minds in a circle again.

Dyannis never once considered telling Harald she'd changed her
mind. She had given her word, as Ridenow, as *Comynara,* and, for the
last time, as *leronis.*

With a heavy heart, she allowed Rella to bathe her face and hands,
dress her, and arrange her hair for dinner with the King.

Dyannis followed Harald and the bright-eyed page sent to summon
them to the royal wing. In the central chamber, a table had been set for
an intimate family meal. Banks of candles cast a honey-soft glow
across the polished wood, the ornaments of gold and white. Maura
Hastur-Elhalyn, once *leronis* of Hali and then Tramontana, and now
Queen, stepped forward to greet them. She had not worked in a Tower
since her marriage to Carolin, but she still held herself with quiet re-
serve. Her flame-bright hair was simply dressed and she wore her favorite colors, sea green and gray.

How good it is to see you again! she spoke mentally to Dyannis.

Dyannis had only a moment or two while Harald was still bowing.
For a wild moment, she thought of sharing her sorrow with Maura, as
one *leronis* to another. Maura, of all people, would understand her situation. But if Maura then spoke to Carolin on her behalf, he might intervene—

No, Dyannis thought, it was dangerous to think such things. Hope
would weaken her resolve, erode her acceptance. Her fate was in the
hands of the gods.

The moment vanished as quickly as it had come, leaving a wave of
longing. *Blessed Cassilda, give me strength!*

Whatever distresses you, my dear?

Varzil! From the clarity of his thought, he must be quite near. She had been so caught up in her own misery, feeling so isolated, that she had missed his approach.

The next instant, the door at the far end of the room swung open and Carolin entered, along with Varzil. There were exclamations all round as the two brothers, Varzil and Harald, greeted one another. Much to everyone's amusement, Varzil behaved just like a doting uncle, remarking how Lerrys had grown.

"I met your father once, *Dom* Harald," Carolin said, as they sat down at the table and servants began bringing in the meal. "He was at Arilinn for *Comyn* Council season while I was a student there. You look very like him."

"I did not know you had ever met," Harald said. "He never spoke of it."

"He did not know me as Carolin Hastur, but only as the nameless courier who chased him down on his way to Sweetwater."

"Father had just refused to let me study at the Tower," Varzil said, smiling. "Everything changed when news came that Harald had been taken by the catmen. We were only a half-day's ride out of Arilinn, and there was no possible way of getting home within a tenday. Carolin arranged for an aircar and then insisted that Father take me back."

"So you are responsible for Varzil being there, to bargain with the catmen as no other man could have done," Harald said, inclining his head. "For that, *vai dom,* I owe my life to you as well."

"At the time," Carolin said, "I thought only that someone of Varzil's talent must be given a chance at the Tower. I don't think any of us realized what would come from it—the Compact, the rebuilding of Neskaya . . ."

"It is unwise to claim personal credit for those things that are the product of the dedication and good will of many men," Varzil said.

"And women," Maura said.

"Indeed," Carolin answered her, "sometimes I think that women do more to reshape our world than we do, but so skillfully and modestly that no one ever notices."

"No one notices?" Maura teased. "How can you miss Lady Liriel, your own kinswoman? Or Queen Taniquel, or Romilly MacAran, or even Jandria in her red vest, fighting as bravely as any man?"

Varzil, it turned out, had returned to Hali Tower for a season. "At least," he said lightly, "I think I have. I've been running around the countryside so much, I sometimes wake up not quite sure where I am."

Carolin laughed. "It was selfish of me to take you from Neskaya to act as my emissary to Asturias, but there was no one else who could have carried it off."

"A difficult business, that," Varzil replied, as the others looked up, eager to hear the story. "It was a politely disguised exchange of hostages, while attempting to spread the Compact—I say *attempting,* for the Asturias lords would have no part in it. I think they are too frightened to give up their *laran* weapons."

"Which makes them even more dangerous," Harald said tightly, "for they will not live in peace with their neighbors, as the folk of Marenji have learned to their sorrow."

"They released our kinsman, *Dom* Eiric, before I could interview him," Varzil said, "and he is under truce oath not to attack them for another half year, so something good may yet come from that quarter."

"Friends," Carolin interrupted, "let us not diminish the joy of our reunion with talk of war. There is time and enough for sorrow. Here we have occasion for celebration. We have honored guests, and cherished friends. I don't believe the four of us have been together since that first Midwinter at Hali."

"Goodness!" Maura laughed. "Has it been that long? What a wild bunch we were in those day! Orain was with us then, and Jandria, before she pierced her ear and joined the Sisterhood of the Sword, and your other friend from Arilinn—what was his name, Carlo?"

"Oh, do you mean Eduin?" Carolin shook his head slightly. "It has been a long time, hasn't it? I heard he came to a rather bad end. Was he ever seen after the battle of Hestral Tower?"

Dyannis lowered her eyes and pretended to be absorbed in her soup. They all carefully avoided mention of either Rakhal or Lyondri, the cousins who had usurped Carolin's throne and then instituted a reign of terror across the land. Why could they not forget about Eduin, too?

"For tonight, however, let all hearts be merry." Carolin raised his wine goblet. "May that time come speedily when people of good will everywhere will have similar reason to celebrate."

"We have yet another occasion for gladness," Maura said. "Dyannis is back among us. The folk at Hali will rejoice at her return."

Dyannis felt the blood drain from her cheeks, leaving her suddenly cold. She raised her voice above the murmur and clink of goblets and knives against fine porcelain plates. "Your Majesty," she said formally, "I regret—that is not the case. In fact, the opposite is true. I have come here with my brother to be betrothed to a cousin of the wife of Carolin's kinsman, Geremy Hastur. All that remains is the permission of my Keeper and Carolin's blessing, as his overlord."

There, it was said. She could not turn back now. Even though she knew she had done the only honorable thing, Dyannis felt sick at heart.

Silence dropped like a thick blanket over the table. Varzil sat motionless. Then he broke out into an enormous grin. Beside him, Carolin and Maura barely suppressed their own smiles.

"Hali will indeed have cause to rejoice," Harald said.

"Please do not mock me!" Dyannis cried.

"You tell her, Harald," Varzil said.

Harald turned to Dyannis. His eyes glowed as if the sun had risen behind them. "My dear sister, did you really believe I would let you enter into a marriage that was not your wish? When I realized what I had done, I sent word to Varzil the very next day to enlist his help in finding a way out of our quandary."

"But—but an agreement was made," Dyannis stammered. "*Dom* Tiavan's family—the alliance—"

"Which is not nearly as important as having you, a powerful *leronis,* serving all of Darkover," Varzil said. "As for your intended bridegroom, Maura herself came up with a solution."

Maura described how, while Dyannis was on the road to Thendara, she had arranged for an equally advantageous match between *Dom* Tiavan Harryl and Rohanne's youngest sister, who had nothing but her sweet disposition to recommend her. Everyone had assumed that as the last of six daughters of a poor but noble family, with no dowry or connections, the sister would die a spinster. Upon their arrival, Harald had agreed to give her the income from a nice stretch of pastureland for her lifetime, with the land itself to go to any children. He felt sure that with such a dowry, and the blessing of King Carolin, the Harryls would be more than content.

Dyannis listened in amazement. She turned to Harald. "How can this be?"

"Do you not wish to return to Hali Tower? If so, I have most grievously misunderstood you."

"Oh, yes! But—"

"*Breda,* did you think for a moment that your brothers do not love you?" Varzil broke in. "That we don't care for your happiness? How could you be content anywhere but a Tower, using your Gifts? When Harald sent word what had happened, how could we not do everything in our power to help you?"

For a long moment, Dyannis could not speak. Her throat closed up with tears. Only the self-control achieved by years of training kept her at her seat, head lifted. She took a deep, shuddering breath. Even so, her voice came out in a whisper. "I have no words to thank you enough, both of you."

"You can thank me by using your Gifts to the fullest," Varzil said. *By being in truth what you are, a Keeper.*

"We did not act solely for your benefit, *vai leronis,*" said Carolin, "but for the good of all. The Tower needs you. Will you not reconsider Varzil's proposal that you train as a Keeper?"

"You and the gods have clearly conspired against me!" Dyannis said, recovering a small measure of composure. "I came to Thendara, prepared to uphold the honor of my family and serve a greater purpose than my own personal desires. At the time, I thought that was to be the marriage Harald had arranged for me. Now I see another destiny in service to you, to Hali Tower, perhaps to all of Darkover." She turned to Varzil, and her voice trembled a little. "If you and Raimon, who are my Keepers, say I am fit, then I will undertake to train as one of you with all my strength and will."

For a long moment, no one spoke, and she realized their silence represented a profound respect for her choice. Then Carolin raised his goblet to her. "This is a moment we will tell our children about," he said solemnly, "the day Dyannis of Hali joined the ranks of the very first women Keepers." Dyannis found herself far more deeply touched by the quiet dignity of the moment than by any expressions of mirth.

After a bit, Carolin turned to Lerrys. "What about you, *chiyu?* I hear you are to pass a season at Hali Tower, and learn what you can from the wise folk there. Will you follow in the footsteps of your brother and sister, and become a *laranzu?*"

The boy ducked his head. "Your pardon, *vai dom,* but my place is back at Sweetwater. I will go to Hali Tower if it is my father's wish, but I will be counting the days until I return home."

"Well enough said," Carolin said, "for without men to till the land and raise fine sons, there would be no one for the Towers to serve."

He then called for another toast, and this one Dyannis joined in with a whole heart.

33

The dinner concluded with good spirits and expressions of fellowship. Dyannis said little, for she was emotionally drained from the sudden reversal of her fortune. As they headed back to their quarters, however, she gathered her strength and asked Harald if they might talk a little. She still did not understand why he had changed his mind, and gone to such great lengths to preserve her freedom. Although the hour was late, he dismissed their servants, leaving them alone in the sitting chamber. A small fire had been lit, and Dyannis went over to it, although she did not feel cold.

"I saw that no matter how advantageous the match might be, the cost was even higher," he said. "At first, I assumed you had given up your place in a Tower, that no matter what else you did, it would not be to use your *laran*. But then, when I truly understood . . ."

He went to her and took her hands in his. Dyannis sensed the deliberation in his touch. He wanted her to read his mind. Caught between the light of the fire and the row of candles on the mantle, his features bore a striking resemblance to their father's. But *Dom* Felix Ridenow would never have spoken as Harald did now.

"I of all men know how important—how rare and precious—*laran* is to our world and its people." His voice was low and husky. In his mind, she saw images, layered one over the other—

—moonlight on flashing swords, the musty reek of catmen, furred bodies twisting and slashing, fire piercing his side, the spurt of hot blood—

—the desperate flight through the hills, running headlong into a cave—down a series of tunnels—the torch sputtering—fever chills shuddering through his body, lights flickering in his mind, the sweetish rankness of a wound gone bad—

—*HARALD!* Varzil's sure mental voice, calling him back from delirium, torches in the distance, more catmen, a sword at his throat—

—*no hope, no hope at last*—

—Varzil stepping forward from the rescuers, his eyes glowing as if lit from within, glaring at the catmen's leader, speaking without words, reaching out to that terrified, inhuman mind—

—the sword falling away, the catmen melting into the darkness—

What happened next was part of family history. Harald had persuaded *Dom* Felix to allow Varzil to return to Arilinn to train his remarkable *laran* talent.

"He has done what none of us thought possible," Harald had argued, "he has made a bargain with the catmen. Surely such a Gift must be developed to its fullest. To do anything less would be to throw it back into the teeth of the gods who bestowed it."

Now Harald gazed at Dyannis with an expression of awe and determination. *What if Varzil had accepted Father's verdict, that he had no talent worth training? What if he had given up, gone along with what was expected of him? How can I ask the same of Dyannis?*

A hush fell on the room, broken only by the soft fall of embers deep within the fire.

"I could never ask that of you," he repeated aloud.

She bent her head, moved beyond words.

"I cannot say that I have much faith in women joining the ranks of Keepers, even as one of Varzil's experiments. But this much I do know: you must return to Hali and whatever destiny awaits you there. To force you into a marriage, no matter how advantageous to the family, would be as ill done—and, I suspect, as dangerous—as chaining a dragon to roast my meat."

— ✦ —

Harald set out again in two days, for even his paxman, Black Eiric, could not long run Sweetwater without him, not with autumn rapidly approaching. Lerrys went directly to Hali. By the time Dyannis was ready to follow her nephew, she had had her fill of court life at Thendara. The castle here had been the seat of many generations of Hastur Kings, and the weight of centuries of elegance and ostentatious wealth bore down upon her. Everywhere she looked, velvets and jewel-studded satins vied with silver lace or ornaments of copper for brilliance. Perfume hung like a miasma in the air. Within an hour of her arrival, it seemed, everyone had known who she was, whose sister she was, and had rushed to curry her favor. Within a day of their arrival, moreover, Thendara buzzed with news of Varzil's presence.

"How can Carolin bear living in the midst of such decadence?" she asked Varzil as they rode along the road to Hali.

They had made an early start that morning. Bridle rings jingled in the dew-moist air as the horses pranced in eagerness.

"Perhaps, if he were not who he is, it would be difficult to remain unaffected," Varzil said. "These lordling courtiers may seem like the worst of sycophants, but they wield influence beyond their personal sphere. It is from their lands and tenants that armies are raised and fed, that grain and meat flow to the cities, and taxes to the treasury. Carolin grants them the prestige of the court, but he is careful to be even-handed in his favors. Thus, he keeps them striving against one another, each eager to gain some small advantage."

Dyannis remembered coming to the court at Hali that first Midwinter Festival, and how awed she had been by the ladies and courtiers in their holiday garb. Compared to the simple comfort of Sweetwater and the austerity of the Tower, the palace seemed like a gorgeous dream. She wondered if the place itself had not imbued Eduin with a romantic glamour. Certainly, she had thrown herself headlong into his arms against all the rules of proper decorum.

As they rode along, Dyannis and Varzil enjoyed a measure of privacy, for the two guards Carolin had sent along stayed some distance in front, and the pack animals and attendants trailed behind. Even though she knew she ought to seize the opportunity, she hesitated.

"What is it, *chiya?*" he asked gently.

She took a deep breath. "I felt so strongly you must be mistaken about Eduin playing a role in Felicia's death and the attacks upon Carolin. I tried to remember every scrap of conversation, every nuance, just to prove you wrong."

Varzil turned slightly in the saddle. His slender body moved easily with the horse's stride. Eyes shadowed, face impassive, he waited for her to go on.

As she switched to mental speech, the story tumbled out, how she had revealed Felicia's identity to Eduin.

I don't know what I was thinking, she concluded. *If you had wanted me to know who she was, surely you would have said something. It was wrong for me to eavesdrop on your thoughts—you were so much in love with her—but even more wrong for me to pass it on.*

"Varzil," she faced him directly. "I would give anything to unsay those careless words. If, knowing what I have done, you now feel I am unfit to work as a Keeper or in any Tower position, I will accept your decision."

He stared straight ahead at the road, broken by shadows cast by the line of willows. She could not read a single hint of emotion from him. At last, he broke the silence.

"One thing is certain, and that is the Dyannis who spoke so impetuously, who acted so rashly, could never have behaved with such dignity and restraint as you did in accepting your obligations, first to your family, then to the future of the Towers and Darkover itself. If you are speaking of your fitness as a Keeper, it is by your present actions you are to be judged, not a foolish mistake in the past."

Moved as she was by his compassion, Dyannis could not let the issue pass. "Yet we are still responsible for those 'foolish mistakes' when they result in terrible harm to others, are we not? I am still guilty of an action that eventually led to—" *to the death of the woman you loved, a fellow leronis, a person who had as much right to fulfill her promise as I do. How can I then aspire to become what she was, a woman Keeper, with her blood on my hands?*

"Let us not speak of guilt and retribution," he answered her gently, "or at least, not yours. Did you hold a knife to Eduin's throat and force him to kill Felicia, or command Hali's attack upon Hestral? You are in no way to blame for his actions."

"I spoke without care, heedless of the consequences," Dyannis said miserably. "If I had not betrayed her, Eduin might never have discovered who she was."

"You do not know that. He was resourceful and tenacious. I believe he would have found out eventually. Besides, how could you have known he was not trustworthy? You had been lovers once, and he was still a *laranzu*. No, let him alone bear the responsibility for what he chose to do. You have more than repaid whatever harm you caused."

For a long time, they rode on in silence. The land began to rise, but not steeply. Dew rose from the earth as the great Bloody Sun climbed higher. Birds sang from the hedgerows and then fell silent, only to begin again.

Life was like that, Dyannis thought, full of beginnings and endings. Joy surged in her, as well as excitement for the new life that awaited her.

There was one aspect of Felicia's death that still gnawed upon her mind. Well before they reached the Tower, she spoke of it to Varzil.

"Why would Eduin want to harm *both* Felicia and Carolin? Carolin must surely have made enemies, first as prince and then as king. What powerful lord does not? Perhaps he injured Eduin in some way, and Eduin pretended to be his friend until he could strike back."

"I have wondered that, too," Varzil answered. "At the time, I believed Eduin resented my friendship with Carolin out of jealousy, but it could also have been because I came between him and his intended victim."

"That does not explain Eduin's assault upon Felicia," Dyannis pointed out.

Varzil sighed, a barely-audible whisper of breath. "Before Felicia came to Arilinn, she and Eduin had never met. I am sure of it. More than that, I cannot believe he hated her personally."

Dyannis frowned. "It doesn't make sense—Felicia and Carolin came from different branches of the Hastur family, and so far as I know, none now remain of Queen Taniquel's lineage. That's why the crown passed to Felix of Carcosa when King Rafael II died. You see," she added with a smile, "I have been studying my history. If you are right, Eduin killed Felicia not because of anything she herself had done, but because she was the last remaining child of Queen Taniquel."

"There was this, too," Varzil went on. "As I followed the mental trace of the Blue Lake assassin into the Overworld, I caught a glimpse of a castle whose banners bore a white-and-black diamond pattern."

Dyannis frowned. "I'm not familiar with that one."

"That's because it no longer exists. It belonged to the family Deslucido."

"The one from the ballads?" She remembered the stories from her childhood, although few harpers sang the songs these days. King Damian Deslucido had overrun his smaller neighbors, including Acosta, home of the famous Queen Taniquel. She fled the slaughter and, with the aid of her uncle, King Rafael Hastur II, returned with an army at her back. "How could that be the connection? It was a generation ago."

"You of all people, a Ridenow among Hasturs, ought to know that hatred and suspicion do not resolve themselves overnight."

"I meant only that if the family was extinct, there should be no one left to carry on the feud." A thought shivered through her. "Could Eduin have had some connection with them?"

Eduin had never spoken of his childhood or his relations. Dyannis had supposed he was ashamed of coming from poor or ignoble folk, and she was too caught up in the romance of the moment to care.

"I think he must have," Varzil said, "although we may never know what it was. If Eduin were involved in the attacks on Carolin, including the Blue Lake attempt, then his motive went beyond personal hatred or resentment. The exact word the dying assassin had in his mind was *revenge*."

Varzil and Dyannis stayed briefly in the city of Hali, in the old palace of the Hasturs. They intended to pass through it to the Tower itself, but Varzil's business delayed them.

When Dyannis had a little free time, she went into the palace library to see what she could discover about the war with Deslucido. She hoped to find some record of those followers of King Damian who survived, perhaps even the name MacEarn. If any such record existed, it was uncataloged and forgotten, for she never found any trace of it. Indeed, the entire victory seemed shrouded in such vague, flowery, and poetic language, she felt sure that the chronicler had never seen the battle with his own eyes. Half of what she read seemed to be traditional descriptions that could have applied to almost any battle, and the other half were filled with oddly incomplete details. Just as in the Archives at Hali, these records seemed to be a deliberate attempt to mislead by omission. What, Dyannis wondered, were they trying to hide?

Dyannis decided to do a little investigating on her own. Perhaps there was some elderly courtier who might remember King Rafael or Taniquel herself. If she could draw that person into reminiscence, she might learn of some connection, some forgotten grievance never recorded in the chronicles.

She remembered the palace from her first visit, that Midwinter Festival when she had met Eduin. Although still in use, the rooms seemed shabby around the edges. The woodwork had lost the fine, hard gloss of daily polish, and the tapestries that softened the stone walls had gone dusty with the years. Still, she found her chambers comfortable, the evening fires generous, the feather bed soft, and the food well-prepared.

While Varzil was about some errand or other for King Carolin, Dyannis made her inquiries. Most of the older courtiers had long since gone, and those few who remained lived in Thendara. Lady Bronwyn had already been elderly on that first Midwinter Festival, and Dyannis was half-expecting to hear that the old lady had died.

"Oh, no, *vai leronis*," the maid said, curtsying for the fourth or fifth time, "though these days, the only ones who see her are her own personal companion and sometimes *Dom* Raimon, when he comes from the Tower. She has no other visitors, and I don't think she's left her own chambers these five years."

Dyannis sent a page to inquire if the lady would meet with her. A few hours later, she received an invitation. The page guided her to the old royal wing, past suites of rooms that were now shut up, unused. Lady Bronwyn's quarters must have been built for some long-ago child princess, for the doorway, carved like two trees arching toward each other, was narrow and almost too short for a normal woman.

Dyannis lifted the latch and entered. The beautifully proportioned octagonal room was lined by windows and deeply cushioned seats. A small fire burned merrily in the hearth of Temoran marble, carved with sea-maidens trailing real inset pearls from their long, intertwined locks of hair. Thin rows of translucent blue stone rose upward to join in a star pattern on the ceiling.

An old woman lay on a divan beside the fireplace, her form hidden beneath the lace-edged blankets. A cap of snowy gauze framed her face. She lifted one hand, the knuckles huge and twisted, and beckoned Dyannis closer.

Dyannis felt as if she ought to curtsy, just as the maid had done. Then she felt the presence of the older woman's mind, a ripple of silvery bells.

Forgive me, I had not realized you, too, were a leronis.

"Oh, yes, although my power is but a shadow of what it once was." The voice was thin and uncertain, the words broken by pauses to draw breath. "I cannot speak to your mind in return, so it is you who must forgive me."

Dyannis drew up a footstool as she was bid. This close, the old woman's face was like a faded flower, the skin pleated into a hundred tiny wrinkles, each reflecting a moment of her life, of pain, of joy, of strength. Soon they were speaking easily to one another.

"So you are the sister of young Varzil, who was Felicia's love. Very interesting boy, that Varzil. He and Carlo are at that age, you know, when they think they can change the whole world." Lady Bronwyn had surely seen several generations of young men filled with idealistic zeal.

"Tell me about Felicia," Dyannis said. "I believe you knew her mother, Queen Taniquel."

"Tani? You remind me of her. Not the hair, for hers was black, you know, but something in the way you hold yourself. No, it was Coryn I knew best, from the time he was a boy. I was escorting Liane Storn to Tramontana—that was before it was burned to the ground—and I remember . . . Such clarity of voice," she tapped one temple. "Such force. I thought half the Hellers must have woken from his call." Lady Bronwyn fell silent and her gaze dimmed, as her eyes turned inward toward a past only she could see.

Gently, Dyannis said, "Coryn helped Taniquel to defeat King Deslucido. Do you remember that?"

"I remember Deslucido, and the terrible things he did, setting one Tower against the other." A shiver ran through the old woman's frame, visible even beneath her wrappings. "So many talented *leronyn* lost their lives, and even more lived on as cripples. Bernardo, whom I loved as a brother, could never work again after that. His heart was badly damaged, so the healers said, but I think the worst hurts were not to the body but to the spirit."

"Could any of that family, the Deslucidos, have survived?" Dyannis asked, leaning forward.

"I hardly think so. Rafael hanged both father and son after the last battle. Strange, it was not like him to take such a harsh measure, not when victory was already his, but he must have had his reasons. Men do not always behave honorably in battle. Still, what was to be gained? Deslucido's army was shattered, his conquests in rebellion. Rafael had never been cruel, and never was again. I was sorry when he died."

"I thought there was a brother, the *laranzu* who commanded Tramontana in the battle that destroyed the Towers."

"Ah, yes. Rumail. He was *nedestro,* but never had any ambitions to the throne that I heard of. Had a reputation as a bad sort. Neskaya expelled him for unethical use of *laran* and I fear he never forgot the insult."

"What happened to him?"

"Oh, he surely perished when Tramontana burned, for he was never seen again." Lady Bronwyn's head nodded, and the companion who had been hovering in the back stepped forward.

"She must rest now."

Dyannis made her apologies and withdrew, not sure whether she had learned anything of value or not. Although it seemed unlikely, Eduin's own family must have been among the few who remained loyal to the Deslucidos. She was troubled by the portrait of Rafael Hastur and the legendary Taniquel as vindictive, slaughtering a helpless, defeated adversary. Whatever Damian had done, he had already been removed from power. He could have been exiled with his son retained as hostage, as was the usual practice.

Why kill both of them? What was so evil or so dangerous that they both must die? Or had Rafael and his niece acted out of malice and the exercise of power because there were none left to oppose them?

Dyannis had not given much thought to her return to Hali Tower, beyond her longing to take up the work she loved among the people who had been her dearest friends. Since she had first come to Hali as a very young woman, she had never been away for this long. The Tower and its community had remained unchanged in her mind, while her own life had gone on. Quickly she realized her very absence had created a change. She was welcomed with warmth, but her place in the circle had been taken by others, her quarters had been occupied by someone else; relationships had shifted, work had been completed, messages had been sent and received.

When Rorie commented on how she had changed, she shrugged. He meant that he found her cold and distant. She shrank from his overtures, unsure how to avoid causing pain. Seeing him, hearing his voice, she felt more confused than before, and she could not afford the distraction of such emotions, not when all her concentration must be focused on her training.

Night by night, Dyannis worked within the circle, learning the skills of an under-Keeper. It was not unlike the role she had played in rebuilding the walls of Cedestri Tower, only this time she was fully aware of what she did. When she was not working in the circle, she studied with either Raimon or Varzil. She would tumble into bed, too exhausted to do anything but sleep. Even if she had wanted a personal relationship with Rorie, she had neither the time nor the energy.

BOOK V

34

Lord Brynon Aillard's entourage descended from the gentle slopes of Kirella into the heart of the Plains of Valeron. Winds swept down upon them, edged with the dust that arose from the vast fields of wheat and tallgrass. When they stopped to rest their horses, Eduin stood in the stirrups, looking in every direction at the endless rippling gold. Valeron was unlike any place he had ever seen. Without mountain or forest to delineate the horizon, the sky seemed enormous. He felt as if he were suspended between heaven and earth.

Sometimes they saw dry lightning in the distance. The wind shifted, bearing the acrid taste of ozone. Eduin glanced north, toward the far Hellers and Aldaran, whose wizards were reputed to summon storms from a clear sky. He remembered the strange weather that had afflicted Thendara in the days before the riot at Hali Lake. How long ago that seemed, he thought, and how many things had happened since. Here, in the vast flatness of the Valeron Plains, nature held sway, dwarfing petty human concerns.

He felt a change in the air some days before the city of Valeron came into view. The height and texture of the grasses altered, more gray-tinged green than the dull gold of the Plains. The horses mouthed their bits and picked up their pace. The air seemed fresher, moister, tinged with the aromatic scents of growing things he could not name but which evoked a subtle resonance.

Eduin first spied the city of Valeron toward sundown, when for a moment, the light of the great Bloody Sun bathed its towers. On the far horizon, in the bend of the distant river, the city glowed like copper and brass, silver and steel. He held his breath, straining against the brightness. It hurt his eyes to gaze directly at it.

Saravio, riding just behind him, spoke, but Eduin scarcely heard the words. When he looked back at the city, the light had shifted, leaving only ordinary stone in the setting sun.

The following day, they reached the city walls and Castle Aillard. Behind them lay the Plains and before them, an expanse of salt marshes cut by the River Valeron. They passed army encampments and a field where three aircars sat, their sides scored with lines of greasy smoke.

At the gates, guards demanded their names and bade them wait while word was taken up to the castle. They proceeded through a city filled with preparations for the festival of Midsummer. Garlands and bright pennons, many in the Aillard colors of scarlet and gray, hung from every doorway and balcony. Peddlers and merchants thronged the streets, selling flowers, fruit, and the gaily-beribboned baskets that were traditional gifts for female relatives.

The castle itself was set on the only high place for leagues around. Its battlements, also bedecked in holiday finery, commanded a view in all directions. One turret in particular rose above the others, separated from the main structure. It was, Eduin learned from one of the Kirella guards, the home of a small Tower.

Eduin lowered his *laran* barriers minutely, listening for any mental activity from the Tower. He sensed several matrix lattices of the sort used to charge batteries for the aircars, apparatus for making *clingfire* as well as the more ordinary sort of fire-bombs, and relay screens to send messages to other Towers. The few minds he sensed were either deep in slumber or else so focused on other matters as to be unaware of his presence. The rulers of Valeron were clearly confident of their invulnerability to attack. He must persuade them that they did, indeed, have an enemy.

Once within the castle walls, a steward came forth to give directions for the stowing of baggage, the feeding and stabling of their animals, and the housing for both the noble family and their attendants. The Kirella guards were directed to the barracks in another area of the city, all except those few Lord Brynon kept for his personal use.

"We will attend the Lady tonight," Lord Brynon told Eduin just before they separated. "Be ready to come with me. Even though it is Midsummer Festival, we have sterner business to conduct."

Eduin nodded, satisfied that Lord Brynon was prepared to introduce the issue of Varzil's conspiracy at the first opportunity. With the might of Valeron aimed at his destruction, not even the legendary Keeper of Neskaya could long escape. Sooner or later, Varzil must leave his Tower fortress, perhaps on some mission for Carolin.

And then . . . then I will have him and with his death, Carolin Hastur will fall. My father's ghost will be appeased and I will at last be free.

— ◆ —

The Aillards were a matrilineal clan, and Queen Julianna held full rights in the *Comyn* Council, as much as any lord. Eduin had known great ladies before, although most of them derived their status from important kinsmen. In his years at Arilinn, and then at Hali and Hestral, he had been introduced to Lady Liriel Hastur and Maura Elhalyn, who was now Carolin's Queen.

The presence chamber was a small one, austere in its furnishings. The style was unfamiliar, the wooden chairs gray or gold, simply shaped with clean soaring lines, the cushions and tapestries in pale, muted colors, unlike the dark, rich ornamentation of the court at Hali.

This evening, only a few counselors stood in attendance. Eduin sensed the trained *laran* of one of them, a woman who appeared to be only a few years older than Romilla. She held herself apart from the others with the composure and slightly distracted air he remembered in Maura Elhalyn when he first met her. He had best be on his guard.

Eduin turned his attention back to Julianna Aillard. With her thick body, unadorned black gown, and taut mouth, she conceded little to the softness of a courtly lady. Chestnut hair frosted with white was coiled low on her neck in a severe, old-fashioned style. Her throne was tall and high-backed, carved from wood polished to a faintly iridescent sheen. Behind her and to one side stood a younger woman, alike but for the untouched brightness of her hair and the steel-slim figure.

Lord Brynon stepped forward as the herald announced him, halted a respectful distance before Queen Julianna, and bowed. She watched him, her expression unreadable. Then she gestured for him to rise and, coming forward, held out her hands in a kinswoman's greeting.

"I am sorry you could not be with us last Midwinter, as has been our custom," Julianna said. Her voice had an odd, husky quality, lower in pitch than most women's. "A joy lessened at one time is increased at another. You are most welcome to Valeron."

"I am honored to be here, kinswoman," he replied, "yet our joy must be tempered with consideration of recent events. I have come not only to celebrate, but to take counsel with you."

"If you mean the dreadful events at Isoldir, rest assured that at the proper time, we will speak of them. For tonight, however, be at your ease." The Lady of Valeron shifted her focus from the single man standing before her to encompass his entire retinue. "May the season lighten all your hearts. Let us feast together and, in due time, hear your concerns."

Lord Brynon bowed and made ready to withdraw. He had clearly been dismissed and must bide the Queen's pleasure. Any objection might well jeopardize his welcome.

The next days passed with preparations for the festivities, rest for Romilla and her ladies, and care of the men and beasts. Although Eduin chafed at the delay, he was powerless to hurry an audience with the Queen.

Eduin used the time to become acquainted with the household staff. He had not realized before the advantages of an inferior position. Maids and underlings were willing to speak to him with a frankness they would never have shown to either a courtier or a *laranzu*.

Eduin's experience working in the stables at Thendara gave him an ease born of familiarity with those who tended the horses. He soon found a groom eager to exchange news and gossip.

"A little over a year ago," the man said, leaning on his pitchfork as he paused in mucking out the stall for Romilla's fine palfrey, "the folk at Isoldir sent an aircar at us, carrying all manner of vile sorcery. Now, we hadn't been exactly friendly, but there weren't no call to do such a thing. Sneaking cowards, the lot of them. Zandru's own luck were with us, though, for the Lady sent out our own and shot it down. Story was, they blew it to bits, scattered for leagues around and all its poison with it."

Eduin agreed this was indeed a stroke of luck.

"Then what was we to do? Let them have another shot at us?" The stableman shook his head, digging the tines of the fork deep into the hay to scatter it over the wooden floor.

"How could you?" Eduin said, coarsening his own accent. "Let a nest of scorpion-ants grow, and next thing you know, they'll be coming up under your house."

"Exactly what I think. But the Lady, she held off. She sent to firebomb their Tower, all right, so they could make no more terrible weapons, but she left the castle and villages and all."

"Why would she hold back? Is she not afeared that Isoldir will rise against her once more?"

"Ah, but any who'd think that don't know our Lady. Tough as salt, she is. Besides, there's many a man, both here and there, who's asleep nights in his own home with his own family that would otherwise be meat for *kyorebni*." The man spat in the corner and bent once more to his work.

That very night, Julianna Aillard held an informal council with Lord Brynon, Lady Romilla, and her most trusted councillors. Her brother and general, Marzan of Valeron, attended, along with two of his lieutenants. They sat around a table in a chamber that was clearly a working office, perhaps the very same from which the counterattack upon Isoldir had been planned. The Queen's daughter, Marelie, stood behind her chair, watching and listening, following every gesture and nuance with a touch of *laran*.

Upon their arrival at Valeron, Saravio had sunk into a lethargy and was not yet sufficiently recovered to attend. Eduin found himself relegated to standing behind Lord Brynon, like a common attendant. Other than Marelie, who used her untrained *laran* without any awareness of what she was doing and probably thought of it as intuition, none of the council had any psychic abilities. Queen Julianna and her heir both had enough latent talent to be accepted by the *Comyn* Council, but neither had spent any time at a Tower. Valentina Aillard, whom Eduin had known in his years at Arilinn, was the daughter of a collateral branch; he had also met her cousin, Ellimara, at Hali. The talent ran deep in the Aillard bloodline, but in this generation, at least, all energies had been turned to the ruling of the land.

Julianna, Queen of Valeron, was no innocent and weak-minded soul, but a shrewd woman accustomed to the intrigues and uses of power. She listened to Lord Brynon's information with quiet calculation. Eduin sensed the workings of her mind, evaluating, weighing each point.

As the discussion progressed, a picture emerged of two lands, one mighty, the other small but proud. Valeron and Isoldir had been at each other's throats many times over the last three generations. The aircar attack from Cedestri Tower may have been unprovoked, but it was hardly without cause. Faced with Julianna's political ambitions, the Isoldir lords must surely have seized upon whatever weapons came within their reach. It was only through Valeron's prompt interception that an even greater devastation was averted, for the Cedestri aircar carried a particularly virulent form of bonewater dust.

Lord Brynon responded to this news with a gesture of abhorrence and Romilla looked visibly shaken.

"We had not believed Cedestri capable of such a thing," Julianna commented.

Eduin did not think that Julliana herself would have any scruples about using whatever weapon came to hand. Her concern was solely that a previously weak neighbor had gained control of such a weapon.

Even as the groom had described, the Cedestri aircar had been destroyed, but not before its cargo had been scattered over hundreds of leagues, rendering the land uninhabitable for generations. From Julianna's description, Eduin realized that the troupe of musicians from Robardin's Fort must have passed through one of the contaminated regions before the roads could be marked. He remembered the kernels of poisonous blackness in the bodies of his friends.

Raynita's voice hummed softly at the back of his mind, rising and falling like the flight of some wild bird. She had not cared for his parentage or credentials in offering the simple comfort of her friendship.

I traveled with them, ate their bread, sang their songs, Eduin thought.

Outrage and pity whispered through him. The echo of his father's voice urged him to discard such thoughts as weak and useless. If a few insignificant minstrels perished because they ventured where they should not, it made no difference in the overriding need for revenge.

"Isoldir has been a thorn in our side for longer than we can remember," General Marzan said, "but it is not wise to turn a thorn into a sword. Therefore, we did not destroy them, for it is not possible to kill every last one of them, and any that remained after an overpowering strike would nurse their vengeance to the grave."

Aye, and beyond. Eduin shuddered inwardly, as if touched by a knife so chill and hard, it came straight from Zandru's coldest Forge. He felt as if he were two people listening to the council. One, the son of his father, kept searching for any opening, any leverage he might use to shape the fears and hatreds of these people into a weapon against Varzil Ridenow and through him, Carolin Hastur.

At the same time, another part of him understood what had been done to him, yet was unable to free himself from his destiny.

Injustice had begotten vengeance, and vengeance fed upon itself until there was nothing left—not his brothers, not his dreams of a life in the Tower, not his friendship with Carolin Hastur, not his love for Dyannis . . . nothing. In that instant, he saw, as if in a waking dream, the figure of a woman cloaked in shadow, with eyes like burning ice, turning toward him, reaching skeletal fingers toward his heart . . .

"We chose instead to render them incapable of a second such attack," Julianna continued. "We left them strength enough to maintain order within their own boundaries, for a land racked by chaos quickly becomes a danger to all of its neighbors, breeding outlaws and malcontents of every sort."

What if Rafael Hastur and his accursed niece, Queen Taniquel, had thought in this manner? What if his father had not been forced into exile? What if his uncle and cousin had been left with their lives and a shred of dignity? What if he himself had been free to follow the dictates of his heart and his talent?

"However," Julianna said, her voice edged, "we did not consider the intervention of outside aid. Cedestri Tower has already been rebuilt with the help of Varzil of Neskaya."

"Varzil!" Lord Brynon exclaimed, as if echoing Eduin's thought.

"Why should such a powerful Keeper bestir himself for an inconsequential little kingdom as Isoldir?"

Marelie bent to her mother's ear. Eduin could not catch her words, but understood their sense. *Because Cedestri was somehow able to make a major* laran *weapon, and that is against King Carolin's precious Compact.*

"Carolin Hastur would make certain that Cedestri is rebuilt as *he* wills it," Julianna said, "even as he rebuilt Neskaya Tower. To that end, he has sent his emissary, Varzil of Neskaya, knowing that whatever remained of the Tower circle would welcome their help without asking the price."

"The reach of the Hasturs grows long," Lord Brynon said. "The shadow of his ambition lies upon every land. Why else would he seek to disarm everyone who can stand against him?"

Queen Julianna's face turned hard, her eyes glittering like chips of obsidian. "Carolin sent an emissary here two summers ago, urging me to sign his Compact. I told him I would have none of it. During the last Council season, it was all anyone could talk about, for or against. It is easy to indulge in such idle talk when no aircars bearing *clingfire* are threatening you. Only then, too late, do you realize your sole protection is the threat of an overwhelming retaliation."

Good, Eduin thought as his father's ghost roused as if scenting blood. The Lady of Valeron was already disposed to distrust Carolin and his lackey, Varzil. Now to turn that suspicion into open hostility . . .

Julianna nodded, as if secretly agreeing with herself. "In time, this madness will pass. The great lords will return to the eternal truth that the only way to peace is through the balance of power."

Eduin felt even more estranged from the conversation. Once he would have argued that not only were powerful weapons like *clingfire* and bonewater dust necessary, but they should be controlled by the people who created them—the Towers. Now those arguments seemed as insubstantial as dayflies. It no longer mattered whether Arilinn or Hali or Cedestri remained standing and who ruled there. He stood alone in the ashes of his dreams.

Julianna deftly turned the conversation toward those courtesies that brought the meeting to a close. Eduin felt a sense of frustration, of unfulfilled expectation, for Lord Brynon had not put forth his own accusations against Varzil Ridenow.

Instead, Lord Brynon had seemed content to yield to Queen Julianna. Perhaps, Eduin reassured himself, he was only waiting for a suitable opportunity. They were new-come to Valeron, and there was much other business to attend to, not the least of which were the festivities of Midsummer.

35

Eduin and Saravio, as well as the other servants accompanying Lord Brynon, had been given quarters in the wing reserved for the men of the household staff in one of the older parts of the castle, a row of small rooms lining a drafty corridor. Their chamber was usually reserved for the personal servants of visiting nobility, and was a shade better quality than the others. Although it was cramped and had only a single slit window, there was a small brazier for warmth and a thick carpet, not Ardcarran but some local weaving. Best of all, they had the chamber to themselves, instead of sharing it with two or three others.

The Tower at Valeron stood apart from the rest of the castle, both physically and psychically. None of the household staff with whom Eduin had become friendly had ever seen the Keeper. The *laranzu'in* who tended the aircars went about their business silently; only the young *leronis* who served the court, Callina Mallory, had any public presence.

Callina had visited Romilla on their first night at Castle Aillard, as a courtesy and to inquire if she needed any care. They quickly fell into a routine of spending most of their daily hours together. When Eduin brought Saravio to Romilla's quarters the next morning, he found the two girls giggling together.

Eduin bowed. "*Vai leronis, vai damisela,* I give you both good morning."

Callina rose from the window seat where she and Romilla had been watching the soldiers drill in the courtyard below. Her red-gold hair, drawn back in a simple, unadorned style, caught the morning light.

Eduin had expected Callina to be like *Domna* Mhari of Kirella, but she was quite different. Mhari had a natural sense of politics and had been hardened by her own struggles with the physician. Callina was far younger, from one of the minor *Comyn* families near Temora. She had trained at the Tower there, but none of the servants knew why she had left to take a post so far from home.

"Sandoval!" Romilla cried, going to Saravio and taking his hand. "How happy I am that you have come! I was just telling Callina how you helped me. She says she has never heard singing like yours."

Saravio stared at the little *leronis* and seemed to actually see her. Eduin sensed the girl's self-confidence like a brittle shield. A darkness lay upon her, which not even her time in a Tower had dispelled. Perhaps, Eduin thought, she simply lacked the determination to overcome it. Now he felt Saravio's response to Callina's unhealed emotional wound.

Callina turned to Eduin. Despite her youthful complexion and bright hair, she looked plain, almost quenched. The dark eyes that met his were both innocent and knowing.

I sense the Gift in you, she spoke silently. *Can you hear me?* Her mental speech was slow and careful, as if she had made the most of a small talent for telepathy.

Eduin formed his reply to seem clumsy, unskilled. He expressed surprise and humble thanks at the notice of a Tower *leronis*. *I—I was told that my father had* nedestro Comyn *blood,* he stammered, letting the truth of his words come through. His father, Rumail Deslucido, was indeed the illegitimate brother of King Damian, and had the full Gift of *laran*. He had trained and worked at Neskaya Tower before it was destroyed, and should have been named Keeper, would have, if only—if only—

Yes, Callina replied. Eduin saw that she had sensed his thoughts, but misinterpreted them to mean that if only his father had been recognized and received proper training, he himself would have had a place in the world.

"Now I serve my brother, Sandoval the Blessed," Eduin said. "I ask no greater honor."

Deftly, Eduin placed Saravio at the center of the room and the women in subordinate positions. Romilla chattered about her former melancholy, heightening the other girl's anticipation.

Under his breath, Eduin murmured to Saravio, "Bring the joy of Naotalba to these women."

The mere speaking of the name of Naotalba was enough. Saravio began humming, almost too softly to hear, but with the full impact of his Gift.

Eduin felt the opening notes as a silvery thrill along his spine. His breath caught in his throat. Romilla's gaze turned inward, listening, opening her heart to what she knew would follow.

> *"Oh, the lark in the morning,*
> *She rises in the west,*
> *And comes home in the evening*
> *With blood upon her breast . . ."*

The words pierced Eduin, familiar and yet subtly altered. For a heartbeat only, he struggled to remain apart from the slow burning awakening of pleasure. The sensation began as a low vibration through the core of his body, so subtle as to be imperceptible by ordinary senses. Promising himself it would be for a moment only, he shut himself away from the outer world and gave himself over to the soaring pleasure.

The world of flesh and time fell away; he no longer felt his physical body. He floated in a silvery mist. A landscape condensed around him, graceful trees that swayed in a secret dance. Figures moved between them, their voices interweaving with the slow harmonies of sky and tree and rain. They turned their luminous eyes toward him . . .

The vision darkened like the sudden fall of night. The last thing he saw were the glimmering eyes and then they, too, disappeared. He was back in his body, his stomach clenched around a jagged rock. Thirst clawed the back of his throat, yet it was not physical drink he craved.

Saravio had fallen silent as the last reverberations of his mental manipulations faded from the minds of his listeners. Eduin cursed himself for surrendering so completely.

Romilla's eyes were still closed and he sensed her lingering, drawing the moment out, savoring the peace and euphoria in her memory.

Callina was another matter. Although susceptible, she might still become suspicious. Eduin nudged her mind with his *laran*. As he expected, very little remained of her psychic barriers at the moment. It was a small matter to implant a suggestion that the effect of pleasure and relaxation was due only to the beauty of the song, nothing more. It was entirely natural to respond in this way. Sandoval the Blessed and his assistant spoke only truth; they were to be trusted.

A moment later, Eduin released her. Color flushed her cheeks. She blinked. A shiver ran through her thin shoulders, then she collected herself. "Thank you," she said to Saravio. "That was very interesting . . ." she hesitated slightly over the next word, "music."

"My brother's songs help us all to look within ourselves," Eduin said. "For it is there, by the grace of the gods, we find true healing. You have the benefit of training at a Tower; tell me, am I mistaken in this?"

"No, no," she answered quickly. "You are correct. Sandoval is extraordinary, to have wrought such a change in Lady Romilla's condition. I see why Lord Brynon values you."

Eduin inclined his head. "We serve in any way we can. I believe it is a good thing, and the will of the gods, that we have come to Valeron at this time."

"It is indeed a troubled world we live in," Callina said, rising to her feet. "Any morsel of hope is welcome."

Romilla said eagerly, "At first, when I was ill, I could not see beyond the next day, even the next hour. With Sandoval's healing, as you see, I am well and strong."

"Then you will soon sit at council with Her Majesty, as is your right," Eduin said.

"Why, yes," Romilla said, clearly pleased. "If I had not fallen ill, I would surely have done so before now. I shall take my place this very evening."

Callina looked dubious. "Will not your lord father object to your taking precedence?"

Romilla tossed her head. "I am sure he will be happy that I am able to do so. Does the Blessed Sandoval not agree?"

"Most certainly, *vai domna,*" Eduin hastened to reply, "for only in this way can the perfidious influence of certain persons be opposed."

"You have seen this?"

Saravio took that moment to intone, "It is the will of Naotalba."

"Naotalba," Callina repeated in a dreamy voice. "I remember hearing that name as a child, in stories meant to frighten us. I always imagined her as a tragic figure, the Bride of Zandru of the Seven Frozen Hells. Now she seems so comforting."

"Much of what we were taught as children changes in the light of truth," Romilla said. "If Naotalba represents a descent into hell, then she also brings us hope, for she is a bridge between the human and the divine."

"But she doesn't exist, not really," Callina protested.

"To Sandoval she does," Eduin said. "Perhaps she is only a symbol that allows him to focus his vision and insight, for there is no question that he can see many things beyond the scope of ordinary men."

"Has he the gift of Allart Hastur, to see into the future?" Callina asked.

"Saravio's vision does not lie in a heritage of strange *laran* from the breeding programs during the Ages of Chaos," Eduin hastened to say, for Callina had come uncomfortably close to the truth. It was one thing to present Saravio as a man touched by the gods, whatever they might be, and entirely another to arouse the suspicion he might be a renegade *laranzu.* "In the end, what difference does it make what Naotalba is, so long as she protects us against our enemies?"

"We must stand together in these perilous times, Kirella and Valeron side by side," Romilla said breathlessly. She slipped her hand confidentially through Callina's elbow. "*You* must help us."

Callina blushed and looked confused, for she was, after all, very young. "I am sworn to the Queen's service, but whatever I can do, I will."

— ✦ —

During the days that followed, Eduin found many opportunities to interact with Callina and others of the court. Courtiers here, as elsewhere, were always alert for the latest rumor or hint of favoritism, possibility for advancement or influence. Within a few hours of their arrival, Eduin had sensed the first tendrils of their curiosity. The stable-man whispered to his friends, as did the chambermaids who served Romilla and Callina.

A word dropped here and there, accompanied by a psychic nudge, was enough to fuel the growing fascination with Saravio. Eduin soon heard of miracle healings, of clairvoyant trances, of haloes of light surrounding the holy man.

Before long, stories of "the Blessed Sandoval" reached beyond the servants' quarters. One morning, a page knocked on the door of the room Eduin and Saravio shared. One of the Queen's ladies-in-waiting had a headache, and, having heard how Romilla had been cured of a terrible affliction, begged him to come to her aid.

Eduin doubted the lady had any ailment beyond those generated by boredom, rich food, and confined living space. "Come," he told Sar-avio, "the disbelievers call upon us once more to prove Naotalba's power."

At these words, as at every mention of the name of the demigod-dess, Saravio's eyes brightened. "They, too, will come to know and serve her. Lead me to them."

The lady and her own attendants received them in a surprisingly comfortable room in the royal wing. Like much of Valeron Castle, its walls were fine-grained stone polished to a soft gloss, the furnishings pale wood, cushions and drapes a pastel shade of gray-green. Bowls of white rosalys scented the air.

The dough-faced matron, encased in layers of silver-edged lace over Aillard scarlet and gray, sat moaning and wiping her forehead with an embroidered handkerchief. Her chair, a graceful piece, seemed more suited to a young *damisela* than one of her girth. Beside her, an equally elegant table held a platter of delicacies, the kind of concentrated sweet foods Eduin had often eaten after strenuous work in a Tower circle.

He bowed while the page announced them and pronounced the lady's name. Eduin realized with a start that she was Linella Marzan, the wife of Julianna's formidable general.

"Oh, my head is very bad," the lady whimpered to Saravio. "I have such palpitations in my breast, I can find no ease. I do not think any power can cure me, but sweet Romilla, the dear girl, said that your singing brought her so much help. What can it hurt?"

She paused to scoop up a handful of sugared nuts. "It is for my nerves," she said, noticing Eduin's gaze. "I am so sensitive, you see, that every possible little thing devastates me. You see the condition I am reduced to. The slightest disturbance in the etheric aura! I should have been trained at a Tower, only my health would not permit it. I could never withstand the stress."

She paused briefly to eat the nuts and fan herself with her limp handkerchief. Eduin murmured how fortunate Her Majesty was to have such a talented lady-in-waiting.

"Oh, yes, she quite depends upon me. And now you know how important—how *essential* it is that I maintain my health. My head torments me most cruelly. I don't suppose there is any help for it. I never complain, but bear my affliction as best I can. It is the price of talent such as mine, to bear such burdens. Ah!" She heaved an enormous sigh.

Eduin made a few reassuring comments and then began arranging the room, placing chairs for Saravio and the lady's attendants and deftly removing the table of food. He did not want any competing pleasures once Saravio had begun singing. One of the attendants, a pretty girl from one of the minor noble houses, brought out a small bowed viol and seated herself on a tufted stool at the lady's feet. Clearly, one of her duties was to play and sing for her mistress.

Lady Linella continued to bemoan her sufferings even as Saravio began singing. She had no strength of will or personality to resist, but slipped easily into the state of euphoria. The girl with the viol provided a simple harmony. She bent over her instrument, her cheeks flushed, eyes dreamy.

When the lady was secured, Eduin skimmed the surface of her thoughts. He searched for some bit of memory or fragment of conversation, anything that would tell him how much influence she had over her husband, or even the things he might confide in her. Perhaps the general spoke to her in bed, or when he was weary with the cares of his position. Even a silly old woman might make a sympathetic listener.

Eduin found little of any immediate use. Eventually, he might induce her to drop a phrase or two, a pointed question, a mention of Varzil in a negative context. He decided that the best course was to create a dependence upon Saravio. It would be simple enough to do, given her initial susceptibility. He would leave her with a mental suggestion of well-being and many reassurances of being at her service.

She might think of Saravio's singing as an enjoyable pastime until she tried to do without it. Then the craving would begin. She might fight it for a time, if she had the wit to realize what it was, but in the end, she would lose.

Then you will do anything to hear Sandoval the Blessed sing for you again.

Even if Lady Linella proved to know nothing, she would tell her friends. More would come to hear the healing song, and some of them might have influence over powerful men. Perhaps word would reach the Queen herself. . . .

— ✦ —

On the night of the Midsummer Festival feast, Romilla and her father sat in the places of honor at the royal table. The hall was bedecked in wreaths of straw and field flowers. Tables creaked under the massed weight of the food. Roasted stuffed fowl and platters of artistically arranged, honey-glazed vegetables sat beside baked casseroles of mushrooms and cheeses carved like flowers. The centerpiece was a sculpture of an eagle in silver-foil-covered peaches and apricots, its wings edged in crimson cherries to reproduce the Aillard colors. Windows stood open, so that the lingering twilight filled the air with a pearly radiance. Ladies, even Queen Julianna herself, wore garlands of flowers, and tiny beribboned baskets of fruit had been set beside each woman's place.

Eduin and Saravio had been relegated to a lower table, along with those guests unworthy of royal notice.

Above the murmur of the crowd, Eduin heard Romilla exclaim in a high, girlish voice, "I, who am heir to Kirella, fell ill with melancholy some winters ago. Neither our household *leronis* nor the physician could heal me. It was not until this man, Sandoval the Blessed—" she gestured to the lower tables, where Saravio and Eduin sat, "—came to us that I emerged from the dark time. Not only that, my father watched with his own eyes as Sandoval healed a mortal wound."

"Extraordinary," one of Julianna's councillors said.

The Queen's voice rose above the others. "We shall see. Is that the man, seated at the lower table with his interpreter?"

Saravio, as if sensing her attention, began to rise from his seat. Eduin grabbed Saravio's arm and pulled him down, too late. The Queen gestured them forward.

"Come here, fellow, so I can see you properly."

Eduin bowed deeply, doing his best to imitate the awkward efface- ment of a poor man among his betters. Saravio held himself proudly, regarding the Queen with a level gaze. She might be the Lady of Valeron, but in Saravio's eyes, she was no match for Naotalba.

Lord Brynon stirred. "*Vai domna,* will you not hear this man? Truly, he has restored my daughter to health and strength when all other help had failed. In doing so, he himself became the target of a nefarious plot that even now stretches out its grasp for all of Valeron."

Hope and exultation flared in Eduin's mind. Impolitic as it was to in- troduce such a serious topic at a festive meal, Lord Brynon had done it, and in such a way that no suspicion of influence could fall upon ei- ther Saravio or Eduin.

Julianna regarded Aillard, one eyebrow raised. "Pray continue."

"An attempt was made upon the life of Sandoval the Blessed by that same physician who failed so miserably to cure my daughter. In fact, I have since come to suspect that his ministrations contributed to her decline."

"And you believe this physician was part of a larger plan?" the Lady inquired.

Zandru, she was sharp! Eduin's heart beat faster and he leaned forward, muscles tensing. Cold sweat damped the palms of his hands. *Go on,* he silently urged the Aillard lord, *say it!*

"Under questioning, the physician revealed his affiliation with none other than the Keeper, Varzil Ridenow," Lord Brynon announced, drawing himself up to his fullest.

"And this is the basis upon which you suppose a plot?" The eyebrow hitched a fraction higher.

"Surely you must see the pattern. Varzil's machinations are every- where, from the shores of Hali to the Tower at Cedestri. He may al- ready have infiltrated this very castle and suborned your own people even as he did mine—"

The Queen cut him off with a sharp, humorless laugh that sent Eduin wincing. "Really, Aillard, you must not go imagining schemes and plots everywhere, simply because you have an incompetent physician. Of course, this wandering entertainer would concoct such an accusation in order to advance his own position. Such men can have considerable power of persuasion. They are useful enough in counteracting the vapors of young girls, but no one of any strength of character takes them seriously. Mind you watch that his influence does not grow beyond the ladies' bower, or the results will be your disgrace and not his."

Lord Brynon flushed. Anger shimmered like an aura around him. Eduin thought that if Julianna had been a man, even an overlord, Aillard would have struck her.

Julianna continued, "I think it best that neither he nor his companion be allowed to attend any further councils, lest they seek to use what they overhear to their own advantage. They are servants; let them keep to their own while they are within the borders of Valeron. As for your charges, you cannot expect me to take such things seriously. There are few things more pathetic than the blame-mongering of a lord who cannot keep his servants in proper order."

With a visible effort, Aillard mastered his temper and, bowing, made another attempt.

"What you say is true, and would be my own shame, were it not for the testimony given under oath—under truthspell. The traitor *admitted* his reverence for Varzil the Good. That cannot be explained away as mere jealousy."

For a moment, Julianna looked thoughtful. "The Keeper of Neskaya Tower may be many things, but a fool he is not, and only a simpleton would use such a weak instrument as your physician seems to be. No, I think you had best look to more ordinary causes for the unrest in your household."

When it looked like Aillard would rouse himself to one more effort, she said, "We will hear no more of this, *kinsman*."

As Aillard murmured apologies, Eduin pulled Saravio back to their places at the lower table. It was going to be even more difficult than he'd thought to influence Julianna.

The Midsummer festivities continued long into the night. The windows of the great hall had been thrown open, and the multihued pastel light of three of Darkover's four moons flooded in, to blend with the glow of torches and the cold blue light of a few costly *laran*-charged glows. Professional dancers, minstrels, and jugglers performed, most more enthusiastic than talented. Every woman present received the traditional basket of fruit and flowers, in remembrance of the gifts that Hastur, son of Aldones Lord of Light, presented to his beloved Cassilda. A pile of baskets, many of them elaborately gilded and beribboned, overflowed the foot of Julianna's throne. Romilla received a number from her father, General Marzan's son, and several male admirers.

It had been long since Eduin had any woman to whom to present a Midsummer gift. He had no sisters and had never known his mother. The only basket he had prepared with any delight was for Dyannis, and she was better forgotten. He could have, following the older custom, left a small token for Romilla or Callina to discover outside their doors, but he had lost the habit of thinking of such things. It had been too long since he had felt any such bonds of love.

Eduin and Saravio crept away while the dancing, begun sedately with the older couples leading the *promenas,* turned wilder and more licentious. Lord Brynon, after dancing an obligatory round or two with Queen Julianna and his daughter, had retreated to a corner where he proceeded to get thoroughly drunk. The smell of the wine, combined with the heady blossoms and swath of moonlight, felt both intoxicating and nauseating to Eduin. There was too much temptation, too much danger in the swirls of tartan and gown, the bright cheeks of the ladies, the clash of goblets and voices raised in raucous song.

What was the old proverb, that nothing that happened under the four moons need be regretted? Or was it the opposite, that much of what came about in the wild celebration of such times lingered for a lifetime?

There were not four moons in the sky on this Midsummer Festival. The gods had held back that final benediction; whatever happened now became entirely the responsibility of men.

There was no one from whom to beg leave to depart, certainly not Lord Brynon. Romilla was dancing with General Marzan's hatchet-jawed son. Exercise and wine flushed her cheeks and she giggled as he held her closer than was seemly for someone not her promised husband. The sight disgusted Eduin. He took Saravio by the arm and guided him back to their quarters.

As Eduin led Saravio back to their room, he fumed inwardly. He could not rely on Lord Brynon or anyone else to convince the Queen of Valeron to search out and destroy his enemies. Julianna was too crafty and strong-willed to be subject to any man's influence. She would never start a war with Carolin, but she might be persuaded to eliminate Varzil if she believed he was the real threat. Now, more than ever, Eduin needed Saravio.

Saravio lay down on one of the narrow beds. His eyes were open and he lay as if in a trance. This present lassitude boded ill. What if Saravio were to fall into a coma, as he had upon their arrival at Kirella? Or, worse yet, suffer a seizure where he might be seen?

"The storm is nearer now," Saravio whispered. "Can you not feel it?"

Eduin lowered his mental shields to search Saravio's thoughts. He caught the fleeting image of fire rising against the sky, and the sweep of a shadowy cloak.

Good, he decided. That feeling of dread, of impending doom, was one he could use.

He went to the cot and sat beside Saravio. By tightening his throat, he made his voice hoarse and rasping. "I have terrible news."

Eyes widening, Saravio lifted his head.

"I have discovered that our enemy, Varzil Ridenow, is on the move. The Tower at Cedestri—" Eduin paused minutely, caught the flicker of recognition, for it was at this Tower Saravio had first trained, and plunged on, "—sent a vicious attack against our friends here. You remember, we heard as much at Robardin's Fort. In retaliation, Cedestri was destroyed—"

"As it deserved!"

"Indeed," Eduin went on. "But what we did not know was that Varzil himself went to rebuild the Tower."

"Varzil? Rebuild Cedestri?" Shaking his head, Saravio sat up. "Why would he do that? They were not worth saving after they turned away from Naotalba."

"Why, indeed?" Eduin said. "What profit might Varzil reap for his trouble, except to make alliance with the new Tower? Can you not see? This way, the malefactors will join forces with Varzil against Naotalba's loyal servants. You know that Varzil seeks to put an end to anyone who follows her. He is creeping up on us, extending his power over one land after another." Eduin waited for the impact of his argument to sink in.

"Varzil—he brings the fire?" Saravio asked.

"Yes! He brings the fire!" Eduin repeated, and felt the answering leap of anguish in Saravio. He jabbed at Saravio's mind, intensifying the fear and hatred.

"He must not—" Saravio stumbled over his words, almost babbling in terror. "Must not—"

"Naotalba will not forsake her faithful," Eduin shifted to a reassuring voice. "We must do our part. We must stand against Varzil and the agents of Cedestri, who turned against Naotalba and cast you, her chosen, out. Here in Valeron, there is the strength to do so, if only there is the will."

"We must persuade them!" Saravio cried. "But how? What must we do?"

Eduin bowed his head in a gesture of reverence and held it for a long moment. "We must pray for her guidance. Perhaps she will speak to us in dreams or visions, as she has so many times before. Rest now, that you may receive her word."

"Receive her word," Saravio echoed. "Rest."

Eduin lowered the other man to the bed and helped him into a comfortable position. He brushed his fingers over Saravio's eyelids, closing them. Saravio's brief spurt of energy faded, leaving him in an even deeper state of lassitude.

"Sleep," Eduin whispered, reinforcing the command with his mind. "Sleep."

Within a short time, Saravio fell into a deep slumber. Eduin felt the change as Saravio's breathing shifted, deeper now and slow. Saravio's mind lay open and vulnerable. He would not resist. He would surrender willingly.

Eduin got up and began pacing, using the movement to harden his resolve. Bile stung his throat at the thought of what he must do. In desperation, he asked himself if there were any other way, if he could not just let events take their natural course. Sooner or later, Queen Julianna or some other powerful ruler would tire of Varzil's interference, or perhaps some bandit or outlaw would seize upon him as easy prey.

Why go to the risk and trouble to force matters to a crisis? He could return to Kirella and live quite comfortably there, except for the whisper at the back of his mind.

Why not crawl back into the bottle? Or live a slave to Saravio's singing? It was either that, or fulfill his father's command.

Eduin had come to the end of the room, facing away from Saravio. His hands curled into fists, so hard and tight that the muscles in his forearms threatened to cramp. His body trembled.

Words rose to his mind, thoughts from another desperate moment but now, it seemed, the very touchstone of his existence. He had not realized how true they were.

I will live life on my own terms or I will end it.

The trembling stopped, replaced by determination. He bit down hard, clamping his jaw shut, and turned around.

Saravio lay as if arranged on his own bier, his legs outstretched and hands folded upon his breast. His head had fallen to one side, exposing his throat.

Eduin crossed the room in a few long strides. Barely pausing, he lowered himself to the bed, settling his body as he had learned to do at Arilinn. Breathing deeply, he found a position he could maintain while his mind ranged free. He closed his eyes, and all awareness of his physical body receded. Distantly, he felt the energy fields arising from the other man's energon channels.

Eduin's first action was to scan his surroundings. Callina or one of the *laranzu'in* who tended the aircars below might sense what he was doing. There was no hint of a trained mind, not even the presence of the Keeper of the Tower.

He sensed nothing beyond the babble of commonplace minds. They brushed his thoughts like the faint rush of a stream over rocks, and he shut them from his awareness as easily.

Eduin gathered himself, shaping his thoughts into a spear point. It was his favorite image, the tip piercing to the core of the problem, with but a single objective, never wavering or turning aside. Then he hurled himself into the swirl of Saravio's sleeping mind.

The last time Eduin had forced such a rapport, he had found a place both darkly bizarre and familiar, sky and rock and storm-wracked sky. Now he saw a landscape of tattered ruins, part Overworld, part pallid chaos, a twisting of light and form. Saravio's mind had disintegrated almost past recognition. No wonder he spent so much time in a trance-like state, barely conscious of his surroundings.

Naotalba! Eduin called silently. He used the name as a focal point. If anything could bring order to this twisted disorder, it would be that figure, central to Saravio's delusional passion.

NA—O—TAL—BA . . . Unseen winds tore the word to syllables and sent them whirling, scattering in the shifting currents of light.

Eduin sensed a distant stirring of recognition. There must be an imprint of Naotalba's image somewhere, one he could evoke and use.

Glancing around, Eduin was struck by the resemblance of this mental place to the Overworld. It was as if Saravio had taken a bit of that strange dimension inside himself, or perhaps this was the residue of his madness.

In his years of Tower training, Eduin had learned to use the primordial thought-stuff that composed the Overworld. A man Gifted with *laran* and disciplined in its use, as he was, could impose shape and form in an imitation of physical reality.

In the Overworld, Eduin had seen Towers raised, reflections of their true shapes, had encountered other *leronyn* as solid and vivid as they were in life. He shuddered inwardly, remembering those times he had encountered men who existed only in this unearthly plane. For a sickening moment, he caught the evanescent form of his father as he had seen him in the Overworld, a ghostly mirror of his living shape.

The vaporous mouth opened once more, exhaling a breath that gave no life but chilled the blood within Eduin's veins. Lips curved, shaping words. *"You swore . . . You swore . . ."*

For the space of a single beat of his heart, Eduin froze. The icy tendrils of his father's command curled around his heart. His temples throbbed with urgency. He knew what had been done to him, and why. He had never had a life of his own, had never been anything beyond an instrument of his father's obsession for revenge. When he tried to resist, from love for Carolin, from compassion, from decency, his own will had been wrested from him.

Just as he now stood poised to do to this helpless man before him. What choice did he have? He could not even seek the oblivion of his own death. If he tried, his father's shade would haunt him for eternity.

Forgive me, he whispered in the confines of his own innermost thoughts, and knew there could be no mercy for what he was about to do.

Eduin set to work. He bent to scoop up handfuls of thought-stuff, sculpting it like soft clay. He was not much of an artist, but he did not need to be. Once the basic shape was established, he had only to imagine her features.

He was doomed either way, to torment and despair if he failed to fulfill his oath, or else to the certain consequences of his actions—the violation of the most basic moral principles of *laran* work. He had sworn never to enter unasked into another man's mind, and this promise had been given with full adult awareness and consent, not with a child's unquestioning obedience. How many times had he already broken it?

I would rather be damned for what I do than what I fail to do.

Either way, he would be forsworn, beyond redemption.

As Eduin worked, he thought not of who Naotalba might have been, a living woman caught up in the stuff of legend, or a figure embodying some deep primordial emotion, but only of what she represented to him.

Into her emerging form, he poured all his own desperate malice, his years of resentment against Varzil and those who stood with him. From the very first Keepers at Arilinn who refused to train him as a Keeper, to Carolin Hastur with his dreams of peace and brotherhood, to the still-raw wound of his separation from Dyannis, to the years of wretched drunkenness, he took each moment of pain, of hatred, of vindictiveness, and shaped it into Naotalba's lineaments.

As Eduin did so, he became aware of an even darker power flowing through him, a bitterness that shivered through his bones, so cold it seared whatever it touched. It was not only his own personal hatred for Varzil, his determination to be free through the destruction of the man who had stood so many times in his way, but his father's enduring vengeance. That which had shaped him, twisted his own life and made him what he was, now coursed through him and into the statue of Naotalba.

When at last Eduin was finished, he stood back to gaze at his work. She was again the woman he had first glimpsed—human, desolate, achingly beautiful. Or did she break his heart because of her sorrow? He watched as she turned toward him with those luminous gray eyes, blind and all-seeing at once.

Naotalba! he called, and watched as she inclined her head in acknowledgment.

A voice shivered through the fiber of his being. *I am here. What do you seek of me?*

A shudder ripped through the firmament that was Saravio's slumbering mind. Awe, recognition . . . terror.

Eduin faced the goddess he had created, and answered her. *Freedom.*

Colorless lips curved in a smile that held no trace of warmth. Eyes glinted like frozen steel. Her cloak rippled as if it were alive, stretching out its shadowed folds. Instinctively, he drew back from it. In its penumbral darkness, unspeakable desires curled like smoke.

Freedom? Naotalba asked. *I see in your heart all that must happen for you to be at last free. You wish a death.*

I do.

A death, you say, but it will require many deaths to make the world right again. Do you still wish this thing?

The wrong was done before I was conceived in my mother's womb! The cry burst, unbidden, from the deepest recesses of his mind. *I have no choice but to go on! There is no other way. This quest, terrible as it is, was chosen for me, and none of my own making.*

Once you have set your foot upon this path, you cannot turn back. Naotalba's voice rang out, resonant as the tolling of a death knell.

Though he trembled as if he stood upon the brink of an abyss, Eduin bent his head in assent. *I wish it, no matter what the cost.*

Very well, you shall have your death.

As long as it rids me of Varzil the Accursed, I am content.

36

Darkness seized him. For a time he knew nothing, felt nothing. Gradually, like the seeping of brightness from the east on a foggy morning, he returned to himself.

Eduin floated in a place that was neither the Overworld nor the physical realm, nor that strange convolution of consciousness that was Saravio's sleeping mind. Around him, within him, lay a world without vision, without hearing, without taste or movement. Strewn across an invisible field before him, he spied nodes of thought-energy and knew that each was the innermost consciousness of a living person. Saravio lay the closest, with Romilla and the household *leronis* a little farther off. There were others he did not recognize or else dismissed as of little use. Lord Brynon's presence was so dim as to be barely reachable. Queen Julianna was not present at all.

Eduin sensed another presence, this time behind him, as if someone were watching over his shoulder. He could almost feel the stirring of breath along the back of his neck, the heat of another body a hair's breadth from his own, the pulse of another's heart.

This is how it is done, a silent voice whispered in his mind. It echoed, leaving ripples of familiar pain. *You reach out thus, and twist thus, and leave, indelible, the mark of your own will.*

So it had been done to him. So he would do in his own turn. Naotalba, the figure he had created from his own hatred, stood on one side, and the shade of his father on the other. Implacable determination and malevolence surged through him, and it seemed these feelings were not his alone. He gave himself over to them, surrendering to them, abdicating all vestiges of generosity or kindness or compassion. No one had ever offered these to him; certainly, his enemies and the tools he must use to reach them deserved none.

This way . . . The whisper was doubled now, as if two voices spoke with a single thought.

Eduin reached out with his mind to Saravio's. This time, his thoughts were not shaped like the point of a spear, but a grappling iron with barbed, talonlike hooks. He set it deep within Saravio's mind.

Whenever Naotalba is mentioned, in word or thought, there will be joy, he commanded. *But whenever the name of Varzil Ridenow of Neskaya, he who is called Varzil the Good, rises to men's minds or lips, there will be pain. Pain and fear and bitter hatred.*

For a long moment there was no response, and he wondered if Saravio's consciousness was too disordered to accept the command. Then he saw how the other man's mind had become reorganized around the new, vengeful figure of Naotalba. Saravio had lain quiescent, caught between awe and terror, waiting only for the doctrine that would bring his mission to life once more.

K–k–kill, rattled the scorpion, only this time it spoke not with his father's voice but with his own. *K–k–kill Varzil!*

Eduin watched long enough to be certain that Saravio would serve him even as he had served his father's compulsion, with thought and deed and *laran.* When he opened his eyes, he saw that Saravio, too, was stirring.

Saravio's eyes glowed against the paleness of his skin. His lips moved, then words formed. "You were right, Eduin. Naotalba has answered our prayers. She has spoken to me and shown me how to defeat her enemy. I must go out among these people and search out every trace of his vile influence. Will you help me in this holy work?"

Slowly, Eduin smiled. "I am now, as ever, in her service."

An hour or so later, a tapping, light and hesitant, sounded on the door of their chamber. Eduin opened the door to find Callina standing there. She had changed from her gown of pale gray, embroidered with snow lilies along sleeves and modest neckline, to a loose robe like the ones universally worn for Tower work. For any other woman, appearing at a man's door in the middle of the night would have occasioned irretrievable scandal. Callina wore her innocence like armor.

Eduin bowed and stepped back for her to enter.

"I am sorry to disturb you, but I searched for Sandoval the Blessed in the great hall and could not find him." Her gaze flew to Saravio's face. Pain and hope radiated from her.

"My child," Eduin murmured, taking her hand in his.

Despite the warmth of the evening, her fingers were like ice. Although he had not intended to read her thoughts, the physical touch catalyzed a telepathic link between them. As vividly as if she had drawn the portrait in paints, he saw the face of a young man, earnest and laughing, his sword bright in the morning sun, with features that mirrored her own. In the image, the man swept Callina into his arms, and Eduin knew it was the last time she had seen her twin brother alive.

The darkness Eduin had sensed in her rose up like a tide. With the twin-bond to heighten the power of her Sight, she had ridden with him, had smelled the blood and ashes of the battlefield, had felt the sword slash through his side as if it had her own. Curled alone in her Tower room, she had suffered every moment of his long, festering death.

Then fragments of other memories brushed against him, fragile as *mariposa* wings. He felt the touch of her Keeper's mind, the fatherly concern.

"Poor thing, to have Seen the battle, too tender and maidenly to be exposed to slaughter. Women are too sensitive for such work."

The same voice, now speaking aloud, explained that she must leave Temora for an easier post, to live among ladies and perform duties no more taxing than preparing sleeping potions or testing children for *laran*. With time and rest, her mind would recover.

Then came the numb sickness of dislocation, the loneliness that ate like a cancer into her bones . . .

"You do not need to explain," Eduin said with a rush of compassion. "Sandoval the Blessed understands that some sorrows cannot be spoken aloud. He knows you have come for the healing comfort of Naotalba."

"Oh!" she cried, half a sob.

Now, summoned by an appeal he could not defy, new energy suffused Saravio's features. His eyes glittered.

"Come," Eduin said, gesturing to the two chairs arranged in front of the small fireplace. No fire had been lit, for although the temperature was already falling, no one was expected to pass this night in his own bed.

Eduin placed each of them in a chair. Within a few minutes, Saravio began to sing. Eduin felt the instant response within his own body, the pulse and leap of pleasure.

He ached to give himself over to it, just for a moment of ease, an island in the storm of events.

Surely a brief rest would help him . . . a moment among the silvery trees, the graceful weaving figures. Longing rose in him, sweet and bitter all at once. He had closed his eyes, swaying with the silent melody, the waves of *laran* stimulation. No ancient forest, no echo of *chieri* song reached him. Instead, shadows curled and fire sprang up. A voice whispered to the flames, feeding them with his substance and spirit until nothing remained but the shadow, the ashes.

No! The cry tore from somewhere deep within him. He could not give up, not now, not after all he had gone through. Varzil—and the peace his death would bring—was not yet within his grasp, but would be, and soon.

Eduin bent his attention to the young *leronis*. Beneath the youthful appearance, the slender girlish body held a core of power. Her *laran* shimmered like a mirror of steel. She was Tower-trained.

But he, he was Eduin Deslucido, and the blood of sorcerers and kings ran in his own veins. If he could hide his secrets from the Keepers of Arilinn and Hali, two of the most powerful Towers Darkover had ever known, then insinuating himself into the mind of even a trained *leronis* should be easy. He softened his psychic presence to a whisper, the gentlest shimmer. She had only the flimsiest barriers in place, barely enough to screen out the psychic chatter elsewhere in the castle. Under the influence of Saravio, she had softened all other defenses.

Like mist, like silk, he twined himself through the outer layers of her mind.

For that moment, Callina's mind lay open, receptive and unguarded. Eduin could control her, shape her animosity toward Varzil, urge her to use her influence on the Queen without understanding why. Instead, he had a different use for her, not only for her talents but for her position. Unlike the other inhabitants of Valeron Castle, she had access to the Tower and all its facilities, most particularly the relay screens that linked them to every other active circle.

A thrill rose in him, chill as the wind from Zandru's Forge. Through her, he could search the world of the Towers for Varzil's location. Then, when the time was ready, he would know where to strike. Or perhaps some opportunity would present itself, some circumstance in which Varzil was on some mission, away from the protection of Tower or Carolin's guards.

Find Varzil... The command reverberated through the girl's mind.

Find Varzil... She answered with all the solemnity of an oath.

37

A tenday after Midsummer Night, heralds signaled the approach of a diplomatic party from Isoldir, traveling under a flag for truce. Queen Julianna placed her own forces in readiness, so that Isoldir found a guarded welcome, one prepared from the security of strength.

Upon Isoldir's arrival, Eduin and Saravio crowded into the central hall, jammed in behind the mass of courtiers and more highly-placed servants. Romilla stood near the front, beside her father. Of Julianna, Eduin could see only the curve of pale gray that was her throne and a drape of ice-blue brocade gown. He could hear nothing above the chattering of the courtiers, not even when the Isoldir envoy began to speak. In frustration, he tried to push past a tall, thick-muscled arms-man.

"Keep back, or you'll find yourself outside with the pigs," the man growled, adding a phrase indicating Eduin was no more than a lady's plaything.

Eduin bit back a reply. Saravio touched his sleeve and bent toward him. "Naotalba is at work here. I can sense her presence."

Instead of trying to hear and see, Eduin reached out with his *laran*. He dared not drop his psychic barriers entirely, for that would leave him open to the barrage of emotions from the crowd. Instead, he focused narrowly on Romilla. He knew the pattern of her thoughts, the imprint of her visions of Naotalba and fire. The despair that had once spurred her to seek release in death had receded to a shadow, dormant.

Images formed at the back of Eduin's mind, hazy and indistinct, but without question those from Romilla's own eyes. When he caught a phrase or two, he heard it echoed, more clearly, from her ears.

The introductions were drawing to a close. Eduin caught enough of the speeches to realize the head emissary was none other than *Dom* Ronal, Lord of Isoldir. The answering exclamations of surprise and suspicion drowned out what came next and snapped Eduin's tenuous telepathic rapport with Romilla.

Fuming in frustration, he tried to reestablish the bond, but there was too much confusion, too many churning thoughts. Pandemonium battered him. He flinched under the onslaught, his *laran* senses reeling. He slammed his barriers into place, as hard and tight as if he were back at Arilinn. For a long moment, his vision went dark, so intense was his inner concentration.

His neighbor, a heavy-set man in Aillard household livery, shoved him, snarling, "Watch it!"

Eduin gestured an apology. The nearness of so many people rasped along his nerves. For most of his adult life, he had either lived in a Tower, where casual physical touch was forbidden, or else he had been too sodden drunk to care. Not even his *laran* barriers could shield him from being shoved from every direction or the smell and heat of so many bodies. In this commotion, he dared not risk another attempt at mental contact.

Having wrestled his aggravation under control, Eduin shifted to ordinary senses. There wasn't much to learn, although he had no trouble gleaning those few events from the mutterings of those closer to the throne.

Dom Ronal had indeed presented himself to Julianna, and under flag of truce. She had offered him a guarded welcome and protection, suitable for one who had been an enemy and whose current intentions were unclear. He and his men had been given quarters that, while undoubtedly heavily guarded, were nonetheless appropriate for his rank.

Julianna rose, indicating that the audience was at an end. The Isoldir contingent bowed deeply and withdrew under their escort. With their departure and that of the Queen, the rest of the crowd began to disperse.

"What did they come for?" one of the house servants near Eduin asked. "You'd have thought they already learned their lesson."

The other, the burly man who had shoved Eduin, shook his head, replying, "They arrived under truce, didn't you hear? Whatever it is, we'll hear once the Lady has dealt with them."

Eduin, having left Saravio safely in their chambers, paced the public halls where courtiers gathered and gossip was to be heard. He had long discovered that he was, like any other servant, regarded as invisible, but he heard little of substance. One graybeard insisted that Julianna was even now torturing *Dom* Ronal, or at least forcing him to watch the torture of his kinsmen, in order to gain knowledge of their true mission at Valeron. Others insisted that the Isoldir party had come to arrange a marriage treaty of *Damisela* Marelie, Julianna's heir, to one of Ronal's sons or possibly to the Isoldir lord himself.

Eduin had come to trust the servants more than the perfumed, beribboned sycophants. He went down to the stables, put on a canvas smock, and lent a hand caring for the Isoldir horses. Julianna was taking no chances, and had arranged to take the beasts under her own control.

"Now, why would the Lady want to throw away such an advantage, and on a man she could have beat into the ground?" the stableman snorted at the idea of a marriage alliance. He bent to examine the near hind hoof of the roach-maned dun he was grooming. "Will you look at this? Poor beastie's got a crack right through the wall. Bad shoeing job, too. I'll get the smith to make him a better, 'fore he's lamed for good."

Eduin straightened up from picking out the feet of the next horse. Neither mount was of the quality he would expect from the lord of even as small a kingdom as Isoldir. Any noble who could command even a single aircar could certainly afford better horses. There was the one with the damaged hoof, his own a swayback with crooked hocks, and the next had one opaque, whitened eye. None of them, he judged, were fit for battle, but they were probably the best to be had. He said aloud that, given the state of their mounts, he doubted the Isoldir party was in a position to bargain for anything.

The stableman slapped the rump of the dun, who turned his head and began playfully nibbling on the man's hair. Laughing, the stableman went on to the next, the blind-eyed mare.

"If you take my meaning, Isoldir's come to keep what the Lady's left him with, but I can't think what he might offer her that she can't take for herself. Oh, if he's worth anything, they'll be parleying long and hard on this one, I can tell you that much."

"Privately, I suppose," Eduin said in a careless tone.

"And how else, for the likes of us with wagging tongues and knowing aught but how to keep their horses sound?"

Eduin bent to his work, currying away the dried mud on the horse's fetlocks, and reflected that the stableman knew more of the affairs of state than any ten courtiers.

On his way back to his chambers, he stopped to chat with one of the cook's assistants, a snub-nosed girl whose freckled cheeks suggested she might have *Comyn* blood. She balanced a basket of root vegetables on one hip, only too happy to share what she'd learned.

The party from Isoldir had brought news from along the road. A new plague, called the masking sickness because of the black sores covering its victims, had arisen in the countries to the north. Frictions between Ridenow and the kingdom of Asturias had escalated, and Varzil had gone to the capital of Asturias to negotiate on behalf of Carolin Hastur.

I hope they seize him as a spy!

"Who told you this?" Eduin asked. "The men from Isoldir?"

"Oh, no, they only talked about the masking sickness. Pepita, who waits on Lady Romilla, she heard *Damisela* Callina talking about Varzil the Good. They're saying that unless *Dom* Varzil can make a treaty, Queen Ariel will go to war. Oh, that will be a terrible time, when kinfolk take arms against one another!"

"Yes, indeed," Eduin said as he patted her shoulder and sent her on her way.

So Varzil had gone to Asturias. Eduin knew little of the quarrel there. Asturias was defended by a ruthless general known as the Kilghard Wolf, and had recently occupied the neighboring kingdom of Marenji. Such a man might not take kindly to unctuous words of peace, or be willing to surrender his military advantage for Carolin's Compact.

There was nothing Eduin could do, nor did he see any way to use the news to intensify suspicions of Varzil. There was no point in trying to create further hostilities with Isoldir. The only thing to be done was to watch and wait.

38

The evening following the arrival of the Isoldir emissary, Eduin and Saravio attended Romilla in her chambers. She sent a servant to summon them. Word had flown about the castle that Queen Julianna and her advisers had already met in secret with *Dom* Ronal. Eduin hoped Romilla had been one of the council. If so, he intended to use whatever means available to learn what had happened.

When they arrived at Romilla's chambers, they found her pacing the length of her sitting room. Rows of expensive beeswax candles filled the chamber with golden light, burnishing the silver inlaid furniture. Some woodsy incense had been added to fire. One of Romilla's attendants stood holding a goblet and decanter of amber-colored wine.

Romilla seated herself, arranging her skirts with a mannerism she had copied from Julianna. "Take that away," she told the attendant. "I will not need it, now that Sandoval is here."

"Naotalba already knows what troubles your heart," Eduin said, and watched the flicker of reaction in her eyes. "She will answer you through Sandoval the Blessed—"

"Of course," Romilla interrupted. "I must prepare myself." She sat very still, but the broken rhythm of her speech betrayed her agitation.

At the mention of Naotalba, Saravio began humming softly. Eduin, even with his *laran* barriers in place, sensed the pulse of psychic emanations. The effect upon Romilla was immediate. Her eyelids softened, her breath caught and then slowed. The color in her cheeks heightened minutely.

"All will be well," Eduin murmured. "Speak aloud what troubles you, that Naotalba may pour the balm of her healing upon you."

"It—surely it is all foolishness—born of my old fears. I should not have such—such doubts. . . ."

Her voice trailed off, the jumbled phrases stilled, and for that moment she looked very young, her pride and self-assurance only a brittle shell over the nightmare-haunted girl Eduin had first known. He remembered that first audience back in Kirella, the bruised darkness of her eyes, her fingers tugging at the white bandages on her wrists.

So she had been. So might she be once more, if there were any advantage in it for him.

"I thought it would be so easy to sit in council," she continued, "the judgment so clear."

"You are in Naotalba's care," he said in a soothing voice, "and it is by her will you take your rightful place as heir to Kirella. As long as you remain faithful to her and submit yourself to her guidance, she will not abandon you."

Romilla closed her eyes, an expression of relief washing her features, and drew a long breath. The flush on her cheeks intensified, along with Saravio's humming. "I knew that I would see things more clearly in the presence of Sandoval the Blessed. Yes, that is better."

"Rest with your eyes closed," Eduin said, shifting his tone from reassurance to command. "Sandoval will sing to you now and let the blessing of Naotalba flow into you. Through him, you need never be alone."

With another sigh, Romilla settled back in her chair. Eduin spared a glance for her attendant, who, having put away the medicinal wine, had taken a stool in the corner and was now listening with half-closed eyes.

> *"O the lark in the twilight*
> *She rises from the west . . ."*

Saravio lifted his voice, stronger with every phrase.

"And she flies o'er the battlefield
With blood upon her breast . . ."

A wave of *laran* energy swept across Eduin's mental barriers. He sensed its power, dark and intoxicating. All he had to do was open himself and let the flood of orgasmic pleasure take him. The schemes of great lords would no longer matter to him, or the bitterness of unfulfilled revenge and blighted dreams. He would walk among the silver trees and hear the song of the *chieri,* eternal and unchanging.

Necessity held him back. He must stay vigilant, or the opportunity would slip by him. Romilla's mouth had fallen open and her hands were draped loosely over the arm rests of her chair, fingers twitching. Her attendant was for the moment oblivious of everything else except her own inner bliss.

Eduin gestured to Saravio to stop singing. "Naotalba has spoken to me, has given me a message to deliver to the *damisela.* She is well pleased with you."

Saravio bent his head, accepting the praise as if he had just emerged from the Dry Towns and had been offered a cup of spring water. As often happened after Saravio had used his psychic abilities, Eduin sensed the languor seeping through him, weighing his limbs, dulling his awareness. In a short time, Saravio would slip into a lassitude as mind and body recovered from the expenditure of energy.

Eduin reached out with his *laran* into the sleeping mind of Romilla. Her dreams were more brightly colored than before, and the shadows, while still present, had retreated to a distance. He saw the glances of the young men who had placed baskets of flowers at her feet, had bowed before her at the dance; he felt the heady thrill of sitting beside Julianna at council.

More, show me more . . .

He thrust against the barriers surrounding her memories. Pain flared, the instinctive protection against psychic invasion, but he drew upon his own power to overcome it. He needed more than fragmented dreams and the emotional reactions of a young girl, untried in matters of war and statecraft. If the Isoldir party had spoken the name of Varzil Ridenow, or had been tainted by his influence, Eduin must *know.*

The scorpion of his father's command roused. *Find . . . K–k–kill . . .*

Tatters of thought and color fell away. Gradually, as if emerging from a ground-hugging mist, Eduin became aware of his surroundings as Romilla had seen them. The memories were hazy, bearing little sense of distance or solidity. He could see and hear, although in a distorted fashion. The room around him was narrow and dark, without outside windows. Cold white radiance diffused from four *laran*-charged glows, casting blurred shadows on the faces of the people who took their places in a circle. Romilla's gaze shifted from Queen Julianna to the man opposite her. Eduin could see little else, but he supposed Lord Brynon must be present, as well as General Marzan and the other senior councillors.

The meeting began by fits and starts, as if Romilla could not bring herself to pay proper attention. Her emotions, anxiety and exhilaration predominating, overwhelmed everything else. In moments, Eduin caught snatches of speech, enough to recognize opening formalities. Abruptly, both words and vision came clear.

Dom Ronal made as if to approach Julianna, but a pair of Aillard guards stepped forward. He halted and bowed deeply.

"Your Majesty, gracious Queen, the time has come to put an end to the hostilities between our two kingdoms. From before the time of our fathers, we have distrusted and sought to injure one another. Suspicion and fear have driven us to seek ever more terrible methods of destruction. Instead of increasing the security of our lands, the result has been the opposite."

"As you have learned to your sorrow," Julianna commented dryly.

The Isoldir lord inclined his head. "I have no justification for my actions, except to ask in all respect if you would not have done the same, had our situations been reversed."

"You dare to say such a thing, when it is by the Lady's own mercy that your castle still stands?" Lord Brynon's voice came from the side.

Julianna waved him to silence. "Let the man speak. I would hear what has brought him here. I assume," she now directed her words to the Isoldir lord, "you are come to sue for peace."

"If that is what I must do to bring an end to the enmity between us, then yes," *Dom* Ronal replied. "Only a fool clings to his enemy's throat when his own house is burning. Lord Brynon speaks the truth; you have been merciful to us, more so than we would have been to you. Yet if our attack had been carried out as we had planned, it is you who would now be on your knees in Isoldir."

One of the councillors shouted in outrage and a guard moved forward, hand upon sword hilt. Romilla's vision faded in a wash of emotions, but only for a moment.

". . . three airships set out from Cedestri Tower that day," Ronal was saying, "but only one continued upon its course, only one for you to defend against. The other pilots turned back of their own accord because they had become convinced of the folly of *laran* weapons."

"*Three* aircars, carrying that hideous new form of bonewater?" General Marzan said. "We saw two at Cedestri Tower, but did not know they had participated in the attack. Had we known, we would not have left a single stone upright or *laranzu* able to draw breath. Your Majesty, if even one of them had succeeded, all our own lands and castles would have been laid waste until the time of your children's children."

"So," Lord Brynon said in a voice that only Romilla could hear, "*Dom* Ronal would have an empty victory, land he could not use and those few souls left alive now sealed to vengeance—aye, they and their sons and their son's sons."

"Why, what could they then do to Valeron, except to wish us ill?" Romilla muttered in return.

In her dreaming memory, her father's features loomed, brows drawn together, mouth tight. "Do not underestimate hatred, my child, or dismiss the consequences of such a terrible injury. Fallen men do not always remain powerless, and injustice has a way of turning back upon itself."

"Father, how can it be wrong to defend oneself against an unprovoked attack? Would that not put an end to the quarrel?"

Before Lord Brynon could answer, Julianna resumed the questioning. "Have you come all these leagues to tell us that you meant to harm us even more than you did? Why should I not have your head struck from your shoulders at this very instant, rather than leave such an enemy alive to strike again?"

Even through the blurred images of Romilla's dream-memory, Eduin saw the Isoldir lord's face pale and his hands tremble.

"Because," *Dom* Ronal said in a voice edged with emotion, "I would no longer be your enemy. I would see peace between us and all through these lands."

Julianna's eyes narrowed. "The only way that will happen is your immediate surrender."

Silence, like a velvet hush, enveloped the room. Slowly, as if the movement were deeply painful, *Dom* Ronal lowered himself to one knee and then the other.

"Then I surrender, not only myself and Isoldir, but our one remaining aircar, for the other was demolished during your retaliation. I ask—I beg you to use it more wisely than I have."

"What is he playing at?" Lord Brynon said under his breath to Romilla. "This must be some ruse to catch us off our guard, lull us into complacency, and then attack. *No one* surrenders unconditionally unless the only other choice is destruction."

Dom Ronal, still on his knees, turned his head to face Lord Brynon. Eduin, watching through Romilla's eyes, saw the Isoldir ruler's expression. It was not that of a defeated man, but of one who has gathered all his courage into his two hands. The surrender was not an act of desperation, but of faith.

If only I had been there! Eduin stormed. *I might have been able to read his true motives!* Instead, he must content himself with Romilla's patchy memories.

"I would of course prefer an alliance by marriage or exchange of fosterage," *Dom* Ronal said, "for such ties often lead to deeper understanding and mutual respect. I am here to do whatever I can to put old resentments to rest. If I must give up my kingdom—" and here his voice faltered, "—and turn over the lands and people that have been the care of my family since the Ages of Chaos, then I must."

"What conditions do you put on this surrender?" General Marzan asked.

"None save that Your Majesty will swear to be a good and just queen to my people as well, accept our fealty, and not to demand that we forswear our other oaths."

Even through Romilla's eyes, Eduin saw the leap in tension in Julianna's body. "Exactly what might those *other oaths* be?"

"*Vai domna,* we have sworn to abide by the Compact of Honor, as presented to us by Varzil the Good. It is at his urging that I present myself here."

Varzil! I knew it! Varzil sent him here! Eduin raged inwardly.

Had Varzil discovered their location and did he now seek to extend his power over the court at Valeron? Or was he simply doing what he had always done, meddling in affairs that were no business of his own?

"You ask a great deal, Ronal of Isoldir," Julianna said.

"Why, when he presents no threat whatsoever?" the General asked. "He has surrendered, and is in no position to demand anything."

The lady sighed, almost imperceptibly. Eduin would not have noticed, except for Romilla's own sigh. The girl had enough statecraft to see what the General had yet to realize. To accept Isoldir's surrender would be tantamount to agreeing to the Compact. If Valeron tried to use either Isoldir's men or the *leronyn* of Cedestri Tower in any aggressive enterprise, they might well face rebellion throughout their own lands as well.

General Marzan cursed softly under his breath. "Better the sandal-wearer had stayed home."

Julianna silenced him with a raised hand. "I accept, but under these conditions. Valeron and Isoldir will make no more war upon one another. You and whatever is left of your armies will swear allegiance to me. In exchange, Valeron will extend its protection to you. Any threat to Isoldir will be defended by Valeron, and all Isoldir soldiers will fight under my command. Isoldir itself may continue to manage its own local affairs, and I will appoint you governor under personal fealty to me. Whatever arrangements you have previously made may continue, so long as they do not nullify your primary oath to me. This shall be sworn by each of us, under truthspell, binding both ourselves and our descendants. Do you agree?"

"Lady, I had not expected such a fair and generous response. Summon your *leronis* and I will so swear."

With a sidelong, humorless smile, Julianna gestured to an attendant. "Whether my offer is *fair and generous* remains to be seen. You will get no better one from me."

A few minutes later, Callina stepped into the room. Instead of her usual gray gown, she wore a loosely-belted, cowled robe. In it, she looked older, more grim. She halted in the center of the room and drew out her starstone from a silken cord around her neck. Eduin noted that the stone had already been freed from its usual locket, as if she were expecting this summons.

"Cast the truthspell," Julianna said, "and we will prove who is in earnest and who dares come before us with thoughts of treachery in his heart."

"In the light of this jewel . . ." Callina began speaking the ritual formula in her light, girlish voice. Even though he heard the words through Romilla's dreaming memory, Eduin felt a shiver of resonance. He himself had cast this very spell, under which no man could tell aught but the truth, or the light of the gemstone would vanish from his face. But he had also stood in that very light, shielded by the psychic manipulation his father had called the Deslucido Gift.

Callina's starstone gave off a pale blue light, spreading from one face to the next as it encompassed the entire chamber. It glinted on the unshed tears in *Dom* Ronal's eyes and washed the color from the Queen's cheeks, so that she resembled a marble sculpture, cast General Marzan's cragged features into the aspect of a giant raptor.

The room hushed, expectant, as Ronal of Isoldir clambered to his feet and began the recitation of his intentions and oath to Julianna. He lifted his face, though at one point his tears spilled over his pallid, blue-washed cheeks, so that everyone could see. There was not the slightest flicker in the truthspell.

As he spoke, an almost palpable ripple of relief spread across the room. Even Julianna softened. Impossible as it seemed, the man had come in earnest.

Ask about Varzil! Eduin urged silently. Then he reminded himself that these events were not actually taking place, they were memories only, seen imperfectly through Romilla's dreaming mind.

You are such a fool, Julianna, for all your oaths and treaties. If you only knew how easy it is to lie under truthspell, to say one thing while holding another truth in your heart . . . The only sure way to end this is to slit the throat of every man who might stand against you.

But she did not know, and he dared not tell her. The secret must die with him.

The dream images tore like fine gauze in a wind as Romilla stirred, restless. Eduin caught fragments of Julianna's face as she promised in turn to treat Isoldir with honor.

Success was slipping through Eduin's grasp. Even as the tatters of Romilla's memory fell away, he saw Julianna turning a gracious eye toward Varzil, the man who had brought about an end to the conflict with Isoldir. Perhaps she might even consider an alliance with Hastur. He, Eduin, would be surrounded by his enemies. Desperately, he wondered if he could convince General Marzan to act on his own, to take a preemptive strike against Varzil in Asturias. Perhaps through the General's lady wife—no, Marzan would never defy Julianna.

Eduin could not rely on anyone else. Somehow he must find a way to convince the Queen that Varzil was not only dangerous, but treacherous, that he could not be reasoned with but must be destroyed before his insidious poison could spread.

Thrusting himself deep into Romilla's waking consciousness, Eduin drew on all his trained *laran*. He wakened the place within his own mind where his father's voice still whispered its compulsion.

Julianna must know the truth and only Sandoval the Blessed, speaking through his interpreter, can tell her.

I hear you, came the faint trace of Romilla's thought, *I hear and obey.*

Then tell the Queen this; that you believe Varzil hides his true purpose behind a veil of lies and appearances. That even now, he stretches out his hand to a terrible laran weapon. Worse by far than clingfire or even bonewater dust. It was for this that he helped to rebuild Cedestri Tower. It is for this he journeys to Asturias, to make alliance between them and King Carolin. Tell her you fear Carolin Hastur plans to strike at Valeron, the very heart of Aillard territory. Tell her that Sandoval the Blessed comes to testify of the potency of Varzil's new weapon. We saw proof at the riot at Hali Lake. She must hear us so that she can judge for herself!

Yes, she must judge . . .

39

"**M**y lords! My lords!" The page stood on the threshold of Eduin and Saravio's chamber. He was one of the youngest, not more than six or seven. Exertion flushed his round face. He must have run all the way from the far side of the castle.

"Why, whatever is the matter?" Eduin lowered his *laran* shields slightly, but could make no sense of the boy's agitation.

"Her Majesty—she has sent—for you—to come—immediately—"

"And you are to bring us now?" Eduin frowned. He would have preferred to let Saravio sleep, for the periods of recovery were growing longer as each "healing" session seemed to drain more and more energy from the singer.

"We'll be but a moment," Eduin said, waving in a reassuring manner. "Wait out here."

Saravio roused slowly from his near-stupor. Eduin could sense how low his vital energies had dipped. He touched the other man's mind and found Naotalba's tattered image wrapped in storm clouds. Spiderweb lightning enveloped her like an aureole. Ashen smoke tinged the psychic atmosphere. Eduin could superimpose some approximation of order upon Saravio's mind once more, but that would disintegrate just like his last efforts. He feared Saravio was near the point where no one could reach him, and the thought filled Eduin with both sadness and anger. For a moment, he contemplated appearing alone before Julianna, rather than risk greater harm to Saravio.

Fortunately, Saravio was able to get to his feet. His eyes focused, although there was no way to tell what he really saw. He made no response when Eduin spoke to him, although at the mention of Naotalba, he put forth a wave of pleasure. His awareness might be impaired, but the mental commands Eduin had placed still held him in their grip.

Stronger than flesh, perhaps stronger than life itself . . .

Eduin paused before opening the door, caught for a moment in a sense of kinship with this poor, unfortunate man. He wondered if, when he himself was at last dead, his father's voice would remain, whispering its tortured commands to nothingness.

They went down the corridor, following the page. As they passed through the servants' quarters, Eduin searched mentally for any hint as to what was so urgent. He found nothing more than the ordinary, daily concerns. Perhaps they did not know.

Shortly, he found himself in Queen Julianna's private presence chamber. General Marzan flanked her, his face deeply furrowed. Marelie sat at Julianna's other side, coolly enigmatic, and beside her, Romilla, her hands folded on the table before her so tightly that her knuckles shone like marbles, her cheeks like ice. Lord Brynon was not in attendance.

Eduin bowed, schooling his features to reflect the proper deference. As usual, Saravio seemed oblivious of what was expected of him.

The Queen leaned forward, elbows resting on the table. Her eyes gleamed like onyx, unreadable. She drew the moment out, watching Eduin and Saravio like a falcon hovering over a rabbit-horn den.

No, Eduin thought. Not a falcon, but a starving wolf circling fresh meat, wary of a trap. He saw the pattern of her thoughts, a dozen tiny pieces at last come together.

Varzil rebuilding Cedestri Tower, where terrible weapons had been created . . . Varzil scheming from afar, influencing lesser men to act . . . Varzil hiding behind a mask of goodness and King Carolin's favor . . . Varzil now at Asturias, ostensibly negotiating peace on behalf of Hastur, but perhaps on some other, far more deadly mission . . .

"So it seems," Julianna said, "that you may have something to tell us, after all."

Eduin suppressed a smile. In that brief moment, she had lost her capacity to intimidate him. Indeed, it was *she* who had fallen within *his* power. Since an answer seemed to be called for, Eduin bowed again and murmured that he attended Her Majesty's pleasure.

"I didn't mean you, I meant *him*." She indicated Saravio.

Saravio remained impassive and unresponsive. Romilla clenched her hands so tightly, her knuckles popped.

"I must serve to answer for him," Eduin said. "It is ever his way. What would Your Majesty ask?"

"I believe you and your brother were in Thendara at the time of the disturbance at Hali Lake."

Ah, Romilla had done her work well.

Word of the riot must surely have spread through the Towers to every corner of Darkover. Every competent monarch must keep alert to such populist uprisings, or be caught unawares when the tide turned against their own rule. It was only a small step from a handful of penniless refugees, howling in protest against the wars that had taken their lands and families, to a mob bent on revenge against their *Comyn* rulers.

Julianna was on guard, scenting a threat. From the way she was looking at Eduin, she considered it very likely that he was among the troublemakers.

"Alas, the Blessed Sandoval and I happened to be present at the lakeside on that fateful day," Eduin said. The statement, with its insinuation of innocence, would not fool Julianna, but that was not his aim. He wanted her to ask more questions.

"You were among those who attacked the circle from Hali Tower as they gathered on the shores of the lake?"

"*Vai domna,* I swear to you we were not."

She paused, watching him with those glittering black eyes, weighing his words. Eduin saw the tightness of her mouth, the preternatural stillness of her hands. *Then what were you doing there?* she asked him silently. *And will you tell me the truth?*

Julianna gestured to the guard standing beside the door on the far side of the room. An instant later, Callina glided into the room. She wore the loosely belted robe of a Tower worker and her starstone hung, unshielded, on its silken cord around her neck. Carefully avoiding looking at either Eduin or Saravio, she halted facing the Queen.

"Cast the spell, child," Julianna said.

Every other time Eduin had witnessed the setting of truthspell, the *leronis* or *laranzu* had bent over his matrix crystal, murmuring the ritual words while the psychoactive gem flared to life. Callina slipped the cord over her neck and held hers aloft. The stone glittered, blue and white, between her fingers. Her eyes went soft with inward focus. She began chanting in a low voice. Although Eduin could barely hear her words, he watched as the stone grew brighter with each phrase.

First, a radiance rose over Callina's face, then it engulfed her in a cone of blue-white brilliance. By the time she was half-way through the ceremony, the room glimmered as if caught in perpetual twilight, at once brighter and darker than any truthspell he had ever seen. For a long moment, no one dared speak, or even breathe.

"Now," said Julianna, in a voice that sliced through the stillness. "Now we will learn the truth of this matter."

"Sandoval the singer, called the Blessed, stand forth," General Marzan called out.

When Saravio did not move, Eduin nudged him forward.

"Do not interfere!" The general's voice rumbled like thunder on the peaks. "Each man must answer only for himself."

Eduin let his hand drop. Let them make what they would of Saravio's unresponsiveness.

"Were you at Hali Lake? What happened there?" Several times, General Marzan put questions to Saravio, without any visible reaction. Finally, the general raised his hands, as if giving up, and turned to Julianna.

"They say he speaks only upon your command," she said to Eduin. "Order him to answer."

"You must tell these good people about the lake shore riot," Eduin said, enunciating every word with care so that there would be no misunderstanding. "Do you remember how we went there? We saw the circle, and the Lake of Clouds, and Varzil Ridenow had gone down into its depths."

At the mention of Varzil, recognition flared in Saravio's eyes. He sent a pulse of anguish through the room. Eduin slammed his *laran* barriers into place.

"Varzil was there," Saravio murmured. "Dragons came from the sky. The lake churned. The air turned dark. People ran away. Those that remained . . . died."

"Varzil the Good?" Julianna repeated. "So he *was* there, after all. He is loved in Hali, or so I have been told. I wonder why he did not speak to the people, to quiet them."

"Let us proceed with the questioning," said General Marzan, "now that Sandoval has recovered his tongue. What did you mean, *dragons came from the sky?* And where was Varzil the Good when this happened?"

Saravio flushed with emotion. He cried out, his voice like the raucous shriek of a *kyorebni,* "Varzil—he brings the fire, he brings the fire! Aiee, Naotalba, have mercy on us—" He flung himself down upon his knees, burying his face in his hands.

Terror and pain flooded from his mind to engulf the room. Romilla uttered a cry like a dying bird, quickly stifled.

"Have mercy," Saravio cried, "or we shall all perish!"

"Your Majesty, great Queen, worthy lords," Eduin held out his hands beseechingly. "You see how my brother fares." He referred to their disguise as "Eduardo" and "Sandoval." "This questioning is too harsh for one of his sensitivities. The tragedy at Hali Lake almost destroyed him. I beg you, let me take him away before he swoons."

"The fire! Naotalba, save us!" Saravio burst into wailing. He beat the sides of his head with his fists.

Even through his tightly-raised barriers, Eduin felt wave after wave of fear emanating from Saravio. Romilla paled to the color of unbleached *linex* and appeared on the verge of fainting. Even the General's ruddy complexion faded. Julianna sat very still. Callina trembled like a leaf in a Hellers blizzard, but did not break her concentration. The truthspell remained, unwavering.

"Take him away," Julianna said. "Not you," to Eduin, "you stay here."

Two guards lifted Saravio to his feet. Saravio could barely stand, but he stumbled along between them, still moaning. The residue of his psychic emanations gradually died down.

"I don't know how much of that we can trust," Julianna commented to General Marzan. "Certainly, the man himself believed every word he spoke. As to how reliable a witness he is, that is another matter entirely." She turned her attention to Eduin. "I sincerely hope you are able to give a more coherent description."

"Lady, I know only what I saw and what was said to me," he replied.

"Proceed, then."

Eduin stepped forward, placing himself so that Callina's truthspell would directly illuminate his face. He could say anything now, and so long as it was not frank raving, his words would be accepted. No one could lie under truthspell, or so they all believed.

"The Blessed Sandoval and I were living in Thendara when we heard there was to be a great working of sorcery at Hali Lake," Eduin began. So far, this was the truth. "Some said that a spell had been laid upon the heavens, for there was much lightning. I heard one man say that the Aldarans had done a mighty weather-working, but I do not know if that was true. So we went to the lake, and saw many other people there. They told me that Varzil, he who is Keeper at Neskaya, had gone down into the lake itself, beneath the waters of cloud. What he did there, I cannot tell, but I heard that the infernal device that caused the Cataclysm, changing the water to mist so long ago, was still upon on the bottom, and he had gone to seek it."

Eduin sensed rather than saw the ripple of response. He shook his head as if he himself were uncertain what to think. Something whispered through the back of his mind, a ghostly echo, *Yes . . . Set the trap for Varzil . . .*

"We had not been there very long," he plunged on, "when I looked above the circle and saw a—I don't know—it was long like a serpent, with hideous wings. It dove down upon us, slashing and striking. When it breathed, men choked and died. There was no place to hide, no where to run."

"How is it *you* were able to escape?" the general asked.

"Oh, it was terrible!" Eduin let the despair of that moment tinge his voice. It *had* been terrible when their plans turned against them and Naotalba's army, formed to bring them victory, dissolved into frenzied retreat. "No man could stand against the thing. I don't know how many died. The lucky ones ran away. We hid, and it missed us. Just then, when it seemed it must see us, the dragon disappeared. It was gone, just like that. I looked toward the lake, and I saw Varzil with my very own eyes."

"Varzil—you saw him, truly?"

"He was walking out of the water, just as if nothing had happened, and *he was smiling*." Eduin conjured a picture in his own mind, half true memory, half a vision born from his hatred. Over it, he poured that unique form of *laran*, the Deslucido Gift, which his father had shown him years ago. He could hear his father's mental voice even now:

Now that I am completely sure of your loyalty, I will teach you how to defeat truthspell. You will be able to swear to whatever serves our higher purpose, and no laranzu *on Darkover will be able to tell the difference.*

No laranzu *on Darkover* . . . And whatever he said would be trusted so absolutely that men might live or die, kings go to war or make peace, based upon a simple word.

How many times had his father used the Gift and watched certainty dissolve into bewilderment, accusers themselves become the accused, men and armies turn away from their own ends and become instruments of another's will? Had his uncle, King Damian, stood in the blue light and lied and been believed? Had his cousin, Belisar?

A shudder passed through Eduin as he realized that *this* was the reason Damian and Belisar had died, this terrible secret. Not ambition, not misjudgment, not lack of military power. Only a trick of fate had spared his own father, who had lived on as a crippled, revenge-obsessed fugitive.

The Deslucido Gift was a weapon too terrible to wield, far more than crystalline bonewater or even whatever dreadful *laran* machinery had created the Cataclysm at Hali Lake. These things destroyed a man's body, perhaps even his mind. The Deslucido Gift struck at the trust that bound men together and made them more than vicious beasts.

Only men sing, only men dance, only men weep. So went the ancient proverb. *Only men place their lives and honor in each other's hands.*

All this, he could undo with a word. He trembled with the knowledge.

No one else seemed to have noticed, although the room had fallen silent. General Marzan glanced at Julianna as if to ask if she were satisfied. After a long moment, she nodded, dismissing Eduin to return to his chambers.

As he heard the door of their room close behind him, Eduin felt a strange, dark jubilation. Varzil now stood condemned in the eyes of Queen Julianna. She would never believe Varzil had innocent motives for descending into the lake. Her canny mind would put together the Cataclysm device and Varzil's role in rebuilding Cedestri Tower. Indeed, she would see Varzil's shadow over Kirella, over Asturias to the north, reaching even now toward Valeron itself. . . .

Eduin found Saravio slumped, barely conscious, in a chair. Saravio's hands twitched as if jolts of energy coursed through his fingers. His eyes had rolled up in his skull, showing crescents of white between half-parted lids. Julianna's guards must have left him there, in all likelihood unwilling to have anything further to do with him. Many soldiers were frightened of madness, as if it were some disease that might infect them, too. Perhaps they saw the mark of the gods as unlucky.

"Poor fool," Eduin murmured and he drew Saravio's arm across his shoulders and hefted the other man to his feet.

Saravio retained just enough shreds of consciousness to stumble to his bed. As he had so many times before, Eduin loosened his clothing and arranged his arms and legs. On impulse, he laid one hand along the side of Saravio's neck. He felt the skin, clammy with sweat, and the thready leap of pulse along the artery.

With the physical touch came a wave of mental images. A figure drifted slowly across a landscape the color of ashes. For a moment, Eduin did not recognize Naotalba, her form was so colorless and translucent. Even the light overhead was slowly fading, quenched, exhausted.

Eduin reached out his mind to the phantasmic form, but even as his fingers brushed the outline, it vanished. Poor Saravio, he had not even enough mental energy to preserve the image of his goddess.

Under Eduin's fingertips, Saravio's pulse stuttered. Once or twice, he thought it had stopped entirely, but it went on, caught in a ragged dance. He did not know if Saravio would ever waken again, or if he did, whether he would even know his own name or where he was.

Go in peace, he prayed. *You have served me well. There is nothing more you can do.*

Although it chilled him to the bone to do so, he was already thinking what use he might make of Saravio's death, how he could make it seem that Varzil had a hand in it. Julianna would be furious that King Carolin's agent could reach into her own castle and take a man's life. But at this moment, he felt too heart-sick to care.

A gentle tapping on the outer door roused Eduin from his musings. He left Saravio to see who it was, but before he reached the door, it swung open and Callina slipped in. She carried a small dark box that he recognized instantly as a telepathic damper.

"I am so sorry to disturb you. Is he asleep?" Callina tilted her head toward the bed where Saravio lay. "What a terrible ordeal he must have gone through! Who would have thought that behind the mask of goodness lay such a monster? Varzil, I mean," she added quickly.

"You are convinced, then, that the Keeper of Neskaya moves with evil purpose against Valeron?"

"How could anyone doubt it? It could not be more plain if I had been there at Hali Lake and seen with my own eyes! But I am forgetting myself. Here, I brought him this," she held out the telepathic damper.

"I know that Sandoval the Blessed has *laran*," Callina said, "and that is in part how he accomplishes his healing work. Now he is the one who requires rest and quiet. This damper will insulate him from any outside mental energies. It will also make it difficult, if not impossible, for him to use his own abilities. Therefore, his mind can rest completely, which it must in order to recover."

Eduin listened with a carefully respectful expression while she explained what it was and how to operate it. He was long familiar with such devices. Since his early years at Arilinn Tower, he had used one in his own chamber at night to prevent any inadvertent thoughts or fragments of dreams from betraying him. Later, he had found that the insulation granted a blessed respite from the continual need to appear other than he was; within its influence, he could at last relax. Only with Dyannis had he known such peace.

"I thank you for your concern, *vai leronis*," Eduin said, "but I fear that not even your magic can help him."

A glimmer of fear passed over her features, as quickly suppressed. "Then I must see him immediately."

Callina bent over Saravio's sleeping form. She went about monitoring his condition in an orderly, competent manner, although clearly this was not her strength. There was no danger if she discovered some lingering trace of Naotalba, if such still existed in the emptiness of Saravio's mind, for he had often spoken of the Bride of Zandru. As for what Eduin himself had done, he had no fear. After all, the Keepers of Hestral and Hali Towers, far more skilled than this young *leronis,* had failed to detect what his own father had done to him. He was safe on that account.

Callina worked slowly and carefully, often pausing to search more deeply. At last, she sighed and drew back. "Alas, I fear you are right. I would send for Tomaso, our monitor in the Tower here, but I do not think there is anything he can do, either."

"You will not insist on a physician?" Eduin asked, furrowing his brow.

She smiled, a little sadly, and shook her head. "No, I understand why you would not want that. With your permission, however, I will inform Lady Romilla, so that she might prepare herself."

Eduin nodded assent. Before she left, Callina set the telepathic damper beside Saravio's bed and turned it on. Eduin felt the familiar blanketing silence. After living so long without such a device, it now felt as if he were suddenly rendered half-blind, half-deaf.

40

Eduin awoke, sweating heavily. He thought he had been dreaming, or wandering in the Overworld, although he could not remember why. Flame and ash and a terrible sense of suffocation enveloped him. He struggled to sit up, pulling away the twisted bedcovers. As he filled his lungs, breath after gasping breath, it seemed his chest had gone brittle, a cage of twigs, and that the pounding of his heart might shatter it at any moment.

The nightmare must be the result of sleeping within the field of a telepathic damper. After all, he had lived so long without it that it would naturally take time for his mind and body to readjust. He told himself that the effects, while unpleasant, would soon pass.

By the light streaming through the single narrow window, the time was well into morning. He had slept longer than he intended, but in this season of long days and lingering twilights, that was of no matter. There would be plenty of time to do whatever must be done that day.

Yawning, he dressed. In the night, one of the servants had taken away his clothing, washed and folded it, and laid it neatly on the small chest. The shirt smelled of sweet herbs. He held it to his face for a moment, remembering when he had taken such pleasures for granted, clean clothing, a warm bed, well-cooked food. Sometimes, in the long years of hiding, a crust of moldy bread and the meager shelter of a half-crumbled wall had seemed like luxuries.

Varzil, it was Varzil who had taken away everything good and bright in his life.

I survived. That's all that matters. Once Varzil is dead, and Carolin's reign is ruined, I'll never have to think about those years again.

Saravio was still alive, although in so deep a slumber he did not rouse, not even when Eduin placed a hand upon his shoulder and shook him gently. Eduin was not sure if he'd expected otherwise.

He has done his work. I no longer need him.

Eduin ran his fingertips over Saravio's brow before leaving him. He felt no mental contact, for that was impossible within the field of a working telepathic damper, only a deep sadness. Surely the man who had pulled him from the Thendara gutters, fed and housed him, deserved some memorial of the heart. Saravio had given him so much more. They had shared the joys and privations of the road, had understood each other, exiled *laranzu'in,* as perhaps few others could. More than that, Saravio had been his only friend, or as close as anyone could be.

The telepathic damper sat on the wash stand beside the door. This close, Eduin felt its effect like a faint buzzing along his nerves. Since Saravio was clearly beyond any help from such a device, Eduin turned it off.

The change in the ambient psychic atmosphere of the castle almost brought him to his knees. Gone was the surge and play of holiday merrymaking, as well as the anxieties of the situation with Isoldir. Instead, framed against the fractured babble of ordinary minds, he felt a singleness of purpose, a shift like a river in flood.

Something had happened, but he could not discern what.

Cold burned deep in his belly. A voice whispered in the back of his mind, *Kill* . . . and he realized with a terrible certainty that it was no longer only his father's voice.

Eduin raced down the corridor. A maid carrying a basket of soiled linens made way for him. He slowed his pace.

"What's happened?" he shouted.

In response, she cringed against the wall, shaking her head. "I—I know nothing! Don't hurt me!"

The stableman would surely know of any comings or goings. Eduin flung himself down the back stairway, taking the steps two at a time. A pair of servants in Valeron house livery jumped aside. What did they know? He had no time for more useless answers. Urgency spurred him on. Hallways flew past and then he burst into the courtyard.

Everything looked normal, the household staff finishing their morning labors. Eduin found the stableman leading Lady Marelie's favorite mare to the watering trough.

"What has happened?" Eduin cried. His heart pounded and his breath rasped in his throat. He knew he looked like a madman, racing through the placid late summer morning as if half the demons in Zandru's Seven Hells were on his heels. How would he explain the sense of disaster that seared every nerve?

The stableman turned to look at him. "Oh, they were off before dawn and that's all any of us knows."

"Off? Who? Where?"

The stableman stroked the mare's neck. She had buried her muzzle in the green-tinted water and was sucking noisily. Then she raised her head and blew out foam, shaking her head to scatter droplets in every direction. The stableman laughed.

"Where?" Eduin repeated.

"Oh, we'll be finding out soon enough. Whatever the Lady's up to, she'll keep her own counsel until everything's done and settled. Times like these, with all the merrymaking, folks come and go, and you never know whose tongue might wag."

With an effort, Eduin controlled himself. "Someone went somewhere. That much you know."

"Crept out quietlike they did, from the Tower to the field. This little lady," he indicated the mare, "was being no lady at all, but about to kick her stall down, so I was awake to hear."

"From the Tower to—*the airfield?*"

"The very same—"

Eduin did not stay to hear more. He bolted for the gate leading to the outer courtyard where the aircars were kept.

The yard was empty except for an old servant in a homespun smock raking the dirt field.

"You there! Halt!" a man's voice rang out behind him.

Eduin turned to see three Valeron soldiers hurry toward him. The foremost wore the badge of a captain and a frown.

"Who are you and what are you doing here?"

Eduin stammered out the false name he used, adding that he served Lord Brynon, before blurting out, "What happened? Where did they go?"

"You'd best get your answers direct from your master," the captain said. "There's no harm in telling you the aircars took off two hours before dawn. They're safely away now. There's nothing any man can do to stop them now."

Two hours before dawn! While I slept—

It could all be perfectly innocent, but he knew it wasn't. He felt it in every mote of air around him, every beat of his heart. A peaceful mission would have left in daylight, without any need for stealth. It had to be an attack, one planned in secrecy and shrouded with dread.

The thoughts of the *laranzu'in* piloting the aircars hung in the air. *We have no choice. We must seize the chance . . . But if we should be wrong . . .*

"I—I thank you," Eduin stammered, making his retreat. "I am sure my Lord will tell me whatever he wishes me to know."

He hurried back to the castle proper and made his way, at a more decorous pace, to Lord Brynon's chambers. To his surprise, he was refused entry. Lord Brynon was not within, but closeted with the Queen.

Eduin's gut twisted. Frustrated and furious, he reached out with his *laran* and plunged through the aide's flimsy defenses. While he'd slept, exhausted and numbed by the telepathic damper, the Queen had met with her advisers. General Marzan had been summoned, several of his most trusted officers, Lord Brynon . . . and the *laranzu'in* of Valeron Tower.

Forcing himself to calm, Eduin bowed and took his leave. The Queen had convened a war council, that much was plain. She had commanded the *laranzu'in* to set out in the aircars. Doubtless, they were loaded with *clingfire* or some other powerful weapon. The speed and secrecy of the attack and the lack of movement of ordinary soldiers suggested it was meant to be a decisive strike.

Against Isoldir? Eduin frowned, pausing to let one of the under-*coridoms* hustle past him. Had Julianna come to doubt the sincerity of *Dom* Ronal's pledge? Did she suspect he might have betrayed an oath made under truthspell?

He shuddered. Then another thought lifted his heart. She might also have finally seen the hand of Varzil Ridenow in Isoldir and sent the air-cars to destroy the newly-rebuilt Tower.

Whatever the mission, it was clear he would get no answers from the servants. He had not dared to approach any of the Tower folk, for fear of detection. But Callina might well know something. At this hour, she was often in Romilla's bower. He quickened his pace in that direction.

He was admitted without question, where he found Callina sitting with Romilla over cups of *jaco* and plates of little flower-decorated pastries. Callina looked pale, the delicate skin around her eyes dark, her energy brittle. Romilla, however, glowed. Her eyes glittered with a hectic fire.

"Good morning to you," Romilla said, looking up. "Where is the Blessed Sandoval? I hope he is not exhausted after the audience last night. Callina said he needed rest and quiet."

Eduin had all but forgotten Saravio in his need to discover what had happened. He replied, "I fear that he has, *vai damisela,* and worse than ever before."

"If he has not recovered under the damper, there is not much more I can do," Callina said. "I do not suppose either of you would accept a physician's ministrations. Shall I send for the Tower monitor?"

That was the last thing Eduin wanted, although he did not think that what he had done to Saravio was detectable even by a trained *laran* healer. He bowed and said that if the Blessed Sandoval did not rally, he would leave the next step to Callina's discretion.

"I will pray to Evanda for his recovery," Romilla said.

"If you must pray, let it be to Naotalba, who is his special patroness," Eduin said.

She turned to him with a look of radiant triumph. "Sandoval's warnings have not gone unheeded. This very morning, Queen Julianna sent a strike force to destroy Varzil Ridenow."

Exultation and dread tightened around Eduin's throat.

"*Domna* Romilla!" Callina said sharply. "Is it wise to speak of such things to one who is not in the confidence of the Queen?"

"Nonsense!" Romilla replied, "Eduardo here has spoken for his brother, Sandoval the Blessed, since they first came to Kirella. Sandoval has brought us nothing but good—for me, for all of Kirella. It was he who first warned us of the perfidious intentions of Varzil Ridenow. Now the shadow of Varzil's influence reaches out to engulf Valeron itself. By his own testimony, this man has given the Queen the evidence she needed to act. Why should he not learn the outcome and the elimination of so subtle and implacable an enemy?"

"Varzil—" Eduin's thoughts churned. Nothing made any sense. Varzil was no longer at Cedestri. Everyone knew that. "She has—she must have attacked Varzil at Asturias?"

"I think you are right, Romilla," Callina said. "These men were the first to give warning, and they have been constant friends to the throne of Aillard. I sensed the menace growing day by day, as has the Queen. Each new piece of news was like a stone in the tomb of Valeron."

"The Compact is but a diversion, a ruse to disarm everyone except his own masters," Romilla said, her brow tightening. As she spoke, she paced a few steps, then reseated herself. "I would not be surprised to learn that Cedestri Tower is once again making dreadful weapons. Only this time, they serve not Isoldir but Hastur. If we do not stop Varzil now, in the single moment he is vulnerable, we may never have another opportunity. Valeron will bend to the yoke of the Hasturs, or else be destroyed."

Eduin, too stunned to form a question, stood and listened. The women went on as if he were not there, continuing to discuss the night's events.

"I felt this need, do you see, to know where Varzil went, what he might next be scheming," Callina said with an expression of satisfaction.

"It is just as well he has not returned to Neskaya," Romilla said. "It makes a difficult target for aircars, being in such mountainous terrain. I do not think Her Majesty would risk a strike there. She has but this one opportunity before she loses the advantage of surprise. In addition, if we diverted our forces to Neskaya, we would leave Hali Tower intact and fully able to retaliate. What would it profit us to eliminate Varzil and yet leave such a powerful force as our enemy?"

"You believe Hali Tower does not mean to abide by the Compact it has signed?" Callina asked.

Eduin too was surprised by Romilla's assertion. The heir to Kirella had never spoken mind-to-mind along the relays. She knew only the sort of spoken promises that might as easily be broken.

"I have not witnessed their oath under truthspell," Romilla temporized. "I would not put it past them to give out that they had done so, and yet secretly continue to develop even more powerful weapons. I believe that Varzil means to bring all Darkover under his influence, and woe betide anyone who has crossed him."

"You speak as if you hate him," Callina said. "I did not know you ever met him."

Romilla paused, her mouth working. Eduin sensed in her the lingering effects of Saravio's emotional manipulations, for which he himself had been responsible. Romilla was already attuned to the heights of euphoria that Saravio's singing produced; she had been equally vulnerable to the fear and anger that accompanied any mention of Varzil.

"I do not need to know the man personally to see what he is," Romilla retorted. "When I name Varzil a menace, I do not indulge in baseless prejudice. This is a matter of state, not of petty personal taste. I certainly have no reason to think ill of the folk at Hali Tower, except that they have fallen under his influence. For all I know, they are even now raising the Cataclysm device so that Varzil may use it to crush anyone who dares stand against him."

She paused, swallowing. Eduin saw tears glimmer in Callina's eyes for an instant.

"I—I have spoken with many of them through the relay screens," Callina said softly. "I will regret their passing."

Eduin's vision leaped into crystalline focus. "Varzil is at *Hali Tower?* You sent aircars to firebomb *Hali Tower?*"

"Calm yourself," Romilla told him. "There is nothing to fear. They will not suspect an attack from this quarter. Callina assures us that as of two days ago, Varzil Ridenow was within the Tower walls, and as you know, the Tower stands some distance from the city. No innocent people will be harmed. Even as Julianna spared *Dom* Ronal in the destruction of Cedestri Tower, so will she leave the city of Hali standing, with the *rhu fead* and all its ancient splendors. Without his pet Keeper and the *laran* resources of Hali Tower, King Carolin will not dare to strike back. The circle at Neskaya will be without its Keeper, so they cannot aid Carolin either. It is a brilliant move, to end a terrible threat with so little loss of life."

She smiled, her lips dark with blood. Eduin had not noticed the cruel lines of her mouth, the arrogant tilt of her chin. Blessed Cassilda, he had thought to control a tormented child and instead he had unleashed a monster.

Hali Tower!

Images washed across his mind, blotting out the room in which he stood. The two women faded like ghosts as he watched the aircars, sleek silver engines of death, bear down on Hali. The Tower stood at the far end of the cloud-filled lake, reaching its slender whiteness to the heavens, shimmering in the morning brightness. The light caught the extravagance of translucent blue stone so that, for an instant, the entire Tower glowed like a matrix crystal. He felt the minds of the *leronyn* within, men and women he had lived with, worked with, linked minds with across the relays. The Tower would be psychically quiet now, the circles resting after a night's labor.

In his imagination, spheres of glowing orange and eye-searing vermilion arced across the sky, heading toward the blue-white Tower. He felt the unnatural fire within them, straining for release, hungering for flesh and bone . . .

Screams . . . charring heat . . . dark smoke filling the sky . . . a woman's body burning . . .

"No, this must not be!" The words burst from him. "We must stop it—call them back!"

"Why, whatever for?" Romilla said.

"What is the problem?" cried Callina. She had caught his terror. Her face paled.

Dyannis is at Hali Tower!

Callina rose and reached out one hand as if she would touch him. "You cannot save her, or any of them. Even as we speak, the aircars draw near their target. It is too late."

"No, you don't understand!" An emotion he had no name for came roaring out from the very depths of his soul.

In that moment, Eduin saw Dyannis as a young girl wreathed in silvery radiance, the personification of everything good and noble in his own life. She had given herself to him freely, and for the first time, he had seen himself, reflected in the eyes of his beloved, as someone worthy of honor and love. Their time had been brief and long ago, but some kernel of its glory had nestled in his innermost heart, a place not even the whispers of his father's ghost could reach.

Surely, she had forgotten him. That made no difference, so long as she lived.

"We must send word to the pilots of the aircars!" he gasped. "Use the matrix screens of the Tower! Tell them there has been a dreadful mistake. They must return at once!"

"You cannot reach them, not even with the power of an entire circle," Callina said. "Queen Julianna feared that Varzil might sense an attack, and use his powers to turn the pilots from their course. To shield them, she equipped each aircar with a masking talisman. It is like the matrix stone in a telepathic damper, only it permits the use of *laran* within its field. It simply isolates the pilots from outside influence. As far as you are concerned, they might as well be deaf."

"There must be some other way, then—is there another aircar we can send after them?"

Before Callina could reply, Romilla said, "You are showing an unusual degree of interest in this expedition." She narrowed her eyes. "Why should you wish to stop the attack? You yourself warned us about Varzil Ridenow. Have you changed your mind, perhaps because you have sold out to him?"

"I don't care if Varzil escapes this time. There will always be another chance," Eduin said. "You must not attack Hali Tower!"

"*Must not?* Eduardo, you forget your place, as servant and guest. Who are you to say what Julianna Aillard, Lady of Valeron, must or *must not* do?"

Behind Eduin's eyes, his father's ghost writhed in fury. *You swore . . . K–k–kill Varzil!*

Eduin staggered under the onslaught. Pain lanced through his head. He doubled over, clutching his belly. Silently, desperately, he fought back against the compulsion spell that wound all through his guts, entangled his very soul. He clung to the only weapon he had—the only shred of sanity—*Dyannis must live, no matter what the cost.*

"Romilla, there is more to this than we previously realized—" Callina began.

"There is no time to waste!" Eduin gasped, hauling himself upright. "While we stand here bickering, the attack may already have begun. At least let me try to bring them back!"

"I have told you," Callina said in a voice like the tolling of a bell, "there is nothing you or I or any of us can do." Her eyes softened, and he saw in them the grief she had carried since she watched as her twin brother died in battle, that terrible powerlessness. She could not shut out the memory any more than she could burn away her own *laran*.

If Dyannis dies, I die with her. He saw his father's skeletal hands reach for him, trailing rotten flesh and shroud.

He grabbed Callina so roughly that she let out a shriek. "The Tower—the relay screens—take me there now!"

"Release her this instant!" Romilla cried. "How dare you lay hands upon a *leronis*! And to give her orders—insufferable! You shall be whipped for such behavior!"

Callina went rigid, staring at Eduin. The physical closeness created a psychic bond.

Who are you? she cried.

For an instant he hesitated. Years of hiding, of drawing in upon himself, died hard. He could not bring himself to give her his true name.

I am a laranzu, *trained at Arilinn Tower, and then at Hali.* Never mind Hestral, and all that had happened there, how he had plotted and brought about the death of Varzil's Felicia, how he had bespelled the Hastur forces and then fled in Hestral's destruction. *I seek only to save the life of one* leronis *at Hali. For this, I will storm your own Tower here, I will lie, I will kill anyone—even you—who stands in my way.*

You will die. The words flowed from her mind with quiet certainty. Behind her, another woman spread out her shadowy cloak.

I don't care—just so long as she lives!

Callina pried his fingers from her shoulders. He could not resist her. "I will take you, although it will do no good. We are all of us caught up in this thing, and it will not release us until it has run its course."

She led the way to the door. Romilla watched aghast for a moment, then rushed after them.

"I will not leave you alone with this madman!"

"We will see," Callina shot back over her shoulder without missing a step, "who is truly mad."

Corridors and stairwells sped past in a blur. Callina led them, not through the courtyard where they might be challenged by armed soldiers, but by an inner route. She used her *laran* to project a wall of force, clearing the way ahead of her. Her stride was so determined and her expression so fierce that no one, not even the household guards, challenged them. A few bowed before scurrying out of the way. If anyone spoke, Eduin paid them no heed.

They crossed over a small stretch of yard to the entrance to the Tower itself. A servant in Aillard livery hurried to open the massive outer doors. The wood was dark, almost black, inlaid with fine copper wire with the emblem of a gigantic eagle, wings outstretched. As he passed between the doors, Eduin remembered the old proverb about the prey that walks from the trap to the stewpot.

"Hurry!" Eduin urged Callina. She plunged on, with him on her heels and Romilla gamely following. Romilla had given up asking questions.

Inside, the central room of the Tower was smaller than he expected. It must have housed only a single circle and a small one at that, perhaps a half dozen.

Where is the Keeper? he asked Callina.

You will not see him, she replied with such a chill in her mental voice that he wondered for an instant if the Keeper were no longer alive. He did not have time to ask how a circle could function without one, for Callina crossed the room, gathered her skirts, and proceeded up a flight of circular stairs.

In every Tower Eduin had ever known, the working chambers were placed at the highest levels. This close to a bustling castle and city, the circle needed every degree of separation, of insulation. As he climbed, trying to avoid treading upon Callina's skirts, he felt as if he were leaving the ordinary world behind.

Something waited at the top of the stairs, in the circular chamber at the very top of the Tower. For an instant, Eduin regretted his rash words. It was too late to draw back now. *It* was aware of him, drawing him in. His feet flew over the stairs. Behind him, Romilla started sobbing.

The stairs led to a shallow landing, with a wide slit window to one side and a door to the other. Callina, her chest heaving, took hold of the latch. The door opened inward on soundless hinges. Callina stood back and gestured Eduin forward.

"Go in."

"The relay screens—"

"Are within."

And what else?

He had no choice. He had come too far to turn back.

41

Eduin's first impression upon entering the top chamber was one of light and spaciousness, although the floor could not have been more than five or six paces across. The room was round, its unadorned walls following the contours of the turret itself. On the far side, a relay screen sat on a narrow table. A padded bench was drawn up beside it, ready for use.

An intricate metallic armature dominated the center of the room. Silver wires meshed to form a five-legged base, soaring upward, dividing and recombining so that the effect was a frozen, freestanding waterfall. Eduin recognized it as a housing for a matrix device. He had designed and built similar structures, arrays of starstones integrated into higher-order matrices. He knew how to link individual stones, to amplify their powers, to attune them to a particular use. It was such a device he had used to assassinate Felicia Hastur-Acosta.

He had never seen anything like this one before. Instead of resting on a table, it stood alone, reaching as high as his chest. Near the top, surrounded by a mesh of fine fibers, a single starstone had been set. It pulsed blue-white like the beating of a heart, filling the entire chamber with its brilliance. Instinctively, he recoiled from it.

Callina caught him before he could retreat. Her fingers dug into his arms like grappling hooks. With preternatural strength and quickness, she whirled him around to face the matrix.

How could he have been so credulous as to think her a weak maiden, still grieving over the death of her brother—if that had not also been an illusion. At this moment, he would have believed her capable of anything.

Once he had seen resin-trees, caught in a wildfire, send sparks like a horde of glowing eyes into the night sky before the white-gold flames engulfed them. So now her mind, her entire being, flared hotter than any smithy's furnace.

Before him, the blue light of the starstone intensified. Within its shifting radiance, he sensed a stirring, part psychoactive crystal, part intelligence . . . part hunger. He struggled against Callina's grasp, but it was no use. His flesh had gone heavy and numb.

What—what is that thing? And what did it want with him?

Behind him, Romilla whimpered, "What are you doing? What's happening?"

"Silence!" Callina's voice, raucous as the cry of a *kyorebni,* shot out. She brought her mouth close to Eduin's ear. "You know what it is. You know what it wants."

If his father's spirit had placed itself into a starstone and condensed all his determination into that crystal lattice, it might have resembled the device Eduin now faced. Only this one was no mere repository of past hatreds; it *sensed* him.

Now he knew why no one had seen the Keeper of Valeron Tower, why the few *leronyn* went mutely about their duties.

The Keeper's crystal blazed with light. It perceived his nearness, his Gift. Within the depths of his mind, the compulsion command left by his father shrieked out in warning. The crystal vibrated with desire. Like a double image to its brightness, a figure cloaked in shadow stretched out ethereal fingers.

You feel it, don't you—the curse upon this place? Callina's thought jittered across the roiling chaos of his mind. *They sent me here out of concern for my health, or so they told me. A place of safety, they promised! They told me it would be an easy position with nothing more troubling than making possets for babes with the colic. The Lady was kind, and Valeron at peace. No more bloody battles, no more deaths! I could rest and recover my strength, and yet still be of service.*

Her mind slammed into his, and for an instant, he watched as a young girl, her brother's death still raw and fresh in her memory, climbed the stairs to meet her new Keeper. She followed a gray-robed *laranzu*, his hair white, his face incised with lines she assumed were caused by suffering. She thought his absence of telepathic overture was a gesture of respect for her sorrow. She did not yet know how wrong she was.

Callina had stood, even as Eduin did now, gazing at the starstone in its silver mantle and wondering where the Keeper was. Confusion fell away as she sensed the adamantine will encased in crystal, the depth of craft and ingenuity.

The Keeper was here, not in body, but in mind, preserved and sustained in the matrix device. Callina had no idea how long he had been there, perhaps from the height of the Ages of Chaos. There had been no limit to the *laran* experimentation in those days. Perhaps a few extraordinarily powerful *leronyn* had managed to cheat death in this fashion. Fascinated and horrified, she had drawn closer to the crystalline array and watched it brighten at her approach.

The Keeper's consciousness, part human, part something else, had brushed hers. Years, decades, centuries past unfolded before her.

Long life and *chieri* blood had given the ancient Keeper knowledge of many things that were now but whispered legends. He had been alive a millennium ago, when men dreamed of reaching out into the depths of space with their *laran,* of delving into the very germs of life, of creating talismans to control fire.

As his body failed, he lingered in the twilight shores of death, this Keeper who had outlived his own name. He waited and watched for a successor, someone to carry on his vision, perhaps even someone whose mind he might overshadow, giving him a new life. The wisdom he had won at such hard cost must not be forgotten.

The men who attended him were too small and brittle to contain him; their minds would break under the strain. More and more, he withdrew into his starstone, seeking the perfection of its unchanging, inanimate structure. His circle gathered, and from the stone, he commanded their linked minds.

At last, he knew he could not hold his own death at bay any longer. He was too decrepit by now to even speak. Commanding his circle through his starstone, he directed the construction of a lattice to amplify his mental patterns. Accustomed to unthinking obedience, they hurried to comply. As he felt the last of his life energy dwindle, the Keeper gazed on the device of his immortality. It would sustain him until he could find another living mind to take for his own.

Older *leronyn* died or moved away, and the younger ones, fewer each year, never questioned his absence. At his direction, they willingly poured their mental energies into charging *laran* batteries for aircars and glow-globes.

Unimaginable years later, Callina, newly-come to Valeron, had faced the Keeper's starstone. In its pattern, she had sensed a desperation turned to despair. It had at last found a mind with the necessary strength and pliability—but that mind belonged to a woman!

A useless woman! stormed the Keeper. Yet, she might serve some purpose. On the brink of thrusting her away, it paused. She might not be able to serve as Keeper, but her life-force could feed his.

In her dreams, it battened upon her like a ghastly leech, feeding off her vitality. From that day forward, she was no better than a chained prisoner. The Keeper's mind permitted her to go as far as the castle, but not beyond. As she slept, it pillaged her memory. In particular, it fed upon her memories of the battle—the pain, the fear, the killing rage. The blood.

Sometimes she thought she would go mad. She considered taking her own life, but even as she drew her dagger, she knew she could not. If only . . . if only she could give the Keeper what it wanted, it might release her.

Then two strangers arrived, in the entourage of a minor Aillard lord. Rumors had flown before them, stories of healing miracles. She had scoffed at such tales, until she had felt the euphoric touch of the Blessed Sandoval. For the first time since she had come to Valeron, she felt the faint stirrings of hope.

In an unguarded moment, she sensed a trained mind on hers, with power enough to mask her own perceptions for a time. Sandoval's *laran* was soporific, balm to her tattered nerves. His singing might have even made her life here endurable. But Eduardo, who masqueraded as his brother, was something more. She did not care why he hid who he really was, or what crime he had committed, why he wandered the length of Darkover in such strange company.

Here he is! she shrieked at the thing in the crystal. *The Keeper you have been waiting for! Take him and let me go!*

Too late, Eduin saw his own danger. How could he have missed the subtle wrongness? No one had seen the Keeper . . . he never left the Tower. . . .

He had been so caught up in his own mission, building the case against Varzil, always Varzil, always his father's whispering voice, *K–k–kill . . .*

I ought to give myself to this thing, Eduin thought furiously, *and let them fight it out between them.*

He could not do it, turn his own mind and heart into a battlefield from which neither could emerge victorious. He was not ready to slit his own throat, not when Hali Tower—and Dyannis—depended upon him.

The relay screen lay only a few paces away. It hummed softly in response to the presence of two Gifted minds. He glanced at it, tearing his eyes away from the silver armature. He could reach it in an instant, but he would need a distraction, something to occupy the Keeper.

Eduin twisted in Callina's grasp, using his weight and the power of his muscles, built up from hours of heavy labor in the stables. Her nails bit into his flesh as he wrenched free. He almost knocked her off her feet. She gave a little shriek as he grabbed her in turn. Her arms were so thin that his hands almost encircled them. He pivoted her to face the matrix device. The crystal blazed, more white now than blue.

Take her instead!

Fool! roared through his mind. *A woman cannot become a Keeper!*

A woman has!

Incredulity answered him.

He summoned his own memories, shaping them like a weapon. When he had come to Hestral Tower in search of the daughter of Queen Taniquel, Felicia had already begun her training as under-Keeper. Arilinn Tower had refused to train her, despite the fact that she had, under emergency conditions, taken on a Keeper's role. Only Hestral, small and experimental, had dared to allow her to develop her extraordinary abilities. Eduin had sat in her circle, felt her sure mental touch as she gathered up the massed psychic energies of each worker. In the centripolar position, channeling immense power, she had never faltered. What she could have become, what she might have accomplished if he had not put an end to her, he would never know. But she *had* worked as a Keeper, as powerful as any man. All this he summoned to hurl at the crystalline Keeper.

A silent howl reverberated in the chamber. Eduin shoved Callina at the armature. She crashed into it and went down in a flurry of skirts and silver wire. Romilla shouted, but he had no time to spare for her. He leaped for the relay screen.

Even as Eduin bent over the screen, bringing it to life with a touch of his mind, he heard Callina struggling to free herself. He glanced around. Romilla had backed against the far wall, hands over her mouth, eyes staring. The impact of Callina's fall had toppled the matrix device, but the central crystal still blazed. White-hot fury seared his vision for a moment.

Callina thrashed on the floor, shrieking like a hamstrung animal. Her panic reverberated through the room.

He turned to the screen. It was tuned to another's mental pattern, but he had no time to make adjustments. He must drive his message through by sheer mental power.

Hali! He threw all the force of his *laran* into the call. Across the leagues, across the years, he cried out.

Hali Tower! Can you hear me?

It was day, he realized with a sickening jolt, and therefore unlikely that a worker would be sitting at the screen. Almost all relay messages were sent at night, to avoid the low-level psychic chatter from ordinary minds.

Behind him, the sound of Callina's struggle changed. He heard the screech of metal on stone as she shoved the armature aside, then the rustle of her skirts.

HALI! Oh, gods, may someone be there! Answer me!

What if he were already too late? What if the silence from Hali were not daytime rest but the absence of all *laran*-trained minds in the Tower, gone up in smoke and ash, in flame and screaming?

No, surely he would have sensed it if Dyannis had suffered such a fate. He would know because a part of him would have died with her.

A moan reached his hearing, so raw and low he barely recognized it as human. Without looking, he knew that Callina had risen and now stood, clutching the Keeper's stone, unable to tear her gaze away. The brightness of the day paled in the pulsating radiance of cold blue light. To the side, Romilla sobbed incoherently.

HALI!

Eduin reeled with the effort. His vision grayed, blurring. He felt the faintest hint of response, a distant stirring like the lightening in the east before dawn. The *leronyn* of Hali were as powerful, as sensitive, as highly trained as any on Darkover. It was not impossible that he had reached any of them.

Even as Eduin gathered his strength to call out once more, a silent roar lapped at his mind. It was like his father's dying command, and yet different. No words came to him, no compulsion to act, to kill. Hunger, like a ravening beast, reached for him.

Eduin twisted around on the bench. Callina had turned toward him, holding out the crystal that now blazed with eye-searing, colorless light. Her mouth gaped in a death's-head rictus, her features distorted almost beyond recognition.

Reflexively, Eduin raised one hand to shield his eyes. Tears stung. His physical vision failed in the blinding whiteness, the burgeoning *laran* presence.

He saw then the thing that the Keeper had become. It had been a powerful mind, and its single motivation had been honed over years, decades, a lifetime and more. It had no care for anyone or anything else. There was nothing human left, no hint of compassion or joy or loyalty, no ties to king or kin, no old loves or long-dead *bredin*. Nothing but a single imperative, to imprint itself upon a living mind.

Eduin staggered under the onslaught. His thoughts crumbled. All awareness of his body, of the room in which he crouched, the relay screen, the message he must send, all fell away.

How simple it would be to just let go. He would feel no pain, no indecision or regret, none of the torment that had been his own life. His body, his mind, his very thoughts would belong to another, with another's purposes.

As if it sensed his weakness, the crystalline Keeper flared even brighter. Within him, the gut-wrenching compulsion that was his father's legacy burst into flame. It had never been attacked before and after that day in his father's cottage, he had never had the will to resist. Now, like some wild beast, it sensed the threat to its very existence. All that was left of his father was the driving need for revenge. All that was left of the Keeper was an equally desperate need for survival. They were mirror images of one another.

And he himself, caught between them, what was he?

All his life, Eduin had been a tool for someone else. He had never been allowed to choose his desires, or even know what they were. He'd sacrificed Carolin's love, a place in the Towers, whatever bizarre fellowship he might have had with Saravio, everything. Only in Dyannis had he found the smallest measure of happiness. To his father, he was a thing to be used, taken up and discarded or remade in a more useful, obedient mold, but in her clear eyes he had seen himself as something more, someone worthy of love. He would never see her again, or hold her in his arms, but if he could prevent her death, even at the cost of his own, even if it meant letting Varzil live, then he would do it.

Anguish rushed through him, pouring forth from some hidden recess of his being.

I will live my life on my own terms, he raged, *or I will end it!* Against them both, the twin ghosts of father and Keeper, he threw all the passion of that cry.

The physical world rose up around him. His eyes focused on wall and window, the tangled web of gleaming metal, the ash-pale woman standing before him with a handful of sun-bright gemstone. He had won that much.

He hurled himself from the bench at Callina. Too late, the Keeper realized his intention. Callina jerked backward like a puppet, but not before Eduin reached her. He dared not try to take the crystal. It was somehow working through her. He took a long stride, turning sideways, and swung a backhand punch. His blow connected, spinning her around. The instant the starstone left her grasp, he felt a lessening of the Keeper's mental attack.

Callina staggered but kept her feet. She screamed out a curse in *cahuenga.* The crystal rolled across the strip of bare floor toward the door. She lunged for it.

Eduin grabbed Callina around the waist and hauled her back. It was like trying to hold a furious cloud leopard. She twisted, kicking and scratching. Her nails raked the side of his face, drawing blood. She spat in his face, for a moment blinding him. Her weight unbalanced him. He fell back, landing against something low and hard-edged.

The two of them went crashing down amid splintering wood and shattered glass. Too late, Eduin realized they'd fallen on top of the table holding the relay screen.

They were on the floor now, rolling over the debris. Callina kept clawing at him, aiming for his eyes. Eduin tried to grab her wrists. She shoved a knee into his upper thigh, hard enough to numb the nerve. He released her.

She scrambled to her hands and knees. He rolled up and caught her on the temple with a roundhouse punch. It was poorly aimed, with little power behind it. He wasn't much of a fighter, but he'd learned a few things on the streets of Thendara. He came at her again. Her body spun away and she landed, limp, a short distance away.

Eduin turned back to the relay screen, but he already knew what he would find. The delicate mechanism lay shattered past repair. His mind caught no hint of resonance.

The Keeper's crystal still glowed, although not as strongly as when Callina's mind had fueled it. Grimly, Eduin hauled himself to his feet. He walked the few paces over to where it lay on the stone floor and brought one boot smashing down on it. It shattered with an almost human wail that hung for a long moment in the air and then died away into silence.

Eduin stood, chest heaving. His muscles trembled and his stomach churned. Blood trickled down his face where Callina had gouged him. *Dyannis . . .*

He had failed. There was no way to get a message to Hali Tower, even if it were not already too late. Not even Varzil could reach so far with his unaided mind.

Eduin's knees buckled under him and he collapsed. The hard stone floor stung his knees. He bent over, curling himself around the knot of pain. Moment by moment, one heartbeat after the next, it swelled until he was no more than a shell of agony. If there had been a dagger or any weapon to hand, he would have ended it.

In that vast and unchanging Overworld, he wondered, would he find any respite? Would his soul wander there, forever tormented, forever torn, until time itself came to an end?

An idea took shape in his mind, so fantastical that he would not have dreamed it had he not been so distraught. In the Overworld, neither time nor distance had any meaning. A *laranzu* could travel to a Tower halfway across Darkover, could shape thought into reality. He had been warned many times about the lands of the dead, which bordered the Overworld.

What if he could travel through the Overworld to reach Dyannis? Just because it had never been done before did not mean it was impossible. The worst thing that could happen was that he would remain there, without hope or home or meaning, long after his body had fallen into dust.

What was the risk in that? He was already doomed. He had nothing to lose.

Eduin felt his body drop gently to the floor even as his mind reached out.

He must have been partway into the Overworld to begin with, for he had never made the transition so smoothly before, not even with a trained Keeper to guide him. Perhaps his own desperation fueled the leap.

A featureless gray sky arched above an equally unbroken plain. Eduin turned slowly, scanning the distant horizon, but saw nothing. The light was diffuse, betraying no direction, but a chill breeze brushed his cheeks. He glanced down and saw himself clothed in a gray robe, loosely belted. A shiver passed through him, for he had not worn such a garment since he last worked at Hestral Tower. He wondered if he might encounter Felicia in this realm, and what he might say to her. Better that her spirit flee him, as the dead were supposed to do.

Valeron Tower had created no structure of mind and thought to mark its location. That was hardly surprising if its workers never ventured forth to the Overworld. Without such an anchor, he might be unable to return to his own place, his own body, but at this moment, he did not care.

He had no idea in which direction Hali Tower lay, but that made no difference. Here in the Overworld, only will and thought had any meaning. He must remember Hali as he had known it from the inside, the essence of the place, the mental signatures of Keeper and circle. These were the true landmarks of a Tower. It had been many years since he lived and worked there, but such communities had their own stability. Workers might come and go, novices complete their training, and Keepers pass away, but the spirit of the place, the ways of thinking and working together, these changed slowly or not at all.

Most of all, Dyannis would still be there. She would have grown. Certainly, she had increased in strength and skill. Her astonishing performance at Hali Lake proved that. Yet, he felt he would know her anywhere.

Dyannis . . .

The unearthly stillness of the Overworld swallowed his cry. Again he called, pouring all his love, his longing, his anguish at lost hope, into that name.

Dyannis . . .

Gradually, he felt a change in the air. He could not judge distances across the plain, but he sensed a ripple, like space folding in upon itself. The light shifted, charged now with a heightened energy, an imminence.

A figure condensed as if from mist, standing before him. His first reaction, joy and relief, faded as the outline became clear. It was too large, too thick, too stooped to be Dyannis.

His father stood before him, wavering and indistinct, yet unmistakable. Straggled locks framed a face as pleated and ashen as the tattered funeral shroud. Marble spheres veined in gray filled the eye sockets. Charcoal lips moved silently and a skeletal hand pointed a bony finger at Eduin.

That tyrant voice whispered once more through his skull. *You swore . . . revenge . . .*

For an instant, the old habit of obedience paralyzed Eduin. He heard his own voice, now a child's, now a man's, pleading, promising, begging for mercy.

"I won't fail you, Father! I won't fail!"

"Please don't die! I'll do anything . . ."

"No, don't—please, don't!"

But those words had been spoken long ago and far away, distant in both time and space and the unfathomable geometry of the heart.

"Get out of my way!" he howled, "or by Zandru and all the demons in his Seven Frozen Hells, I will walk right through you!"

Eduin's belly cramped. He knew his body here was only a mental fabrication, yet he felt the twisting as physical agony. Anger flared in response, spreading like a wildfire through a grove of pitch pine. Fists clenched, teeth bared, he strode toward the ghostly figure.

Zandru? But it is Zandru's Bride who owns you now!

The figure shimmered, as if light itself crumpled. Instead of the lineaments of an old man, stooped and bearded, a cloak swept back to reveal the bone-pale features of Naotalba. She lifted her chin. Her white throat glimmered in the gray light.

A death, you said, but you did not say whose.

"Not hers! I never meant hers!"

Fool of a mortal! Do you think to bargain with me now? Naotalba shifted, and he sensed all the legions of frozen demons at her back. Her breath touched him, icy as the coldest grave.

Eduin drew back. He realized what he had done. He had poured all his hatred, all his rage, all his father's twisted need for revenge into the figure of Naotalba. She was as beautiful as when he'd first seen her in Saravio's mind, a human woman with the power to stir men's hearts. But there was no pity left in her. She had become as hard and unfeeling as any stone.

Because he had made her so.

Once Eduin had been innocent, full of hope and trust. In his own madness, his father had taken him, twisted him, crippled him. He had no choice in what he had become, and yet in a terrible way, he was still responsible for his deeds.

He could never undo what he had done, the things he had set in motion, the lives he had ruined. But he could choose what to do now.

Eduin set his jaw and plunged through the shadowy figure. Whiteness shocked through him. He could not see or feel or breathe. It was far worse than passing through the coruscating *laran* Veil that guarded Arilinn Tower.

The next instant, Eduin stumbled free.

A Tower stood there, slender and shining. A woman, her robes the crimson worn only by a Keeper, darted toward him. Curls bright as flame streamed down her back. Her gaze was steady as she met his in recognition.

Dyannis.

42

Dyannis passed from sleep to waking in the space of a heartbeat. Pulling aside the summer-weight bedcovers, she sat up. Her room at Hali Tower and the corridor beyond it lay quiet. With her *laran*, she felt the slow rhythms of sleeping minds and, farther off, the hum of activity from kitchen and yard. Milky predawn light filtered through the partly-drawn curtains. A gentle breeze, cool and fragrant with night-blooming flowers, barely stirred the air.

The fragments of her dreams slipped away, leaving only a sense of unease. She had been working regularly long into the night until Raimon urged her to relax more, to take time for fellowship and exercise.

"You will be of no use to yourself or to the circle if you are too exhausted to work properly," Raimon said. "Knowing your limits and respecting your own needs are as much a part of the training of a Keeper as anything you do in a circle."

Varzil had watched her uncritically, with that sympathy of mind, that deep understanding. He was the only one at Hali Tower to truly understand why she dared not stint or hold back, why she must prove herself. It was not because she was a woman. Ellimara Aillard, whom

Varzil was training as a Keeper back at Neskaya, felt no compulsion to work harder and better than any five men.

If I am to have the power and authority of a Keeper, then I must also have the discipline to use it wisely. Never again would dragons fly, born of her unthinking rage. Never again would a careless word cause another's death.

Her strategy was working, for as she gained in skill, her fears had diminished. Little by little, she began to trust herself. Varzil's arrival at Hali Tower had strengthened her faith in herself. In his clear vision, she glimpsed her own goodness.

Varzil never told her not to work so hard, or attempted to soothe her with bland reassurances. He refused to offer advice, and she knew why. If he told her what to do, he would then become responsible for the consequences. If she were to rely upon herself as Keeper, then she must be free to make her own decisions.

Varzil . . .

Barefoot, not bothering with a shawl, she hurried through her sitting room and flung the outer door open. Her brother stood there, holding a *laran*-charged glow. In its light, his gray eyes glinted.

She put her hands on her hips. "Do you have any idea what time it is?"

"It is time to say good-bye."

"In the middle of the night?"

"Just so."

For a long moment, she stared at him, not quite sure she'd understood. "Then we need to talk."

Varzil dipped his head and stepped inside. Dyannis excused herself and went into her bedroom to change. As an under-Keeper, she enjoyed larger quarters than she had as a mere circle worker. When she'd objected, saying that she had no need for two separate rooms, Raimon had pointed out all the times she had met with him in his own chambers. Now she was glad to be able to hold a private discussion in some place other than her bedroom.

It took only a few minutes to wash her face and hands and pull on a sleeveless tunic over a simple underdress, the kind of loose, comfortable clothing she preferred. Her hair was still braided for sleep in a single plait reaching almost to her waist.

Varzil stood beside the window overlooking the courtyard. He'd lit several candles, enough for them to see each other's faces. He turned at her approach, and they settled themselves in the two cushioned chairs beside the hearth.

"Now," she said, "tell me what this is all about. I thought you were to stay here until the end of autumn."

"So did I, and so it must be given out."

That confirmed her suspicion that his departure was to be kept secret. "Is it some mission for Carolin?"

"Very astute, little sister. As I once said, you have an instinct for statecraft."

She shrugged. "I made a lucky guess, that's all. It wasn't hard. You brought us good news from Isoldir, that *Dom* Ronal was prepared to make his peace with the Lady of Valeron, but these are shifting times, and even the best intentions may not hold. Nor is that the only brewing storm. Asturias still threatens our own kinsmen at Serrais. From everything I have heard of him, their general, the man known as the Kilghard Wolf, is not to be trusted. And—"

Varzil held up his hands in a gesture of surrender. "You need not elaborate further. For every kingdom or Tower that has sworn itself to the Compact, there are three others who are ready to set all the land ablaze in their quarrels."

Dyannis nodded. This must be some business having to do with the Compact, then, and one that demanded secrecy. If Varzil's mission were known, rumors would fly before him, possibly placing his cause in jeopardy. Varzil had already gained a considerable reputation among the *Comyn* lords as either a savior or a madman. His revolutionary ideas had made him a traitor to his class in the eyes of more than a few members of the Council.

She asked if there were any way she might aid his mission.

"As a matter of fact, there is. Carolin has a horse waiting for me by the lake, and from there I will travel with a party of traders in salt and furs."

Dyannis nodded. The cargo would not be rich enough to tempt bandits to risk an attack against numbers. In plain clothing, mounted on a lackluster beast, Varzil could easily avoid any particular notice. That is, if no one were looking for him.

And no one will be looking, if everyone believes you are still here at Hali.

She caught his affirming nod. No wonder he had been welcomed with such a public spectacle. The king himself had come to the Tower to visit him.

"Hali is big enough, now that we have two full circles at work, that days—even a tenday—might pass without encountering every other person here," she commented.

"You might hear someone mention a person, and that would have the effect of keeping him in your mind, just as if you had seen him," Varzil said.

"That is true. I could let drop, 'Varzil says this,' or 'Varzil did that,' just as if I had come fresh from meeting you. I need not say *when* you had said or done something."

Varzil laughed softly. "You were always a fine conspirator. If we had been closer in age, I think that Father would have been hard-pressed to handle both of us."

"No," she said, her voice coming with unexpected softness, "you, being the elder, took the brunt of it."

I do not think I would have been allowed to come to Hali, if you had not taken my part with Father and then with Harald.

"You would have been married off, with five healthy sons, and never known the difference," he teased.

She met his gaze steadily. "I would have known the difference. Believe me, I would have known."

"I should know better than to say such things," he admitted. "When I was a boy, I thought only of my own misery. I knew that if I had to stay at home and be the dutiful second son our father wanted, I would go mad. I have since learned that women, rich or poor, suffer even more unrelenting confinement all their lives. To have such Gifts—and to have no way of using them—if that is not a living hell, I do not know what is."

"We speak of Zandru as the Lord of the Seven Frozen Hells, but I think he does not rule everywhere," she said. "I think there is a special land of torment for women, in the shadow of Zandru's Bride, Naotalba the Accursed. She was human once, or so the stories go, and so only she can know what has been lost, what—what might have been." Her throat closed up.

Why should the idea affect her so deeply, when she now had everything she wanted? She had the training to use her *laran,* a useful independent life, the rank and privilege—and power—of becoming a Keeper. Why then did thoughts of failed hopes and unfulfilled talents fill her with sorrow?

The moment passed, a mist seemed to lift from her sight, and she saw a mirror to her own sadness in the eyes of her brother. She remembered how he had talked about his lost love, Felicia.

A little shudder passed through her shoulders. She stood, rubbing her arms. "The dawn approaches, and you must be on the road. I will do what I can, and hold you ever in my thoughts."

"As you will be in mine."

On impulse, Dyannis pressed herself against him, hugging him as if she could not bear to let him go. He was one of the few people she could embrace without distress. Their bond, as sister and brother, as fellow telepaths, made the physical contact especially close.

She did not know if the sickness in her heart came from the emotions stirred by their conversation, or some dreadful premonition. Even disguised, even guarded as he would be, the roads could be perilous. Yet, there was nothing to be done. She could not hold him here, not if Darkover were to be freed from the horrors of *clingfire,* lungrot, and bonewater dust.

She pushed herself away. "On with you, then. Walk with the gods, and return to us in their good time."

"*Adelandeyo,*" he answered, and slipped away into the fading night.

— ◆ —

Several days later, Dyannis sat at the window of her outer chamber, cradling a mug and watching the first light creep into the eastern sky. She should be resting, she knew, instead of sipping *jaco* that would surely keep her awake half the morning. A sense of unease, of imminence, had been growing in her ever since she dissolved the circle last night. The work, recharging *laran* batteries, had gone smoothly, uneventfully. What, then, troubled her?

She wondered if Varzil had met with some difficulty along the road. Ever since their parting, a light rapport had remained between them. The connection ran deeper than that of brother and sister. It was more akin to a twin-bond, strengthened and deepened by their shared work as Keepers.

No, she would surely have sensed it if Varzil had met with some harm. She was overtired, and the general anxiety of the world outside had seeped through her *laran* shields. She must take greater care.

A knock at her door startled her from her inner musings.

Rorie.

Pleasure and sadness rose up in her. She had once told herself she could not be sure of her feelings for him until she had resolved her relationship with Eduin. Now that was no longer a question. Other Keepers might take lovers when they were not actively working, remaining loving but celibate companions the rest of the time. They were all men, and perhaps men's hearts and bodies worked differently from women's. Whatever the cause, she knew she was not capable of it. Her entire life had narrowed to a single focus. If she were to be a Keeper—and now she was, irrevocably—she could be nothing else to any man.

She did not want to hurt him, and she greatly feared she would. So she took her time, setting down the mug of *jaco* before she bid him enter.

He knew. His awareness radiated throughout his psychic aura, the way he held himself, the expression in his eyes.

Dyannis managed a small smile and gestured for him to sit. The two chairs had been drawn up beside a small, high table that bore the tray upon which the pitcher of *jaco* and a second mug had been set.

When Rorie looked as if he would refuse, she said aloud, "Please, let us sit together as friends."

"As friends." He lowered himself into the other chair as if his joints hurt.

I had hoped we might become more, his thought brushed her mind.

I know.

She watched him quietly, thinking that the world and the times they had lived through had changed them both. She was not the same girl who had run away in a servant's clothing to dance along the shores of Hali Lake, nor was he the carefree boy who had been her companion since she had first come to the Tower. So much had happened, from the discovery of the treachery of Cedestri Tower to its rebuilding.

Their world was changing, the role of the Towers, the spread of the Compact, the ending of an era. The time of the Hundred Kingdoms was almost over, and no one knew what the new world would look like. In place of scores of tiny realms, powerful new Domains, Hastur the chief among them, were emerging. It was the nature of such things to alter with time. There was no way she could have foreseen how she herself would be transformed.

I did not know, she spoke silently, mind to his mind. *When I set my foot upon this path, I had no idea where it would lead, what it would truly mean to become a Keeper.*

The cost, he said.

Dyannis nodded. Her eyes ached; her heart ached. Then she saw how those unshed tears touched him. She had given him that much, at least.

"I don't know what to do," Rorie said simply. "Can we go on as if I had never had any feelings for you?"

"No, I don't think that's possible." A sigh rose up in her. She let it go, like freeing a captive bird. "The practical question is whether we can work together in a circle. Whether such intimacy of mind would be difficult for you."

"For me? What about for you?"

She shook her head, again feeling a ripple of sadness, of the weight of isolation. It passed, leaving dispassionate calm. "I am a Keeper. Each member of my circle is unique and precious to me, but no one more than any other."

"I see." He lowered his gaze. Moments passed.

"If there is any doubt, it would be better if you worked only with Raimon," she said, hearing the hardness in her voice.

"You *have* changed," he said tightly. "I will grieve the loss of what might have been, but not the woman just beyond my reach. She no longer exists."

Dyannis regarded him steadily. It was true, she had been cruel. She did not know any other way to be.

"I do not want to hurt you," she said.

"I know," he replied, more gently. "It was only a dream, anyway. I could as well have lost you to some head-blind fool in a marriage your brother arranged."

That almost happened. She reached out to brush the back of his hand with her fingertips, a telepath's contact, the only way she would ever touch him. "We always were friends, Rorie."

He nodded. "This much is true. I think it would actually help to work in your circle, for that will make it all the more real to me that the girl I once knew has grown into something else. If you were another man's wife, or a pledged virgin, then I would also turn my thoughts away from you."

Dyannis rose as he took his leave of her. The encounter had gone better than she had dared hope, yet the feeling of disquiet remained, just beyond reach. She thought again of Varzil, this time deliberately searching the psychic firmament for any trace of his presence. A pulse of response, like the faint ripple from a beating heart, distant but bright, answered her. He was well, then, but beyond the reach of ordinary telepathy.

The memory of Eduin rose to her thoughts and the sense of unease intensified. Perhaps she had been right in thinking she must resolve her feelings about him before she was truly free to go on with her life. She picked up her mug, realized the *jaco* had now gone cold, and put it down.

It was all so annoying. She'd known Eduin for only a short time, when she was still a child in many ways. The luminosity that surrounded her memories came from her own inexperience with love—if it were love after all. Here Dyannis got up and began to pace. She *had* loved him, with that intense, never-to-be-repeated exhilaration of first awakening. What might have happened, had the relationship been allowed to run its natural course, she would never know. In all likelihood, they would have passed from infatuation to disillusionment and thence perhaps to a lingering affection.

When he had come to Hali Tower, years later, he had changed. A shadow lay upon him, masking the heart that had once seemed so transparent, so infinitely tender.

And then again, at the lake at Hali . . .

Of course, he had become a different man by then. He'd been outlawed, hiding, in the company of other desperate men. She thought, with the ruthless self-honesty of a Keeper, that she did not want to surrender those first memories, to admit that the boy she had once cherished to distraction had become a criminal, possibly even, if Varzil were right, the worst kind of murderer. That must be why he haunted her, like a basso harmony hovering beyond the reach of her senses.

Had she been wrong about him all along, remembering only who she wanted him to be and not who he truly was?

Let him go, she told herself. *Let the past rest.*

Resolving to do just that, she fortified her *laran* barriers and tried to go back to sleep. She hovered on the edge for what seemed like hours, marking the passage of time by the beating of her own heart. Eventually, she slipped into an uneasy jumble of dreams, half-formed and restless. She could not shake the feeling that someone was talking, saying things of importance just beyond her hearing. Though she pushed and twisted through the shifting landscape, she could not make out the words.

The sense of dread intensified as her dreams shifted. Smoking blood dripped from the sky, rocks cried aloud in agony, people she ought to know but could not name ran shrieking past her, trailing snakes instead of hair. She seemed to be in some bizarre version of the Overworld, bounded on every side by walls of fire that grew ever closer.

Dyannis awoke, sitting upright in her bed, shaking. It was full day now and unseasonably warm, yet she had broken into a cold sweat. She shivered as if gripped by a fever. Wrapping her arms around herself, she rocked back and forth until at last the trembling subsided. She wished Varzil were still at Hali so she could talk things over with him, but he had departed on his latest mission several days ago.

Eventually, she was able to get out of bed, wash her face and hands, and call for a servant to help her comb her hair and to dress.

As soon as she had composed herself, Dyannis sought out Raimon. She might be functioning on a daily basis as a full-fledged Keeper, but she was still under his care and command.

When I am truly a Keeper, what then? she wondered as she waited in his sitting chamber. *Who will be the Keeper's Keeper?*

He listened gravely as she described her nightmares. "I am sorry it has come to this," he sighed. "I have seen a similar increase in sensitivity in other Keepers as they progress through their training. Of course, none of them was as hard on himself, as ruthless I should say, as you have been."

They were all men.

"What of that?" he answered her unspoken thought. "If Varzil is correct, there are as many differences between one male Keeper and the next as there are between men as a whole and women. Each of us comes to our own understanding and acceptance of the discipline, just as no two of us join the minds of our circle together in the same way."

Dyannis admitted he was correct. "So you think what happened to me is the result of overwork and worry?"

"That is my first presumption, yes." He sat back in his chair to regard her with that level, pellucid gaze, and refrained from reminding her how he had urged her to rest, not to push herself so hard.

"It is all very well to tell me to take some time off!" she said. Her voice resonated with a heat that surprised her. "Your circle will continue to do the most necessary work. But what if there were not two of us? What if I were alone, the only Keeper of Hali Tower? What would I do then?"

Raimon's eyes darkened. "I understand what you fear, that the time may indeed come when there are so few of us, each Tower has only one Keeper. It is this very fate Varzil is hoping to avert by training women as well as men. For the time being, we shall let the matter rest. There are few things less productive than worrying about a future that may or may not come about. I know you, Dyannis, and I will not allow you to distract me from telling you what you do not wish to hear. If you will not take a suggestion, then I must give you an order. You must have rest and quiet. These nightmares are but a warning. If you do not heed it, they will only get worse. Will you risk your circle as well as yourself by continuing to work when you are unfit?"

"I will not work if I am not able to do so properly," she said stubbornly. Even as she said the words, she knew he was right. "I won't go home again, if that's what you mean. *This* is my home, the place I belong."

"You could spend a tenday or so at Thendara with King Carolin and Queen Maura," he suggested. "I believe you and Maura were friends when she was here at Hali."

That was true enough. Maura had always been kind to her, and she would understand the demands of responsibility. Yet something held her back from leaving Hali Tower. The best she could manage was to agree to think about it.

Raimon knew better than to press the issue. "In the meantime, you might consider the use of a telepathic damper while you sleep. It's not comfortable, but it will shield you from the thoughts and emotions of those around you. You might sleep better for it."

Dyannis frowned. She'd worked with dampers as part of her training and never liked them. "It feels like stuffing my head with wool and wrapping my eyes and ears in gauze. But," she sighed, "at least I'd get some sleep."

Raimon sent a servant to search for one. "It's been a long time since any of us needed such a device. Years ago, when Eduin MacEarn worked among us, he requested the use of one."

Eduin needed a telepathic damper? A shiver ran across her shoulders. Of course, he needed to guard his sleeping thoughts, lest some stray thought betray him. She did not know whether to feel anger, sorrow, or pity.

All of them, I think. Raimon answered her with unexpected gentleness. *How else can any of us respond to such a tragedy?*

You call what Eduin did, how he betrayed our trust in him, a tragedy?

I do. And so should you, and so should anyone who saw the potential in him. Do not embitter your memory of him with recriminations, Dyannis. Let the past rest, but let it rest with all the joy and faith you once felt.

But—

You were not deceived. The good you saw in him existed. And if what he has become is not a tragedy, I do not know the meaning of the word.

43

*R*ap! Rap! Rap!

The knocking would not go away, although Dyannis muttered curses at it. She curled into a ball with her back to the door and drew the pillow over her ears. Her body felt thick and heavy, as if her flesh had turned to clay. Something high-pitched, like the whirr of insects, buzzed along her nerves. She had slept, how long she could not tell. Her body still craved rest, but the racket from the other side of the room continued, louder and faster than before.

Rap! Rap! Rap!

"Gods," she muttered, shoving the pillow aside. The room around her was as dark as her dreamless sleep. No light came from the direction of the window, but she might have drawn the curtains tight before falling into bed. She could not remember.

"I'm coming." Her voice sounded like the croak of a frog.

Rap! Rap! Rap!

Forcing her stiff muscles to move, Dyannis got to her feet. She made the gesture to summon the blue light with her *laran* but none came. Was she so sluggish, then, that she could not perform even this simple beginner's spell? Her temples throbbed, and her head felt like a bag full of curdled cheese.

The telepathic damper was still on. Ah, that explained everything. She stumbled toward it, feeling her way. Her fingers brushed over the control mechanism. The next instant, the barely-audible whine vanished.

She felt the dense, unmoving mineral hardness of the walls, the brightness of the pale translucent stone panels, the intense concentration of a working circle, their minds like flares of inner-lit jewels, the distant murmur of cloud-water from Hali Lake, the vast sweep of night above.

It was almost dawn; she could taste the rising light, the shift in temperature and moisture. She had slept only a few hours under the influence of the damper.

Moving confidently now through her darkened room, Dyannis went to the door and opened it. One of the young novices, an Elhalyn boy, stood with his fist raised to knock again. He held an ordinary candlestick in the other hand, and his eyes bulged slightly, ringed with white.

"*Domna,* I don't know what to do!" The child was trembling visibly. "Raimon is still working in the circle with the others and I dare not disturb him."

Dyannis knew that the night's work involved the synthesis of firefighting chemicals, destined for Verdanta and High Kinally. There were a number of steps in the process when the elements became unstable, handled safely only through unwavering concentration of *laran.* As kindly as she could, she said, "There is nothing to fear. Whatever is the matter?"

"Three aircars—coming in fast—they won't answer us, not even *Dom* Rorie. He sent me to ask you to come."

Dyannis frowned. Rorie was a strong telepath, skilled and experienced, and only trained *leronyn* could guide an aircar. If Rorie could not reach them with his mind, something terrible must have happened. Were the pilots all dead, then, or rendered unconscious by some spell or disease? That didn't seem likely. The aircars, cut off from motive power and guidance, would surely have dropped from the sky and not continued on their course.

"Where is he?"

"In the second laboratory, along with everyone else who is not working in Raimon's circle tonight."

Rorie?

Dyannis sensed Rorie's mind, bent in concentration upon the incoming aircars, but did not press him for a response. They must make preparations in case the aircar pilots were injured.

"Summon everyone with monitor's training and meet me there."

The boy scurried away, visibly relieved to have some definite task.

I will do no one any good if I rush off, thoughts scattered from here to the Hellers, emotions every which way, and still in my nightgown!

Hurriedly, Dyannis pulled on a shift and loosely belted working robe. She shoved her bare feet into a pair of worn suede sandals, using the time to put her thoughts in order. The discipline and calm she had practiced every waking hour since beginning her Keeper's training returned quickly.

She drew out her starstone to see what she could perceive directly about the aircars. Close by, Raimon's circle blazed with energy like a ring of blue fire. She sensed Rorie and several others, their minds also alight. The Tower, which was not merely a physical structure but a psychic one as well, surrounded them all. She swept through its walls and upwards.

Sweet gods, the aircars were almost upon them!

Only a short distance from Hali Tower, three motes like encapsulated emptiness zoomed ever closer. They felt like nothing she had known, certainly not ordinary aircars, more like disturbances in the air currents with only the faintest auras of psychic energy.

Hail, aircars approaching Hali Tower! she called out.

Silence answered her. She might have been shouting into an empty sky.

Do you need help?

If the aircars did not change course, they would swoop over the topmost turrets in only a few minutes. As near as she could judge, they were too high to collide with the Tower. Even unguided, their momentum would carry them beyond. They might crash into the surrounding countryside or— Her breath caught in her throat—they might be heading for the lake.

The lake, and the Cataclysm device beneath it?

No, Varzil had sealed the rift, forever barring access to that terrible *laran* machinery. Perhaps these invaders did not know that. In the process of attempting to recover the Cataclysm device, what disaster might ensue? The cloud-water of the lake retained the vibrational pattern of its transformation. Dyannis knew all too well how readily it could transmit psychic energy.

A series of breaths heightened her trance, freeing her mind to quest deeper. Perhaps if she searched on a wider band, not just the usual mode of telepathy, she could discover something about the intruders. She could not have done it a year ago, before she began her training as under-Keeper, but she had grown in skill as well as strength and confidence.

By shifting her own mode of mental listening, she was able to glimpse the patterns of inanimate glass and metal that comprised the aircars. *Laran* energy sizzled like tiny lightnings along the mechanisms that controlled the flying apparatus, wings and stabilizer fins. The craft were functional, then, and not derelict. Why could she not reach the pilots?

Dyannis pressed her search harder and brushed against a grating vibration. Instantly she recognized an interference pattern like that generated by a telepathic damper. They must have found a way to surround themselves with a barrier impenetrable to *laran* and still be able to guide the aircars with their minds. It was not impossible, just puzzling.

Unless they mean to wall themselves off from any possible communication or psychic influence . . .

Something tugged at the lower levels of her mind, a ripple, an ache, a calling. She paused in her reflections.

It came from the Overworld. Someone was crying out to her with an urgency that transcended the usual separation between the ordinary physical realm and that vast, formless region.

It made no sense that one of the pilots might be trying to reach her. This was no general plea for help, but rather a sending aimed at her specific mental pattern, which meant an intimate familiarity. It could not be one of the pilots.

The call came again, too faint for recognition yet imbued with desperate need. A cold shiver passed through her, as if some demon from Zandru's Hells ran its talons along her spine.

Dyannis summoned the image of Hali Tower in the Overworld, the psychic counterpart that she had helped to establish and maintain. This would be her anchor, as it had so many times in the past. In form and color, it resembled its physical counterpart, a slender structure of white set with panels of translucent stone, a bejeweled finger reaching for the heavens.

The next instant, she stood upon its threshold. The temperature and odor of the air shifted. She blinked, waiting for the distant gray horizon to come into focus. The sky would be overcast and featureless, the light diffuse. A flat plain would stretch in every direction, until she shaped it into something else.

Instead of a gray monotone overhead, an enormous boiling darkness rushed toward her, growing larger and closer with each passing moment. She had never seen anything like it, either in the physical realm or this one. In its churning shadows, she glimpsed the form of a woman, face white as a polished skull, cloak whipping about.

Dyannis!

A man raced toward her, outstripping the storm. Although she could not make out his features, she instantly recognized the touch of his mind.

Sweet Cassilda, it's Eduin! What are you doing here?

Neither time nor distance held any meaning in the Overworld. Between one heartbeat and the next, Eduin stood before her. If she had not known him, she would never have recognized the man who stumbled to a halt, barely able to keep his feet. Hair hung in sodden ropes about a haggard face, creased with lines of suffering. He wore only filthy rags, which might once have been the robe of a *laranzu*, and he looked as if some huge predator, a banshee perhaps, had savaged him. A mangled wound gaped in his belly, dripping blood. Through the tatters of his clothing, welts and scratches marked his body.

Yet it was undeniably Eduin, and for an instant, she wanted nothing more than to take him into her arms. The eyes that glowed in their bruised sockets met hers, both resolute and pleading.

"Dyannis, there is no time! Run, get out of there! Any moment now, you will be attacked!"

"Eduin—what are you talking about? What—"

He turned to glance at the onrushing storm. The cloak of the ghostly woman blew aloft and Dyannis saw that she held in her out-stretched hands three firebolts and was even now preparing to hurl them at Hali Tower.

"You cannot stop them!" Eduin cried. "They are shielded against any contact—please, you must save yourself!"

The first firebolt left the hands of the ghost-woman. It moved faster than Dyannis could follow, faster than thought. Eduin screamed, "No!" and struggled to sculpt the Overworld thought-stuff to stop the missile.

Screams filling her head, Dyannis was jerked back into her room in the Tower. The very stones around her vibrated. The silent cries fell away and she heard Rorie's clear mental voice.

ATTACK! Rorie called. *Anyone who hears this, help us! Raimon, answer me!*

Dyannis pulled the door open and sprinted down the corridor. Only a few of Hali's inhabitants were asleep at this hour, whether they were working in Raimon's circle or not. Some were finishing other *laran* tasks, or keeping to their schedule of daytime sleep. She passed a servant bringing warm water and towels.

"Oh, *Domna* Dyannis, what has happened? Is it an accident?"

"I don't know!" Dyannis did not slow her pace. In her mind, flames encircled the laboratory in which Raimon worked. One of the workers was injured, her mind sending out waves of pain. The circle had fractured; all was in confusion.

She reached the stairwell. Without warning, something burst through the outside wall just above her. Stones tumbled inward, fracturing with a horrendous noise. Orange-white flames poured through the opening. Dust and shards rained down upon her. She ducked, instinctively covering her head with her arms, and drew in the acrid reek of *clingfire*.

Motes of the deadly caustic sprayed the stairwell. She flung herself backward, narrowly avoiding one of the larger drops. Stumbling, twisting, she escaped back into the corridor leading to the living quarters. Smoke and flame filled the air, each moment hotter and denser.

She was cut off from both the laboratories and her only escape.

One of the older women, a matrix mechanic named Javanne, rushed up to her. "Blessed Cassilda, we're under attack!"

Dyannis felt rather than heard her words above the roar of the flame and the crack of splintering stone. Somewhere else in the Tower, another explosion shuddered through the stone walls. She heard screaming, distant and muffled.

"Come with me." With a firmness of touch almost unknown among telepaths, Dyannis grabbed the other woman's hand and pulled her back along the corridor. The *clingfire* would eat its way to them eventually, or the Tower would collapse, but in the meantime, they must find a place quiet enough to create a circle.

The two of us?

Dyannis closed the door of the farthest room behind them. Its owner had been working in Raimon's circle; Dyannis did not know if the woman was still alive.

She went to the window and looked down. Like most of the rooms in this wing, it overlooked sheer rock walls. There was no possibility of jumping to safety.

Safety. What was she thinking? There would be no escape for any of them.

Dyannis pulled the other woman down to sit facing her on the bed and took both her hands, Cedestri-style. Javanne's eyes were glassy with fright.

Gently, with a Keeper's quiet confidence, Dyannis touched Javanne's mind with her own. *Together we can reach Raimon and strengthen his circle. Our only hope is to contain the fire with our joined* laran.

Javanne calmed under the mental contact. She had spent many years at one Tower or another, drilled in obedience to a Keeper.

The *clingfire* crept along the corridor, gaining intensity as it went. Dyannis felt it through her closed eyelids, a heat upon her mind.

Javanne fed mental power to Dyannis. Dyannis seized it, wove it together with her own, and reached for Raimon and his circle. Dyannis thought that with the addition of her own strength, Raimon might be able to regather the circle and throw up some kind of psychic shelter around them.

Raimon!

For a terrifying moment, she could not locate his mental signature anywhere. Then she saw the laboratory through his eyes, wooden floor and furniture ablaze. One figure lay writhing, outlined in eye-searing orange-white. A robed figure tried to reach her, but could not penetrate the fire. Raimon himself sprawled face-down on the floor. Lewis-Mikhail sobbed as he slashed away the muscle on Raimon's upper back, digging for the mote of *clingfire*.

Dyannis! Lewis-Mikhail cried out, recognizing her.

I am here and unhurt, though not for long. What can I do?

Save yourself, little sister, for there is no hope here. Aldones preserve us all! Who has done this thing, and why?

I do not know, she answered, and then realization shook her. *But I know who does.*

A blast from above jerked Dyannis back into her physical body. She glanced up just as the ceiling broke open and flaming rock poured down upon her.

44

Dyannis hurled herself into the Overworld. Her only thought was that Eduin had *known* about the attack before it began, that he was somehow connected to the dreadful shadow-woman.

She stood outside a burning Tower, and it seemed to her that the flames fed not only upon the physical structure, but the minds of the people within it. The Tower itself had gone translucent, fading. Its form might persist for a time, even after those who created it had perished.

A shadow fell across her, a blotch of darkness. She turned to see the cloaked woman, shrunk now to almost human size.

Someone was grappling with the woman. Eduin had placed himself between her and the Tower. They struggled silently, twisting to one side and then the other. The cloak flared out like a living thing, seeking to wrap itself around its adversary. Somehow, Eduin managed to keep free from its entanglement, or perhaps that was because he fought with such single-minded determination. Step by shuffling step, he forced the figure backward.

They sprang apart, and the cloaked woman drew herself to her full height. Her eyes blazed like live coals.

"You made a bargain, Eduin Deslucido," she said, raising one skeletal hand to point at the Tower. "Do you now deny me my prize?"

Deslucido? Dyannis wondered.

"I never said you could have *her*," he answered, his voice hoarse.

"A death, you said, and we agreed. You have your death and I will fulfill the purpose for which I was created."

Eduin shook his head. "May all the gods forgive me, I made you what you are. What I have made, I will now unmake!"

The figure turned, and a flicker of human emotion passed across the skull-white face. "You will not find it so easy. Some things, once set in motion, cannot be stopped."

"If you must have a death, take me instead, but let her live! Let them all live—even him—and let it end here."

"You swore an oath, so many times that it is etched into your soul."

"Then I am forsworn." His voice rang with resolve, and at the same time, despair. "I give it up, now and forever!"

"Ah!" The woman in the cloak shuddered as if wounded. At the same moment, the skies convulsed. Winds sprang up, rapidly gaining in ferocity.

Dyannis crept forward. She recognized the figure now. It was Naotalba, the Bride of Zandru, sometimes considered a symbol of noble sacrifice, but as often, an evil omen. How had Eduin come to deal with a demigoddess?

I made you, he had said. Here in the Overworld, the only reality was thought, and once he had been a powerful *laranzu*. Had he indeed conjured up a mythic image and shaped it to his own ends?

He now stood, legs braced wide in a posture of confrontation. Dyannis dared not break his concentration, though a thousand questions boiled up in her mind. In an odd shift of vision, she saw what linked Eduin and Naotalba. Strands of psychic material, some as fine as spider's silk, others coarse and knotted, ran between them. Some pulsed the color of clotted blood, like congested *laran* channels. In places, they twisted together, forming webs and nodes of darkness.

The strands, thick and thin, all sprang from the ravaged wound in Eduin's belly and converged upon a single point deep in the substance of Naotalba's form. Instinctively, Dyannis knew that each was born of some moment of bitterness, of resentment festering into hatred, of twisted dreams and poisoned fears.

Dark Lady Avarra, what could have happened to turn that radiant boy—or any man—into a source of such evil?

Singly and by handfuls, Eduin wrenched the strands free from his own body. Colorless blood streamed from the fresh wounds. If he cried out, Dyannis could not hear it above the shrieking of the storm. The loose ends whipped free in the winds, shriveling. Within moments, they turned into dust that was blown away.

When he grasped the last one, the thickest, it writhed in his hands. He staggered, almost losing his balance. Dyannis had heard of men who, under the control of *laran* spells of madness, had taken knives to their own bellies, disemboweling themselves. She had heard that Eduin had used such spells in defense at Hestral Tower against the besieging armies of Rafael Hastur. She wondered if, in some twisted version of justice, he were not inflicting the same dreadful injury upon himself.

The twisted rope came free in Eduin's hands. Dyannis could not see his face, but she felt the desolation that gripped him, the terrifying aloneness, the absence of the presence that had shaped his entire life.

The storm died as quickly as it had begun. Naotalba lifted her face, no longer smooth and pale, but fallen in upon itself. Whatever strength of purpose Eduin had poured into her was now gone.

Bloodless lips moved, shaping speech. "You have done a brave and foolish thing, Eduin Deslucido."

Deslucido, Dyannis repeated in her mind. That was the second time Naotalba had called Eduin by that name.

"I have seen the world of gods as well as men," Naotalba continued, "and I do not know another who would have chosen as you have. I will return now to the realm of my bridegroom. We will meet there soon."

Naotalba turned away, and the folds of her cloak gathered her into nothingness.

With a cry, Eduin fell to his knees. Dyannis rushed to his side. He pressed both hands over his belly, as if to staunch the flow of blood. Even as she approached, he lifted his hands, revealing unbroken skin beneath the tattered shirt. He looked up at her, his eyes filled with amazement. His mouth moved, but no words came.

Dyannis felt no pity for him, only realization condensing into fury. "You knew about the attack before it ever began! You—you must have sent it!"

He flinched at her words, but did not turn away his gaze. In that moment, she read the bitterness of years reaching back far before she had known him. She saw, but could not understand the driving obsession. A chain of deeds, like loathsome beads strung on a silken cord, stretched into the past. She heard a voice like the slither of scales over rock, whispering, *You swore to kill, k–k–kill . . .*

She saw a stern Queen upon her throne, the rapt look on the face of a pale, dark-eyed girl, the storm-racked landscape of a once-Gifted mind, an old man in physician's robes led away in chains . . . and farther back, the lake at Hali, an army of beggars poised to attack . . .

"Why?" she cried. "Why would you do such a thing? Why destroy an entire Tower?"

"I did not mean to destroy Hali Tower, only one person within its walls." His voice was inexpressibly bleak.

Her heart froze. Had he hated her so much, all these years?

"No, not you!" Eduin cried. "Never you. It was Varzil's death I sought, and to my damnation, I have brought about yours as well."

"But Varzil isn't here!" Dyannis said. "He left on a secret mission some days ago."

"Then it has all been for naught."

She brushed the thought aside. "Why kill Varzil? What has he done to harm you?"

Surely it was not her brother's attempts to foil their budding romance so many years ago. She had rebelled against Varzil's orders, plunging headlong into the affair. Time and distance and some mysterious change within Eduin, not Varzil's interference, had ended it.

An icy thought trickled through her mind. She remembered Varzil sitting with her outside the ruins of Cedestri Tower, remembering his lost love. She could almost hear his words, as appalling now as when they were first spoken.

"Felicia was Hastur and Eduin tried to kill her—did kill her. Eduin tried to kill Carolin, another Hastur, and failed, for which he probably hates me even more."

"You hated Varzil because he stood in your way of destroying first Carolin Hastur and then Felicia of Hestral Tower," Dyannis said. In his eyes, she read the truth of her words.

She took a step closer. He was trembling. She wanted to lash out, to hit him, hurt him. Yet he made no move to defend himself, either in word or action. He saw himself as utterly damned, irrevocably lost, and she, for whom he was prepared to sacrifice everything, would be his judge and executioner.

She lowered herself to the ground in front of him. Her anger drained away. "Why?" she repeated. "Why did you hate the Hasturs so much?"

"Felicia was the daughter of the witch-Queen Taniquel," he said. "And Carlo—gods forgive me, I tried to kill him even though I loved him!—was the heir to the throne of King Rafael. Together, they destroyed my family."

"Of course! Naotalba called you *Deslucido*, not MacEarn. How can that be? Everyone thought that family extinct. I see now they were wrong. But the war against King Damian ended years before either of us were born."

He nodded. "As you may have guessed, I am the only surviving member of that once-great family. After the last battle, my uncle and his son Belisar were executed, but not my father, the *laranzu* Rumail Deslucido."

"I've heard of him," Dyannis said. *And how he was responsible for using bonewater dust in the Battle of Drycreek.* "I thought he perished in the fall of Neskaya Tower."

"No, he escaped to the wild lands beyond the Kadarin. He married a local woman, took her name, and raised my brothers and myself, swearing us to only one purpose."

Revenge.

Dyannis shuddered, both at the obsession that had driven Eduin's father and the harshness of Rafael's victory. Such things did occur in war, she supposed, although many times, the conquering lord would exile a worthy adversary, keeping his sons as hostages to ensure a lasting peace. Perhaps Rafael had an overriding reason to treat his enemy with such ruthlessness.

"Even if King Rafael acted out of malice, surely it should have ended there," she said aloud. "He had no sons, so the throne passed to a collateral line and thence to Carolin. Surely that is justice enough."

"There can be no justice for such a crime as his, save for the complete obliteration of his line—and hers," Eduin said bleakly. "After all, that is what they did to *us*. Without his sorcerer's skills, my father would have perished. Their slaughter would have been complete. I do not say that my father's vengeance was right, only that it was justified."

So many lives lost or ruined, Dyannis thought, whole stretches of land poisoned for generations, villages laid waste, families bereft of loved ones. And for what? To fuel some King's greed for power?

Yet everything she knew about Rafael Hastur and Queen Taniquel suggested they were not senselessly evil.

Her astral form shivered, and she knew that in the physical realm, a hail of burning stone and wood had fallen across her and Javanne. Droplets of *clingfire* struck her in a dozen places. Her hair and gown caught fire. She looked down at her psychic form to see the pale flames rising. In another instant, she would feel the agony of burning. Here in the Overworld, however, she could slow the passage of time, long enough at least to learn why she and so many others must die.

She reached out to Eduin, grasping his arms. "Why? What started it all? What caused such hatred that men would treat one another in such monstrous fashion?"

"They could not—" Eduin's voice stumbled. "They feared to let us live."

"Why? What had your family done?"

"It was not what we did." He sounded even more desolate than ever. "It was what we *were*. It was because of the Deslucido Gift."

"And what was that? Some relic from the Ages of Chaos?"

"I do not know how it began, by design or some accident of breeding, only that if anyone found out, it would be the death of us all."

"What was this Gift, that Rafael Hastur and Queen Taniquel would commit such barbarity to eliminate it?"

Eduin gazed at her for a long moment. The ingrained secrecy of a lifetime rose up behind his eyes, holding him immobile.

Screams shivered through the Overworld. The flames grew brighter, tinged now with the orange-white of *clingfire*.

"At least tell me before I die!" she cried.

He blurted out, "We can defeat truthspell."

"What! That isn't possible!"

"Believe me, *carya preciosa,* it is more possible than you imagine. I have done it myself, stood in the blue fire and spoken things I knew to be false."

Abhorrence rose up in her like bile behind her throat. As Varzil had said, she had an instinct for seeing the political implications of things. She knew immediately what it would mean if truthspell could not be trusted. Without such assurance, no pact or treaty would stand, and even a King's honor would be suspect. The only certainty would lie in power, and the key to power was *laran* weaponry. Varzil's Compact, and any hope of a lasting peace, would perish like dayflies in a Hellers storm.

"This Gift," she said thickly, "all of your family possessed it?"

"Only my father and I had it in full measure. My uncle, King Damian, and Prince Belisar could do it only with the aid of my father."

"So the Hasturs—"

"Somehow, King Rafael and Queen Taniquel must have found out. But they thought Damian and Belisar were the only ones left alive. They didn't know my father survived—or that *he* was the one responsible for Damian's ability to nullify truthspell."

"Ah!" The cry burst from her. She knew why Rafael and Taniquel had slain their conquered foes, out of fear for their entire world. What were the lives of two men, or two dozen, against the very foundations of truth?

The Hasturs, Rafael and Taniquel, had killed the wrong men. That single act of injustice gave rise to a revenge that consumed the lives of everyone it touched. Nor would it end with the destruction of Hali Tower. Her vision went black as she looked upon a charred and smoking landscape.

Carolin would not rest until he discovered who had launched the attack, and all the wide lands would be set ablaze. Men would reach for their most powerful weapons in the name of righteousness. The *clingfire* that even now consumed her flesh would be only the beginning.

45

Only the beginning . . .

The thought echoed through Eduin's mind. He watched Dyannis sink into herself, defeated. Her robes glimmered like red flames. In moments, the *clingfire* would consume her. He reached out, praying that his own insubstantial flesh might ignite and burn along with hers.

Dyannis looked up, and he saw in her eyes a surge of indomitable will. She had always had a temper, but it was now refined, mastered.

"It must not happen," she said tightly. "And it *will not*. Eduin, I am as good as dead, as are all the others at Hali Tower. We must not waste our deaths."

What did she mean to do? Reach into the lake for the Cataclysm device and drag all of Darkover into the conflagration?

"The only way to ensure that no more such weapons are ever used is to prevent their creation. The only people who can do that are we *leronyn* ourselves. Think, Eduin! Would you or I or any of us be willing to make *clingfire* or bonewater dust if we truly knew what it did to its victims? If we were linked, mind to mind, with our fellow *leronyn* as they die?"

Eduin shook his head. Once he had believed that those who created the terrible power of *laran* weaponry ought to be the only ones who decided how it was to be used. What Dyannis proposed, however, was absurd. She meant to use the dying agony of her own mind, and those of her colleagues at Hali Tower, to convince anyone with *laran* of the horror of what they had done. Even as he marveled at her courage, he knew it was in vain.

"It is impossible," he said. "Even through the relays, you cannot reach so many."

Dyannis grasped both his hands and spoke with quiet certainty. "Alone, I cannot. But together, linked with the circle at Hali, *we can.*"

She was no longer the inexperienced novice with whom he had first fallen in love, nor the matrix worker content with a subordinate place in the circle, nor even the *leronis* who had summoned the dragon over Hali Lake out of her own rage.

Dyannis had become a Keeper, powerful and adept, and what was more, she saw in him that same strength. He did not know if she were right, or if he could fulfill her trust in him. He only knew he had to try, as he had never tried before.

Eduin felt Dyannis bring his mind into full rapport with hers. Her mental touch was unlike that of any male Keeper he had ever known, yet supple and vital. She drew upon his strength as she reached out to the others in Hali Tower.

. . . an older woman, her face bathed in flames . . .

. . . a man bent over a relay screen . . .

. . . a child, his talent still raw and new . . .

. . . a Keeper's voice, *Let me be, Lewis-Mikhail, for there is no hope for any of us* . . .

. . . and then a sudden surge in power as one after another, a circle of trained minds joined them . . .

Dyannis gathered up the concentrated mental force and shifted its resonance. Like water, like the cloud-stuff of Hali Lake, it became an exquisitely sensitive medium for transmitting *laran* impressions. Only then did she open their combined minds to physical sensation and emotion.

Pain surged through the unity. Eduin reeled with it, but he held on. Throughout Hali, others were doing the same, pouring everything they felt into the hands of their Keeper. Even as the fire ate into her own flesh, Dyannis held fast. The intensity mounted as the circle became a crucible.

In a single, sweeping movement, Dyannis released the pent-up forces.

Flaring light . . . searing pain, past all bearing . . . flames that rose and struck inward, consuming . . . mounting fire, smoke . . . walls crumbling and falling . . . voices raised in shrieks, wild lamentations . . . death raining down from the sky . . . a woman's body blazing like a torch, the smell of burning hair, charred bone . . .

Like a fireball of pain and terror, the mental sending blasted out in all directions. Eduin rode with it, sensing its impact upon each vulnerable mind.

In the city of Hali and all through the Venza Hills, every person with a scrap of *laran,* men and women and children, cried out in anguish. In Thendara, Queen Maura collapsed screaming into the arms of a stunned Carolin. Along a trail, a *leronis* in a green cloak jerked her horse to a violent stop, her face contorted. Across the Plains of Arilinn, workers shuddered, momentarily blinded. Someone sobbed, "Death, death falling from the sky—the fire—the screams—"

Triumph rose in Eduin and as soon faltered. For every mind they reached, there were still more beyond their range. The initial broadcast had reached many, but the Hundred Kingdoms stretched wide and far. Even now, the circle created by Dyannis was beginning to fall away. Raimon's mind went silent, an aching emptiness. Others were still alive, but rapidly losing the ability to concentrate, to hold their minds open. Hearts stuttered, lungs choked with smoke, consciousness faded.

They would never reach Dalereuth, home of the illegal circles that made *clingfire* and worse for any lordling who could pay, or Temora on the sea coast, or far Aldaran. These kingdoms would swoop down, unhindered by Compact or scruple, upon the Lowlands. The Hastur reign might come to an end, its *leronyn* helpless to defend their lord, and its place would be taken by a tyranny far more terrible.

Denial raged through him. Whatever he had done to bring this disaster about, he must undo, and more.

In the Overworld, he rose and stepped away from Dyannis. She followed him with bleak eyes, for she was nearing the end of her own strength.

There was a source of power that he could call upon. He could not command it, only ask.

The next instant, Naotalba stood before him in a dissolving mist, a wind rippling through her cloak. As her features came clear, he recognized the pale skin, the ebony hair rising from a widow's peak, the gown the color of a moonless sky.

Wordless, he knelt before her.

"What would you have of me, Eduin Deslucido?" The voice bore none of its former cruelty. Instead, Naotalba sounded weary, almost desolate.

Whatever she had been, he had turned her into a creature of hatred and destruction. He had torn out her human heart, leaving only the bitterness of vengeance. Then he had turned away from the path set by his father so many years ago, but the events he had set in motion still unfolded. She was as much a prisoner of that destiny as he. He had no right to ask, nothing he could use to compel.

Redemption, he thought.

"Ah!" she cried, shuddering, and he realized that she had understood it to mean for her, as well.

"Help me," he pleaded. "Help me to undo the harm I have done."

A glimmer of a smile passed over Naotalba's lips, and the faintest blush of rose touched her cheeks. She stretched out her arms. Her cloak flared wide, dissolving at the edges. It grew, covering sky and ground, but its shadow was no longer the icy cold of Zandru's realm. Instead, warmth, sweet as a summer dawn, suffused him.

The next instant, he was once more linked to Dyannis and the two of them formed the heart of the expanding circle. Their unity included not only the workers at Hali, but every mind they touched. All resonated to the same pattern; all burned and wept.

From the shores of Temora to the farthest reaches of the Hellers to the borders of the Dry Towns, every telepath on Darkover joined for one brief, bright moment.

No more! The words passed from one mind to the next, building into a ripple, then a chorus, then a roar. The cry arose from the innermost hearts of *leronyn* across Darkover.

No more terrible weapons!

No more enslaving the Gifts of the mind to destruction!

No more war at the command of men who hide in safety behind their walls!

The moment passed, and Eduin realized that Dyannis, too, was slipping away from him. She no longer burned with orange-white flames. The light in her eyes dimmed. He reached for her hands, as she had reached for his. His fingers passed through her flesh as if she were water.

Had the gods no mercy? To have come so far, to have found her at last, and now to lose her after so short a time!

I will not leave you.

Eduin could not be sure which one of them had spoken, for their minds were still linked.

Wherever you go, so will I.

Like the sun coming out from behind a cloud, her image strengthened. Color returned to her lips and her robe of Keeper's crimson. He felt warm flesh, hard bone, smooth skin beneath his fingers. A scent like wildflowers filled his nostrils.

I have brought you back, he thought in wonder.

No, dear heart. You have come here with me.

He glanced behind her and saw not the familiar unchanging gray of the Overworld, but green rising to meet a golden sky, and then all color dimming to silver. Within the mist, trees bent and swayed. Slender figures moved in a secret dance, their eyes luminous, their hands beckoning. Music, like the faint chiming of bells, hung on the air.

Eduin's last conscious thought was of a figure not of shadow but of light, as it bent to gather both of them in its embrace.

EPILOGUE

Slowly, Varzil Ridenow climbed the stairs leading to the private quarters of his sworn brother, Carolin Hastur. The guards in livery of blue and silver stood watching. Some of them bent their heads in token of respect for his grief. One or two had tears in their eyes.

He could not remember a time when he had felt so utterly empty, and yet so filled with pain. When Felicia died, it had been as if half his heart were torn away. Hestral Tower had been under siege, and all their lives depended upon his swift actions. There had been no time to feel the loss. More than that, he had not felt Felicia's death as if it were his own.

He had been with Dyannis, his mind merged with hers, her pain as real and vivid as if it had been his flesh that burned. His throat had gone raw and then numb with screaming until he could no longer breathe the greasy smoke. His own bones had splintered in the heat.

Aldones, let me not remember! He paused, for the moment unable to go on, and ran one hand over his eyes. *Let me not forget.*

Every telepath across the face of Darkover, trained or raw, had heard the massed voices of the workers of Hali. Even in their death agonies, they had somehow held their minds open. It did not seem humanly possible, and yet they had done it. For days thereafter, relays lay silent, their workers too stunned to operate the screens. By the grace of the gods, Varzil had already completed his diplomatic mission for Carolin when the blow struck. He had hurried back to Thendara, dreading what he would find.

Hali Tower lay in ruins. Only the *rhu fead* with its holy things, housed in a separate location under layers of *laran*-keyed insulating fields, and part of the foundation had survived. It would take a generation to reassemble a working circle and rebuild the physical structure. He intended to offer Carolin the services of Neskaya Tower in healing and reconstruction, as well as volunteers to create the germ of a new circle. The balance of their powers, Crown and Tower, required the formal offer and acceptance. Perhaps he would send Ellimara Aillard, who had almost completed her Keeper's training.

Varzil reached the top of the stairs and Carolin's paxman, who had been leading the way, paused to let him catch his breath. Varzil managed a half-smile and gestured for the man to continue. A few moments later, he was escorted into the presence of his friend.

Carolin had aged visibly since Varzil had last seen him, although it was but a few tendays ago. Carolin had only a modest Gift, telepathy the least of his talents, but clearly he had been caught in the psychic blast of Hali's dying circle. More than that, the loss of so many talented men and women under his rule and care had slashed him to the bone.

They greeted each other formally, and then the paxman withdrew. Carolin crossed the space between them and held out his arms in a brother's embrace.

Although physical contact was difficult at best for most telepaths, Carolin was one of the few people Varzil trusted with such intimacy. They had shared much, dreams and struggles, laughter and betrayal, and now this overwhelming grief.

Varzil felt the strength of Carolin's grip, the muscles hardened from years of regular sword practice, the quick indrawn breath, the steadiness of mind. There was no need to speak. Their understanding ran deeper than words. He found the silence far more comforting than any empty phrases.

At last, they drew apart. Varzil felt a lightening of heart, as if some portion of his *bredu's* strength had seeped into him.

Carolin led him to two cushioned chairs drawn up near a small fire. The day was warm enough to make it unnecessary, but Varzil welcomed the homey touch. He sank gratefully against the pillows.

To Carolin's inquiry, he replied that he was not yet recovered, but that he was doing as well as could be expected. They all would, given time.

"Indeed," Carolin said with a grave nod. "Such a thing ought not to be quickly forgotten."

"It is said that when one age dies, another is born from its ashes. I believe we are living in such a time." Varzil went on to present his formal offer of assistance.

Carolin accepted with phrases of gratitude. "So we will have a woman Keeper at Hali, after all. Soon, our world will have changed so much that our fathers would not recognize it. Yet, is this not what we have dreamed of and striven for? We did not anticipate how it would come about, the dreadful cost, yet the reality may exceed our expectations."

"That much is true," Varzil said. "Neither of us could have foreseen such a cataclysmic change."

Carolin gestured to the desk at the far end of the room, heaped with scrolls. "Messengers keep coming from every corner of Darkover, even as far away as Dalereuth and the Hellers. They have all sworn to abide by the Compact, and many small kingdoms have thrown down their arms and sued their neighbors for peace." He shook his head. "It is indeed the beginning of a new age."

Carolin rose and went to the desk. He picked up a scroll and read it briefly. "This is perhaps the strangest news of all. Valeron has signed the Compact, but also sends word of its own tragedy. Within their small Tower, several *leronyn* were found dead, their minds apparently burned out in the conflagration."

He looked up, brow furrowing. "One of them was our old friend, Eduin."

"Eduin! What was he doing at Valeron?"

"The Lady's message says only that he and a companion had arrived with a party from Kirella, one of their provinces. Perhaps he had found some useful employment there, some place in the world. He apparently concealed his name from them. Only the Lady herself suspected anything, but it was Eduin's companion, a sort of simpleton, who revealed enough to establish his true identity."

"I did not know Eduin was at Valeron," Varzil said, carefully feeling his way through the tangle of truths and suspicions, "but he was part of the Hali circle. How he was able to join them over such a distance, I do not know. His talent was great; he could have been a Keeper. He was with Dyannis at the end."

"I remember how they fell in love so many years ago," Carolin murmured.

"During those last moments, I learned the truth about Eduin. Carlo, this is difficult for me to say, but he was indeed responsible for Felicia's death, and very nearly for yours."

"We were friends. He loved me, I'm sure of it."

Varzil told Carolin who Eduin really was, how he had been shaped into an instrument of revenge, how at the last he had tried to undo the harm he had caused. He did not mention why the Deslucidos had been executed. Their secret must die with him, finally ending the cycle of retaliation.

Carolin looked thoughtful. "In a way, each of us was right about Eduin. He was both good and evil, and in the end, he chose the good. May the gods grant him peace."

"So ends another era," Varzil said.

They must look to the future now, to the new age taking shape around them. It was a heavy burden, to carry through what so many had perished for, but he would not have to do it alone. Carolin stood at his side. Everywhere, men and women of good will had joined together to end the menace of *laran* weaponry forever.

The ring on his right hand, with the white stone holding the imprint of Felicia's mind, glowed softly. His heart lightened and he could almost feel her smile, her warmth, her enduring hope.

In a moment of clarity, he glimpsed circles dedicated to healing instead of death, women as well as men clothed in Keeper's crimson, mighty kings meeting in Council instead of battle, poisoned lands growing green and fertile, children laughing beneath the great Red Sun.

Felicia would have rejoiced to see it, as would have Dyannis and all the others who had given their lives. He met Carolin's steady gaze and knew that together, they would surely bring that vision into reality.